In the Mix

THE GEG SERIES
BOOK 2

JACQUELYN AYRES

In The Mix

Cover Design: Cover to Cover Design

Editor: Rebecca J. Cartee, Editing by Rebecca
Editing Consultant: Jess Huckins
Proofreading Services: BNW Author Services
Formatting: Champagne Formats

ISBN: 978-0-9863069-1-4

Also by the author

The Lost & Found Series
Goodbye Caution, Book 1
Goodbye Secrets, Book 2
Goodbye Uncertainty, Book 3

The One

The GEG Series
Under Contract, Book 1

Dedication

For Susan Powers, my aunt, who was taken from this world far earlier than anyone should. Your strength, struggle, humor, and most of all, your kindness has had a bigger impact on my life then you ever imagined it would. I am beyond grateful for the lessons I learned from you in the short seventeen years you were in my life. The greatest lesson was that of friendship; to see the person within and not what everyone else sees on the outside. My life has been blessed with the most wonderful friendships because of it. Thank you. I love you and I miss you.

Ps. Sorry for the snail mail, next time I'll use a Ouija board. ;)

For Wendy Colby, my friend, you inspire me every day. You know, they say that everyone has a choice of how they could handle the things that life throws at them, and I do believe that. However, some people, like you, are just born with the right stuff. The stuff that makes you strong without ever really trying. I see it every time I talk to you. It's in your concern for others, the excitement you find in things, especially your books, and your continuous dreams of the future. And when things do get to you, I love that you have a double barrel salute up, through your tears, while you blow raspberries at life. Supergirl. I love you. No one and nothing will ever snuff out that light you walk around with—it's too bright.

Thank you for all of your help with our Shannon. And it is an honor to be your CiCi (Goddamn it!).

And finally, to everyone else who has been affected by MS (Multiple Sclerosis) whether personally having it or watching the people you love suffer from it, I ask you to join me by raising your fists up like MS is standing in front of you. Let those birds fly and yell with me:

FUCCCCCKKKKK YOOOOOUUUUU!

Prologue

The balls know . . .

Kyle

I look up from my laptop as soon as I hear the door to my office slam open. “He’s not here, miss!” Erica practically yells at the woman charging through the threshold.

“My name is CiCi, bitch—remember that shit!” she barks at Erica before bringing her attention to me. “Where is he? Where is that dickless son of a bitch?” She charges towards me.

Holy shit—she’s fucking hot!

“Who are you talking about?” I get up and walk around to the front of my desk.

“Mitch—motherfucking, pussy breath, ballless wonder of the world—Colton!” she yells in my face.

Her eyes are gorgeous.

She smells incredible.

That fucking mouth on her . . .

I widen my stance due to unforeseen circumstances. "He's not here. Can I leave a message for you?" I lick my lips, fighting the urge to nip at hers.

"What the fuck are you smirking at?"

"Do you want me to call security, Kyle?" Erica pipes up from the doorway. Talk about a delayed reaction.

"No, Erica, close the door; we'll be fine." I command without averting my eyes from this woman's gorgeous ones.

"Ha! You may want that security, Kyle," she laughs threateningly.

"Yeah?" I get closer to her, breathing in her face. "Fuck, you're beautiful . . ." I trail off. The tension in her face lightens up for a moment and, as if she remembers, she furrows her brow.

Oh shit! Oh shit!

She has my balls!

Don't yelp like a girl.

Don't yelp like a girl.

"You have a really nice set of balls here, Kyle." She leans in near my ear. "I'm pretty sure you want to keep them. I'm also pretty sure they sound fantastic slapping the ass of whomever you are fucking. If you want to keep it that way, I suggest you tell Mitch that he had better call me or I will not only rip your balls off, but his as well. Capisce?" She lightens the grip. All I can do is nod and try my hardest not to get a full-on erection. But then . . . she gives me a soft caressing rub.

I may have just groaned.

"Feel good?" she whispers in the most seductive tone I've ever heard in my life. "It won't feel like this anymore if I don't hear from Mitch, *you got me?*" she threatens and, good God, gives me another squeeze. "I will have your balls, Kyle!"

I can confirm right now—she already does.

I want her.

Before I can say another word, she lets go of me and leaves my office as quickly as she arrived. I pick up the phone and dial Mitch. I'm not wasting a single moment. What the hell did she say her name was? She said it. I was just too busy being hypnotized by her eyes for it to register.

"Hey, Kyle," Mitch answers.

"Mitch—holy shit!"

"What's the matter, man?"

"I just met the woman of my dreams!"

"What?"

"She came in here looking for you. Well, to rip your head off. Christ, she's gorgeous! She's got long, dark brown hair, a nose ring, and those eyes, Mitch—her fucking eyes. They're green like fucking emeralds, man! Shit, I bet she has a hot tattoo in a hot place! I want to find that tattoo, Mitch." I finally take a breath and wait for his response.

"CiCi?" he asks after a moment.

"CiCi," I sigh. He laughs. "Mitch, this is no joke. She left here not five minutes ago, and I'm completely obsessed," I say, getting lost in my thoughts of her.

"What did she say to you?"

"Man . . . I don't know. She had me by the balls—literally had her fingers wrapped around my balls! Her hand fit them good, Mitch," I state, the desire to have her hand there again, growing in me. "At times it was a little painful, I have to admit, but my balls were made to fit in her palm. Mitch," I take on a more serious tone. "I have found the keeper of my balls, Mitch. I'm ready to hand them over. Who is she? An ex of yours?" I ask, ignoring his roar of laughter.

"No. She's Charlotte's sister."

"Did you patch things up with her? Please tell me you did," I beg.

"Yes. Well . . . sort of."

"What do you mean, *sort of?*"

"We haven't discussed things yet."

I sit at my desk and start doing a google search on her. What? I'm just going to check her out on Facebook and stuff. "Well, discuss, make up, and tell me where I'm meeting you guys for drinks tonight," I say quickly as I click onto her page.

"Drinks?" Mitch asks.

"Yes, drinks. You, me, Charlotte, and CiCi."

"A double date?" he asks apprehensively.

"Yeah! Shit. Mitch, is CiCi involved with anyone?"

"I don't know, actually—I don't think so." He hesitates for a moment. "You sure you want this, man? CiCi's sort of different. I mean, in a good way—like crazy or eccentric." He hesitates again. "She has no filter, man. You're kind of straitlaced."

"Yeah, I'm boring, Mitch—thanks to you!" I say. "I wasn't always like this, by the way. Maybe I need someone without a filter."

"All right, man, I'll see what I can do." He takes in a deep breath and exhales loudly.

"Great! Call me and let me know!"

"You got it. But before you go, I want to get one thing straight."

"What's that?"

"What's my name again?" he asks then laughs.

"What?" I ask a little confused but then I realize what he's referring to. "Oh, that's easy. It's dickhead!" I hit him with a delayed, yet witty comeback. He's quiet for a while. "Dude? You there?"

"Yeah. Sorry. So, I'll text you the time and place."

"Thanks, man! Later!" I say then hang up. I settle in to studying her timeline.

Oh yeah, I want her.

No. I'm not being a creep.

Really? She just had my balls in her hand!

That's what I thought.

Smirk

Carry on . . .

Chapter One

Secret Packages . . .

Ever have a nosy neighbor? Maybe a family member? Somebody who was always in your shit because they thought it smelled funny like, like—scandal?

I have several of those people in my life, but the most annoying one is my fucking mail lady. *Nosy bitch!*

Here she comes, up my walkway with her fucking frizzed out *please don't dye me again* red hair. I know what she has in her hand. She knows what she has in her hand.

So much for discreet shipping!

I open the door before she can embark on her annoying melody of ring, knock, ring—must be fucking OCD. "Mrs. Magee!" I say cheerfully with a slight hint of stink-eye.

"Carissa Catherine O'Brien?" She looks down at the package, asking.

She's known me my entire life.

"Yes, Mrs. Magee, I haven't gotten the sex change yet nor am I in the witness protection program." My pleasantries can only last so long. She's past my ten-second mark.

"You have a package here." She darts a suspicious eye up at me.

"You don't say?" I step out and look at it in her hands. "From whom?"

"It has no name of the company." She clears her throat and adds a disapproving look.

Does she really think she's going to embarrass me? *Me?*

Bitch, puhlease!

"Ooh . . ." I widen my eyes. "Why, Mrs. Magee, I bet this is from that dildo company I order from!" I tap her hand excitedly.

Mrs. Magee shifts from foot to foot—a bit uncomfortable, I might add.

But no—that's not enough for me!

"I've been waiting on this one!" I take the package. I lower my voice. "This is my new toosh-trainer anal vibrator."

Mrs. Magee gasps.

"It's the intermediate one. I'll only have one more to go before I can finally take some nice cock up my ass. I'm so excited!" I bounce a little for emphasis.

Mrs. Magee places her hand over her heart and stammers over her words. "Hav . . . va . . . nice . . . d-day," finally comes out before she heads down my stoop. She steps and turns. "Here's the rest of your mail." She hands me the stack. She then races (at an elderly pace) back to her mail van.

Some bitches be crazy, yo!

I definitely be one a dos bitches.

No. I'm white.

That was me, living the thug life for a sec.

I wave as Mrs. Magee pulls out of the driveway. She shakes her head at me and then heads to the next house. Well, that was fun . . .

I walk back in and glance at the clock on my cable box. I don't have to be back at Bark Avenue for another hour. Hmm . . . what to do for an hour? I could clean. *Nope.* I could pay bills. *With what?* I really should just be the smart consumer that I am and test this bad boy out! Get it out of the way . . . off the list of things to do! "Yes!"

I agree and kick off my sneakers as I head into my bedroom with my new "friend."

I sit on my bed (still not made so like, *hello!*—tell me that's not a sign!) and open the white package. My tongue licks my lips at the anticipation. This is supposed to be the *motha* of all vibrators! I am supposed to see stars and have a permanent smile on my face.

I slide it out of the package. "Now *this* is what I'm talking about!" I stare at it in all its magnificent glory. Purple silicone—soft to the touch. Yeah, I said purple. What? It's my favorite color! Look at all of these settings! I reach into the package, grab the batteries they supply, (cuz' there good like that, ya know?) and slip those puppies in. I hit the first button. "Holy shit!" This thing is gyrating in circles. I hit the arrow to up the tempo. My eyes grow wider. I hit it again. It's off! No, I mean like . . . ride 'em cowboy! I hit the other button and the rabbit ears spring to life.

I may be a little scared.

All I can think of when I look at this silicone swinging meat is a rodeo. No! A rodeo bar where you get on that fake bull and have to try to stay on. You're holding on with one hand. The other arm is up in the air, swinging around in a circle? That's what my new vibrator is doing. It's an arm, swinging around for balance. I turn it off and stare at it some more. I can feel the heat rising to my cheeks as I think of this one-armed bastard swinging around inside of me like a disco ball at a party.

Ohhh . . . imma 'bout to get my groove on . . .

I place it gently on the bed then proceed to tear my yoga pants down like there's a gun at my head. I whip my top off and flop onto my back. "Ok, Ceese . . . who is the lucky guy today?" Marky Mark? *No. Although I'm sure I'll get some 'good vibrations'!* Kyle . . . *Shut up, Ceese!* Henry Cavill. *He is super, but no.*

Damn the way he kissed me the other night!

Kyle it is! I close my eyes and think about the way he pinned me up against my door. He was in my face, all angry and sexy and . . . and . . . *fuck the way he smells!* I don't even remember half the shit he was telling me. Something about how *when he knows what he wants, he goes after it until it's his.* All I could do was stare at his lips, wondering when the fuck he was going to do something better with them, like kiss me. There was something else on my mind as my eyes took in the scruff on his face. Being the classy lady I am, I told him what was on my mind. *"This,"* I touched the stubble across the right side of his jawline, *"is going to feel so good rubbing against my pussy when you're eating the fuck out of it."* Yeah. I totally fucking said that! I couldn't believe it, either. I mean, of course, I have no problem saying shit like that. Just not to guys like Kyle. Good guys that I don't belong with.

What did he do? He smirked. He's a smirker—that one. Then he eskimo kissed me. Yeah, weird, right? He softly kissed my eyelids then leaned in to my ear and said, "I don't do one-night stands, beautiful." He kissed my cheek and lingered there for a moment. Just when I thought he was pulling away, readying himself to leave, he palmed my face, and said, "One night could never be enough with you, so I'd like to leave you with something to think about. Something, I hope, will encourage you to consider a chance with me." It was dark, but I could still see how crystal blue his eyes are. I just stared into them—cemented to the ground. His palms held my face with a bit more aggression and then . . . he laid the mother of all kisses on me.

Slowly, I let my hands travel up to my nipples. I roll and pull on them as I think about the way his tongue swirled around in my mouth. The way he sucked at my bottom lip and dove his tongue back in for more.

I hated it.
I hated every moment that I loved it!
Fuck!

I reach over and grab Purp. What? He's purple and the way he moves around makes him a little suspect. You know what I mean?

I spread my legs and guide Purp down my center. Yup, no lube required this session! I thrust Purp inside quickly; encouraged by the memory of the way Kyle's tongue plunged into my mouth. *Faaaaccck!* My overzealous movement now requires a moment of acclimation. Holy crap! *I wonder if Kyle has a big dick. Does it wiggle around like Purp does?*

Shaking my thoughts away, I feel around Purp with my right hand trying to find the magic rodeo buttons. *Finally!* "You got eight seconds, Purp. I'm gonna time this shit!" The rabbit ears are working a good rhythm at my clit. It's time to disco, do the hustle, shake my groove thing—whatever! Let's see what this bad boy can *Holy . . .*

mother . . . of . . . God!! "Oh hell fucking yeah!!"

Seven seconds flat.

You know what I'm talking about.

I may be whimpering a little as I come down from this. My toes are still curled almost as if they know just to stay that way cuz' I ain't done! I calm my breathing, gathering energy up for the next round. Everything is finally quiet in my head.

Then . . . I hear it.

Brzzzjrrr.

I close my legs a little.

Bbbrrzzzzjerrrrzzz.

And suddenly I feel like Betty Cocker (Yes, I said Cock-er), getting busy, mixing a cake in here. Why do they have to make these things so loud? I mean—*oh . . . oh, holy fuck of all fuckkkkerrrs! I'm not even holding it! Shhhhit! Yessss!*

Ding!

Cake's done!

I immediately turn Purp off; otherwise, I won't be able to walk today! This thing is lethal! *I love it!*

I barely walk through the door of my shop and the phone is already screaming at me. "Bark Avenue, this is CiCi, how can I help you?"

"Did you lose your fucking cell phone again?" Julie asks. Fuck, she sounds annoyed.

"No! I just don't have it attached to my ass like some people I know. What's the matter with you?" I glance down at my appointment book then up at the clock. This bitch has fifteen minutes for me to solve her problems.

"What's the matter with me?" She does that sarcastic laugh that makes me want to throat punch her. I'm not really a violent person—just pms-ing. "Let's see!" Oh boy. "My best friend, who tells me *everything,* forgets to mention a certain rich, hot-as-fuck, CEO-type dude she's met. Same dude who ruffled her feathers so much, I've barely heard from her in three weeks since said event!"

"Dude," I sigh.

"What?"

"I talked to you yesterday."

"So?"

"I have hung out with you just about every other day!" Bitch just lost ten minutes! I'm not in the mood for this shit.

"So?"

"So . . . what the fuck are you talking about?" I throw my free hand out before using it to shove the swinging door open to my back room.

"Just because you are here doesn't mean you are fucking present. What is going on with you? What happened?" Her tone dials it up a notch.

"Julie, I can't do this right now. I have a client coming in any minute." I grab the shampoo bottles.

"It's a dog—not a client!" she yells.

"Dogs are my clients and they're people, too. Stop acting like they don't matter." I grab the brushes.

"They are *dogs,* you Asswhore—not humans!"

"You know what I mean." Nobody ever understands the way I feel about animals. They don't suck. People suck. Well, except for Buddy, that dog sucks—the life out of me!

"Whatever. We're going for drinks tonight and I want the truth, the whole truth, and nothing but the truth or so help me God . . ."

"Ok, Judge Judy. Now will you shut the fuck up and let me get to work?" I head back out to the front as I hear the bell.

"Yeah, yeah. I'm only doing this because I love you," she claims.

"You're only doing this because you're a nosy bitch," I say quietly and wave to my customer. "And I love you, too. Bye, bitch!"

"Bye!" she says in her usual carefree tone. I hang up. She thinks she's won, but there is no way in hell that I'm going to talk to her about Kyle. No way! I've been dodging that bullet for three weeks now and I will not cave in. This phone call, though, only tells me that Julie has hit level two of being a pain in the ass about it. I'll need to step up my game.

"Hey, CiCi, I hope you didn't get off the phone on my account." Addie smiles as she puts Pearl up on the counter. Pearl is a two year-old Pug and she's just, well . . . a pearl!

"Oh, no, not at all. You actually saved me from my meddling

best friend." I say with a sigh of relief. "Hello there, Miss Pearl. Are you all ready to get the royal treatment?" I lift her into my arms. She answers with an assertive licking of my face.

"She loves spa time with CiCi." She gives Pearl's head a little scratch. "How are the numbers coming along for the fundraiser?" she inquires and my heart sinks.

"Slow, but I've added more advertisements. I'm going to see if my sister's boyfriend will help me out. I'm sure he'll be able to." *Bastard better after the way he fucking treated me!*

"That'll be good. I know I've been driving people nuts about it. They just don't understand how much the shelters need their help. Most people think about people and not these defenseless little dolls." Addie says sadly. She speaks the truth. I'd do anything for these little guys—all animals, really. Even Buddy—that little fucker! That's why I've teamed up with Addie every year to raise money. Sometimes, twice a year. I try to do as much as I can. Being a small business owner that focuses on animals does help in reaching the right people to get to our goals. However, with the economy being the way it has been, it's been rough. Not only are people bringing their animals in less to be groomed, they are actually giving them up to the very shelters that we are trying to help maintain.

"You look tired today, Addie." I cock my head a bit to the side.

"I am," she nods slightly. "I had to let go of another person and I'm just not getting the volunteers that I used to. I've been working more hours lately." She holds back on her frown a bit. Addie never complains about anything. She has a heart of gold, that woman. She's one of the very few people I like. I suppose I could say she's one of the very few people who like me!

"What day could you use me the most?" I ask.

"Oh, Ceese, I couldn't—"

"You didn't. I'm offering. I want to! What day?" I ask again.

"You are an angel. You know that, right?" Her smile hits her bright, blue eyes as she grabs my hand and squeezes it. *She really doesn't know me that well.* "Whatever day you find the time, dear." She pats my hand.

"Ok. I'll call you and let you know when I can head over." I pull away slightly. I have a hard time getting compliments. It freaks me out. Maddie calls it Doxophobia. I told her *'Well at least I don't have*

Dicksaphobia! That would suck!' She said, *'Seriously, what would you do with your mouth then? You'd have to pick up a nasty habit like smoking or something!'*

"CiCi? You alright?" Addie breaks me out of my thoughts.

"Oh yeah, sorry." I smile. "Well, Miss Pearl should be ready for you by two but you know she can stay here with me till I close up." I hug Pearl to me.

"Good, I'll be back around five." She smiles and scratches Pearl's head again before heading out.

I head in to my back room again or *le spa,* if you will, and set Pearl down in the pen. I want to send Mitch a text before I get started on her. Fucking bastard owes me!

Chapter Two

Interception . . .

Kyle

"Ugh!" Mitch pushes his phone away from him on the table.

"What's wrong? Who is that?" I look up from last month's financials. We're getting ready to buy out another company and merge them with ours. It was impromptu and we've pretty much been at it around the clock for the past week. We want this merger to go as smoothly as if we have been working on and planning it for months. This would be a lot easier had we been working on and planning it for months. However, we just got wind of Trox, Inc. going down. They have been one of our biggest competitors. To be ahead in business, you gotta stay ahead. If we let this go and another company grabs it, I'm not going to lie; it could hurt us. Hence—us grabbing this thing by the balls. It's getting down to the wire and every call is making us jump or pace. It has nothing to do whatsoever with the forty-two cans of Redbull lying around.

"CiCi. I don't have time for whatever bullshit she's spewing my way." He grabs his can of RB and chugs the rest.

"Uh, can I see what she wants?" *What am I—a fucking teenager?* It's just driving me crazy. I thought I'd hear something from her by now. It's been three weeks. She hasn't even mentioned me to Charlotte, as far as Mitch knows. I'm trying to be cool about this and get a game plan going. Only, I don't know what game she's playing so I can plan my strategy out.

"Here." He slides his phone down to me. "But I'm going to tell you one thing!" He holds a finger up and shakes it at me. "Whatever you do better not get me in trouble with Charlotte. I'll kick your fucking ass. I'd fire you but that would be the equivalent of kicking my own ass. So that won't do. Don't fuck with my home life, Kyle!" he warns again.

"Dude, why the fuck would I do anything to get you in trouble? What I will do for you though, is take you to the doctor's so you can get your balls reattached. Would you like me to do that for you? Where does Charlotte keep them—a compartment in her purse?" I smirk.

"Fuck you, *Mr. I've found the keeper of my balls, Mitch.*"

"You're gonna play that card, huh?" *Why the fuck did I say that to him? He's never gonna let me live it down!*

"Dude, I'm gonna play that card till neither one of us remembers why the fuck I'm playing it!" He gives me a smug smile. *Asshole.*

I look down and go into his text.

I need your help, Asshole.

Don't fucking ignore me or you'll get no Puss 'n Boots!

"From the look on your face, man, you need some translation done for you!" Mitch laughs.

"Do they have an App for this?" I shake my head. Mitch throws his head back, laughing harder. I'm guessing he's familiar with "CiCi speak."

"What did she say?" he asks. I tell him. "She's threatening to get Charlotte to hold back from me."

"Did you take a course on this?" I stare at him in awe.

"Yeah, a crash course." He rolls his eyes.

"Can I?" I shake his phone a bit.

"Go ahead, be my guest! Just don't complain to me about your headache later!" he says then gets back to the financial reports.

Nobody comes between me and my Puss 'n Boots!

What do you need help with?

Puhlease!

Anywho . . .

I'm running a fundraiser for the shelter I work with.

I'm having a groom-a-thon where I donate all of the proceeds to the shelter.

A groom-a-thon?

Yes, dipshit! I groom as many as I can in one day.

Will you groom me?

Why—you need your vagina waxed?

"Dude, stop laughing like a girl over there!" Mitch barks at me.

"Fuck you!" I flip him off.

No. But I know somebody who would love to groom yours!

I told you, Mitch, I'm not fucking you!

I stare at those words for I don't know how goddamn long. I am doing everything I can not to flip the fuck out here. I glance up at my boss. My friend. I study him, waiting for the answer to the question I don't know if I can bring myself to ask. Mitch looks up quickly then looks again when he notices my stare. I'm sure from his perspective, it looks pretty intense. I'm feeling pretty intense. His phone pings. I look down.

Are you whacking off to my picture again?

Which one?

The one you've been dreaming about me sending, Asshat!

"Kyle, did you just get mind-fucked by her?" Mitch asks cautiously.

"Yep. I'm good now, though."

"Alright. Let me know if you need any more help translating." He gets back to work.

What can I do to help?

A generous donation for a start.

But mostly, if you can get people down to my shop.

For?

Blowjobs of course!

What do you think, moron?
You have an odd way of asking people to help you!
Sorry.
I don't speak 'Dumbass' fluently. *shrugs*
Unlike the language of 'Bitch.'
Exactly!
Can you nudge the people you know with pets to come down?
Please?
I'll even take volunteers to help if somebody wants to.
Really?
Yes! I can use all the help I can get.
Don't even fucking say it!
Say what?
Fuck you, Mitch!
I didn't say anything!
You don't have to!
What day?
Sept. 7th. It's the Sat. after labor day!
So none of your pansy-ass employees can say they can't!
Um . . . that's only 1.5 weeks away!
So?
I'll see what we can do . . .
Who's 'we'?
The company and . . .
No!
No?
No Kyle, Mitch!
What's wrong with Kyle?
I'm not his type.
How do you know what his type is?

This is ridiculous. I know she likes me. At least, I think she does. Her kiss certainly didn't tell me any different. Why won't she bother with me?

It's just not me.
He really likes you, CiCi. He asks about you every day.
Well, tell him not to waste his time.
I'm not worth it.
The fuck you aren't!!!

Why do you say stuff like this?
So let me know if you can help me out!
Thanks! Bye!
Asshole!
CiCi!!!!

She doesn't reply. I put the phone down, staring at her thoughts about being with me and rub my temples. I have no idea as to what I should do.

"Walk away, man," Mitch says as he stretches in the chair before getting up to head over to me. He picks up his phone and reads the texts.

"I can't walk away, Mitch. There's something about her." I shake my head.

"Are you sure you really want to be with her because you like her or because she's a puzzle you're dying to figure out?" He cocks an eyebrow up at me.

"Honestly?"

"Yeah."

"Both." I lean back in my chair and rub my face. "I've got to figure something out. I've got to get some plan of action going, preferably by next Saturday."

"Well, if anyone can do it, it's certainly you." He slaps my shoulder.

"Thanks, man. I've just got to find her weakness."

Chapter Three

Secret Weapon . . .

CiCi

I drive down the main drag, hoping to catch a glimpse of a mob scene outside Bark Avenue. Nope. Nothing. Well, it is a half an hour before I actually open. Still, I fantasized seeing a long line. How sad is that? Me—fantasizing about a line of people with pets outside of my shop. Better than fantasizing about Kyle again. I don't know why I can't shake him out of my system. *It pisses me off!*

I turn right after my building and down the alley to the parking lot in the back. Hmm . . . why's Addie here so early?

"CiCi!" she bellows out as I park and turn the ignition off.

"Hey, Addie, everything okay?" I ask, opening the car door.

"Holy mother of God, girl! I just can't believe it!" She does this running jump sort of thing towards me. Actually, I don't know what the fuck she's doing. She may be having some sort of weird seizure. "I tried calling you!" She smacks my arm. Pearl barks at our feet—not sure who that was directed towards.

"What is it?"

"We got an anonymous check today from a donor!" she screeches.

"That's great but, uh, why is it *that* great?" Seriously, the shelter gets checks like that a few times a year.

"It's for fifty thousand dollars!" She bounces. I have never seen a smile this huge on her face before. *Oh shit. Crrrrrrrappppp!* She's starting to cry. Shit's about to get real. I don't like it when shit's about to get real. "Do you know what this means?" she asks through her tears.

"We won't get upset if no one shows up today?" I ask slowly, unsure of how to handle all of this emotion.

"Nope. It also means we won't be shutting our doors anytime soon!" She pulls me in for a hug—the same one I'm suffocating from.

"Addie, that's awesome!" I pat her back, hoping she gets the message to let me go.

"Yes it is!" She pulls away. "Well, let's get inside and set up for whatever crowd we have."

"Do you have the volunteer list for the people who are helping me today?" I ask as we walk around the building. I unlock the door and we walk in.

"Yes, it's right here." She pulls it out of her purse and hands it to me. I set it down on the counter and hang my purse underneath on the hook. I take a moment to look down at the list. It's filled with the usual people, mostly the ones I drag in here.

"Who's Lindsey?" I glance up and give her a strange look.

"I don't know. Her brother set it up with me, though. I guess we'll find out." she smiles.

"I guess so." I return it with a meek one. I hate meeting new people. Well, I just hate having to hold myself back a little from who I am. I hit the stereo and The Go-Go Girls come on singing about their lips being sealed. *I haven't heard this song in forever!* Just then, the bells at my door ring as it opens.

"Loxy!" Charley yells as Loxy bolts in. She loves her Aunt CiCi. Vader follows suit, heading right for Pearl. Pearl is Vader's best friend.

She's small but thinks she's big and he's the opposite. On some weird level, they've connected over this. That's animals for you.

"Do I have to stay the entire two hours if it's slow?" Charley asks exasperated. Bitch is lucky Addie is here. See, I hate holding my *crazy* back—pisses me off! I give her a look. Being sisters, we get all telepathic and shit.

"No. I actually have a lot of people signed up for today. I just hope I have work for those people." I throw her an apron.

"I don't want this one!" She throws it back.

"Put it on!" I throw it back at her.

"*It says I ♥ Puddy Tat!* I'm not wearing it," she growls and throws it onto the shelf.

"Here." I roll my eyes and hand her a different one. She opens it.

"Ceese! *My bird is bigger than yours?* Why does every apron have to have a sexual reference? You don't even groom birds!" She turns it inside out and puts it on.

"It's a conversation piece." I shrug.

"What the hell kind of conversation are you going to start with that besides inappropriate ones that have nothing to do with animals?" She throws her hair up in a ponybun aggressively.

"Exactly." I smirk.

"We need to find a cure for you soon!" She shakes her head and takes Loxy and Vader into the back.

"I love you!" I bellow out.

And out of nowhere . . .

The bells go off and five people walk in with their pets as if they are in a parade. *What the . . . ?* Ok. I was not expecting this! I get them situated and give them their pick up times. And just like that, the shop comes to life and we are crazy busy.

11:00 a.m.

"Excuse me, I'm looking for CiCi." I hear a woman say. I look up from the schedule.

"That's me." I'm a little caught off guard. She's a short woman, about Maddie's height, at five foot nothing. She has light brown hair and piercing blue eyes. She also has downs syndrome. So, yeah, I was caught off guard at first but, I'm not a complete douchebag, so I bounce back.

"Ooh . . . you are pretty." She smiles as her eyes widen. *Huh?*

"I'm sorry, did you have a pet you wanted groomed today?" I ignore the compliment.

"No. I'm here to help. I'm Lindsey and I signed up to volunteer." She smiles.

"Lindsey, that is some fucking cool shit right there!" I say and goddamn it, I mean the shit out of it! How awesome is she? "Come on to the back. We've been getting slaughtered and can definitely use your help!" I show her the way.

"You cursed!" she giggles.

"I did. Are you ok with that?" I look back and arch my brows up at her.

"It's fucking awesome," she laughs. "Is it ok if I curse? I'm not allowed to at home."

"Only around me. Not the customers." I chuckle. I'm gonna love the hell out of this girl—I can feel it.

"Cool!"

"Alright, Ceese, I'm outta here. Buddy is next." Charley takes her apron off and runs her arm across her forehead.

"Fuck," I sigh. Buddy is not one I want to give Lindsey. "Thanks for your help, Charley."

"I'll see you for dinner tonight, right?" She leashes Loxy and Vader.

"Am I cooking?" I ask.

"Uh, no." She looks at me weird.

"I'll definitely be there then."

"You wouldn't be there if you were cooking?" She asks cuz she falls for this shit all of the time.

"No. My cooking sucks." I shrug.

"So, you would cook then leave?"

"No, I just wouldn't show up. I don't want to be guilted into eating my own food." I shrug.

"Your food wouldn't be there if you didn't show up in enough time to cook it."

"Exactly."

"You make me want to be a better alcoholic, Ceese." She shakes her head and walks away.

"See you at AA!" I shout.

"What's AA?" Lindsey asks.

"Asswhores Anonymous." I shrug.

"Oh, I always wondered what that was," she sighs. I should tell her the truth, but I think I'll just leave it alone for now, especially since the damn door is jingling away.

"Is this Buddy?" Lindsey asks just as I'm about to go out to greet the other customers. I turn to find her opening his cage.

"Lindsey, no!" I say quickly but not quickly enough.

Holy Fuck!

I stand here rooted to the floor, jaw open, and eyes staring in disbelief. Buddy is loving on Lindsey like she is his long lost friend. He has *never* responded to anybody like this. Not even his owner, DeeDee.

"You ready to get all cleaned up, Buddy. You are sooo cute." She giggles at his kisses. "Should I take him over to the wash station?" She looks up at me.

"Um, yeah . . . that one over there." I say in disbelief. "I'll be right back."

"Ok."

I head out to the front, still in shock. Wow. Just, wow. I grab the next few clients and bring them into the back. Lindsey is rinsing Buddy down. I walk over to them to instruct her on what to do. Buddy barks at me as if to say *Back off, bitch!* Gladly, dude.

I grab Delilah, the poodle, and take her over to the next station. I keep an eye on Lindsey. She's wonderful with Buddy. She's calm and gentle. He's like a completely different dog.

The last few hours have flown by. Actually, the whole day has flown by! I can't believe how busy I was. I wish that were the case on a more regular basis. Although, many of the customers today were very happy with my work—our work—and said they would be coming back. I could really use the boost in clientele!

Lindsey stayed with me the rest of the day. She was only supposed to do two hours but she loved it and I loved having her here! We've really connected. There's something so simple between us—acceptance. We both sense it, I think. Her brother is picking her up soon and I want to talk to him about her working here part-time. She's awesome with the animals, she does a great job, and honestly, it's hard to find good people who care as much. She shouldn't be wasting her time bagging groceries. *Hell no!*

I walk out of the bathroom and hear chatter coming from the front. I hope that's her brother she let in here and not a stranger! I push the swinging door. Looking up, we lock eyes.

Faaaaaaaaccccckkkk!

"CiCi, tell him!" Lindsay shrieks. Kyle's eyes continue to burn into me. You bitches saw that coming, didn't you? Mother fucker!

"Tell me what?" he asks and licks his bottom lip. I lick mine involuntarily. His brows dart up. *Fuck the butterflies in my belly!* Why does this guy affect me so much? Jesus, I haven't felt butterflies in my stomach like this since . . . since—Drew! *No!*

"I have nothing to tell you." I'm suddenly not feeling so good.

"CiCi, you said you would like me to work here part-time, if I could." Lindsay reminds me. Her voice so quiet, it's almost as if she's ready to accept the disappointment in the fact that I lied to her. *Shit.*

"Right." I smile at her. "I'd love for Lindsay to come and work for me." I look back at him.

"Really?" he asks with a look. I don't know what that look is. Is he in shock?

"Yes. She's a good worker, loves the animals, and they love her back. I'd love to have her here." I avoid his eyes now; they pierce right through me.

"CiCi, that's wonderful. I'm sure my parents wouldn't mind at all." He crosses the room to me. Shit . . . why is he crossing the room to me? His hands grasp my upper arms gently. "Thank you, Ceese," he says softly. His eyes are full of warmth. He squeezes my arms a little for emphasis. I bite the inside of my cheek because I'm all levels of uncomfortable right now. "You have no idea how amazing you are—how amazing your offer just was," he almost whispers now. His fresh minty breath pleasantly travels up my nostrils. He leans in closer to my face.

And . . .

He eskimo kisses me.

I know, right?

"Ceese," he breathes then leans in more to kiss me. I pull away.

"So, here's my business card, Lindsay, with the store hours on it." I say as I round the counter to get one. "Just let me know what hours you want to work. You can set your own schedule, sweetie." I smile nervously and walk the card over to her—completely avoiding her brother.

"You ready, Linz?" Kyle asks her as he walks up behind me. He places his hand on my back and slides it up to my left shoulder. "Thanks, Ceese," he says into my ear then plants a prolonged kiss on my cheek. My stomach leaps up to my heart.

"Can I come this Monday?" she asks.

"Sure!" I pull away from Kyle again. "Thank you so much for all of your help today." I give her a hug. I'm not much of a hugger. I only don't mind hugging my family. I don't mind hugging Lindsay at all. Hmm . . . strange.

"C'mon, Linz." Kyle says as we break from our hug. He puts his hand on her back in a protective manner as they head to the door. I turn away from them, grab the box UPS dropped off today, and take it to the back room. Placing the box on the table, I open it, and put the product away before I leave. The sound of the swinging door grabs my attention. I turn my head just as Kyle reaches for my arm and turns my whole body to face him—aggressively. I gasp (like a fucking Disney princess). He forces me to back up against the wall. His right hand grasps me by the back of my neck. I try to push him off; my heart is racing so fast, I feel it may explode out of my chest. Kyle grabs my hands and slams them up against the wall above my head. He shifts so that his left hand encircles both of my wrists. His right hand reclaims the back of my neck.

"Get—" I try to yell but Kyle's mouth is quick to shut mine up as he slams it against me. His tongue licks hard into my mouth. I try to fight him. Every time I do—he licks harder—taking my breath away. Finally, a slight moan of defeat escapes my throat and I give into his demands. Kyle then kisses the ever-loving fuck out of me. You know what? I give that shit right back to him. *Mother fucker!* Invading my mind every day, the way he does—he deserves it!

Kyle groans as I suck the shit out of his bottom lip. He finally frees his lips from the clutches of my teeth. He stares deeply into my eyes, barely able to catch his breath. My lungs match his tempo. He releases my arms. Just when I think he's going to back up, his hands quickly reach down behind my thighs, above my knees, and he lifts them and me up. He wraps my legs around his waist and pushes my back up against the wall again. My arms flail in a panic and I grab his shoulders. Slowly, he leans up to my mouth and lays the softest kiss on them. He does it again and again. His tongue slides across the slit of my lips. I part them for him and his tongue darts in caressing mine so patiently, I whimper.

His hands slide up my thighs and around to my ass. He cups me possessively and gives a little squeeze as he grinds into me, taking his time exploring my mouth. I have never been kissed this gently in my life. I feel like he's savoring every second our mouths are locked. I may be doing that as well, but I won't commit to that statement.

"CiCi." He pecks.

"Hmm?" I feel so lightheaded.

"Give me a chance; I'm not such a bad guy." He kisses me again.

"No. You're one of the good ones." I pull back. "Which, to me, means you are bad." My head clears up. "Put me down, Kyle. It's never going to happen. Get off of me." I look away from him.

"You. Are. Wrong!" he says angrily.

"No, I'm not." I bring my eyes back to his. "Put me down. I don't want this. I don't want you." I push at his shoulders.

"You're a fucking liar. You want this and you want it with me," he says through his teeth.

"If I fuck you once, will you leave me the hell alone?" I try to act indifferent and roll my eyes.

Kyle drops me. I almost fall to the floor but catch myself. He stares at me intensely. His jawline twitches. "Lindsay will be here on Monday and I promise to stay the fuck away from you," he states calmly. Well, as calmly as one can when you're angry as hell.

"Good." I widen my eyes in a snarky manner.

He stares with angry eyes.

My eyes continue their snark at him.

His hands grasp my face so quick, I may have gotten whiplash. His mouth smacks mine hard. He sucks my lower lip painfully . . . that is until he bites it so hard I yelp before he lets go. He let's go of my head, pushing it back a little. My fingers reach up to comfort my lip. Kyle shakes his head at me—same angry look intact.

He turns and hits the swinging door open. It hits the wall on the other side making a loud *bang* sound that makes me jump. I listen for the sound of the bells on the door to jingle. They do within seconds. I run out to the store and quickly lock the door. I go to the backroom again where there are no windows. No chance of anyone having the ability to see me.

All alone.
The way I like it.
I cry.
Fuck my life!

No. It's a figure of speech. Don't get all *I'm gonna psychoanalyze this bitch!* I've got Maddie for that—thank you!

Chapter Four

When in doubt . . .

Kyle

It's been two weeks. You think I could get her out of my mind for at least one fucking day? No. I've tried everything. Tonight I'm trying something new. I'm going on a date with someone else. Paige from finance. She's cute. We've been working a lot together. She's done more than drop a hint or two that she's interested. *Fuck CiCi!*

So, here I go. Hey, maybe it will work out. Maybe I'm not really meant to be with CiCi. *Fuck.* I just said that. You know what that means, right? I'm not going to get her or those fucking gorgeous green eyes off my mind all night!

I get out of the car when I see Paige heading down her stairs with a spring in her step. "Hi." I smile and kiss her cheek before opening the door for her. She smells like sweet candy and flowers. *Crap.* I bet she was a cheerleader.

"Hi!" she giggles. Why the hell is she giggling? What's so funny? She gets in and I close the door. I look up at the sky for some sort of divine intervention. I fear this may be the longest date of my life. It already feels too long. *Bad attitude, Kyle.* I shake my head and head over to the driver's side.

"Where are we going?" she asks when I get in.

"Dinner?" I look over at her and study her for a moment. Her blonde hair is just above her shoulders—not a hair out of place. It sort of looks like a helmet. I start laughing. Her hair looks like Twiki's, Buck Roger's robot. She giggles. I laugh harder. She giggles more. *Fuck . . . it's going to be a long night, for sure!*

I head out onto the main road and drive to the restaurant. I'm taking her to La Bella's in Salem, New Hampshire. This is not just a pleasure trip. It's business. Mitch has his eye on it for Charlotte. She loves to cook and I have to say, I've had the pleasure of eating her food. Amazing! So I'm casing out the joint for him.

"Ooh . . . I love Italian!" Paige says like it's her first time ever visiting a restaurant. Of course, this is followed up by a giggle. Someone, someday will appreciate her giggling. Thirty minutes into the date, I can tell you I am definitely not that someone.

We've finished our dinner. Thank Christ! Not only is Paige a giggler, she's a slow eater. Like ridiculously slow. I've been done for forty-five minutes. She's talked and giggled me into a fucking migraine!

"Oooh!" She gets wide-eyed. She also says *Oooh* a lot! "There's a new karaoke place up the road! We should go there!" She taps my hand. *Shit!*

"Hold on! Let me ask my friend about it. He lives up here." I smile as I pull out my phone to text Mitch and Trent.

MAYDAY!!! HELP!!! SOS!!!

I finish my text and look up at her. She flashes me a huge smile . . . with a huge piece of something in her teeth. Should I tell her? She gestures that she's going to run to the bathroom as soon as my phone rings. I nod and smile. I answer once she's far enough away.

"Dude! Help me!" I greet Mitch.

"Not working out, huh?" he chuckles.

"Man, my head is ready to explode! What are you guys doing?" I ask desperately.

"We were thinking of going out," he says and sighs like he's still contemplating.

"Good! Meet us at the karaoke bar up the street from this place."

"Uh, Ok. How's the restaurant?" he asks quietly.

"Nice! It has a great location here just off of 28. I think she'll love it!" I smile. "Fuck. She's coming back! Meet us there, ok?" I beg.

"Ok."

"And, Mitch?"

"Yes?"

"Hurry . . . please!" I give a final plea. He just laughs at me. *Asshole!*

I hang up just as the waitress brings my card back to me. I stand up. I can't sit another minute here with her. "Ready?" I smile.

"Sure. You didn't want to have coffee?" she crooks her head.

"Nah. Let's go!" I'm not even about to ask her if she wants coffee.

We head out to my car and take the drive ten minutes down the road.

Twenty-three times.

Sorry.

Giggle count: Twenty-three times.

In ten minutes.

Ya feeling me?

You're asking *why,* aren't you? Why am I continuing with this date if I'm miserable? Two reasons. 1. I work with her and she's generally a nice girl so I don't want to be a jerk. 2. CiCi.

Got it?

We get to McPherson's Karaoke bar and head in to get a table. I let Paige know that Mitch and Charlotte will be joining us. It just occurred to me, when she got giddy and giggled, that I may have been sending out the wrong message by making this a double date. *Fuck.* I think she now thinks that *I* think things are going so well, I want her to hang out with my friends. Yes, she knows Mitch but the fact that this is Mitch makes it even worse. *Oh well!* I sit back and watch the clock. Ugh!

Finally, after fifteen minutes, Mitch walks in with Charlotte. And . . .

Faaaaaccccckkkkk!

We lock eyes. I proceed to do what I do next when we lock eyes. Yes. I fuck her. I fuck her with my goddamn eyes every time. You know what? She fucks me back. I know it. My dick knows it. We eye fuck. We give *good* eye fuck.

"Hey guys!" I stand up and shake Mitch's hand. I kiss Charlotte on the cheek. I stare at CiCi—thrusting into her one more time.

Paige? You know what Paige is doing . . . hee hee. *Christ!* CiCi widens her eyes at me when Paige's giggling fit rolls into the next. I widen mine back at her.

We both snort.

We all finally sit. Paige grabs my arm and puts it over her shoulder and snuggles into me like one does on a first date. *Awkward.* CiCi, probably for the pure pleasure of seeing me uncomfortable, is laughing her ass off. Part of me wants to laugh with her, but then I remember. I remember that she's the one who's supposed to have my arm around *her.* She's not and it's her fault. So instead of laughing with her, like I want to, I pull a dick move. I bring my forefinger under Paige's chin to lift her face up and I kiss her. Then I deepen the kiss. Giggling aside—Paige can kiss and she seems more than happy to be kissing me. A minute or so later, I pull away after giving her another quick peck. Paige snuggles into me a bit more as I bring my eyes up. My eyes find CiCi's. She's not laughing anymore. She seems uncomfortable. *Good.*

CiCi gets up and goes up by the DJ's to look through the song choices. CiCi sings? Hmm. I bring my eyes back to Mitch who is staring at me like I've got eight heads. Charlotte is glaring as opposed to staring. I shrug. Charlotte mouths *Asshole* at me.

"We have CiCi up at the mic!" the DJ announces. Guess there wasn't a long wait! We all turn to give our attention to her up on stage. Within seconds, the music is playing and she starts singing. God . . . she has a beautiful voice. She's singing "Human" by Christina Perri. I love this song. She's staring right at me as she sings about losing her strength to not be vulnerable. My heart aches. I want to run up to the stage. I want to save her from whatever negative thought that is keeping her from being with me. I pull away from Paige as CiCi continues to sing. Jesus—she's fucking running her tongue up my neck. It's annoying. I give her a look to knock it off. She giggles. *Idiot.* My eyes go back to CiCi. She's amazing. You would think this was *her* song!

CiCi finishes the song and the room claps their hands off for her. Some guy *Woot Woos* for her. I scan the room to find this guy who is woot wooing my girl. *My girl?* What am I thinking? She's not my girl. She doesn't want to be my girl. I wish I was a quitter. I'd find it much easier to walk away from her. But . . . I'm not. I've just got to find a way to reach her.

Think.

Suddenly, it hits me! As soon as CiCi sits down, I get up and head to the front by the DJ. I request a song and due the earliness of the evening, I'm able to go right up. "This is for you, Ceese." I say before the song comes on. I want to make sure *Giggles* doesn't get the wrong idea. I can see CiCi's rapid breathing from here. She's seems unsure—uncomfortable. Yet, I can tell she's glued to her seat. The music begins and I don't take my eyes off her as I sing "Perfect" by Pink to her. She seems shocked. The whole table seems shocked.

Yeah. I know my way around a note or two!

CiCi starts chewing at the inside of her cheek. Nasty habit but I love it. It tells me that a window is being cracked open. It's a small crack, but it's opening. How long will I have before she slams it shut again? I finish the song and am a little taken aback by the applause I receive.

"Dude, I'm booking you for the company Christmas party! We'll call you the singing ninja." Mitch laughs. *Asshole.* I offer my usual salute of a smirk and hand gesture. He unloads both barrels at me. I sit next to Paige, still laughing at Mitch. CiCi and I lock eyes. My smile drops. My heart races. I lick my bottom lip slowly. She does the same. If anybody is talking to me, I couldn't tell you what they are saying. The only person in this room is CiCi. "Stay" by Rhianna and Chris Brown plays in the background. Ever have that moment when you're feeling a certain way that is indescribable then . . . out of nowhere . . . the perfect song comes on. No other words needed. The song explains everything. Our eyes stay focused on each other's.

Making love.

"Can you take me home, please?" Paige elbows me. I break away from my stare down with CiCi to look at Paige. Oh, she's not happy . . . at all!

"Yeah, sure." I nod. She stands up and grabs her purse aggressively before slamming her chair under the table. She storms off to the door to exit.

"I'm guessing there won't be a second date." Mitch says as he watches her.

I stare at CiCi—locking eyes with her again. "There should've never been a first one," I say then proceed to follow Paige.

"Is she your ex-girlfriend? Did you know she was coming here? Did you only kiss me to make her jealous? Do you even like me? Did you really even want to go out with me? Why didn't you just take me home if you didn't want to be here with me? Are you going to answer me?" Paige unloads her questions like her mouth is a Tommy gun. I stand here staring at her—mouth open. "Kyle!" she yells.

"Get in the car, Paige," is all I say and hit the unlock button. She gets in angrily. "I'm sorry. I wasn't expecting her to be here. But I do have feelings for her that I can't seem to quash. It wasn't my intention to use you. I mean, I'm not using you. I don't think it will be wise for me to pursue you. It wouldn't be fair to you." I say after I start up the car and start driving away.

"So, what was this?" She throws her hand out.

"This was me, trying to move on from her. I'm sorry, Paige." I give her the courtesy of a glance while I apologize. "I should've never taken someone out from the office. Isn't that, like, rule number one—don't date co-workers?"

"Yeah, well, it's not an easy rule to follow when the only people you ever meet are co-workers. Let's face it, Kyle; we're both slaves to our job. When and where are we supposed to meet someone? I'm not down with the online thing," she states. I think she's finally calming down. She actually isn't too bad when she's not giggling every minute. Ok, yes—she still has Twiki hair.

"I guess you're right." I shrug.

"Do you want to talk about her?" I see her cringe a bit out of my peripheral vision.

"Uh. No. There's really not much to say, except that she has a wall up that I keep trying to knock down." I jump onto the highway. Within ten minutes, I'm turning off at her exit.

"Kyle," she speaks up again.

"Yeah." I glance over.

"I really like you."

"Uh, Paige—"

"No. I know." She waves her hand dismissively. "I just want to put this out there." She takes in a deep breath. "When and if you are done chasing her. If I'm free," she adds quickly. "Don't hesitate to ask me out again." She gives me a half smile as I pull up to her house. Wow. I was not expecting that. I don't even know what to say.

"Um, ok. Thanks, Paige." I give her a curt nod.

"Goodnight." She smiles and leans over to me for what I like to call *awkward hug.* You know what I'm talking about. She gets out and we both follow up with *awkward wave.* I head off—not fast enough—believe me.

I have to say, I'm fighting every fiber of my being, not to go straight to CiCi's. I doubt that will help. So, I'm going to take this drive home to do what I do best—analyze. What do I know about CiCi so far? When in doubt . . . always find something you can use to your benefit.

She loves animals.
She loves my sister (what a huge bonus that is!)
She can sing her ass off.
She's beautiful.
Has amazing eyes.
Gives good ball hold. (Yeah, I still think about it!)
Her kiss makes me breathless.
Mmm . . . her curves.

Shit! I've gotten off track. Ok animals, my sister, and music. I'll start there!

Chapter Five

Singing Assholes . . .

CiCi

"CiCi! You back there?" I hear Todd, my mailman, yell from the front of the store. I put Gimpy (terrible name, right? Poor thing!) back into his cage and hit the fan for him to dry off. Grabbing a hand towel to dry off myself, I head out front.

"Hey, Todd, what's up, man?" I ask as he hands me a huge stack of letters, magazines, etc.

"I have a few boxes for you, too." He smiles and kicks them gently. "Also, I need you to sign this certified letter." He turns it over for me to sign the postcard attached to it. *Oh boy! Never good news!*

"Thanks, Todd!" I try to put on my fake smile as I flip through all of the bills with colorful papers beaming through the windows. Yeah, you know what that means. Ugh! Todd bids me a good day and heads out.

I slump down into my chair and slowly open up the stack, putting it in some sort of order. I don't know how I'm going to pay for any of this but putting it in order makes me feel like I have a plan.

"Hi, Ceese!" Lindsey walks through the door—cheerful as ever. I love this girl. She's so good with the animals. They trust her. I trust her. But . . . I should not have hired her. I don't know what I was thinking. Sometimes, you've just got to face the facts, no matter how hard they are to face.

"Hi, Linz!" I get up and give her a hug. I still find it strange that I like to hug her. There are only certain people I will hug. Hell, I hate hugging my own twin! I don't know . . . there's something so special about her. Makes me want to recite cheesy lines from movies.

"Is Gimpy here?" She smiles as we head to the back.

"Yes. I had to put him in the cage because Todd stopped by. You want to take him out and give him the royal treatment?" I ask.

"Yes! Of course!" she says and puts her stuff in the cabinet we use for personal shit. "Hold on, Gimpy!" She smiles over her shoulder to him.

I need to leave the room.

I can't let her go. I have to figure out something. I can't afford to keep her on. I thought business would pick up from last month's charity event but it hasn't. *Fuck these tears that are forming.*

Just then, a man comes in through the door. "CiCi O'Brien?" he asks.

"Yes?"

"Kyle Cooper has a message for you," he says. He then stands up straight, clears his throat, and blows a note into a harmonica and proceeds to sing "Get Me Some of That" by Thomas Rhett.

I stare blankly.

After a few minutes, he finishes. He stares at me. "Is that all?" I ask.

"Yes, ma'am." He smiles.

"Well, thank you. Um, you have a nice voice." *Awkward!*

"Thank you! I'll see you tomorrow then!" he offers and begins to head out.

"Wait!" I stop him. "Why will I see you tomorrow?"

"I'm scheduled to sing to you again."

"Why?"

"I don't know, ma'am. I don't ask why. I just collect my pay for a song and a smile."

"How old are you?" He's like a seventeen-year-old, trapped in old man's clothes. Fucking bowtie and all! He's a cute kid, though. Brown hair that could use a cut and blue eyes.

"Twenty. I have a girlfriend, though."

"Oh. Wait . . . what? I wasn't picking you up!" I say shocked.

"Too bad." He looks me up and down before he takes off. Yeah, I'm not going to lie—total ego boost!

"Was that the singer my brother was sending you?" Linz says from behind me. I turn around quickly.

"Apparently."

"Kyle really likes you." She smiles and winks at me before she heads to the back again.

"Guess so," I say under my breath as I follow her.

"Are you just going to sit there and stare at me or are you going to talk?" Maddie asks across from me at her desk. She takes a swig of coffee.

"Every day for a week now," is all I say.

"Ok." She smiles. "Can we have that in English now?"

"He sends me singing assholes, every day." I bounce my knee.

"You know I'm actually visualizing assholes singing to you, right?" she asks then immediately bursts into laughter. I may be chuckling a little with her, as well. Yep, the visual popped into my head, too.

"What's that about?"

"Ceese, Kyle has made it known several times now that he's very interested in you."

"He shouldn't be." I chew the inside of my cheek.

"Why?"

"He should have a trophy wife."

"I'd put you on my mantel any day, Ceese."

"Thanks, bitch." I kiss the air at her.

"Why do you feel this way? What's wrong with him wanting you?" She writes notes down.

"Don't be writing shit down! I'm not a patient!"

"I'm not charging you! I need to write notes," she says defensively. "Ceese, I shouldn't be doing this! I told you to see one of my colleagues."

"You're my best friend. I'm not going to see some asshole who thinks they have me figured out. I don't have me figured out! Besides . . ." I sigh. "I don't have any insurance. Most importantly, I know you would never say anything to anybody."

"Ok. Well, best friend aside, you are still avoiding my question as your therapist." She raises a brow at me.

"He's a good guy. I don't belong with a good guy. I don't want to get blindsided again." I look down.

"Again?" she asks. I look up at her. I fight off the tears that want to form and shake my head.

"I don't want to talk about it," I say quietly.

"Is this about Drew?"

"I don't want to talk about it."

"You never told me what happened. Maybe you will feel better," she offers.

"I'll never feel better. I don't want to talk about it. And I don't want to be with Kyle!"

"Does he look like Drew?"

"Shut up, Maddie! I don't want to talk about it!"

"What happened?" She gets up.

"Nothing! Nothing worth talking about. Kyle isn't my type. How do I get him to leave me alone?" I stand up and step back from her. I don't want a hug. Hugs are not comforting. "I'm going to lose my business," I say to distract her.

"What? Why?"

"Not enough clients." I rub my face. "Ok, I'm done."

"We've barely talked," she points out.

"I'm done!" I widen my eyes. She knows to back off.

"Yoga tonight?"

"Fuck, yeah!" I say and finally give her a hug. Because it's a *later* hug not a *there, there now* hug. Whatever—I'm weird. Suck it!

"Good! We'll go out to eat with the girls tonight," she states as she heads back to her desk.

"Oh, I would but I've got some mean Ramen Noodles at home, calling my name." I grab my purse.

"My treat, Asswhore." She rolls her eyes at me as she retrieves her lip balm out of her desk drawer and applies it.

"Getting your lips ready for your next john, cocksucker?"

"Nah . . . Tuesday's blow job day around here." She smirks.

"Ah . . . I keep mixing that shit up with Titty-fuck Thursday." I shake my head and make my way to the door.

"It's an honest mistake. It's hard for me to keep the schedule straight."

"Speaking of things that are hard—what's up with the Viking?" I turn abruptly.

"He may have bought me a coffee." She smiles coyly.

"What? You're fucked now—he knows your weakness! Damn caffeine junkie!" I smack her arm.

"When it comes to him, I wouldn't say that's my weakness." She blows her bangs out of her eyes. "For the love all things fucking holy—he's Australian! Motherfucker just had to have an accent!" she sighs with frustration.

"Let me guess—"

"Yes—extra panties on Wednesdays!" She cuts me off. It's crazy—the level us sick bitches get each other!

"I would be dry humping the furniture in here, listening to him, myself. Christ!" I shiver.

"Jeebus . . . he could probably command an orgasm from me! I have to wear thick padded bras on Wednesdays," she says quietly.

"Why?"

"I get one look at him and the girls are poking out to chisel his Zeus-like chest. They want to carve my name right into that bitch!" she says with bite.

"You're gonna dry hump the furniture now, aren't you? You sound a bit hostile," I tease. "Wait! Is that why all of your fucking plants die? Are you shoving the stems up your—"

"Oh my God—goodbye, Ceese!" And with that, she opens the door fully and shoves me out. I kiss a bird off to her. She returns the gesture. God, I love that bitch!

Chapter Six

A Way In . . .

Kyle

I pull up to my parent's house. Dad gives me a wave as he finishes mowing the last patch of grass in the front yard. "Hey, Dad!" I call out as I hit the lock on my car and walk up to him.

"Hey, bud!" He wipes his forehead with his handkerchief.

"Dad, you should have somebody do this for you." I don't know why I bother to say anything—I always get the same answer.

"What for?—I ain't got Polio!" He takes my extended hand in for a shake, hugs me, and slaps my back.

"Mom and Linz inside?" I ask as we head in.

"Yeah, supper should be ready any minute now." He pats my back for me to go in ahead of him.

"There's my handsome son!" Mom heads over to me with a skip

in her step. I love my mom but it's like somebody turned on TVland and plucked her right out of a *Leave It to Beaver* episode. She even wears a goddamn apron all day long. Yet . . . I love that about her. How brave was she to not burn her bra and go all gung-ho women's lib like all of her peers. My mom just wanted to have a nice family and a nice house. She stood her ground while most people put her down for it. She was always confident in knowing that she had the most difficult job and damn if she isn't good at it! I give her a lot of credit and respect for not wavering. When Linz came along, after ten long years of trying, Winnie Cooper (my mom, not the chick from the Wonder Years) was on top of the world—gracious for God's gift. She doted over and bragged about Lindsay as if nothing was wrong with her at all.

One particular visit home from college, my mom hosted some other moms from the PTA and I overheard a conversation, neither I nor my mother, were supposed to hear. Two of the women were pitying my mother and my sister, for that matter, over my sister's condition. They had bet that my mother's demeanor was a façade, of some sort, as to how she really felt.

"Mom, are those ladies for real?" I was pissed.

"I feel sorry for them, son." She gave me a slight frown and shake of her head.

"Why do you feel sorry for them? They are putting you down and calling you a liar!" I wanted to kick those bitches out. They didn't deserve to be in the presence of my mother!

"Kyle, those poor women out there can't see past their own negativity. I will never see Lindsay as anything but a blessing to me. I love that girl as any mother would love her daughter. No. That's not true. I believe I love her more. I love her more because she is a wonderful, caring, and thoughtful human being. That aside, she has overcome so much—given her disability. I'm so proud of her accomplishments." She stretched her neck a bit to see if the ladies were still far enough away not to hear us. "They see your sister as a curse. I feel sorry for them that they are so miserable and negative that they can't see Lindsay. They only see her diagnosis. They are missing out on the person she is. They are missing out on the warmth of God's love when that beautiful girl wraps her arms around you. They are missing out on kindness that is so pure, it makes you want to be a better person.

Finally, they are missing out on the innocence. Innocence that the world has taken away from us at such a young age—Lindsay gets to hold on to hers much, much longer. What a gift. What a treasure she is." Her eyes teared up and if I'm going to be honest—mine did, too. I knew exactly what mom was talking about. "Yes. I feel very sorry for them. What a shame to walk around with such a gloomy sky above you. Right, son?" She palmed my face. "How lucky am I, to be blessed with such a loving family. You and Lindsay are my greatest life's work and I am a proud artist." She shook my head a little for emphasis before giving me a quick kiss. She let go and grabbed her tray of goodies to take out to the women. "Ladies, so sorry for the delay! I do hope you have brought your appetites!" My mother greeted them as if they never gave her anything to pity them for. I always respected my mother growing up, but that was a pivotal moment for me. That was when my respect and pride in my mother reached a new level of maturity. That was the day I realized just how strong she is. Not giving into the pressure of her peers to become the liberal woman they were all striving to be. Finding gratification in her chosen path and not imprisonment, as it was portrayed. To be handed an extra side on the plate of life and graciously accept it while others complain that it's too much. To raise Lindsay and me with thought, instead of action. To see God in everything she does, find a smile to cross her face, no matter the situation—my mother is strong—and I am honored to be her son.

"Something smells good, Mom." I smile and take in a big whiff.

"Stuffed peppers, sweetie."

"My favorite!" I say in an excited gaspy manner.

"You say that every Sunday, no matter what I'm making." She laughs at me. It's true. What can I say?—My mom knows her way around a kitchen! "Alright, you kids set the table while Dad takes his shower. Dinner will be ready in twenty." She pats my cheek and heads back to the kitchen.

"So, anything new?" My mother hints as we all get ready to dig in.

"I don't know, Mom, you think Lindsay left anything out in her reports?" I inquire with my sarcastic charm then shoot a playful smirk at Lindsay that makes her giggle. I could never get mad at my little sis. I reach over and poke a finger at her side.

"I'd like to meet her." Mom announces.

"Oh, I don't think that will happen for a while. Well, that is, unless you go in with Lindsay one day." I shrug. There's no way I'll get Ceese here to *meet the parents,* I can't even get her to go on a date with me!

"You will love her, Mom. She's my best friend!" Lindsay beams and my heart grows just a little fonder of CiCi. "She always tells me I do a good job and when I make mistakes, she never gets mad. We just go over it again. She's a really good person."

"Well, she sounds like a good egg to me!" Mom's eyes light up at Lindsay's declaration. I know my mom already loves CiCi just because CiCi treats Linz the way she does—like there's nothing wrong with her. "I just question her judgment when it comes to who she lets court her," she says and shakes her head with an added sigh.

"What do you mean, Mom?" I shoot her a quizzical look. Is CiCi dating someone that I don't know about? Did my sister tell her and not me?

"I don't know why she's making you work so hard for a date with her." She switches out her fork for her glass and takes a sip.

"She's just afraid."

"Afraid of what? You're a good guy! You're successful, have your head on your shoulders, and, if I do say so myself, you are quite attractive." She raises her brow and gives me a proud smile.

"He gets his looks from his mother," my dad pipes in.

"I don't know, Stu, I see a lot of you in him." She tilts her head at him in a flirty fashion. My sister and I catch each other's eyes and roll ours, then chuckle. Dad leans towards her and pecks her lips. I know it sounds silly, because I'm still young, but at thirty-eight, I can't help but feel my time is running out to find and have what they have.

"CiCi likes Kyle," my sister announces before shoving a mouthful in.

I clear my throat, "She does?" I try to act as nonchalant as I can, pushing food around on my plate, only glancing up for a second.

"Yes. She smiles a lot when the guys sing your songs to her. She smiles most of the day. But then, she stops." She shrugs.

"She stops smiling?"

"Yes."

"Why, dear?" Mom asks.

"I asked her that yesterday."

"And?" I grab my drink and swig.

"She just said she wishes you would stop."

"Why does she wish that if she likes the attention Kyle is giving to her?" Mom is officially in her *I'll get to the bottom of this* mode. Yeah—good luck, Mom!

"She just said she's not the right girl for him and that she's not really interested. She feels bad that he's wasting his money." She takes her last bite. My sister could be the champion of any race that involved eating. Sometimes I call her *The Hoover* but that usually warrants a slap on the arm from my mom.

"Well, then, son, you shouldn't waste any more money on her," dad says as if he's solved a problem.

"Stewart Eli Cooper! Where is the romantic man I married?" Mom turns his way and slaps his arm. She's a dainty woman but she really packs a wallop!

"What? He's not getting any younger." Dad points his hand in my direction. "I want some grandkids before I'm too old to enjoy them.

"Thanks, Dad! You've always had the amazing ability to lift one's spirit." I smirk at him. *Asshole*—I mean that lovingly, of course.

"Always happy to help," he chuckles.

"I wonder what's she's done that makes her feel like you deserve better." Mom says, though I think it was mostly to herself.

"I don't know, Mom." I shake my head. "I really like her, though. Yet, I really haven't gotten to know her much. I've learned more about her through Mitch and Charlotte than from her. Heck, even Lindsay knows more about her." It sort of makes me feel like a shmuck. There's just something there. Something that ignited inside of me from the very first moment we met.

No. Not that.

Well—a little bit of that. I am a man.

There's a pull there. I can't say that I've felt it—ever—with another woman. I look into her eyes and I just feel that those are the eyes I was meant to look into. Her kiss—guts me. Every night, I replay the kiss outside her door—the night I went all *ninja* at the bar and the kiss at her shop. *Oh man—that kiss at her shop.* I think my knees were weak for days.

"Why don't you try to get to know her better?" she starts. "Don't roll your eyes at me! I know you've been trying to *date* her. Instead, just get to know her. Ask her a question or two about herself when you run into her. Make sure you run into her more. Maybe the serenades are too much for her. You might be pushing her farther away, son." And with that, she puts her concentration back into eating.

I think she may have something here. I am going about this all wrong. I think I know just what I'm going to do!

Throwing the gear into park, I'm beginning to wonder if maybe this was a really bad idea. I turn off my car and thumb a beat at my steering wheel as I stare straight ahead at the *Home For Good* animal shelter in Hampstead. I roll through all of the questions she could possibly hammer at me. My answers, I think, are pretty solid. That's it—no more sitting here! I'm gonna go in before I pussy out!

I climb out of my car and head up to the door while checking my watch. It's 11:00 am and she should've been here for an hour already doing her Sunday of the month that she volunteers for. Yeah, I got her schedule down pat, so what?

With a big breath, I open the door and head in. CiCi has her back to me as she is on the phone. I walk up to the counter and wait.

And . . .

I may be taking inventory of her nice ass.

I lift my eyes up quickly as she hangs up the phone. She turns with a smile that quickly drops. I would've rather had an actual slap across the face then the imaginary one I just felt. *Stay cool, Kyle, this is a way in. Form a connection other than the heat you two feel.*

Oh the fucking heat I feel for this girl!

"What do you want?" she asks as she starts shifting papers around. Busy work. I get it. I also get that I am affecting her the way she is affecting me. Why does she fight it so?

"Lindsay's birthday is this week." I start. Her eyes widen in surprise and warm up a bit at my sister's name. "So, I thought it was time to get her a dog. It seems like she's doing a good job working for you.

She's responsible and knows what to do now—thanks to you." I add with a nod of my head. "She's always wanted a dog. So I thought it would be perfect. I thought it would be even better if I got the dog from here. She's always talking about the shelter and wishing she could find all of the animals homes right away." *Fuck, I'm overdoing it! Shut-up, Kyle!*

"I'm sure there's a shelter where you live."

"There is." I agree. "However, this is the one she's always talking about because of your involvement here. So, I think she would be thrilled to know I got her dog here. Shall we look?" I ask quickly to thwart her from any ideas of putting me out to get the dog somewhere else.

"Um . . . okay," she says hesitantly but then comes out from behind the counter. "This way." She gives me a half smile before walking ahead of me. And yes—I check out her heart shaped ass again. It may not really be heart shaped—but there are hearts flying out of my eyes at it. *Yum!* I'd like to take a bite out of that crime. "What kind of dog do you think she'd want?" She turns abruptly to me.

"Who?" I ask as if I'm in a daze. I suppose I am . . . or was. Oh, fuck it! I'm screwing this up already! How do I know? Call it hunch, but I'm going by the look of suspicion on CiCi's face. Her raised eyebrows are screaming "liar!" at me. "Sorry," I say quickly. "My mind wandered away." I open the door behind her that leads into the back. "After you." I wave her in.

"Well?" she asks as she walks ahead of me again into the other room.

"Well, what?"

"Kyle!" she yells with frustration, turning on her heal again to face me.

"What?" I throw my hands out and try not to smirk. It's quite the challenge. We all know how I like to smirk.

"What kind of *fucking dog* does she want?!"

"Preferably one that isn't a *fucking* dog; that could be embarrassing when she takes him out for walks." I tease.

"What are you doing here?" she seethes. Damn it, she's even hot when she's angry. Maybe hotter.

"I told you. I'm here to get a dog for Linz."

"I think you're here to provoke me," she challenges.

"I am not here to poke you. Well, not today at least."

"I said *pro voke,*" she says slowly, breaking up the syllables for me like I'm five.

"You definitely said poke."

"I did not."

"You must want me to poke you." I continue to bait her.

"I do not!" she says through clenched teeth. I step closer to her to the point where we are nose to nose. I note the tempo change of her breaths. It matches my own. Our heads struggle against what seems like a magnetic force wanting to join our lips. Mine brush against hers, slightly.

"Why do you fight it so much?" I murmur.

"Fight what?" she asks breathily.

"This. Us. Let me in, Ceese." I grasp her face in my hands gently.

"No." She tries to pull away.

"Let. Me. In." My hold firmer with a slight shake at each word.

"No."

I slam my mouth against hers.

Not two seconds go by and she's giving it right back to me, fisting the ever-loving fuck out of my hair, I might add. I don't care. She can angry kiss me all she wants, just as long as she's kissing me. Slowly, the anger dissipates and our tongues explore each other's mouth at a savoring pace.

Reluctantly, I pull away. One more swift peck and . . . an eskimo kiss. "C'mon, let's find a dog for my sister."

"Um . . . do you know what kind she um . . . would want?" she stammers.

"You'd know best." I let my hands drop down to hers, squeezing them before I let go of her left one. I lace my fingers with hers and tug her along a bit. "C'mon." I jerk my head towards the cages.

"A lapdog," she mumbles.

"Ok." I smile. "Show me what you have." I run my thumb over the top of her hand. She looks down at our entwined hands as she follows along. "Let's look at the oldest ones first. I think she'd feel best about giving one of them a home," I say to distract her from any thought of pulling away from me.

"That's a great idea, actually." Her eyes widen. "I have just the dog for her!" she says excitedly and drags me towards the right instead. I stare at her in amazement. These animals bring out such a light in her; I'm half-jealous of them. *She lets them in.*

"Are you sure about this?" I ask her for the hundredth time. Mickey is cute and all . . . ya know . . . with the exception of his continuous growl and several attempts on my life already. Let the record show: I've had him leashed and next to me for all about five minutes now. I may be sweating profusely at the thought of traveling home with him.

"Just give him space and you'll be alright." She goes to pet him but quickly backs up when he nips.

"Do you have a muzzle for him?" I ask impatiently. I can't believe she's serious about me taking him. "You know, I'm starting to wonder if you are doing this on purpose."

"What do you mean?" She shoots me a look of confusion that simmers my boiling pot down. I'm overreacting. *Fuck.* This dog is scary as hell. It's a white terrier-mixed-something-or-another with beige spots. However, all I see are his fucking teeth, grinning at me with an evil smile. It's not a smile, though. It's an "I'm going to eat your nuts for lunch, Kyle" vicious grin. "Kyle?" She touches my arm, tearing my gaze away from Mickey "The Man Eater." "Are you ok? You don't look so hot."

"You don't think I'm hot?"

"I said you don't look so hot."

"So, you don't think I'm hot. Should I work out more?"

"No. I think you're hot . . . I mean . . . you don't need to work out more. It's nice. You . . . it's nice. Oh fuck! Why are you doing this to me today?" She throws her hands in her hair and paces around a little. Mickey seems nervous by her actions. Me? I'm smirking.

"Doing what?"

"This!" She throws her hands out. "You've never done *this* before!"

"What? Get you flustered?" Still smirking . . .

"*Yes!* What the hell?!"

"I'm taking what I can get."

"What the fuck does that mean?" She widens her eyes. Her beautiful—*I so want to stare into them the rest of my life*—eyes.

"Until I can get you flustered the way I want to get you flustered, this will have to do." I take a step towards her, crowding her personal space. Our eyes track back and forth like we're watching a tennis match. But you know what we're really doing, right? "You're losing your edge, gorgeous." I step back but then lean down near her ear. "I can almost taste your pussy on the tip of my tongue," I breathe. Her lungs push air in and out rapidly. I straighten up and slowly begin to back away from her, taking Mickey along with me. "See, you have me pegged as a *nice guy* and I am. However, I have no problem being bad, Ceese. In fact, I'm pretty good at it, baby." I raise an eyebrow to join my smirk. Checkmate. She's speechless as I leave with the man-eater. Although, after that stare down, he seems to know I'm the boss now. He even gets into my car with no problem.

"Woo!" I howl after closing my door. "Did you see that?!" I ask Mickey. What? There's nobody else around. "I totally beat her at her own game! You see, she usually says something inappropriate to throw people off, but I did it! And it worked!" I grin at him. His upper lip curls and . . .

I may have just thrown up in my mouth.

I quickly start the car up and roll down the windows. This fucking dog is going to kill me one way or another—I swear!

Chapter Seven

Lights out . . .

CICI

Flick on . . . flick off.

Flick on . . . flick off.

"Fuck you, Mr. Miyagi, and the bastard from the electric company," I groan quietly and hit the flashlight on my cell phone. I walk in fully to my house and shut the door behind me. I look down at the little green shut-off slip from the electric company. *Oh good!* I only have to pay $358.03 to have it turned back on—that's the deposit.

Fuck my life.

Well, I can't sit here and act like I didn't know it was going to happen. It was either the electric at the shop or here. I think my customers would find it odd if I handed their pets back to them soaking wet.

Looking around in the darkness, I decide to do what I do best: mess with my sister. You'll see what I mean. Bitch falls for it every time! I quickly pack a few things and run back out, locking the door behind me. This will be better for me anyhow. I don't want to spend another night replaying, what I now refer to as, The Kyle—what the fuck was that?—Incident.

I jump into my car and start it up. Yes, there should be enough gas in this baby to get me to her house. *Fucking hell, I feel like a goddamn teenager!*

"Hey, sorry I'm late!" I say out of breath as I charge into Charley's house.

"Late for what?" She turns around with a look of confusion.

"I'm watching the kids tonight for you guys. Do I have the wrong night?" I ask, giving her my "what the fuck is wrong with you?" face.

"Uh . . . we haven't asked you to watch the kids." she states but I can see she's trying to ponder whether she did or not. See? Bitch always falls for it.

"You totally did. What the fuck is the matter with you?" I ask as I saunter over to the sauce she's cooking. "Mmm . . . whatcha got going on here?" I stir it then suck down a mouthful from the spoon.

"Ceese, goddamn it! Stop!" She smacks my hand.

"What?!" My mouth full. Mm . . . I haven't had normal food in three days. "Did you make enough for me?" I ask, though I don't know why I bother.

"Of course, but I wasn't expecting you." She nudges me over to open the oven.

Just then, I hear the garage door open. "I guess vagina breath is home."

"Ceese, knock it off!" she gasps and swats me.

"Um . . . according to you, it's true." I bite back my smile.

"I did not say he has . . . vagina breath," she says the last bit quietly.

"Hey, Ceese! What a pleasant surprise!" Mitch bellows behind me . . . sarcastically. Don't get me wrong, Mitch and I love each other.

Things have just been a little off because of the whole Kyle situation.

"According to Ceese, we asked her to watch the kids tonight," Charley informs Mitch before planting a kiss on his lips.

Yeah. I'm jealous. So what? I'm also happy for my sister. I can live vicariously through her. I know I'll never have this. You know, the 'Hey, honey, how was your day?' shit. *He* ruined all my hopes of having that. I'll never allow myself to trust like that again. It's been fifteen years and it's no less painful or traumatic. I'm always amazed how people handle things so differently. You ever think about that? What happened to me, I can just about guarantee, has happened to other women. I don't know who they are but I wonder if they've moved on from it. I have. In many ways, I have, except when it comes to trusting.

"CiCi!" Mitch snaps his fingers in my face and I focus back. "Where'd you go in there?" He taps my temple.

"I'd tell you, but then you'd want to tag along next time." I grab some grapes out of the bowl on the counter and pop them into my mouth. "Where are the kids?" I ask with my mouth full.

"Mom and Dad's for the night." Charley raises a brow at me. *Damn it.*

"Why did you do that since I was coming over?"

"I didn't know you were coming over." She rolls her eyes. I mentally chuckle. No one ruffles her feathers like I do. I'm quite proud of that record.

"Why the hell else would I be here? Don't you think I have better things to do?" I throw my arms up.

"*No!*" They bark in unison.

"But, I'm glad you're here," Mitch smiles. Not the normal smile you get from somebody who's generally happy. More like a smile from someone who has something up their sleeve but you're not quite sure what it could be.

"Why?" I ask slowly and suspiciously.

"We've missed you, that's all!" He smiles broadly and pulls me in for a hug. *Awkward hug.* Just then, the doorbell rings. "Ah! That would be our dinner guest." Mitch announces, pulling away.

"Dinner guest?" I mouth to Charley when he leaves to answer the door. She ignores me by turning to grab dishes out of the cabinet.

"Here, at least set the table," she says as she passes them to me.

"I can go."

"Nope," she quips and goes back to getting things ready to bring out. I walk out to the dining room with the plates.

"Oh . . . so you are alive! What's the matter, Ceese, you can't call a brotha back?"

"Jay . . . first of all," I turn to face him, "you're white. Second, I've been busy."

"Busy avoiding people," he mutters under his breath.

"Only meddling bitches." I smile sarcastically.

"Oh, shut the fuck up and give me some love!" He grabs me and pulls me into his Hercules-embrace. Jay's got a body to die for. The kind that makes you want to outline muscles with your tongue. He smells good. He's handsome and when he smiles, those killer dimples get you every time. He's one of my dearest friends and the only guy I thoroughly trust. Oh, and . . . he's gay . . . as all the good ones are. I could hug him forever.

"What the hell is this?" A voice, that is becoming very familiar to me, asks in an accusatory tone.

I lift my head off Jay's chest. "This is me, hugging my gusband. Why? You jealous?" I ask straight-faced. "Jay, I think Kyle wants a hug from you." I look up at Jay and chuckle.

"Damn skippy, I want a hug from him." Kyle says, placing his hands on his hips. "I can't believe you're stepping out on me like this, Jay. I mean, I know she's beautiful but I thought we had something," he adds.

"Listen, man, if she don't give it up soon, you just come swinging my way and I'll show you just what you been missin' your whole life." Jay laughs and throws his hand out for one of those slap-shakes that only guys can pull off. I don't know how Jay pulls it off, either; my balls are definitely bigger than his.

"How the hell do you two know each other?" I finally ask.

"Kyle and I go way back!" Jay shrugs and let's his embrace on me go.

"Way back since when?"

"Since last Tuesday." Kyle grabs my hand and pulls me to him. "Hi," he breathes into my face. *Fuck the way my heart pounds like crazy when he's this close. Just fuck it!* And then he does it. He leans down and sweeps my lips like we've been together forever.

And.
I hate it.
I hate every second that I love it.
Eskimo kiss.
Damn it, I love when he does that.

"Ceese, can you grab the rest of the stuff for me?" Charley asks as she walks into the dining room with one of her masterpieces.

"Sure." I try to pull myself together. Kyle gives me another quick peck then pats my ass before letting me go. I turn and head through the threshold of the dining room into the kitchen. And yes, I totally misgauged the doorway and smacked my shoulder into the frame, but I'ma keep walking like that didn't happen.

"Owww!" I complain lowly as I make it into the kitchen and out of view. I rub my shoulder. *That is so going to bruise.* I head over to the cabinet to grab the glasses.

"Psst . . . hey!" Charley hisses behind me. I turn to her. "Are you guys together now?"

I shrug.

"No! You don't get to just shrug as if I asked you a simple question. This is a *very* loaded question that deserves a *very* loaded answer!" She crosses her arms.

"Since when do you wear aprons and who gave you that one?" I try to divert her inquisition.

"I didn't want to slop up my outfit. Kyle's mom gave it to me. I like it," she adds.

"Kyle's mom? When did you meet her and why did she give that to you?" Ok, I'm a little irritated that my sister has met my boy . . . er . . . Kyle's mom before I have. Not that I want to meet her. Lord only knows what she'll think of me. Actually, I'm pretty sure she'll think me not good enough for her son. I don't blame her. In fact, I agree with her.

"I met her last week. She invited us over for dinner. She's really nice. You'd like her." She smacks my arm lightly for emphasis.

"Well, I'm sure she wouldn't like me, so I'm in no rush," I mutter.

"On the contrary, we had a very nice chat about you and she's already decided she's a big fan of yours, although, she's not pleased with how you're stringing her son along." She raises her brows. "Which brings me back to my question, the one you so nicely avoided; are you two together now?"

"Why is she a fan of mine?"

"The way you treat Lindsay."

"How do I treat Lindsay?" I knit my brows together.

"Like a person and not a diagnosis."

I give her a slight smile. "I love that kid." I hand her the glasses I had retrieved so I can turn around for the last of them.

"Ceese, are you going to answer me about Kyle?"

"Jesus." I sigh. "You're a pain in the ass!" I complain. "I don't know. I guess I'm letting some walls down. I'm not sure about anything in my life right now."

"What's that supposed to mean?" She jerks her head back as I turn again.

"It means I'm hungry and I'm not sure if you're ever going to feed me. Now, come on." I nudge her shoulder as I pass her, heading back out to the dining room.

"I'll take those," Mitch says, grabbing the glasses from me to place on the wet bar. "Go sit down." He nods his head in Kyle's direction. Dutifully, I head over. Yeah, I said dutifully. I'm a little off my game tonight—so what?

I head around the table to the chair next to Kyle and take a seat. He gives me one of those smiles that hits his eyes. It makes me feel giddy inside like a fucking moron.

I hate it.

I hate how good he makes me feel.

Here's the thing. I know that if I give this "a go," eventually, I'm going to fuck up and then his eyes will change towards me. He'll look at me with hatred. That's why I hate this so much. Kyle is normal and good and Goddamn it if I'm not falling for him, but I don't trust normal and good. I'm very scared of it.

But with him . . .

Just maybe.

Kyle leans into my ear; his hand softly rubs my back, "How was work today, Ceese?"

"It was ok. Slow." I say truthfully before grabbing my glass of wine from Mitch.

"I thought you guys did a killing at your charity thing. You haven't gained any new clientele from that?" he asks.

"No." I answer abruptly and grab my plate to put some eggplant parm on it. I grab Kyle's when I'm done and give him a portion. "Bread?" I glance at him quickly.

"Yeah. Thanks," he nods. "I don't get it. Lindsay said so many people were happy with the service and promised to come back."

"I don't get it, either. I also don't want to talk about it." I add.

"Can I look into this for you? You know, business is sort of my thing." I can see that he's treading lightly. I sit back and stare at him for a few.

"It'd be smart on your part to do so, Ceese. Kyle'll figure that shit out in no time. It's why I keep him around." Mitch points his forkful at me before shoving it into his mouth. He then rolls his eyes back and my sister grins excitedly. *Dorks—both of them!*

"I don't run a car part business. I deal in cuddly fur balls." I roll my eyes and take a sip.

"Business is business, babe." Kyle mumbles and butters his bread.

"Well, this is *my* business and I'd prefer you to keep your nose out of it. Ok, *babe?*" I snap, throwing his endearment back at him sarcastically.

"Fine!" He forks into his eggplant aggressively. "Just when I thought your fucking self-protective wall had vanished, you whip it out like a fucking magic trick. Bravo, Ceese!"

I didn't mean to be like that. I meant to keep my wall down. I just . . ."babe" felt very possessive. I couldn't help myself. I'm such an over achiever—I'm fucking things up before they even get started. I stew in this, silently, as I eat my food.

"So, let's talk design, shall we?" Jay pipes up.

"Yes!" Charley's voice jumps excitedly at the mention.

"I was thinking that since your menu is comfort food with no specifically themed ethnicity, we'd design around the comforts of home. Plush, couch-like seating for the booths. Tables will be more like dining room tables instead of restaurant quality. Only input I'd like is what kind of comfort theme are you looking for in style and color? Personally, I'm thinking Southern. Pay homage to your hero, Paula Dean. What are your thoughts, sweetie?"

"What do you think, Ceese?" Charley asks me excitedly. *Fuck.* I'm sitting here, battling tears because I feel so fucked up and emotional and she's expecting me to give her my opinion on . . . on . . . wait—what the fuck are they talking about?

"What are you guys talking about?" I try to keep my voice steady.

"Mitch bought me a restaurant. He just surprised me with the deed last night!" She smacks my hand. My sister and her effin' smacking for emphasis.

"Wow." It's all I can say because I feel a little green monster taking over me. Ever feel jealous of the person you love the most in your life? I don't want to feel this way. I want to be happy for her, but fuck it if doesn't feel like she's gotten everything handed to her lately. I know, I know; I shouldn't be saying that or feeling this way. She's had her fair share of fucked up shit. I'm just hormonal. Yes. I must be due for my lady curse.

"That's how Kyle and I met. He handled the buy for Mitch and met me over at the site to get measurements for me to give the place an overhaul." Jay snaps me out of my pity-party-for-one. "Of course, I thought he wanted my measurements but he was quick to correct me. It seems he's only interested in yours, CiCi."

"Yeah, well, Kyle's realizing that maybe he should change his mind about that. It's not worth it." Kyle mutters . . . in third person. I can't even stop my neck from turning to look at him or stop the tear that finally wins and slides down my cheek. I believe the words, *it's not worth it,* is what pushed it along. I'm guessing that he senses me looking at him because he glances up from his plate and his face visibly softens. I look away.

"I'm going to take my dinner to my room," I say quickly and start to stand with my plate in hands.

"You don't live here, CiCi. You don't have a room." Mitch bellows out with annoyance.

"I have lived here for over ten years!" I snap back.

"You are not staying here! Go home! I'm tired of you inviting yourself all of the damn time! You're not wanted here!" Mitch continues. *Crack.* That was the sound of my heart breaking down the center. Mitch has *never* talked to me like this.

"How dare you?" Charley gasps. I look over at her, expecting that question to be directed towards me. I mean, why not? First Kyle, then Mitch. However, she's looking right at Mitch.

"How dare I what, Charlotte, state the obvious?"

"Who's it obvious to, Mitch? You?" She throws her napkin on top of her plate.

"Baby, what are you doing? You need to eat." He points at her plate.

"I've lost my appetite," she seethes. "CiCi, you're more than welcome to stay here tonight." She looks over at me. "In fact, I think we should make a girl's night of it! Stay in my room with me and we'll rent movies and pig out on ice cream." She smiles.

"Excuse me?" Mitch says through his teeth angrily.

"You heard me." She glares right back at him before bringing her focus over to Kyle, "And you, Kyle, are a fucking pussy! You didn't even attempt to tell Mitch to shut up while he was being a rude fucking prick to my sister. It seems to me that you're not the one who's "worth it" around here."

"Dayum! You know Charley's pissed when the f-bomb is flying out her mouth like it's her job to drop them." Jay adds his two cents before continuing with his meal.

"CiCi, you are not staying here. That's final." Mitch states before taking another bite of his meal.

"This is *my* house and I will say who stays and leaves." Charley yells and I swear to God her face has just turned as red as the damn sauce. I think it's clear that Charley and I are on the same cycle.

"Your house, huh?" He laughs but not the haha laugh, more like the "are you fucking kidding me?" laugh. "You haven't paid one single mortgage payment on *your* house since I met you! I'm pretty sure you've never made a single payment on this house in general. Spreading your legs so your bills get paid won't hold up in court, Char, so I think it's safe to say I own this house just like I own you!" He pushes his plate away.

What are we all doing?

Same as you—staring at him in shock and wanting to choke him.

"Excuse me, everyone," Charley says, barely audible before getting up. "Sorry about dinner tonight. I don't know what happened, but I apologize." She gains some strength back in her voice. "Goodnight," she adds before heading out of the dining room.

"Baby, wait." Mitch tries to grab her arm but she takes off.

"Dude . . ." Kyle says, seemingly in disbelief.

"I can't believe I just talked to her like that. Where do I even begin to try to fix what I just did?" He puts his head into his hands after propping his elbows onto the table.

"Tell her you're sorry. She knows you're still working on what happened to you. She knows that shit flies out of your mouth before you can even think about it because you're still trying to protect yourself. She loves you, Mitch, and she knows you love her. Just tell her, but don't say that you won't do it again. Be honest. Tell her that you're sorry for now and for in the future if and when you do it again, no matter the degree." I offer, knowing exactly why he does it. I do the same damn thing.

"Let me start by apologizing to you, Ceese. I've been a real jerk to you because I see you doing to Kyle what I do to Charlotte." He reaches forward for my hand. "You know I love you. You are always welcome here. I didn't mean that." He squeezes my hand once I place it in his.

"Thanks for saying that. I'm sorry I ruined your evening. The pipes at my place burst or something and it'll be a few days before it's fixed, so I don't have any running water at the moment. I'll go to my parents." A little white lie never hurt anyone.

"Why didn't you just tell us that?" Mitch shakes his head.

"Because that would be so un-CiCi like of me." I shiver at the thought.

"Alright, I'm going to go upstairs and begin my groveling. Wish me luck. If you hear a girl, screaming in fear, it'll probably be me, getting the crap kicked out of me," he says wearily before getting up.

"You deserve it."

"I know I do." He shakes his head. "Goodnight." He gives us a half smile and heads out of the room.

"Well, this was a new spin on fast food." Jay scrapes up the last bite on his plate.

"Dude, I can't believe you just sat here and shoveled that fucking food in your mouth the entire time." I throw a roll at his head.

"First of all, not only was I starving but this is Charley's eggplant parm we're talking about. A fucking bomb could go off or David Beckham could pull up a chair next to me and I would eat that shit before solving world peace or convincing David he's playing for the wrong team!" Jay deadpans.

"Listen, nobody expects you to do any of that on an empty stomach!" I chuckle.

"Right?" he plays along. "Alright, I'm going to head out and leave you two lovebirds alone." He pushes his chair back and gets up.

"You just don't want to do dishes."

"Damn skippy!" he laughs. I get up to walk around the table and give him a quick hug. He leans down towards my ear, "Go easy on Kyle, he really likes you."

"I know." I pull back from him and give him a smile.

"Are you alright, besides everything tonight? You don't seem like yourself."

"I'm a little off tonight. It's been a rough few days. I'll be fine though." I admit.

"Call me tomorrow and we'll talk." He kisses my forehead.

"Sure," I say but we both know I won't do it. After releasing me, he reaches across the table to shake Kyle's hand.

"Sorry about tonight, man." Kyle slaps Jay's shoulder as he stands and shakes hands.

"Look, I got what I came for." Jay shrugs. "Alright, I'll see you kids on the flipside!" And with that, he heads out. I turn back to the table and Kyle.

"Um . . . I'll go." He runs his hand through his hair, seemingly unsure.

"Don't," I say quickly.

"No?" He furrows his brow.

"I don't want to eat alone." I reach across the table and grab my plate before seating myself into Jay's chair across from Kyle. I push Jay's plate over before setting mine down. I grab Jay's fork and start eating while Kyle stares at me in silence.

"You're using his fork?"

"He's my best friend, and last I checked, he doesn't have cooties."

"Jay's right and I'm worried, too." He takes his seat. "You're not yourself."

"It's been a difficult week, Kyle, that's all." I keep my eyes down.

"Talk to me . . ." he trails off. I look up at him and say nothing. I just sit here, studying him. "What?" he asks after a few minutes. If I knew, I'd tell him.

"How are things going with Mickey? Linz didn't mention him

the other day."

"Not about the dog, Ceese, about you! I want you to talk to me about your difficult week." He does nothing to hide his frustration.

"What did you do with Mickey?" I question, feeling a little alarmed.

"I have him till the party."

"You've had him for three days?" I widen my eyes. I can't believe my ears.

"We've come to an understanding. Incidentally, my mother invited you to my sister's surprise party." He grabs his wine and takes a swig.

"What? Why?" I drop my fork.

"Because you're Lindsay's friend and boss. She wants you there."

"Oh."

"And she knows that you're important to me, as well," he adds quickly before throwing a forkful of food into his mouth.

What's that sound, you ask?

Oh . . . just my heart, trying to beat out of my chest.

"All done?" I gesture to his plate as he finishes his last bite.

"Uh, yeah," he says with his mouthful. I quickly grab his plate and pile it on the others as well as mine. I head out to the kitchen to wash them all or . . . you know . . . regroup. I place the dishes in the sink and turn the faucet on. I lean my hands on either side of the sink, listening to the sound of the water rushing through the pipes at full force. Why does he affect me like this? I should be fighting this. It's not good. *He'll hurt me.* Sadly, part of me doesn't even care anymore. I've lost my fight. I've no energy left for self-preservation. Everything is going wrong in my life right now. I could use some "right," even if for just a small moment of time. Just a moment to feel normal, worthy, loved, and most importantly—not alone.

"Ah," I gasp softly as Kyle's hand slides onto my hip. His free hand sweeps my hair away from the right side of my neck over onto my left shoulder before it finds its place at my other hip. Yes, I'm panting like a dog in heat. Wouldn't you be? His breath hits my neck hot and slow.

Lord, help me.

His lips move up to my ear, "All day—everyday—you're there, in my head. I can't get you out. You consume me. I keep trying. Christ,

I try like hell to push you out, shake you off. I can't. I see your eyes. I feel your mouth on mine." His lips skirt down my neck. I close my eyes, relishing in his touch. I place my hands on top of his, guiding them to explore my belly and up my torso. I lean my head back, giving him more access to my neck as I listen to his words. "I breathe the rapid breaths you breathe those moments you let your guard down. I can't stand the power you have over me. I hate it. I hate how much I fucking love it. I want you. I want you like . . . actually, I've never wanted anyone like I want you." He buries his face into the crook of my neck. His hands stop moving. I'm not going to lie—I'm disappointed. They're parked just under my girls.

My girls want to play "Tug, tug, rub and roll."

What the fuck?

"Kyle," I breathe, "Don't stop." I try to nudge his hands along.

"You want me to touch you?" he asks, his mouth back at my ear—breaths matching mine.

"Yes."

"No."

"No?"

"No."

I push his hands off me and grab the sponge, pouring a ridiculous amount of dish soap on it. I'm going to do these damn dishes and I'm going to try my hardest not to stab him with one of these knives for making me feel like an asshole.

"I want to touch you." He slides his hands back on to my hips. His chest presses into my back, giving me no space to turn if I wanted to. "But," he continues, "If I touch you, I won't be able to stop until you're screaming my name while your legs are shaking around my hips." *Is it a little wet in here or is it just me . . . and my panties?*

I bet he'd give me good leg shake.

Also, I may have just whimpered . . . slightly.

"I'm going to go." He pats my hip.

"Go? What?!" I turn around the moment he backs off.

"I can't stay, Ceese." He shakes his head. "If I stay, then I will end up making love to you." Running his hand through his hair, he looks everywhere but at me directly.

"Why is that such a bad thing?" I barely recognize the vulnerability in my own voice.

"It wouldn't be except for the way *I know* you will behave afterwards."

"The way I'll behave?" I knit my brows together.

"Aww c'mon, CiCi!" He raises his voice and paces, seemingly frustrated. "You will go right back to your usual "all walls up, I don't need anyone" self. You'll make comments about it being nothing, that you just needed to get your rocks off and I happened to be there! You'll push me away and goddamn it, I know it will destroy me," he lowers his voice for that last part of his speech.

I take a few steps towards him and hold up my pinky. "I promise that I won't do that."

"Really, Ceese? You think I'm gonna put my trust in a pinky-promise that you will be a good girl after we make love?" he asks, staring down into my eyes, once I make it into his personal space.

"How about a pinky-promise that I'll be a good girl while we're making love?" I breathe as I toe-up and brush my lips against his. He growls lowly before attacking my mouth in a viciously delicious manner.

"CiCi," he murmurs against my lips.

"Yes?"

"You want to get rid of that soapy sponge now? You're soaking the back of my shirt with it." He does his smirkish smile while pulling my arm that is encircled around his neck down—soapy sponge gripped tightly in my hand.

"Sorry." I whisper giggle. Yes "whisper giggle" is a real thing! It's when you laugh through your nose without any sound—just rapid breaths, mimicking a giggle: whisper giggle. Got it? Now stop distracting me; that's Kyle's job. *Mmm . . . Kyle.* I toss the sponge in its dish and rinse my hands. I turn to him, drying my hands off only to find his hand already extended out to me.

Shit's about to get real, people!

Kyle is sporting that hooded "I'm about to get laid" stare. His bright blue eyes have changed a few shades darker. And holy hell if my heart isn't flipping out, knocking on every wall of my chest, trying to get the fuck out.

"Lead the way, beautiful." He squeezes my hand and nods his head. I stare at him. I'm pretty sure I just licked my lips before pulling my bottom one in to nibble on it a little because he growled again and tugged me along.

My feet are moving but my mind is still on the mental image I just had of his naked body all over mine. He feels very muscular and toned. He's not beefcake status, but he's definitely built. I'm imagining a delicious v-line. I'm imagining everything so hard and powerful all over me.

And . . . I may have just whimpered again.

I look over at Kyle.

He's smirking.

Shit. I definitely whimpered.

I lead him up to the pseudo apartment, above the garage, that Charlotte uses for overflow of guests. I use it for overflow of my life's necessities: clothes, makeup, hair products, framed pictures—you know, the usual stuff. Stopping at the door, I reach up on my toes to feel for my key.

"Why is the door locked if it can be entered from the inside of the house?" he asks in a hushed tone.

"I don't want the kids to go through my shit. Actually, I don't want friends of the kids' going through my shit. Kids are fucking nosy, ya know?" I shrug and fumble with getting the key into the hole. I can't help it. I'm thinking about him, putting his key in my hole—unlocking shit.

"I thought you didn't live here."

"I do live here." I open the door and flick on the light. "They just haven't accepted that yet."

"I don't know why. It seems pretty obvious to me that you reside here." He looks around, smiling and shaking his head at all of my stuff.

"See?!" I point out.

"Clearly," he adds, shuffling his hand out at all of my things. "So . . ." he trails off and sits on the bed.

"Don't do that!" I rush towards him when he picks up an old pair of my underwear.

"Don't do what?"

"Don't sniff my panties." I try to grab them but he moves his hand back and away from me quickly. He's laughing, I might add. *Fucker!*

"I wasn't going to, but now you have me intrigued." He holds me back with his free arm as I continue my efforts in reaching them.

"Kyle, they're old! It wouldn't be sexy for you to sniff those! You want fresh-scented CiCi pussy not expired-scented CiCi pussy. God only knows what kind of chemical changes have occurred since I took them off!" I practically yell as I go for the grab one more time. I'm not successful but he does toss them onto the floor before encircling my body with that arm, whisking me down onto the bed, and under him.

Fuck, he really is a goddamn ninja!

I'm trying to control my breathing. I really am. However, he's staring down at me with those ice-blue eyes and strumming his fingers slowly over my bottom lip. They descend my jawline, neck, until he reaches my right clavicle bone. He traces over it and leans his head down closer to mine. Instantly, I feel that magnetic pull neither one of us has ever been able to fight. I lick my lips, anticipating his. Closer. Closer. Closer . . .

Eskimo kiss.

Let the record show that at the time of—I don't have a fucking clock to look at; my panties have become soaked. And let's also give an honorable mention to my confusion as to why the hell it turns me on when he does that!

His lips linger over mine again.

Peck.

Open-mouth peck . . . suck.

Peck.

Open-mouth, slight tongue-peck and . . . succcckkkk.

And so begins our synchronized kissing. His tongue dives deep into my mouth. My hands climb up to his head and thread through his hair, pulling him harder against my mouth. I feel his hand drift down my chest. He pushes at my flimsy V-neck shirt, making it fall off my shoulder. Grabbing at my sports tank, he yanks it down with urgency. *Tug, tug, rub, and roll. Tug, tug, rub, and roll.* Chant with me; you know you want to!

Suddenly, he rips his mouth from mine. His eyes fall down to my right girl, chilling outside my shirt. Oh. *Oh holy mother of all motherfucking hell!* Tug, tug, rub, roll, and pinch. And . . . lick, suck, and bite. Repeat. Yes, I'm trying to hump him. He tears away from me again, sitting up on his knees. His shoulders rise up and down in a quick fashion, matching the tempo of his breaths. He stares down into my eyes and unbuttons his shirt at a God awful slow pace. Ever have one of those moments where you want to get so lost into somebody that you don't even want to remember your fucking name afterwards? Yeah—I'm having one of those moments right now. I lean up and pull my shirt and sports tank off fully. Our eyes staying connected, I place my hands on his stomach and slide them up at the same pace he just took to reveal it. When I reach his shoulders, I slide his shirt off them. I was right. Oh, man was I right, but . . . I would've never guessed I'd find this on top of a very nicely toned chest. Half of his upper right chest and arm is covered in the most beautiful (read: HOT AS FUCK!) Polynesian tribal tattoo I have ever seen. This is the real deal, yo. Not the trendy 1990's, "check out my tribal tattoo, dude, even though I don't know what the fuck it means" tattoo.

"You like that, beautiful?" he asks, running the back of his hand down my cheek while I trace the very intricate lines of this masterpiece with my fingertips.

"Fuck, yeah," I murmur before following the path of my fingertips with short licks and nips.

"I thought you would, especially, when I saw this." He runs his hand down my side, tracing my own, more delicate version of a tribal tattoo. "Do you have any idea how fucking sexy you are, Ceese?" His voice carries through the air all soft and vulnerable—almost aching. His fingers trail farther down, hooking the waist of my yoga pants, and sliding them down. My lips work their way up to his neck. Fisting his hair, I breathe him in and get lost in the sense of his touch. "Don't leave me in the morning," he whispers against my shoulder, his lips painting it gently. I jerk my head back slightly and look into his eyes. "Don't do it," he repeats with a sterner approach, yet calm. I give him a little nod of agreement before leaning in to sweep his lips. The pressure from the weight of his body makes me lie back down on the bed. Abruptly, he tears his lips from mine. He stares into my eyes again for a moment before he begins to travel down my body. His tongue spends some time tracing the details of my tattoo, spanning the length of the left side of my torso. "So fucking sexy . . ." he trails off in a growl before continuing on, whipping my pants off.

He gasps. Pants. Groans.

He gently flicks at my hood piercing.

I lean up on my elbows and study him, not sure of this reaction.

His fingers glide across my clef. "So smooth," he barely utters.

"I don't like body hair . . . on me. It bothers me," I offer.

"Gorgeous. So. Fucking. Gorgeous." His finger plays with my ring gently. He closes his eyes, throwing his head back.

"What's the matter?" I ask, feeling a bit anxious.

"What's the matter?" He lets out a light chuckle. "I'm trying to compose myself. You have no idea how badly I want to pound into you like a teenage boy, having his first go at things."

"Oh . . ."

"Remember the first time we kissed? What you said to me about how good my scruff was going to feel against your pussy, when I eat the fuck out of it?" He situates himself in position and . . . he smirks. This is different from the usual Kyle smirk I get from him. This is sexy smirk. This is "I'm about to rock your fucking world" smirk. *Fucking smirker.* I'm gonna wipe that smirk right off of his face—with my pussy. He lowers his face to my center and glides up it with *one . . . two . . . three* quick, soft, and savoring kisses. The last one, on my clit, had a little tongue slippage action going on and it was hot as hell. "Did it go down at all like this in your mind?" he asks before he lowers back down then shakes his face, rubbing his scruff on my pussy lips and blowing raspberries.

Me?

I'm wide-eyed for a moment until my laughter rolls up from my toes and closes my eyes as I go into hysterics. I stop when he stops. My eyes open to find his smiling ones. I'm about to ask him what in the fuck that was but I'm distracted by the weight of my smile falling. I know exactly what that was. That was him pulling some shit that I would've pulled had the roles been reversed. He pulled a "CiCi." He's been doing that a lot lately. And at this moment, I realize, he's able to pull a "CiCi" because he *gets* me.

Holy fuck . . .

He gets me . . .

"That was so much hotter than I imagined, actually," I say with the most serious tone I can muster, cos . . . ya know, I gotta fuck with him.

"It was the raspberries, wasn't it?" he asks, knowingly.

"It was." I nod. "I mean, you went right for it. No waiting. No planning out when you would take our relationship to vaginal raspberry status. You just went for it . . . like a ninja." I widen my eyes at him. "That's fucking hot, Kyle. I love a confident man who pays no attention to codes, rules, and whatnot. You see a pussy that needs a raspberry blown on it and you go in like a champ!"

"That's my motto, actually—*go in like a champ!* I'm getting bumper stickers made next week."

"I'd put that on my bumper," I say thoughtfully.

"That's nice, Ceese. Thank you for the support but I have other things in mind for your bumper." He flicks his left eyebrow up at me then winks.

Let the record show that I am speechless. Normally, I'd have something here, but I don't. I feel like he stole my line. I feel like I'm bantering with myself. I don't know how to banter with myself . . . with other people in the room.

"Do me a favor?"

"Huh?" I snap my attention back.

"Make sure to tell me how awful I am at this . . . don't hold back, ok?" His tone is still slightly playful but the look in his eyes grows serious, almost predatory like. I nod. "I can't wait to find out how many licks it takes to get to the center of CiCi's tootsie pop." All I can do is pant while I watch him lower his attention to my *Golden Ticket.*

I think I may have pegged Kyle out all wrong. Or . . . I've created a monster who wants to do nothing more than show me just how bad he can be.

Chapter Eight

Where there's a wall . . . there's still a way.

Kyle

Fuck, I love the way her pussy tastes . . .

I should stop and tell her. I'm pretty sure, under normal circumstances, she'd love for me to tell her that; talk dirty to her in general. But she's all over the place tonight. Funny thing with CiCi is that her "all over the place" is everybody else's "normal."

She almost comes to a seated position and pulls at my hair, grinding harder into my face, "Oh God, right there!" she cries out, her pussy pulsating into my face. "Do you have any idea," she starts after coming down, "how many times I've imagined you doing this to me? How hard you've fucked me?" Her voice is so soft and seductive, causing me to mentally talk the "big guy" down. I swear if I get any fucking harder right now, I won't even make it to the unzipping of my pants. "Just the slightest thought of you," she pants, "and my pussy is dripping, aching for you."

"Faaaacccckkk!" I growl, whipping her legs over my shoulders and rising to my knees, sending her back and on to her upper back—almost upside down.

And . . .

I fuck her hard with my tongue, my fingers working their magic at her clit. The sounds coming from her are bringing me closer to the edge than I've ever been. "Come, CiCi! Come!" I snap out of pure need to get her there again so I can bury myself in her. I have never commanded a woman to come before. I didn't even think about it—I just did it. And you know what? She is fucking coming like a champ.

Yes, I'm smirking.

I lay her body back down and attack her lips, unzipping and yanking my pants down before wrapping her legs around my waist. I break away from her mouth and stare into her eyes for a beat. "Please . . ." she whispers. I slam into her and soak in the sound of her whimper.

She feels so fucking good.

My left hand palms her face, my mouth claiming hers as I roll into her over and over again. I let go and reach down to hook her leg, allowing myself to thrust deeper; I can't get close enough. Her whimperish cries hypnotize me like some fucking spell I'm under. I can't stop.

It's intense.

I feel like I'm on a high.

I don't want to come down.

Deeper . . .

"Oh. You. Have. Got. To. Be. Kidding. Me!" CiCi bellows out through another orgasm. She clenches tightly around my cock, causing a long low groan from me.

"Ceese! Stop! Fuck—I gotta pull out!"

"No! Don't stop!" She holds me to her and grinds her hips, finishing off.

"Shit! Shit! *God . . . damn!*" Yup . . . Like a teenage boy, having his first go at things. I pump into her a few last times, unable to close my gaping mouth until I collapse on top of her.

We lay still for some time, trying to steady our breathing.

"Ceese?"

"No."

"No?"

"No, I'm not on birth control," she says quietly.

"Oh. Wow . . . ok."

"I'm sorry." She turns her head when I lift mine up to look at her.

"Me, too. I just couldn't hold back anymore." I try to explain.

"As far as pregnancy, I'm sure we'll be fine. I'm due within the next day or two."

"But?" I move a strand of her hair off of her left cheek.

"Are you," she hesitates, "are you clean?"

"Of course I am!" I bite, making her jump a bit. "Sorry." I shake my head, trying to control the spark of anger that shot out of nowhere. I had better control over my anger before CiCi came along. It's not even true anger, more like some sort of anxiety. I never know what to expect with this woman. All I know is that no matter what . . . for some reason . . . I can't walk away. "I always protect myself and get regular check-ups. I can usually control myself enough to not go too far without a condom."

"Usually?"

"Yes. You're the exception. I can't seem to control any part of me around you." I pull out and roll onto my back. Letting out a big sigh, I continue, "At some point, I should probably quit trying." I turn my head in her direction and bring my hand up to her cheek, grazing it with the back of my fingers. She lies in silence, her breathing hypnotizing me. I stare at her for several minutes just wondering. Wondering what's going through her head, what's going on with her? Something is not right. She's not herself. I'm not going to lie; my anxiety is starting to go through the roof. I can't help but think that's she's planning an exit strategy. I take in a deep breath and close my eyes, unable to believe I'm about to assist her with this. "Do you want me to go?"

Her head whips my way to face me, her eyes open wide. "Do you want to leave?!" she asks in an almost accusatory tone.

I shake my head and give her a half smile (of relief, really). "No. I, most definitely, do not want to leave you right now."

"Why would you ask me that then?" She turns on her side and

props up on her elbow.

"Ceese, why *wouldn't* I ask that?" I prop up as well. "This . . . tonight, was completely out of character for you. You have to understand that while part of me is thrilled that this just happened, another part of me is waiting for you to pull your crap. Wait . . ." I trail off shaking my head.

"What?" She rises up more.

"I'm sorry." I palm her left cheek. "We should be basking in the afterglow, not talking about this shit. I'm screwing this up for us. I analyze everything like a damn robot."

"Yes, Mr. Spock, you should knock that off." Her tone . . . a teasing one. I stare into her eyes. It's not long before she shifts them away, giving my tattoo attention. "Can you tell me about this?" she asks as her fingers trace over the different patterns. I don't think I have to tell you what her touch is stirring deep inside of me. My eyes fall to the area she is circling. She lies back, seemingly waiting for me to explain it all. Although, something tells me she knows what all of these different symbols mean.

"I take it you're familiar with Polynesian tribal tattoos?" I question.

"A little bit. I know some of the meanings but I'd love to hear about them from you and your interpretation of them for your tattoo. Tattoos are very personal. Two people could have the same one—completely identical—yet, have two different meanings. What's the story behind yours?"

"Very true. Well, these right here," I trace the pattern of heads, "are enatas, representing my family. The turtles here and there are about family also, but longevity and wellness, too, since I like to live a healthy lifestyle. The fish are for prosperity and life. The shark teeth represent the warrior in me," I chuckle. "I'm a 10th- dan black belt in Karate, so I wanted to incorporate that. I also have spearheads to do the same. The suns represent leadership. The ocean; my persistence."

"You persistent? No kidding," she teases.

"Shocking, I know." I bite back my smile. "What about yours?" I glide the back of my hand down the length of hers.

"Birkita?" She glances down, smiling slightly.

"Birkita?" I laugh.

"Yes. Birkita. It's Celtic. It means strong," she says shyly. "I decided on the horned dragon because I loved the idea behind the symbolism. *Being mighty with words and actions,*" she adds.

"Birkita . . . the horned dragon . . . with green eyes and purple eyelids. Perfect. Absolutely. Perfect." I plant several kisses on her lips.

"I like purple."

"I like you." I smile against her mouth.

"I like you, too, Spock."

"I'm glad, Birkita." I slowly climb on top of her.

"The horny dragon?"

"My favorite kind." I eskimo kiss her. She growls at me before threading her hands into my hair and bringing my mouth to slam hard against hers. Her hips rock up against me, causing my cock to slide up and down her wetness. Our wetness. *Fuck, that's hot.*

"Kyle . . . please," she begs, ripping her mouth from mine. Just as I'm about to enter her, there's a knock on the door. CiCi's eyes widen in panic.

"Ceese? Are you alright? I wanted to check on you before I went to bed." Charlotte calls through the door.

She opens her mouth, about to answer. "I've got this," I say before giving her nose a quick peck. She knits her brows slightly. I'm guessing she's wondering what I'm going to say. What she doesn't know is that I'm not going to say anything—she is. I slam inside of her quickly, causing her to scream out my name and a prayer or two to God. I pound into her relentlessly. She claws at my back, yelling out things that would only make sense if you were fluent in CiCi Speak.

"Sounds like you're alright to me . . . or working really hard on being so!" Charlotte calls out again. "Make sure to pound her in the ass real good, Kyle, just how she likes it," she adds. I stop and stare at CiCi.

"Oh my God! Don't listen to her! Keep going!" she snaps and smacks my ass. Slowly, I lower my face to hers and caress her lips with mine before biting her bottom one. She gasps as I roll my hips confidently. Her hands grasp my ass, her hips grinding into me at a rushed pace. I grab her hip to stop her. "Ugh!" she groans in frustration. My eyes find hers. They study her as I continue at the pace I want. She tries to look everywhere but straight at me. Look, I know I'm going to sound like a pussy when I say this, but this not looking at me shit is kind of bothering me. I can't put my finger on the reason why, but it is. I decide to stop trying and just give her what she wants.

"Is this what you want?!" I yell through my teeth as I slam into her repeatedly.

"Yes . . . oh God, yes!" she pants.

"You just want to fuck hard and not feel anything else?" I pound harder only to get the same answer from her. I rip myself from her and get off the bed.

"Kyle?" She tries to grab my arm as I walk away and towards the bathroom, slamming it open before going in, slamming it closed, and locking it. I turn to the sink and hold on the edges as I try to steady my breathing. Finally, I look up to face myself in the mirror. Sweat is trickling down my temples, my cheeks puff in and out, and my neck vein is pulsating as I continue trying to control my breaths. The truth hits me like a Mack truck.

She's fucking using me.

Some shit is going on with her and she's using me to escape from it for a while. She's been off all night. I'm a distraction. It's the only logical reason for her sudden change of behavior towards me. Fuck, I really am like Mr. Spock. I let out a deep sigh and head into the tiny shower. I need to calm down and get my thoughts together before I head back out there.

Everyone warned me.

Okay, maybe it was just Mitch, but for one man, he can seem like a damn crowd sometimes.

I can do this, though. I can reach her. I make a living (a very good one) solving massive problems, figuring shit out that no one else knows where to begin with.

I don't know where to begin with her . . .

I thought I did. I thought it was working. My mom was right. I should've just stopped for a moment and gone a different direction. But, at the end of the day, I'm still just a guy. And, being a guy, I totally fucked up tonight and gave in to her vulnerability. I wasn't going to let this happen. I knew it was wrong. Damn it, though; she felt so good, her response to my touch, clouding my judgment. *Great.* Could I have been any more of a dick to her just now? What's even better is that I'm about to walk out there—soaking wet—in the buff to do my back paddling. *Note to self:* Next time you angry "I need to clear my head" shower, make sure you have a fucking towel waiting for you afterwards!

With one final deep inhale, I open the door only to have a towel thrown at my head. *At least it wasn't something hard!* I wipe my face and drag the towel down my body before wrapping it around my waist. I glance up at her. She's sitting on the edge of the bed in a long t-shirt-like nightgown. Her long hair pushed behind her ears. Puffy, reddened eyes stare at me, breaking my heart. I can tell you right now, I never want to see this look on her face again—it's crushing me to the core.

"Ceese," I start.

"No!" she snaps. "Just leave. I don't want to hear it—whatever it is. Just go."

I sit next to her, ignoring her demands. "I fucked up tonight." I shake my head. "This shouldn't have happened."

"God, Kyle . . . please just go." She closes her eyes tightly.

"Fuck, that came out wrong." I run my hands through my hair. "I don't mean *this.* Well, I do, but I mean it shouldn't have happened tonight. Not like this. Not while you're dealing with whatever it is you're dealing with." I grab her right hand, placing it in my palm. My fingers doodle patterns on the back of it as I continue, "I was weak tonight. I should've been stronger. I should've spent this time getting you to tell me what was wrong so I could help you."

"To fix the problem?" she asks quietly.

"Yes." I squeeze her hand and nudge her shoulder slightly with mine.

"That's what I am to you." She breathes with slight scary humor. "You see me as a problem to fucking solve!" She stands up. "That's why you've been chasing me these past few months. You want to be the one who figures out what makes CiCi O'Brien tick!"

"No!" I jump up.

"Yes! That's exactly what you see!" She pokes at my chest angrily. "Well, I'm not a fucking problem for you to solve, Kyle!"

"Knock it off—that's not true! I didn't say that you were a problem I wanted to fix or that I see you that way. All I said is that I want to help you figure out whatever it is you're going through right now." I try to keep my cool. I have to say, though, it's pretty fucking difficult to be accused of something you are not guilty of and trying to keep your cool about it.

"I don't need your help figuring shit out! My problems should be no concern of yours. I. Am. Nothing. To. You!" she bites out.

"That is *your* choice!" I scream in her face before grabbing at my clothes. I take a deep breath, trying to collect myself again. I turn back to her. "If I had my way," I say calmly, "you'd be everything to me."

I can see the fight all over her face. Her nose is flaring, chin quivering, and her eyes sit in a pool of tears.

I wait.

She looks away.

Shaking my head, I throw my clothes on and head to the door.

"Don't mistake my leaving tonight as me giving up. I never quit, Birkita." And with that, I leave. I could almost swear that I felt the heat from a fire hit my back as I closed the door. I definitely did hear a shoe or something hit it.

I go down the stairs and back the way we came earlier only to run into Mitch in the kitchen. "Dude, are you drinking a Capri Sun?" I chuckle at him.

He breaks away from the tiny yellow straw, "Shut-up, man, I'm thirsty. Besides . . . I like this flavor." He shrugs.

"You have another one?"

"Yeah." He opens the fridge. "Here. Hurry up before Charlotte catches us," he says with a bit of urgency.

"Why, is she the juice box police?"

"Affirmative."

"So . . . this has become a problem with you, has it?" Yes, I'm smirking.

"I guess so. Why don't they make this shit for adults? Kids get everything." He shakes his head before slurping the rest up.

"Dude . . . I think you got it all." I laugh again as I put my straw in. Yup . . . I forgot to not squeeze the container while doing so. "I'm glad I'm providing entertainment for you," I say as he laughs and grabs me a towel.

"Here." He throws it at me. "What are you still doing here anyway?"

"Uh, safe to say, screwing things up with CiCi."

"Oh, I'm sure that she's putting in most of that effort."

"No, man, I fucked up tonight." I put the juice down and rinse off my hands. "Do you, by chance, know what's going on with her? I mean, other than what she mentioned earlier?"

"No, can't say that I do. I'd ask Charlotte for you but I've put myself in the dog house, as well."

"You two going to be ok?" I turn and lean against the counter, drying my hands.

"Yeah," he sighs. "We'll be real good once I get cured from this 'foot in mouth' syndrome I seem to suffer from."

"Did you start seeing a therapist?"

"Nah. My first appointment is next week."

"Make sure to mention the whole surrogacy thing. I know that's weighing heavy on your mind," I remind him. A few months back, just when he and Charlotte had come to grips with their feelings, she had informed him that she was going to be the surrogate for Ava and Trent's baby. It didn't go over too well, but in the interest of not losing her, Mitch conceded.

"Shhh!" He puts a finger up to his lips and peaks out of the kitchen. "Don't talk so loud. Especially, about that shit."

"Sorry."

He leans back against the counter next to me. "It took," he says quietly.

"Shit, man," is all I say. I don't know what else to say. I know he doesn't really want this and while this is a wonderful thing Charlotte is doing for her friend, I can totally see and agree with his side of things.

"I know." He blows out a big breath through pursed lips.

"So . . . now what?" I sip my juice.

"Now," he opens the fridge and grabs another one, "we sit back, wait, and watch her have someone else's baby with a supportive smile on our faces." He pops the straw in. We both stand there, leaning against the counter . . . sucking on tiny yellow straws, contemplating life. Within seconds, we're slurping the rest of our juice down. I throw my shrunken, twisted juice pack out and get my car keys out of my pocket.

"Thanks for the juice box, buddy." I slap his shoulder. "See you at preschool tomorrow," I add.

"Laugh now, but you'll be feening for one of these bad boys before you know it!" He warns.

"I'll take your word for it!" I nod before heading out the front door.

It's almost 10pm. My head is swimming (drowning really) in thoughts about tonight. I need to talk to the one person who always seems to help me swim against the current. Go ahead! Call me a Mama's boy; I don't care.

I cut the lights just before I pull in the driveway in case Linz is sleeping. I don't want her around for this conversation. Mom peeks out the curtain in the living room and gives me a little wave. I swear this woman never sleeps. Hitting the lock on my car, I head up to the door that is already being opened. There she is . . . my Ghandi, looking just as pretty and put together in her robe as she is in her dresses during the day.

"What happened?" She hugs me.

"I messed up with her tonight, Mom. I did something I shouldn't have." I walk in.

"Well, what do you mean by that, son?"

I begin to explain everything to her in the most PG way possible while we sit on the sofa, eating cookies. *Jesus,* forget I just said that.

"So what are you going to do now?" She folds her napkin, gliding her fingers across the crease, making it perfect.

"What do you mean 'what are you going to do now?' I'm here to find out from you what I should do next," I say with a little panic in my voice.

"Well, son, you didn't listen to my advice the last time." She shakes her head in a "tsk tsk" way.

"I was going to but then . . ."

"But then what?"

"But then, I didn't. I couldn't help it, Mom."

"I call bullshit, Kyle." Yes, she said that sweetly.

"Mom!"

"Don't 'Mom' me! Start thinking with the right head." She sips her tea.

"When do you think I should call her?"

"Don't call." She shakes her head.

"How can I not call? Won't that make it worse?" I throw my hands out in protest.

"She can hang up. Send her a note." She sips her tea again.

"Should I attach it to a pigeon?" I ask in the most serious, sarcastic way. Mom gives me a closed-mouth smile, leans forward, palms my left cheek then abruptly slaps me upside my head. I had a feeling that was going to happen but then she tricked me by being endearing. Besides, my mother always looks innocent and she works that shit to her benefit.

"Ok, why a note?"

"You have a higher chance of not only screwing up what you want to say on the phone, but of her hanging up on you. With a letter, you can say everything perfectly and though she may fight the urge to read it at first, she's more likely to do so. How would you know if she did, if she doesn't tell you?" She shrugs.

"You're a wise woman, Mother, dear." I wink at her.

"Ugh, you make me sound ninety when you call me that." She complains.

"Mommy dearest?" I raise an inquisitive brow.

"You want me to slap the other side of your head?"

"So aggressive!" I tease.

"Hmm. Speaking of, I need your help with something." She places her cup and saucer on the coffee table.

"What's up, buttercup?"

Leaning in closer, she looks around at both entrances to the room before speaking up, "I brought laundry into Lindsay's room earlier and she started ruffling papers around frantically when I walked in, like she was hiding something. I asked her what she was working on and she said nothing; she was just doodling. Why would she freak out like that if she was just doodling? Something's up and she's keeping it from me. Now you know, I wouldn't pry—I'm not like that—but I have a strange feeling about this. I need to see what she was working on. Can you please, maybe during the party, go into her room and investigate?" she asks in a whisper.

"Why don't you look while she's at work?"

"I don't snoop. I'm not a snooper. Never have been. Never will be," she states matter-of-factly.

"Oh, but you can send me in to do it and be the bad guy?"

"Yes. Because you love your mother, right?" She nudges me.

"Mom, this really is out of character for you."

"I know, but I just have a weird feeling. Please, just humor me." She grabs and squeezes my hands.

"I'll see." I shake my head at her slightly, smiling. "Alright, I better get going. I've got a letter to write tonight and work in the morning." I stand up. "Thanks for listening, Mom. I really appreciate it." I hug her when she stands up with me.

"Anytime, you know that."

"Ok. I'll see you at the party then." I give her another squeeze before letting go. "Love you, Mom."

"I love you, too. C'mon . . . I'll walk you to the door." She slips her arm through mine, hugging it to her as we head towards the door. "Kyle . . ."

"Yeah, Mom?" I turn to her after opening the front door.

"Make sure to do the note thing with your flair," she says.

"What are you talking about?"

"From what you've told me, which I'm sure has been dulled down a bit; you two seem to be over-the-top with each other in one way or another. Don't change that." She pats at my chest, hugging my arm to her one last time before letting go.

"Mom, I'm not sure I know what you mean. I mean—I do—to a point, but what are you getting at?" I grab my keys off the little square table, meant for plants, by the door. We've always "planted" our keys there, instead.

"What I'm getting at is this, if you do something that is completely out of character . . . she's not going to trust it. She knows you overdo things. I'm not sure what it is you *have* to do; all I know is that it has to be consistent so she can trust it. Does that make any sense to you?"

"Slightly, but I'm going to take your word for it and try to come up with something." I lean down and kiss her cheek.

"You'll figure it out, son. Where there's a will . . ."

"There's a way," I finish for her. She gives me a slight nod, smiling, and pulls me in for a hug.

I head out the door . . . on a mission.

Chapter Nine

Feelings and shit . . .

CiCi

"Hey, do have a twenty on you? I left my debit card at home and I'm like on 'E,'" I ask Charley as I breeze into kitchen in a rush.

"Whoa!" She grabs my arm to stop me. "Yes, but I want some details first."

"The only detail I'm going to give you is that I was right about him. Fuck, I hate that I was right!" I try to fight off my anger but not as hard as I'm trying to fight off my tears. "Do me a favor, please?"

"What?"

"Give me the twenty and never mention him to me again."

"Um . . . ok." She hesitates then quickly grabs her purse and gives me the money. I look down and see that I've scored a Benjamin.

"Thanks for the twenty." I wave on my way out.

"I didn't give you a twenty!" she calls after me.

"Who's counting?" I shrug and get into my car before she can say another word. As soon as I turn the ignition, I see an envelope under my driver's side wiper. *What the fuck?* Rolling down the window, I grab it. It's simply addressed "Psst . . ." I open it. But I don't have to tell you that, we all know I'm a nosy bitch.

Birkita,
If you build it (your wall), I will scale it . . .
L.L.Y.P.
Spock (Channeling Kevin)
PS. This message will not self-destruct. However, not knowing what that abbreviation means may kill you. All you need to do is simply text me "Got it" so I know you've read this. You will earn the information you seek . . . eventually! ☺

Is he for real? "Fuck you, Kyle!" I snap at the note and toss it on the passenger seat before putting my car into gear. Who does he think he is? I head to the nearest gas station without giving that stupid note another thought . . . or two thoughts . . . or three. Fucking bastard!

Got it.

What? Oh please, like you don't want to know!

Good.

I continuously glance down at my phone, waiting for another message to pop up, but by the time my tank is filled, one doesn't. So that's it? Just *Good?* Shaking my head, I get back into my car, and head home to grab a few things before I head into work.

Approaching my door, I find another note taped to it. It's addressed **"Because curiosity killed the cat . . ."** I let out a big sigh. Wouldn't want cats dying on my watch, right?

*Hey! *Looks both ways to make sure we're alone**
Mitch drinks all of the kids' Capri Suns . . . with the tiny yellow straw. He sneaks it like a criminal.
Because Knowing is . . . good blackmail material. ☺
I.T.L.P.

Guess who?

PS. Same goes with this one, except please put # written in corner, as well.

Got It.

You're a dork. I'm not playing this anymore.

#2

Shut-up, I meant after this time.

Well, I have to give him credit for that last move. Although, I'm not really sure what the point of doing this is. I'm not really sure of anything . . . except that my electric bill hasn't been magically paid.

Flick on. Flick off.

Fuckers!

I go about opening all of the shades in the house to let some light shine in. Looking around, I realize that I have a major decision I need to make. *I'm going to have to sell this place.* You know what that means, right? If I sell, I will have to possibly live in an apartment or a condex. This means I will have close-proximity neighbors. The thought alone makes me want to hurl. Ugh! However, the idea of closing Bark Avenue is crippling. I know this because I just thought about it for a nanosecond and my wobbling legs almost gave out. We won't discuss why my legs are wobbling. *Fucking smirker could've of at least finished me off!*

Why did I let my guard down? I *never* let it down. I guess just to prove myself right. Also . . . it's been a while—know what I'm sayin'? I'm not going to lie; I'm crushed. Then again, I knew that was going to happen. That's what good guys do to me. From the looks of it, however, with these notes, he's not done. But I am.

Time to refocus!

Yes! Ok, I'm going to sell my house. This much, I know. I need to make a list of my debts; get everything in order so I can figure this shit out. I'm going to need girls for this one. Pulling my phone out, I start the group text (I don't know why we don't have a GEG signal like batman, either!):

Me: ATTENTION ALL GEGs!
Staff meeting—STAT!

Julie: I just got out of a "staff meeting." It was very "informative."
☺

Me: Save the "Snatch Report" for later.
Can everyone meet at Mick & Marley's tonight?
Maddie: I have a late client but I'll come right after.
Me: Come whenever you want . . . she's already late.
Julie: Bwhahaha . . . *snorts* I thought the same thing.
Me: Well, someone needs to sit in the gutter with you! ;)
Charley: Don't any of you work?! Anywho . . . I'll be there.
Ava: I'll be there after the gym!
Me: Jesus, Ava, give it a rest! Your ass is tight enough!
Julie: That's what he said!
Charley: That's what he said!
Maddie: That's what he said!
Ava: That's what he said!
Me: Really? Everyone thought they would be the only one to say that?
Julie: I said it the quickest, so I win!
Charley: Dude . . . we did it at the same time! Besides, my name is Charley so I can be the only one really "winning" here, right?
Charley: Guys?
Charley: Hello?!
Charley: Fuck, you bitches! See you tonight!

I shouldn't leave her hanging. I mean . . . she is my sister. Nah—she'll live! Besides, I need to pack a bag for Julie's tonight. No way am I staying with Charley again. I don't want to take my chances running into *him.* I'm not staying with my parents. My mother will pry and my father will somehow get me to talk my shit out with him. I don't know how he does it. He barely says anything. He just sits and waits for me to do all of the talking, like it's my idea. He's a Jedi Master. I've been convinced of that since I was five. That's what he dressed as for our annual Trick or Treating excursion, circa 1985. I went as Hans Solo (that shit still makes sense, don't it?!) and Charley was Chewbacca. Although, she was so little, everyone thought she was an ewok. Our other three sisters teased us about dressing up in the boy roles. Yes, too bad we couldn't have been as original as they were. It would've definitely been cooler to have five Princess Leia's instead of three. What were we thinking? Our mom was a Storm Trooper—no surprise there.

Grabbing the framed photo of that night off of my bureau, I smile for the first time this morning. We were all so young, especially my parents. That's another thing. Sometimes it's hard for me to see my parents "old" now. Dad's still a piece of work, but Mom is coming out of remission. We all know it; the signs are obvious. It kills me to see her like this, getting so frustrated. I feel helpless. I can tell you—first hand—worst feeling in the world. It makes me want to run and hide. So . . . to support that selfish habit, I'm gonna stay with Julie till lights are back on over here. Also, I know she's going to want me to just live with her anyways. She hates living alone.

"Just so we're clear here . . . you are *not* moving in, permanently! Having a roomie is too much of a hassle. *And* I love living alone; not having to answer to anyone. I'm sorry, CiCi. Temporary is fine—but that's it!"

"Uhhhh . . ."

"Haha . . . gotcha!" she laughs into the phone. "Of course you can stay here! That is, of course, if you tell me what's going on before you tell everyone else."

"Julie, I'm telling everyone tonight—together. I need everyone's input at once. I don't want to have this conversation ten million different times. Just wait until then, please." I tap my pen on the appointment book and look up when the bells chime. "Look, I've got to go. I'll see you tonight."

"Ceese, I'm your number one best friend. You have to have to tell me first!" she pleads.

"I'm thirty-five, I haven't put you girls in number order since the 90's, knock it off."

"I don't believe you. Your number two is Ava," she states matter-of-factly.

"No . . . ! It's Maddie. I gotta go, bye!" I quickly hang up.

"Hey, Linz . . . what's wrong?" I drop my smile for her when I realize she looks as if she's been crying.

"Are you still coming to my party this weekend?"

"Umm . . . eh," I fumble.

"He said you would back out. I didn't believe him." She sniffles and wipes her nose with the back of her arm. "I thought you were my friend."

"First of all, I am your friend." I come around from behind the desk and place my hands on her upper arms. "Second of all, who said this? Kyle? And third of all, why do you even know about your surprise party?"

"Yes. He said he upset you last night and that you probably won't come because of him. It's a surprise for everyone else. I don't like surprises so Mom told me and I get to act surprised," she rambles off quickly.

Oh, I definitely didn't "come" because of him!

Fucker!

"Well, your brother doesn't know me very well then. I will be there—don't you worry." I hug her. I can't believe he did this! Why did he have to pull her into *our* shit? "Ok, go in the back, put your stuff away, and get a smile on your face." I give her another quick squeeze. She nods, smiles, and heads back. I grab my phone off of my desk to text him.

That was a dick move, dragging your sister into this!

I just wanted to prepare her.

Prepare her for what—you being an asshole?

If she hasn't managed to come to this conclusion already, then it's a lost cause.

Make sure to get your next set of notes off of her.

No. I'm done listening to you.

Yes. You'll want to read them.

Just sayin'. . .

Goodbye!

See you Saturday, beautiful.

Fuck you!

That option is ALWAYS available when you want it. ;)

Ugh! He is confusing the hell out of me. This is one of those phone-slamming moments. Yes, I'm dialing his cell on my work phone, an old-school phone that can do the job.

"Hey . . ." he answers.

SLAM!

There—now I feel better. I look up from the phone, watching Lindsey head back in. "All better?" I ask.

"Yes." She smiles. "Who do we have coming in today?"

I look back down at the schedule. Jesus. Another shit day. "We have Pearl and Trixie. That's all." I let out a big sigh. I can't keep going on like this. Something's gotta give.

"Will it pick up in the winter?"

"I don't know. Usually it's busier during the summer and into the fall. I really don't understand what's going on." I flip through the next few days only to find more of the same.

"Yesterday the ice cream truck came around and Mom bought me one."

"That's nice. I totally would've run to get in line with you. I love getting an ice cream cone off a truck. It tastes better for some reason." I widen my eyes and give a slight groan at the thought. Also, I realize that this kid really has some sort of "decency" hold on me. If it was anybody else giving me this random information, I would've been widening my eyes thinking they were a moron or something.

"You should've seen the line!" She says with excitement. "You know what I noticed?"

"What's that, babe?"

"A bunch of people were standing in line with their dogs on leashes." She laughs. "I imagined the dogs were all lined up to get our spa treatment! Isn't that silly?"

She's a genius!

"Actually, that's not silly at all, Linz. There are a lot of groomers that do go around like an ice cream truck to groom people's pets." I assure her. It is something that I have always been well aware of but never thought about it for me. Maybe I *should* look into that. Fuck, that sounds like a big hassle. A: I don't have a truck. B: I don't have money to finance a truck. C: What song would I play driving around—"Who Let The Dogs Out?" My brain already hurts, thinking about it.

"Can we do that?" Her eyes light up.

"Sure! Do you have a truck lying around somewhere?" A little snark never hurt no one!

"No." She slumps in the chair next to me. "Can we rent one?"

"I don't have the money to do that, sweetie, or we'd be cruisin' in a paw mobile in a heartbeat." And with that, we sit there, watching the cars go by outside, in silence.

"Oh!" She jumps up after a few. "I almost forget to give you Kyle's notes." She heads to the back, quickly. *Great!* After a minute or two, she comes back. "Here you go," she says hurriedly. Um . . . ok.

Cici,

I'm sorry that I behaved the way I did tonight. I know that you've been hurt in the past; I've learned that much. However, I think I've proven that I'm more interested in pursuing a relationship with you—not just a one-night stand. There's something about you that makes me feel things. Things I'm not sure of myself. Things I know I'm not familiar with. Crazy. You make me feel crazy! It's a good crazy, though. Well, at least, it makes me feel good. I never know what to expect with you. That's my favorite part about you. That's also the scariest part. This is all scary for me. I don't care how much of pussy I sound like right now—it's true!

We all have a past that has mistakes we've made or bad memories that like to resurface. We can't let it dictate our future. I don't know what that fucking prick did to you but I know one thing—he didn't deserve you! I deserve you. Please give me the proper chance to prove that to you.

I panicked last night. I knew then that you were using me to escape whatever it is that is haunting you right now. I didn't like it then and I don't like it now. But . . . if you were just using me to help you forget what's bothering you and not JUST using me, then I'm ok with that as long as you and me are a "we" . Do you understand what I'm saying to you? Can you commit to me—only me? We'll go at whatever speed you want to. I just need the commitment.

I hope I see you at Linz's party. I know there's a possibility that you won't come and I know I'm to blame for that. But please consider what it means to my sister to have you there. You're so good to her, Ceese. She loves you.

Just one more thing before I end this letter. Being with you tonight (before I had a tantrum) was nothing short of a slice of heaven to me. Touching your soft skin, tasting you, kissing you . . . being inside of you; the sounds that escaped your throat are still loud in my ears. I can't tell you how many times I've imagined us like that. Next time, don't avoid my eyes and let me make love to you. I don't mind fucking at all but I just wanted to savor the moment with you tonight and you wouldn't let me have that. Did you not feel the way that I did? Text me now and tell me "Yes, I felt it" or "No, I didn't." When you do so, I will tell you what that abbreviation meant. ☺

Yours, no matter what,

Kyle xxx

Fuck the way I'm feeling right now!

What do I do? Yeah, I felt the way he was feeling. I also felt a shitload of anxiety with it, as well. I'm feeling that right now! Like I'm in a crowded room with no oxygen.

"Are you ok? You don't look so well." I hear Linz ask next to me.

"I don't feel so good," I answer and get up to walk near the AC duct. Don't hate me but I'm about to punk out right now. This is too much for me. I have too many things on my plate—I can't handle this. I just can't.

I go back to the desk and grab my phone.

I read your first note.

Back off.

I stare at my phone, waiting. Several minutes go by and instead of driving myself crazy, I decide to head into my office and compile the list of bills I need to pay off. Christ, this list is growing by the minute and definitely not helping my anxiety. My phone pings. Nervously, I look down at it.

Mitch: What did you do?

Me: What did I do when?

Mitch: What did you just do to Kyle?!

Me: What are you talking about?

Mitch: You are a fucking piece of work! Smh.

I don't bother to respond again. I don't know what's going on that he would send me these texts but I can imagine that it's not good. Suddenly, the butterflies I usually feel in my belly when Kyle is around me are fluttering in my heart. That can't be good, right? I knew I was going to fuck this up. I told you—didn't I?! I'm not cut out for this shit. *I was once.* That was a long time ago, though. I've learned my lesson. My phone pings again. I look down, expecting a lovely message from Mitch telling me to go fuck myself. Instead . . .

Kyle: *DONE!*

Look, I'm not about playing games, but did you see that? Fucking liar. Was he not the one who said to me last night, and I quote, *"Don't mistake my leaving tonight as me giving up. I never quit, Birkita."*? Still, I'm not going to sit here and tell you my heart didn't just break a little.

Focus . . . focus . . . focus.

Electric: 217.51 due: Immediately!

Vendor (Paws plus): 353.01 due: Immediately! Won't send anymore shipments till paid in full.

Fuckers!

Rent: 1000.00 due: 2 weeks ago—*shit!*

Amex: Fuck that shit . . . I can't even look! Wait . . . $457.63 due: tomorrow. Hmm . . .

Lindsey: 20hrs times 8=160.00.

I fire up my laptop and get into my bank account for business.

$1604.23.

"Booyah, motherfucka!" I fist pump before writing out a check for the rent. I pay the Amex bill online then pay the vendor with the Amex (that will be charged on Monday to give all the money a chance to settle.). That leaves me with . . . $146.60. That plus what I get today will cover the electric and some of Lindsay's paycheck. I pull up my personal account. Um . . . yeah, looks like I'll be visiting the pawn shop later.

Fuck my life . . . just fuck it!

Well, it could've been worse, right? I lean back in my office chair, closing my eyes for a moment. I love my chair. It's one of those that go back so far, you think you're going to fall. I open my eyes back up. "*Fuck!* Jesus Christ, Linz!" I yell, holding my chest, after she scares the effin' crap out of me.

"Sorry," she says sympathetically then begins to giggle. "You should've seen your face; that was awesome."

"Yeah . . . yeah. What's up? Our client here?" I swirl my chair around to face her.

"No. You forgot to open these." She hands the other notes from Kyle to me. I take in a deep breath and let out a heavy sigh, grabbing the notes from her.

Note #2:

I could stare into your eyes forever.

I could draw them for you but I think that may come off as creepy, right?

Yes, that, most definitely, would be creepy.

Note #3:

Remember . . . Spitters are quitters.

Random. Hope it made you laugh. ☺

PS. I felt a little awkward writing that.

Ok. I laughed. *Damn it.* I wasn't expecting that.

"What's so funny?" Lindsay tries to peek.

"Nothing really." I close up the letter and shove it in my desk drawer. "Hey, Linz, I need to talk to you about something. Can you sit?"

"There's no other seat in here, CiCi." She looks around then back at me with her brow furrowed.

"It was just a figure of speech." I wave her off.

"Huh?"

"Never mind. Listen, I'm gonna need to cut back on your hours. It's only temporary." I add the last bit quickly.

"Did I do something wrong?" she asks, her chin beginning to quiver.

"God, no, Linz." I grab her hands. "Things are just really slow right now. It's getting very difficult for me to keep up with my bills. Do you understand that it has nothing to do with you? If I had the money, I'd have you here full-time if you wanted it." I try to reassure her.

"Can I still come in? Can I volunteer some of my time?"

"You'd do that?"

"I love working here. I look forward to it." She looks down. "This is the only place I've ever worked where no-one treats me differently. I'm just Lindsay here. I'm not the girl with Downs Syndrome."

"Have I ever told you how fucking awesome I think you are?" I smile through my tears. I love this kid. Fuck all those people who treat her differently! She is different—she's not a douchebag like most people. She's sweet, sincere, loving, caring . . . you get the idea. She rocks and it's an honor not only to know her but to call her my friend. "If you want to volunteer ten hours and work the other ten, that's fine by me! I can't imagine this place without you. Buddy would have conniption fit if you weren't here when he was." I get up and hug her.

"I wouldn't want to do that to him." She shakes her head.

"Alright, c'mon . . . let's get out there. Maybe a massive rush happened while we were both back here." I side hug her to me as we head out. Just then, the bells jingle and Addie walks through with Pearl.

"Would it look like favoritism if we took Pearl first?" Lindsay leans closer to me to ask. I go into hysterics. I'm definitely rubbing off on her. Probably not a good thing, but it's funny.

"Addie might get upset but she'll just have to understand that we take the dogs first—always!" I play along. Lindsay giggles. I love it when she laughs.

"Where's Ava?" I ask Charley as she arrives—late as usual. Maddie, Julie, and I have already had a first round.

"I'm sorry; did I get promoted to Ava's fucking keeper?" She wraps her purse strap on the back of her chair before sitting. We all hiss at her and put our claws up.

"Sorry. I'm in a pissy mood." She props her elbow on the table and lays her head in her open palm.

"What's up?" Maddie asks then slurps her margarita up in an obnoxious manner that has all three of us staring at her.

"Just Mitch. He says some fucked up shit sometimes. I get it. I know why he does it. My problem is that he catches himself quickly, apologizes, and in the same breath, expects me to be ok. Like . . . let me pissed off for a minute. I'm, like, entitled to my feelings. Just because you, like, apologized doesn't mean I'm supposed, like, get over it that quick!"

"I, like, totally agree with you." I try to keep my straightest face.

"What does Mama Kardashian say about this?" Julie asks in an extremely serious tone. I actually don't know how she is keeping a straight face or any of us for that matter.

"What?" Charley squints her eyes at Julie as if she's trying to figure her out.

"I think she would, like, totally agree with you." Maddie pipes in, clearly knowing where we're going with this.

"What the fuck are you bitches talking about?!" Charley practically yells.

"Have you recently watched a Kardashian marathon or something because you are, *like,* totally sounding like them?" I ask.

"Fuck, really?"

"Like . . . yup," Julie says then laughs. "Here's Ava, now." She adds, nodding her head towards the door.

"Sorry!" She runs up. "What did I miss?"

"Charley spent the night with a bunch of valley girls, that's all," I inform her.

"You whore!" She spits out at Charley. "Were they cute?"

"Not as cute as you." She smiles and goes in for a hug.

"Alright, knock it off with the girl on girl love. I have some serious shit I need to discuss. Order your drinks so you two can catch up to us." I point my finger and wave it between Charley and Ava.

"Eh, I'm going to pass tonight. I'm actually feeling a bit queasy." Charley says as DeeDee walks up to us for their order (Yes, that's Buddy's bitch . . . I mean, owner.). "Just a pineapple and cranberry tonight, DeeDee. I want one of Mick's Reubens, though. I'm wicked starvin,'" she informs her.

"Welcome back to New England." Julie lifts a glass to her.

"Thanks. I've missed it. Such a lovely place." Charley winks. Ava orders the same as Charley and as soon as Dee leaves, all eyes are on me.

"Ok. What are we looking at here—zombie apocalypse?" Ava asks, pulling a white packaged snack of some sort out of her purse.

"What the fuck is that?"

"My granola snack," she says defensively.

"You're a fucking a dork." I shake my head.

"What?" She shrugs.

"You don't come to a bar and pull out your own Goddamn Scooby Snack! You fucking drink a beer and eat some bad bar food that will give you the shits tomorrow," I inform her.

"It's called the bar diet; man's secret for years." Julie offers. "I know this because I'm a model, there's not a diet out there that we don't know years before anyone else. We're like the guinea pigs for the FBA."

"It's the FDA, dipshit." Charley interjects.

"Who cares anyways? What the hell do they even stand for?"

"Fat Dickheads Association!" I yell over Maddie who is, of course, offering the right information. Mine sounds better, though, doncha think?

"What the hell is the FBA then?" She gives us a quizzical look.

"Full Breasted Asswhores . . . they are the sister administration."

"Isn't that the club we belonged to in high school?"

"That was FBLA." Maddie fans herself. Oh boy . . . this is going to be a banner night.

"Which stood for: Fucked Before Legal Age."

"It did not!" Ava laughs, "Knock it off."

"Yes! Can we get back to the topic at hand?" Charley snaps. Man, she is in a pissy mood. Normally I would fuckin' run with this shit but I'm praying she doesn't say anything about Kyle and me last night. If I mess with her, I can kiss that prayer goodbye.

"Alright! Geez!" I say then close my eyes to regroup. You have no idea how hard this is for me (Psst . . . that's what she said). "I think you all know that I've been struggling at the shop for the past few months. Wait! Let me finish!" I put my hand up when half of them open their mouths. Julie, of course, is not. That's because she knows partly what's going on. Don't let her fool you with this whole ditzy model routine; it's all part of her act. She's pretty fucking brilliant and can get info out of you like a twenty year veteran spy. "No, I'm not selling the shop. I've never hit a low like this but I'm sure I can figure out how to fix that. In the meantime, I am going to sell my house, catch up on my bills, and possibly look into another idea I've recently given a second thought to. What do you guys think? I'm going to need help—and by that I mean—I need to borrow money from all of you." I say the last bit quickly. It doesn't matter how fast I just said that; I heard the tires screeching in my head as they all came to a complete stop.

Collectively—they all stare.

I stare back.

It's becoming uncomfortable right about now.

Can somebody please unpause this shit?!

I'm not surprised by their reaction. I never ask for help . . . not like this. Charley clears her throat and leans in from across the table like big brother is watching. "What do you need? You know Mitch and I—"

"No!" I cut her off. "Mitch can't know because he will tell Kyle. I don't want Kyle to know any of this." I tap at the table for emphasis. "That's why I'm asking all of you for help. He won't notice the amount I'm asking for."

"What amount is that?" she asks.

"The amount that he won't notice."

"Which is?" she asks impatiently as DeeDee places all of our drinks down then walks away.

"You suck his dick . . . what amount won't get his balls in a twist?" I shrug. Maddie is now suffering from the misfortune of thinking that it was safe to start her next margarita. A slushy green substance is pouring out of her nostrils as she tries to contain her laughter.

"It's Leaky Lindsay!" We all yell at the same time. Yes, we all had a thing for Garbage Pail Kid cards back in the 80's (I may or may not still have mine . . . shh.). We all throw our little drink napkins at her.

"Fuck, I needed that," she says, finally able to breathe.

"You needed green shit coming out of your nose?" Charley asks, chuckling a bit.

"Better her nose than her vag . . ." Ava pipes up.

"Ewww!" We all screech collectively. I follow up with the "that skeeves me" shiver.

"So, what are you looking at? The grand total, so we can figure this shit out." Julie asks, grabbing half of Charley's sandwich as it is delivered.

"Julie!" she yells as Julie sinks her teeth in.

"What?! It's a big sandwich. I'm helping you!" she says defensively.

"Why didn't you order one?"

"Yours tastes better."

"How do you know?"

"It always tastes better when it's someone else's," she states before taking another heaping bite.

"Honestly, whatever you girls can manage, but let's not be cheap bitches about it, either, please," I finally say after the numbers run through my mind, not making a lick of sense.

"Nice touch, throwing that 'please' in there at the end." Maddie winks.

"I'm working on my charm." I steal a fry from Charley.

"What. In. The. Actual. Fuck, you two?!" She pulls her plate closer and circles her arm around it clearly trying to keep us off of it. I smile and bite into it.

"I need to catch up on some bills on the house, get everything up to date." I go back to the real conversation at hand.

"You'll need money for the repairs then, too." Charley says, taking a bite of her sandwich.

"What repairs?" Julie furrows her brows, looking between Charley and me.

"Charley, do you really think I'd be this calm if I had no water at my house? My electric got cut off," I inform her.

"Is a thousand enough from each of us?" Maddie asks, "Can your parents help?"

"No. They can't help at all. I won't even ask. And yes, that should be a good amount. I have to say that while I'm relieved that you are all able to help like this, it makes me feel like a complete shithead. How the fuck do you bitches have a grand laying around like pocket change?"

"I don't. I have to talk to Trent. That may be too much for us at the moment. We're still hurting from all of the money we've shelled out trying to have a baby." Ava shakes her head.

"I'll pay you back as soon as the house sells. I promise." I reach forward to grab her hand and squeeze it.

"I know you will." She pats the top of my hand with her other. "You never ask for help. I know you hate this. We'll make it work," Ava says with tears in her eyes. *Fuck. I hate when she does this.*

"Only God and the GEGs will judge you." Julie nudges my shoulder with her hand.

Maddie breaks out in another fit of laughter. I'd say it's the margaritas hitting her hard tonight, but she always does this. She thinks of something funny—usually a memory—and goes into what looks like a seizure before she can even tell us what's on her mind. By that point, even if it's not funny, we're all laughing our asses off at her. Chain reaction, if you will.

"*What?!*" we all yell at her in unison.

She gasps.
She snorts.
She may have farted because she's laughing harder now.
We're all now laughing hysterically like a bunch of fucking assholes.

"Do you . . . do you . . . do you . . ." She tries to tell us.

"*What?!*" We sing like a choir. No really, that's how it sounded. Like a choir of Sopranos . . . dying.

"Do you . . . phew . . . remember our pledge in high school?" She finally gets out. We all laugh again before straightening up in our chairs. I take a fork and tap it on my beer bottle three times before putting it down again. We all stare straight-faced at each other (ok . . . we're trying to. There may be some cheek biting to stop from smiling.).

"GEG Roll Call!" I command authoritatively. "CiCi!"

"Charley!"

"Ava!"

"Maddie!"

"Julie!"

"Salute!" I yell. We all flip our birds up. "GEG Pledge!"

"I pledge allegiance to the GEGs
Only God and you girls can judge me.
And to the music of our favorite boy bands
We will rock it out—we will dance
With coordination—and with soul
Promising to never become assholes."

"Boy, did we fail!" Julie laughs.

"We did. But that's a good thing," Ava says, her tears filling her eyes again. Christ . . . she isn't even drinking. We all sit in collective silence, knowing Ava has a long drawn out speech to deliver. "Who has this? Like us?" She throws her hands out. "I know I'm the one out of us five that is the most serious and I give you girls a hard time. I can't imagine it any other way between us. I wouldn't want to! We've been friends most of our lives. We've been through everything together. Sure, we have other friends that are good friends and have been there for things. But . . . not like us. Not everything. No one knows me like you girls. I don't think anyone ever will. There's something special about being friends as long as we have. The ability to act like a complete moron with you girls serves as a form of therapy that, unfortunately, a lot of people don't understand. I feel sad for them. I can't imagine not having this. I can't imagine my life without any of you." She looks around at all of us.

"We do the grown-up thing pretty well, too. We do it differently than most, but that's us . . . different," Charley pipes up, tears conquering her face.

"Here's to laughing our way through life . . . even the tough shit. I love you girls!" Maddie lifts her glass. We follow.

"Cheers, Asswhores!" we all say in unison, clinking our glasses.

"I can't believe it!" A certain Brit, by the name of Blake, yells over the microphone. "Do we have all five of the GEGs here with us tonight?!"

"Oh Christ," Julie groans.

"You are fucking crazy. If I wasn't with . . . if I were you, I'd be climbing that hot piece of ass, permanently." I slap her arm.

"Ohhhh!" they all yell in my direction.

"Floor has been opened by you, young lady!" Maddie taps her glass. "Woot woooo!" she bellows out. Oh . . . she's about one more drink away from being completely shitfaced.

"Take it easy with the drinks, shortstack." I warn.

"She's right . . ." Charley trails off.

"I'm not talking about Kyle." I shake my head.

"Paging the GEGs to the stage! Get your pretty arses up here," Blake says.

"Saved by the Brit!" I smile and get up. "C'mon girls; Julie's boyfriend beckons," I announce then take off towards him.

"He's not my boyfriend!" she yells after me. Yeah right! I don't know why she's so afraid to commit to him. He's a great guy, treats her well, makes her laugh, and is as patient as a nun with her. Did I mention that he's fucking hot-as-hell? I mean, *what is wrong with her?!*

"What kind of mood is she in tonight, Ceese?" Blake asks as he gives me a hug.

"I don't know. It's kind of been about me tonight, narcissist that I am."

"You're no bloody help, lady," he teases me before giving Julie his attention. "Julie, you look revolting tonight. Honestly, I can't even bear to look at you. I don't think I can put you up on the stage tonight. I'm trying to bring customers in, not send them away, for Christ's sake." He throws his hand up. I'm standing here like all. . . . *huh?* He leans into my ear again when he sees my confusion. "Hot off the press this week, Ceese! I'm not allowed to compliment her anymore." He straightens up and rolls his eyes.

"Are you still getting booty calls?"

"Of course!" He jerks his head back like I asked a crazy question.

"Julie!" I grab her attention then lean in. "Blake really hates pounding you in the ass."

"The way you girls talk to each other never gets old to me," he laughs. "Yes, Julie, for Christ's sake, please stop asking me to do that to you."

"Only if you stop making me shove my dildo up yours!" she retorts sarcastically then pushes past him, knocking his shoulder with hers as she does.

"Bloody hell . . ." he trails off then lets out a sigh. "I can't win with her." He shakes his head. "Go on up there, will ya? What are you girls going to sing?"

"'5 Years Time' by Noah and the Whale. We were having a nice *I love you, man* moment before. That song is perfect for it." I pat his shoulder. Poor guy. I don't know why he hangs in there.

In case you weren't aware, Mick & Marley's pub is our local hang out. Blake's grandfather started it. He passed it down to Blake when his son declined. No surprise there, Blake's father is too much of a stiff collar to appreciate the crowd here. Blake has always loved this place. He not only runs it but he's the one who ran it out of the ground when he started featuring local bands. Of course, he's in one of those local bands featured. He plays the drums and he's pretty damn good at it! He also plays Julie's main fuck buddy. I don't blame her—I'd fuck him. Except, I can't think of being with anybody really, not since I met Kyle. Blake is a great guy, though and he's the only one she's ever meshed well with. I wish she would give him an honest chance. He fits right in with us. It's not easy keeping up with the GEGs, as you can imagine.

Kyle could keep up. I'm still trying to digest all that has happened in the past twenty-four hours. This party should be interesting. I don't know what I'm going to say to him. I'm sort of regretting pushing him away today. I'm not sure I am ready for what he brings to the table. It's something I'm so used to *not* having, how am I supposed to learn how to be comfortable with having it. I don't know . . . I'm a fucking mess.

All five of us get on stage. We've been doing group performances since we were teenagers but now we just keep it to Karaoke. We're pretty well known and with good reason—we kick ass on the stage!

Chapter Ten

Motherly advice . . . take two!

Kyle

Back off? Back off?! Can you believe that? No, I'm not pissed. I'm fucking livid! It's been five hours since I've received that text and it's all I see, all I can think about. Maybe she is too much for me. I should cut my losses and walk away. Clearly, she wants no part of any sort of legit relationship.

Anger to the side, the more I go back and forth between her up and down behavior the past few weeks, I'm realizing there are two parts to CiCi. There's the side she shows (boldly, mind you) to everyone and the side (the vulnerable one) she's been showing me here and there. That's got to mean something, right?

Maybe her saying "back off" was a positive thing; I struck a chord with her that scared her, perhaps? Pushing the commitment word probably did it. I just . . . Christ, I wish I knew what the fuck happened in her past. I want to understand this better. I need a bone thrown to me, here. I have no idea what I'm dealing with. I hate that shit. I like to be prepared; have all of my I's dotted and T's crossed.

"Dude!" Mitch barks behind me. I turn away from the window to face him. He lets out a long sigh, shaking his head. "Do we need to have a 'don't be a pussy' talk?" he asks.

I laugh but I think I may actually need one of those talks. "Yeah, I think so, man."

"Don't be a fucking pussy! Call her out on her shit and don't take any more of it. Time for you to fully get in the driver's seat, buddy." He throws his jacket on.

"What happened to the 'walk away' speech?"

"Nah. Forget that. She's got feelings for you. I could see that the other night. Get to the bottom of it with her. You have to figure this shit out. I get the feeling that she really needs you."

"What do you mean by that?" I ask, panic setting in. Does he know something he's not telling me?

"It's just a feeling, Kyle. You know I'd tell you if I knew anything. CiCi has been really off lately. You seem to be the only one getting through to her." He picks his briefcase up. "C'mon, clock out . . . go home."

"She told me to back off. I poured my heart out today in a letter and she told me to back off." I look at him for some sort of explanation, if he has one. I wish somebody had one. I'm not picky—I'll take any bullshit theory somebody can come up with.

"You're getting too close," he offers.

"Too close to what?" I jerk my head back.

"Her heart. See you Monday, man," he says before turning on his heel to leave.

"It's only Thursday!" I yell after him.

"I'm spending the day with Charlotte tomorrow . . . to properly grovel—all day."

"Own that shit, man!" I laugh at him. Fucking shithead deserves it. He turns and shoots me both barrels, fully loaded . . . with *my* signature smirk. *Punk.* I have to laugh. I'm really happy for him. I'm glad he's found his purpose in life and that it's not just work. Nobody's purpose in life should just be work. Yes, one should take pride in what they do but it shouldn't be their only legacy. You haven't accomplished anything if you haven't earned the love and respect of your family, friends, and peers.

I plop into my chair with a heavy sigh. I really don't know what to do. Honestly, I have never put so much thought and fight into winning over a chick in my life. I think it's safe to say, though, that CiCi is in a category of her own and that is, most likely, why I have done so. Should it really be this hard? Why does it seem like for everyone else it's *Poof! They're the one!* I thought you were supposed to fall out of nowhere; didn't even see it coming. That sort of thing? This seems like way too much work.

I like work.

I like figuring shit out.

I'm such a dork.

Fuck it. Sitting in this office any longer is not going to give me the answers I need. It'll just remind me of the things I could be working on. I get up, grabbing my jacket and briefcase. I wish *I could* have the damn day off tomorrow.

"Good Lord, son, you look like hell," Mom states the obvious.

I push my shades up and glare at her.

"Don't give me that tone of look! What happened? You weren't out all night drinking, were you?"

I push my shades back down, ignoring her for the closest seat.

"Kyle! What is wrong with you?" She swats my back when I let my head fall to my arms on the kitchen table.

"I listened to my mother, that's what's wrong with me."

"What on earth are you talking about?" She seats herself to my right.

"I sent her the damn notes!" I lift my head and hand for emphasis.

"What happened?"

"She told me to back off." I grumble.

"So your answer was to get drunk?" she asks, her tone laced thick with disapproval.

"Nope. I waited a day to do that. Then I did something so awesome I pretty much want to shoot myself for it."

"Kyle, don't talk like that!" she snaps. "What did you do?" she asks, softening her tone.

"I drunk-texted her. Ya know, just to make myself seem extra creepy to her. Which, as her texted reply, confirms—I succeeded." I slowly bang my head on my folded arms. The memory shoots back in my mind like a fucking nightmare.

Play this! This is what you do to me . . .

Patsy Cline—I Fall To Pieces—Single Version

What do you rise to?

I think you know the answer to that.

Jesus . . . you had risen!

I shall rise again . . .

Not with me.

Yes, I will. You are mine.

Kyle, you are creeping me out! Please stop.

What did he do to you?

Who?

The fucking bastard, keeping you from me.

I don't know what you're talking about.

I'll make him pay.

Are you drinking?

What if I am?

Stop the crazy talk and go to bed.

Crazy! Another song by the great Patsy Cline!

Are you home? Where are you? You better not drive!

Will you come and pick me up?

Where are you?

You'd come and get me?

Of course!

You don't want anything to happen to me?

No.

So you care about me?

Yes, I'm very concerned about you.

Why?

Because you sound about 2 seconds away from flashing your vagina to everyone.

What?

Stop acting like a pussy!

At least I'm not acting like a cunt, like you!

Wow . . . only took you 5 mins to come up with such a big word.

Asshole.

*^^^ took me 2 seconds ^^^*

I'll give you extra points, though for use of a comma in an inebriated state.

I'm not in a coma. You are.

Commmmma!

Dumbass.

You breathe but you don't live.

You're not living. You're existing.

You're running from me because you are afraid of how I make you feel!

Oh, please!

Fuck, you just made my cock twitch!

What?!

All I hear now is you whimpering, "oh, please . . ." the other night

When I had my cock buried so deep in that tight little pussy of yours.

You think my pussy feels tight and little?

No.

I know it is.

And . . .

It felt amazing, wrapped so sweetly around me.

Do you remember how hard you came all over my cock, baby?

Don't call me baby.

CiCi! Do you remember?!

Yes . . .

I've never come like that before.

The hottest part was me watching you, watching my cock slam into you over and over.

I'm a visual fucker. If my pussy's getting it good, I want to see it.

I gave it to you good?

My pussy is still slightly sore . . .

Wear a dress tomorrow.

Why?

Because the moment I get you alone at the party, I'm going to make sure there's nothing slight about the soreness of your pussy.

No.

If you bother to wear panties, you won't be wearing them after I'm done.

It's not happening.

Dress. No panties. I'm taking what's mine.

I'm not yours!

The hell you aren't!

I won't come to the party, then.

You will come to the party and you will COME at that party!

NO I WON'T! GOODBYE!

You're going to do this to Linz?

Please stop . . .

You better show up tomorrow.

Or?

Don't test me.

I will be there tomorrow but . . .

But what?

Don't bring drunk Kyle . . . he creeps me out.

You do realize you are saying this to drunk Kyle, right?

Yeah, but that's ok.

Why is that ok?

Though drunk Kyle can still text in a grammatically correct fashion, he won't remember doing it.

He will remember.

No he won't. Stop speaking in 3rd person.

You're speaking in 3rd person.

Where?

Where what?

Go to bed . . . you're drunk.

You're beautiful.

Question?

Yes?

I want to know what those abbreviations meant.

Ooo . . . has it been driving you crazy?

Yes, like most things you do.

What do I get?

You're gonna get my foot up your ass in a moment!

Tell me!

Say something dirty to me and I will.

Something dirty to me.

You're impossible.

. . .

L.L.Y.P. = Love licking your pussy.

I.T.L.P. = It tastes like peaches.

Sweet, I should be a hit at the Farmer's Market then!

I'm sure you could sell your line of bullshit there, too.

In the manure section.

Yeah, I got the point. Lol.

I do love it, though. And I can't wait to taste you again.

Bye . . .

Tomorrow?

Today.

It's 3 am.

I'll be waiting.

You had to close out with one more creepy line, didn't you?

So I creep . . . yeah . . .

Shut-up, Left-smirk

LOL . . . I get it!

Congrats! Go to bed now, Asshat!

Sweet talker.

Night, beautiful . . .

Night.

"That was a long conversation," Mom says and shakes her head. Don't worry; I left all of the sex talk out. "Can I give you some advice?"

"Sure! Because the last bit you gave me was so successful!" I reply snidely. She stays silent like she always does when I get short with her. "Please tell me," I soften my tone.

"Don't text when you're drunk."

"You are a wise woman, Mother." I let my head drop to my folded arms in defeat . . . again.

"Why don't you go upstairs and lie down for a few hours before the party?" She rubs my back.

"I came early to help you."

"Help me do what, taste test all of the food?" She laughs.

"Well, that's my job." I lift my head and smile warmly at her.

"I don't recall ever giving you that job. You took on the role of taste tester all on your own."

"I'm good at it." I shrug.

"You're greedy, that's all! You want to make sure you get to have all of your favorites before anyone even walks through that door." She gives me that look that tells me she's got my number. You know that "knowing" look all mothers give their kids. "Now march your butt up those stairs; you look like hell."

"Thanks, Mom." I rub my face and do as I'm told.

Chapter Eleven

Dams will break . . .

CiCi

"Morning, Dolly," Dad says softly from behind me before planting a kiss on the top of my head. My dad has called me "Dolly" since I was a toddler. Apparently, I wanted him to carry me everywhere. I, of course, carried my doll everywhere with me, as well. So, one day he started calling me Dolly. When I asked him why, he told me that since he carried me everywhere like I carried my doll, then I was his dolly. It stuck and he's the only one I don't mind being called a pet name by. He's my dad—an awesome one to boot—why would I mind?

"Morning, Dad. Mom up?" I lean back.

"She's getting dressed. I'm going to take her to Charley's to spend some time with the kids and get her mind off of things. Thanks for staying last night, honey. Mom really needed you." He places his hand on my shoulder and squeezes.

"Did you hear any of our conversation?"

"I heard most of it. I'm glad she got it out." He takes a seat next to me and lets out a big sigh. "You know, you're the only one she can really talk like that to. Everyone else treats her . . . well, you know. I do it, too. I need to take a page out of your book, Dolly." He shakes his head and looks down. I hate seeing my dad so defeated. I hate seeing them both this way. I know exactly what he's talking about with my mom. Everyone walks on eggshells around her. I do, too—to a point. But when it's time, I step up to the plate to listen to her speak candidly about her condition. No one else can manage to do it. They don't know what to say. It's not always about saying anything; it's about listening. *Twerps.* Last night was pretty bad, though. I've never seen her like this. I replayed our conversation over and over again, all night. I hope what I said and what I didn't say helped.

We had just sat down on the couch, getting ready to watch The Little Princess *with Shirley Temple. My mom loves Shirley and that is the only movie of hers I really like, so we compromised. I had just brought some popcorn up to my mouth when she said, "I'm scared, Carissa." I turned my head her way, placing the popcorn in my mouth. I studied her and chewed. Mom looked as weary as she sounded. Her face was a little paler than usual, green eyes that were drowning in tears, and her chin quivering. I put the bowl on the coffee table. I had a feeling this was going to happen. She had been asking me to stay over for a few days.*

"Have you seen the doctor, Mom?" I asked as I turned, on the couch, to face her.

"Yes . . . I'm no longer in remission," she choked on her words. "I can't do this again," she softly cried. "I just can't. I don't have anything left in me." She wiped at her eyes with the tissue I gave her.

"Mom, don't talk like that. You kicked it's ass before, you'll do it again." I tried to encourage.

"You can only kick MS's ass so long before you're too old, tired, and weak. Then, it kicks your ass. This is it, Ceese, I'm not going to make it through this round—I can feel it down deep in my soul. I'm not ready . . ." she trailed off, shaking her head before the shaking transferred to her shoulders as she sobbed silently.

I grabbed my mom into a fierce hug, "I want to scream at you right now for talking like this. Goddamn it, Mom." I didn't though, because sometimes we just need to say what our fears are. Everyone thinks it's bravery not to show that you are scared. Fuck that shit! I think when you are a strong person, like my mom, it's much braver to say what scares the hell out of you. It's also therapeutic. If you acknowledge your shit then you can move onto the other phases like anger and acceptance. How can you form a positive plan of action if you won't acknowledge the very thing that needs a positive plan of action? "Ok, you're scared," I said as I pulled back from her, "Now tell me what pisses you off."

"That Goddamn wheelchair! I swore to Christ I would never sit my fat ass in it again!" she said angrily, balling her hands into fists.

"Uh, Shannon?" Dad interrupted us from the doorway. "I happen to think you have a lovely bottom, sweetheart." He gave her a wink. Mom chuckled and waved nonsense at him.

"Alright, Dad, I love you, but go away." I ordered.

"Ok, Dolly. I'll be in the den if you girls need me." He blew us a kiss and went on his merry way.

"So, we call Tom Kruse, the scooter guy." I said and we laughed.

"Poor bastard! Everyone must get so excited to meet him until they do and realize it's not the actor."

"Yeah, but just think about how many scooters he sells with that name. I'm not sure I really feel bad for him or his suffering ego." I shrugged, firing up the iPad to look at what Tom had to offer.

"Now would you look at those? They are hideous!" She pointed and tapped at the iPad angrily.

"Quit it, Ma! You're going to end up ordering something by tapping the screen like that!" I pulled it out of her reach. "Now," I continued, "look at this red one. It has a basket and side view mirrors!" I said in an exaggerated, excited manner.

She held up her hands as if she was driving a motorcycle then started sounding off the backing up beeping sound. "Move out of my way, asshole, before I run you over! Can't you see how fast I'm going?" she yelled out, looking in her pretend side mirror. I held my stomach, laughing.

"Wait! Do the beeping sound again and I'll be the robotic alert voice thingy." I laughed.

"Beep . . . Beep . . . Beep . . ."

"Approaching douchebag in plaid shorts and hideous shirt in five . . . four . . . three. Immediate impact on douchebag in two . . ."

"Beep! Beep! Beep!" Mom fell back, laughing harder.

"Holy shit! Besides the obvious stuffed Toto dog, you need to put a foghorn in your basket. As you're beeping, you should press that and make people jump!" I was getting so excited, I wanted a matching scooter just to hang and fuck with people all day. I mean, is that not right up my alley?

"I could also just 'accidently' drive in reverse and run into people, claiming innocence," she added thoughtfully.

"We can take you to amusement parks and get to the front of the line."

"When my shakes get really bad, we can tell them I'm seizing and you need to get me through to exit. Then once we're up by the ride, we'll be cool as a cucumber and get on the ride, ahead of all the other gimpy bastards." She points her finger in the air at her clever thought.

"What if you get called out?" I widen my eyes in horror (not really, cuz' we've done that before).

"I'll do what I did the last time—slap my bicep, uncoordinatingly, while flipping them off." She imitated the action, reminding me of that day, the day I actually *pissed myself. Luckily, I was in my bathing suit. I almost pissed myself again, right there. I had to run to the bathroom.*

"FYI, Mom," I said when I came back to the couch, "I don't think uncoordinatingly is an actual word."

"Well . . . let's look around and see if there are any Shannon O'Brien's who give a flying fuck." she suggested and turned her neck to look around the room. "Nope, I don't see a single one." She waved her hand around.

I love my mom.

She simply rocks.

She took back her somber look. "I'm afraid I'll never get to see you truly be happy, Carissa Catherine. That breaks my heart the most." Her tears formed once again. I'll admit it; mine did, too.

"I've met someone, Mom." I don't know why I said that.

"You have?" Her face lit up. Ok . . . maybe that's why.

"I'm scared." That, too. Who doesn't need their mama when they

are scared?

"That's when you know it's the real deal." She smiled.

"What?"

"When you're scared, that's the real deal. There are two reasons why you're scared," she said before I could interrupt again. "First reason is that you're afraid that it's not going to work out and you're going to get hurt. Second reason is you're afraid that he's the right one and your life will change. It will no longer revolve around you; you'll need to make room for this other person. That thought is terrifying; to have someone consume as much of your life as you do."

"Mom," my voice shook.

"Don't fight it, honey. He's not part of your past, don't force him there."

"What do you mean?"

"Don't make him pay for what Drew did to you. Life's too short, Ceese. You deserve to get over what happened to you—whatever that was—and have a happy life." She grabbed my hand and squeezed it.

"I wish it was that simple, Mom. I want to get over the past but it's always there, haunting me."

"I don't care who it is, but you need to talk to someone about what happened. This is the biggest reason why you haven't been able to move on . . . why you push men away." Her eyes filled up and I know she was thinking the worst. I know this because she's asked me so many times over the past fifteen years.

"The next step is forgiveness."

"Yes!" She slapped my leg.

"I'll never forgive him," I bit through those stupid fucking tears that were forming. Goddamn that son of a bitch! Every time I get emotional enough, thinking about what happened, and cry, it just makes me hate him all the more.

"What did he do?" Her question paraded out of her mouth shaky and slow. She seemed to be trying to contain every emotion known to man.

I changed the subject.

"So, what is the doctor's plan of action?" I grabbed the bowl of popcorn and began shoving it in my mouth . . . preventing me from talking.

Mom eyed me. "I know what you are doing." Nevertheless, she gave up and looked down at her hands. "Pills, diet, exercise . . . ya know, the usual. However, he did mention a different more pro-active treatment called Tsybari. It's an infusion that I would have to do every four weeks. There are some risks and they are not sure if it works as well on people over the age of sixty-five like it does for younger adults. He usually doesn't offer this as an option for people my age but given my long remission and my general health, he thought we could definitely consider it. Here's the pamphlet." She pulls up on the coffee table that actually works as a desk and storage bin, as well. That's so mine when we split the goods up in this house! What?! No, I don't want my parents to die. I'm just sayin' . . . gotta stake your claim on this shit early! You're still appalled? Try getting that stick out of your ass. There . . . that's better. ☺

"Mom, you can't do this. Nope!" I averted my eyes from the pamphlet to look at her.

"Too risky?" She bit her lip.

"Uh, yeah! For Christ's sake, you can get Vaginitis!" I almost yelled.

"But the vagina is all muscle! How do you get arthritis there? Oh, the pelvic bone maybe?" She widened her eyes at me.

I stared blankly at her.

Convulsing laughter fully equipped with snorting ensued after.

"It's an infection in your vagina!" I finally informed her.

"Well, I can get cream for that." She defended it.

"Um . . . eww. Also, that shit stinks! I think Daddy would rather you doing your shaky shakes under him; might give him an extra . . ." I winked and clicked my tongue twice. "Vaginitis will only have him hurl whenever he'd try to get near you. Would you rather repulse him or re-enact the 70s when you two would stay at hotels with the vibrating beds?"

"Shh . . . shh!" She held her finger to her mouth, frantically blowing—oh, the irony. "How is it you're the only kid I know that doesn't vomit in their mouth, thinking about their parents having sex?" She chuckled.

"You've had five kids, Ma, I'm pretty certain Dad likes to hit that shit—"

"—Carissa Catherine!" She gasped, cutting me off.

"What?"

"I love you. You're crazy as hell, but, God, do I love that about you." Yes, the tears started up again. "You need a good man who will love that about you, too."

"I . . . Kyle . . ." I hesitated. Admitting to anyone that Kyle was just that guy seemed (still seems) like defeat. Fuck, I hate this flip-flopping 'oh, what am I to do? (spoken in damsel distress voice)' attitude I've been having. This is *not* me! I hate that he's affected me like this. I hate that I love how he makes me feel. Seriously . . . What. In. The. Actual. Fuck?

"Kyle what? Is that his name?" She smiled.

"Yes." That was it. I grabbed the remote and pressed play. My mother patted my lap. I glanced at her a few minutes later only to find a small smile planted on her face. Her eyes fluttered over to me and she gave me a soft wink. I replied with a half-smile.

Mothers are amazing, aren't they? I'm always in awe as to how my mom just knows. She knows when to press me more and she knows just when to stop. When I'm off? She's grilling me for the answer why. I could go on and on. No one knows me as well as she does—emotionally, that is. I used to hope that I would be half as wonderful as a mom that she is. I settled for the title of Aunt a long time ago. I do my best there and it's pretty damn good, I think. That's the closest I will ever get to motherhood. I'm lucky to have that. I don't deserve to be a mom. I would suck at it.

"What are you two up to?" Mom asks from behind me.

"Just contemplating why the hell I'm up so early," I say before bringing my cup of coffee up to my lips.

"Because you're an adult with a business to run," she offers and kisses the top of my head.

"Shit, I never got that memo on being an adult. When the hell did that happen?"

"Come to think of it, you may have been overlooked," she sasses.

"Thanks, Mom."

"You're welcome. So, how's business?" she asks taking her cup of coffee out of Dad's hand. She sits next to me with Dad next to her. *Now's a good time as ever, right?*

"Business is not that great. I've decided to sell my house and use that money to try something else to salvage it." I sip my coffee, waiting.

"What are you thinking of, Dolly?" Dad widens his eyes as if he's anxious to hear about my newest scheme. You know what I love about my dad? This right here! My dad never flips out and throws his opinions at us. He waits to hear our entire plan before putting his two cents in. You know what I love even more about him? He never responds negatively. Nope, Happy Jack O'Brien tends to find his girls very capable and in return, he always hears us out. The only opinion he ever gives us is a thought on how to do something or another better. I asked him about that one time. *"Dad? How is it that you never get impatient with us girls? Every time we have big plans and share them with you, you never flip out or tell us our thinking is all wrong."*

"Dolly, even if I thought your plan wasn't solid, why would I ever make you second-guess yourself? That is the biggest mistake I think a parent can make. I'd rather support you and find the best ways to help you achieve what you want to do to be a success."

"So, if I decided to become a crack dealer, you'd help me find the best way to distribute the crack?" Because I'm a smartass.

"Crack is whack, Dolly! Better off with the weed. It's becoming legal in a few states now."

"The weed?" I chuckled.

"What? They call it something different these days?"

"Yeah, they dropped 'the'; it took too long to say. It's a fast paced business, drug dealing, they gotta keep the line movin,' ya know?" I said straight-faced (well, I think I did).

"Smarty-pants." He chuckled.

Yep, I love my dad. I'm very blessed in the parental unit department. They both have been (still are) wonderful parents. And that's the top reason why Charley and I have stayed around here and do our best to help them out. That and the rest of the girls; they are our family. I can't imagine going through my life without any of them nearby. It's sad to say, but with the exception of Charley, these girls are more like sisters to me than my own sisters. I love Caroline, Colleen, and Caitlyn but bitches stepped out a long time ago. They are holiday and vacation sisters now. I can't tell you the last time I picked up the phone to have a "Hey, sis, whatcha doin'" conversation with any of them. It's sad, I know. Charley and I talk about it every once in a while; it bothers us. You know what, though? Every time we try to call and check in, they've done nothing but aggravate the piss out of us. The biggest problem? Well, it's something that, I think, most older siblings go through. There's always one (in our case, two) sibling that stays near the parents. While they are the ones taking the "rents" to dr's appointments, checking in on them, and doing basically anything that they need, the other siblings sit half or all the way across the country, barking orders. Then they wonder why we get mad at them. Listen, I know that not everyone can handle taking care of their parents, watching them age. But either suck it the fuck up or don't be a douchebag to the ones who are there day in and day out, handling everything. If you think you can do it better, put your swim cap on and dive in, motherfucker!

Yeah—that's what I thought.

All talk.

"I'm going to look into getting a grooming van. I can take a couple days a week and hit up the areas concentrated with seniors. It's hard for them to get out, and they always love their animals the hardest." I pop a piece of toast in my mouth.

"That's a fantastic idea," Mom says as if she's surprised. "For marketing, you can say 'We'll bring Bark Avenue to you!' or something like that."

"Not too shabby, there, Mom." I nod my head in agreement.

"Do you have a place lined up to live?" Dad interjects.

"I'm working on it. I'll be at my house for a while, yet. I need to get some things up to date, ya know, get it show ready."

"We have plenty of room here, honey." Dad pats my shoulder.

"Thanks, Dad. I'll see what happens." I wipe my mouth then push away from the table to get up. "I better head into the shower. I have Lindsay's party today. I don't want to be late. Do you guys need anything before I head out?" I offer, before I run up the stairs.

"We're good, Ceese." Dad smiles up at me. "We're leaving in a few anyway."

"Ok. Give the kids a hug for me." I give them both a kiss on the head and head upstairs.

Chapter Twelve

A party in my pants . . .

CiCi

Ok, CiCi, you've got this. You are NOT going to let him get to you. Pull it together; he's not the only man on the planet.

Oh fuck this pep talk . . .

I get out of my black Honda Civic, grab the gift bags, and close the door. I parked several houses down . . . a half an hour ago. I'm still about fifteen minutes early but I want to offer help. Might as well start on the good foot since I'll probably end up on the bad one. Wait—I didn't mean it that way! I'm not saying anything sexual about me and Kyle. Oh . . . you weren't thinking that? Me neither . . .

Approaching the door, I smooth out my green dress. Well, not any dress. This is the dress that has been in my closet since my birthday, waiting patiently for me to have a good place to wear it. Aunt Clara bought me this for my birthday. She's my father's sister and I swear to God, she has more money than should be allowed. Her favorite store? Saks Fifth Avenue. I can't even begin to tell you the store credit I have racked up at that store. I wish I could turn it into cash. Anyways, every once in a while, Aunt Clara gets something so right that it cannot be returned. She told me she bought this because it matched my eyes. She was right. Also, I am very partial to the designer, alice + olivia (Charley is, too.) This is their tevin satin brocade dress and I'm in love with it.

Before I can knock, the door is whipped open. "You're here! I can't believe you're here!" Lindsay screeches, her face beaming the hugest smile I've ever seen. I don't know if it's because I've been off lately or the talk with my mom but I'm tearing up like a crazy hormonal bitch. *I hate when this shit happens.* Seeing her face though, I know I've made the right decision. No matter what's going on between Kyle and me, I cherish this chick. She's become a wonderful friend to me.

"Of course I came! I wouldn't miss your birthday party!" I hug her. Then it hits me like a ton of bricks—I know no one here! I mean, I know Linz and Kyle, but that's it. Oh man, I hate this fucking shit. You know I hate it. I have no filter and no apology for it. Oh well . . .

Here goes nothing . . .

"Come on in! I can't wait for you to meet my mom," she says quickly and grabs my hand to drag me along. "Mom! Mom, this is my best friend, CiCi," she announces when we make it over the threshold to the kitchen. She made it; I tripped. I look up to find warm, blue eyes, smiling my way.

We both give each other a quick "once over." "alice + olivia!" We say in unison. She's wearing their fila beaded cotton dress. I love that dress!

"Turn! Turn!" she barks at me. I do a slow spin. "Ahh . . . look at that racerback! Oh, I love it, CiCi. It's gorgeous." She beams.

"Thank you . . . uh . . . Mrs. Cooper," I stammer.

"Call me Winnie." She pulls me in for a hug. She's a little thing. Perfectly put together from her well-coiffed, brown hair to her patent leather, sling back Jimmy Choo's. I went with my Fendi, patent leather "Fuck me" pumps. It's clear; we have fashion in common.

"Winnie Cooper?" I ask as straight-faced as I can.

"Yes, I'm afraid so," she chuckles.

"Do you get by with a little help from your friends?" I ask because it couldn't be helped.

"As well as a few smarty-pants." She smirks. Ah-ha! It runs in the family.

"Sorry." I chew on the inside of my cheek. Damn nerves.

"Oh, that's ok, dear. Why don't you put your gift in the living room with the others, then I would love your help. That is . . . if you don't mind."

"I'd love to help. That's why I came early. Uh . . . this is for you, though." I hand her one of the bags.

"Me?" she asks, her face lighting up. And that's where Lindsay gets that expression from. Ok. I might already like their mom.

"Yes, I wanted to give you a little something to thank you for the invite," I reply as she digs into the bag and pulls out an apron. She reads it. I chew on the inside of my cheek again. She roars with laughter. *Thank God!*

"What does it say, Mom?" Lindsay asks as Winnie puts it on.

"Read it." She ties the knot.

"My . . . oven . . . gets . . . hot . . . for . . . big . . . cocks," she reads aloud, slowly. "I like the rooster on there, he looks so real." She lifts the bottom of the apron and inspects it closely. I try to stifle my giggle. Lindsay clearly didn't get the pun of the apron. I'm just happy that Winnie got a kick out of it. I was concerned about it but I thought it best to put my personality right out there. I don't have the energy to be someone I'm not.

"What's going on in here?" I hear a guy bellow out from behind us.

"Stu, come in here and meet Kyle's girlfriend," she greets him, placing a hand softly on my upper arm.

Yes, the wheels in my head just screeched to a stop.

Girlfriend?

"Is this CiCi?" He gives me a full wattage smile and brings me in for a hug, patting my back. Actually, it's more of a *whack . . . whack . . . whack.* "Look at you! You're more beautiful than he said you were." He pulls back but holds my upper arms near my shoulders and gives me a kiss on each cheek.

Uh . . .

Help . . . me.

"Alright, Daddy, let her go." Linz taps at his arm. He lets go. *Oh, thank Christ.*

"Um . . . I'm going to put these out in the living room." I motion my thumb in that direction.

"Let Lindsay do it," Winnie starts, "I need you to go upstairs to wake Kyle. He's suffering from a fool's headache." She winks at me. That wasn't a normal ah-ha wink. It was like an awkward "get my code?" wink. Except, I have no idea what the code is. I know he got drunk. Clearly, she knows. That's where this exchange stops for me and I'm actually afraid to ask what the exaggerated wink means.

"Maybe Lindsay should wake him." I shake my head and go to head to the living room.

"No, dear, I need her help with something." She grabs the bag from me and pats me on the ass to get going.

I'm not going to lie; I'm walking up these stairs with my pussy clenched to the hilt. I can't help it. All I can think about is his piercing blue eyes, shooting right through me. His hands all over my body. My nipples pebble hard. You know what they want.

Tug, tug, rub, and roll . . .

Let's not discuss the wicked things his tongue did to my lady business. The farther I walk down this hall (mindlessly because I didn't ask which room was his) the stronger my body reacts to his proximity. I stop and lean against the wall, panting, ready to bust at the seams.

Holy fuck.

I have a lady boner.

I have *never* in my life felt the need to rub one out real quick just so I could go back to normal function. What. In. The. Actual. Fuck with this guy?! *Pull it together, Ceese!*

Ah! "Kyle's Room" Wow, I can't believe they left the sign on his door. It's like he never moved out. I open it slowly and peek in. He's sleeping peacefully on his old bed. I quietly walk in, closing the door behind me. I lock it . . . out of habit.

Oh, shut-up.

I watch him. Creepy, I know. But, he's beautiful. His brown hair is longer on top; it has a slight wave to it, and has flopped near his left eye. I want to push it out of the way and kiss those fantastic lips of his. My eyes scan down his body, drinking in the sight of his form-fitting, white, V-neck t-shirt. *Yum.* It must be an expensive brand because you can't see his tattoo through it. I continue on with my inspection.

Fuck the way his jeans are hanging at his hips.

Lifting my right leg and bending it at the knee, I reach down and slide off my shoe. When I glance up before switching to my other foot, I'm paralyzed by his stare. Kyle slides to the edge of the bed and sits up in front of me. He reaches out to my left leg and lets his hand slide down it to my ankle. He grasps it gently and lifts, pulling my other shoe off as soon as my foot is in the air. My heart drums loudly in my ears while his hands travel up my legs. That drumming is soon joined by a whole slew of band members parading their tingle-worthy music up and down the channel from my heart to the inner walls of my . . . *oh, God.* I throw my head back as Kyle's hands make it to my upper thighs, his thumbs stretch out to caress me lightly over my panties.

Kyle's breath hits my neck hot and harsh as he stands up abruptly. His hands cup my ass possessively, kneading it. I thread my fingers through his hair as his mouth attacks my neck. Bringing my neck back up, I guide his face to mine. Our rapid breaths compete with each other before our mouths finally slam against one another. His tongue slides against mine so deliciously; I can't help my slight moan. I can feel my dress being unzipped as I give in to this kiss completely. My hands guide his shirt out of his pants, grasp the hem, and pull the shirt up and over his head, causing us to break from our kiss. *Fuck.* The adrenaline is making me shiver. Kyle cups my face, staring into my eyes. I'm about to avert mine but then I remember what he asked me about looking back at him and I keep focused. A small, sexy smile crosses his lips. Obviously, this pleases him. That makes me happy . . . that I've pleased him. And *that* makes me feel all kinds of uncomfortable.

His hands glide down my neck and under the thick-banded straps of my dress, sliding them off my shoulders. He watches intently as my dress slowly falls to the ground. I step out of it. He bends down, picking it up off the floor and laying it over his old computer desk chair.

"It's satin, I don't want it to wrinkle," he whispers, refocusing on me.

"That's ok. It sounds to me like I have a manwhore who knows his way around an iron," I tease.

"Manwhore, huh?" he asks in a whispering laugh. I nod. "You are so beautiful." He touches my cheek with the back of his hand. "I could stare at you forever." He leans in and captures my lips again. Suddenly, he rips my bra from me. Well, it's backless so, it doesn't take much.

"Kyle," I breathe against his mouth. The girls find themselves captive in his hands, being pushed up and squeezed.

And then . . .

Yup.

Tug, tug, rub, and roll . . .

I want to climb him like a wild amazon woman. For right now, I'm just going to wrap my right leg around his and rub one off on him, like so. I feel like we're waltzing as he leads me to turn with him till the bed is at the back of my knees. Reaching down, I work at his belt, yanking it from him. He takes in a sharp breath and sucks my lower lip into his mouth when I unbutton, unzip, and slide my hand into his jeans. I wrap it around his already hard-as-steel cock. I groan, remembering how good he felt inside of me the last time. Kyle was given a very generous amount in the kibbles and bits department and for that, I'm thankful. Look, I don't know who came up with this idea of telling men that size doesn't matter but, it's a big ole' fucking lie. Sure, we don't want to be ripped into two pieces but there's not a girl I know who likes having to ask if he's in, know what I'm sayin'?

My thumb swirls his pre-cum around his tip. "I need to taste you," I say, finally freeing my lip from his. I'm actually going to need a minute to digest what I just said. I *never ever* want to suck a guy off. Nope. Not my thing. I generally avoid it all costs. My mouth is fucking *watering* for him. I take my time sliding down to sit on the edge of the bed. He remains standing in front of me, breathing rapidly, watching me. I can't even begin to tell you how fucking sexy he looks with no shirt and his jeans, hanging on his hips, unbuttoned. All I can say is that my panties are on the verge of needing to be wrung out and no man has ever made me this hot before. Praying that I don't do a shit job at this, I grasp either side of his jeans and shimmy them down. I can feel Kyle's eyes watching me as I take him in my hand. I close my eyes and think about the time Jay and I had watched a marathon of gay man porn (that shit is hot; don't knock it!). I try to concentrate on what I learned from "CockSuckers Take the Shots" . . . it was very educational.

I part my lips, letting my tongue swirl around his fat tip (seriously—how am I walking?), tasting his pre-cum. His dick twitches at this. I raise my eyes to find his. He's biting his lip, his chest puffing in and out at a quick pace. I flatten my tongue and keeping my eyes on his, I run it up from the base to the tip before breaking eye contact to fill my mouth with him. When I can't possibly fit another inch in and I'm almost gagging, I begin the slow sucking process, making sure to add the pressure of my tongue caressing him as I work up his shaft.

Shaft?!

I fucking hate that word!

Retrieving his tip from my mouth, I let a little of my spit spill onto it to work at him with my hand in a smoother manner. I glance up at Kyle. He's watching me with his mouth open and tongue touching his front top teeth. He gives me a nod of encouragement and I get back to work, fluctuating between sucking and jerking him off. I can tell he's trying his hardest to remain quiet as I'm sure the house is starting to buzz to life with guests for the party. After a few minutes, I can feel his dick thickening further (Christ, how is that possible?) and he's now letting out gushes of breath like he's been holding them in forever.

"Ceese, stop! Stop, stop, stop!" He pulls away from me. *Damn, I was getting a good rhythm going!* I'm a little disappointed. I knew he was getting close and I really wanted to taste him. Again . . . that's a very bizarre desire to have, for me.

"Are you ok?" I finally ask, watching him pace a little.

"Yeah. I just don't want to come until I'm inside of you." He stops pacing.

Mayday! Mayday! The little man in the boat is drowning!

"Lie back on the bed," he commands. I find myself obeying. I sucked cock willingly today, why stop there, right? "Slide your panties off," he continues. "Give them here." He reaches out for them after I slide them off. "Oh, baby . . . they're drenched." He balls them in his fist, closing his eyes like he's trying to fight something off—probably his dick from exploding. Seems plausible. I know I'm ready to open my legs and squirt across the room. I'm not a squirter, but today just might be the day. He opens his eyes again and they are darker, full of lust. "Spread these gorgeous legs. I want to see that beautiful pussy of yours." His voice is so low and seductive; it's making that very pussy of mine ache terribly. I do as he asks and groan as I feel my wetness slide down to my ass. Kyle falls to his knees in front of me. "I can't tell you how badly this is making my dick hurt to see you dripping like this for me," he says above a whisper.

"Kyle . . . please," I beg.

"Tell me to taste what's mine."

"What?"

"You heard me, CiCi."

"You're going to ruin the moment with this shit? I can't believe you," I seethe through my teeth in a hushed tone.

"Your pussy is in my face, glistening and beautiful. I am more than willing to please it . . . please you. In order for that to happen, you need to ensure me that I am, and will be, the only one to please it. There are very few things in life that I won't share. You are one of those things. All you need to do is tell me that I won't have to share you." He kisses my inner left thigh. Waiting patiently for my answer, his tongue slides out, slowly licking his lips. *Oh God.*

Shit. This is ridiculous. I know I'm not going to let anyone else near me. I don't want anyone else! I'm still trying to accept the fact that I want him. But here's the thing, I'm stubborn. Shocking, I know. This power struggle is the very thing that is going to ruin this moment. He's saying black and I so badly want to say white. I can't begin to tell you the bells that are going off in my head. However, there is another bell that is going off far louder. One I wasn't even aware I had. It's never rung before.

My pussy bell.

It's so fucking loud! Do you have one of those? Maybe that's what Anita Ward was singing about when she said you could ring her bell.

Kyle rings my bell.

He gives good bell ring.

"While you're thinking about that, I'm going to help you out by guiding you to the conclusion that should come so easily to you," he says, sounding a little perturbed. With that, he licks up my center slowly. His left hand spreads me open, giving him full access. I watch (possibly whimpering) as his tongue does wicked things to me. I rest my head back and join in by working at my nipples. Fuck—this feels awesome.

Suddenly, my breath hitches. Oh my God, what is he doing? I raise my head again to confirm what I'm feeling. His finger is playing with my ass. "Kyle?" I pant nervously as the pressure increases. *Don't finger my ass. Don't finger my ass. Don't finger my ass.*

He slips his finger in my ass.

Where's an "Oh shit!" handle when you need one?

Kyle's finger is in my ass and he's slowly fucking it. I'm not sure how I feel about this. I mean—"Oh, oh, Kyle, please . . . please," I beg. I fist at the quilt underneath us as his tongue plunges deep into my pussy, synchronized with his finger. His free thumb working circles on my clit with perfect pressure.

Ding, ding, ding, ding, ding!

My pussy bell may or may not be on fire.

"Yes! Don't stop, Kyle . . . just like that," I encourage him. He stops.

Dafuq?

"Tell me! Who do you belong to? Are you mine? Is your pussy mine? Tell me, damn it!" he bites.

"Oh, please . . . don't do this to me again. Don't leave me hanging like this." I beg again.

"One word and I take this ache away."

I lie here, silently fighting off tears of frustration. Just as my climax loses its build, he starts up again. He works me up into another frenzy. This time, I take notice how adjusted I've become to his finger's intrusion and am now grinding to meet its thrust.

"Feel good, Ceese?" he murmurs against my raging lady hotness.

"Yes. Kyle." I pant.

"I'll make you feel like this every day. Just one word."

"Please . . ." I trail off.

"Wrong word," he states and works me up again. My pussy fucks the hell out of his face.

"Oh . . ." I arch my back. He stops.

Motherfucker!

"Say it!" His hands slap the inside of my thighs, making me buck into the air. *Just say it, CiCi, just say it!*

"No," I groan.

"Wrong answer. Just so you know, I fucking love the taste of your pussy and I have no problem—whatsoever—keeping up with these charades until I hear what I want to hear, you understand me?" he asks before starting at me again.

I quit.

"Say it!" He pulls away again.

"Please, Kyle." I sit up slightly, cupping his face in my hands; I pull him up to me. "I need you inside of me. Take what's yours," I say, not hiding how vulnerable I feel.

"Say it again," he breathes into my face, the scent of my urgency thick in the air.

"The scent of my pussy on your face is sexy as fuck," I say before attacking his lips.

"Who's pussy?" He breaks away.

"Yours. All yours." I bring him back for another kiss. After a beat, he pulls away again and leans back on his knees. He grabs his jeans and pulls a condom out of the pocket.

"Back up on the bed," he orders as he tears the packet open. I watch as he sheathes himself. "Now." He reiterates. I slide back as he climbs onto the bed and above me. "This is going to be fast and rough. We should've been downstairs twenty minutes ago. Are you ok with that?"

I say nothing. I'm too busy thinking about how hot that fucking statement was.

"Hold your legs; I want to watch myself fucking you." He brings my legs up and pushes them back. I grab a hold of them, looking down, waiting to watch myself.

Kyle guides his cock up and down my between my slick folds. "Always so fucking wet for me, aren't you, Birkita?" he asks sweetly. I love that he calls me this. It's different. He's different.

"Ahh," I gasp as he sinks himself inside of me.

"Fuck . . . you're so tight," he groans lowly. "You ok?"

"Yes."

"Ready?"

"Yes."

"You gonna watch with me?" He smiles.

"I'm a visual fucker," I remind him.

"Don't drop your legs." He leans down, kisses me, then leans back and watches as he slowly slides out of me.

Slam!

Oh God!

He's off! I watch as his cock slips in and out of me over and over again at a fast pace. God, it's such a turn on. Kyle pushes my legs back harder, raising my pelvis in the air. Fuck, it's so full this way. I close my eyes for a minute and listen to his balls slapping against my ass. I love the sounds of sex. I love the tingling I feel in my ass as it gets slapped. I open my eyes again to find his searching mine.

"Harder," I order and look down again. He shifts a little, then pounds into me, relentlessly. I let out a scream that gets stifled by his hand.

"Fuck, look at how your pussy's taking it, Ceese."

Kyle's a visual fucker, too.

Kyle also tends to lose his Boy Scout image in the bedroom.

I'm a fan.

Suddenly, he slows down to an agonizing pace. We watch him fill me . . . pull out . . . fill me . . . it reminds me of a bow sliding across the strings of a violin. I bring my attention to his face as he watches us. Something clicks inside me. I don't know how to explain it but all of the sudden I'm feeling things and shit. I don't like it. I feel like I've lost more control over myself. Possibly sensing my watching him, he looks up and locks eyes with me. He removes his hand from my mouth and releases my other leg, letting it fall around his waist as he positions himself on top of me. He hooks my leg with his arm to shift me a little, thrusting into me at full capacity.

"Gah!" I gasp, reaching down to grasp his ass and help him. His mouth attacks mine and I can feel the slow, sweet climb. "Please let me come," I beg against his lips.

"I'll give you anything you want," he grunts. I can tell he's ready to explode himself. His finger finds my clit and rubs it in a slow, circular motion.

Oh, hell yes!

"That's it. Right there." I dig my nails into him and clench, encouraging his release.

"C'mon, Ceese. Come for me," he demands. My mouth opens in a silent scream. My legs begin to shake.

Kyle definitely gives good leg shake.

He scrunches up his face and breathes those gusty breaths, finally finding his release. I hold on, rocking with him. With one last thrust, he collapses on top of me.

"Please. Tell. Me. That there's. A shower on the. Other side of one those. Doors." I pant through. Kyle lifts his head and chuckles, looking me in the eyes. "We're a hot, sweaty mess," I add.

"We are hot, aren't we?" He kisses me.

"Kyle?" I almost whine.

"Yes." He kisses me again. "There's a ¾ bathroom through that door. We need to be quick, though." He reaches down and pulls out.

I whimper.

He smirks.

We're quite the pair, aren't we?

"C'mon." He gets up, ties the condom to seal it, and holds his hand out for me. I take it and follow his lead into the tiny bathroom. I close the door while he starts the water.

"So," I sigh as he turns to me. "You totally fingered my ass."

"Yup."

"How do you feel about that?" I widen my eyes at him and bite the inside of my cheek.

"It was good . . . in the end," he replies straight-faced. He lets out a little breathy chuckle . . . probably something close to my whisper giggle . . . which I'm now doing. Grasping my hips, he leans into my ear, "Every part of your body is amazing to me. It's softness, the curves, your scent; I'm looking forward to exploring it more and more."

I'm looking forward to being explored.

And conquered . . . let's not forget conquered.

"Ready to wash the evidence away?" He straightens himself out and backs up towards the shower. I nod and follow him. The way he's eyeing me combined with the growth occurring down in the dirty south (I mean that in the best possible way), I'm getting a vision of my face being pressed up against that glass door . . . awkwardly, like . . . like . . .

You know.

Chapter Thirteen

A shift in the force . . .

Kyle

CiCi and I race down the stairs. The party is in full swing and we've been MIA for probably an hour, give or take. I'm pretty sure a few eyebrows will be raised. I don't really care, though. That was amazing. If I had my way, we'd spend the rest of the day in my old room, finding different ways to please each other.

I spin around before we get to the kitchen. This causes her to walk right into me. "What are you doing?" she laughs in a giddy fashion. I stare at her in awe. She seems so relaxed and happy . . . different. I thought she was beautiful before, but this takes the cake.

"I just wanted to do this." I nudge her nose with mine before planting several kisses on her lips. She starts laughing when I become obnoxious with my pecks. She turns her head and I chuckle into her neck. I feel so high on life right now. "Alright, I'll stop. I'm sorry . . . I'm just so happy." I squeeze her to me.

"Most guys are after they get laid," she says near my ear.

I jerk my head back. "No, Ceese. It's not just that."

"Sounds like your mom might need our help." She avoids my eyes and points to the kitchen door. There's a lot of banging going on in there.

"Let's go." I agree, deciding not to push this discussion with her further. I have to say though, that I'm pretty certain CiCi is not feeling the same things I am. It's taking everything in me not to fall into a somber mood but, Jesus Christ, I feel like she just ripped the sunshine right out of my sky. I'm probably overreacting. I'm just going to shake this off.

"There you two are." Mom smiles at us, pulling appetizers out of the oven.

"Sorry, Mom," I offer, placing my arm around CiCi's shoulders and squeezing her to me to kiss her temple.

"I'm so glad you kids talked things out," she says and closes the oven.

"Yeah, I gave CiCi a mouthful." I deadpan. Mom turns to the face the counter and CiCi elbows me in the ribs—hard. I look at her and she mouths *"jerk"* to me.

"You mean an earful, dear." Mom looks over her shoulder. "Get me that plate there, please." I grab the plate and hand it to her.

"What can I do, Winnie?" She heads over to the island. "Want me to pass these out?"

Mom turns around and I read her apron. "Mom! You can't wear that!" The feeling of shock is an understatement. I've never seen my mom wear anything like this.

"You don't like the apron I got your mom?"

I look over at CiCi then to my mom and back. "No! No, I don't like it! That's my mother for Christ's sake! Why would you give her something like that?" I raise my voice.

"Kyle, honey, there's no reason to get so upset." Mom touches my arm.

"What's going on in here?" Dad pops his head in.

I look over at him and point to my mother's apron. "Dad, did you see this?"

"Yes. I damn near fell over laughing." He walks into the kitchen. "True too, huh, Winnie?" He winks at her.

"Oh, Stu!" Mom laughs and slaps his chest. I turn my focus towards CiCi who is joining in their laughter. I shake my head at her and walk across the kitchen to the back door, slamming it as I leave.

No. I'm not overreacting!

Would you want your mom walking around, advertising that big cocks make her oven hot? I didn't think so. That's so like CiCi, isn't it?! She just does whatever she feels like; no thought of consequences involved. And that's exactly why—

I stop dead in my tracks.

That's exactly why . . . I like her.

Shit. I hope I didn't just royally fuck up. I head back to the house, but not before noticing CiCi's car. I chuckle as I read the bumper sticker on the back *"I get a ♥ on for groomed pussies!"* this, of course, has cats lining the bottom of the sticker along with Bark Avenue's symbol in case anyone got the wrong idea. I look at her backseat and notice a duffle bag with clothes coming out. Man, I bet she's still having water issues at her house. I hate the idea of her living out of suitcases. Maybe she'll stay with me until it gets fixed. Too fast? Nah . . .

I stop as I come around to the back of the house. The windows are open and I can hear CiCi and my mom talking as clear as day. I lean up against the siding and try to avoid being seen.

"It's tough, seeing them get older. It kills me that I can't take this away from my mom. I don't know how I'm going to survive, as selfish as that seems, watching her suffer through this again," CiCi's voice shakes.

"I understand. I had a terrible time of it when my mom was dying from cancer."

"I don't want my mom to die. I don't want to see her go through all of this pain only to leave the life she's not ready to give up yet." CiCi chokes and it takes every fiber of my being not to run in there and pull her into my arms like that will save the day. I've only known CiCi for a few months and *only* what she lets me know. However, what I get from others is that this, right here, is not something she does very often. I think she needs to purge some of these burdens she's been facing and if my mother is the one she finally feels comfortable enough to do that with well, then, so be it.

"I'm sorry. I'm being very selfish. I'm sorry about your mom, Winnie."

"Hush now. We were discussing your mom in the first place. I just wanted you to know that I understand."

"Thank you."

"Do the rest of your sisters know? You said you have four sisters, right?"

"Yes. Four. No, I don't think they all know. She only told me last night. I'm always the first one she tells anything important to."

"Why's that?"

"Probably because I'm straight with her. I don't walk on eggshells. We discuss things and after the seriousness gets too much, I come up with a way to find the humor in whatever it is."

"That's lovely. That's exactly how I'd want to be treated. Life's too short, CiCi. You and I may know that a little better than most."

"Speaking of being treated a certain way. I gave you that apron because I love stuff like that. I call them conversational pieces." CiCi laughs nervously. "But, I also wanted you to know my personality right off the bat. I can't stand when people pretend to be a certain way that they're not. In saying that though, I didn't think—which is a common occurrence with me—about whether I'd be offending anyone. I actually didn't think you would wear it. If you're wearing it just to be nice, it's really ok. I don't mind if you take it off. It would probably make Kyle happy to see it off."

I shift at the mention of my name. And that urge to run in there and tackle her in a hug returns to me.

"You really like my son, don't you?"

My breath hitches.

"Yes, I do. I tried not to but he's a persistent fucker . . . shit . . . sorry." CiCi has the decency to sound mortified at her own language. I can't help but grin.

"Why?"

"Why do I like him?" she asks, seemingly trying to clarify.

"No. Why did you try to not like him?" I can hear Mom spoon some sort of sauce or something around in a pan. I hate not being able to watch CiCi's body language . . . or just her body, really. God, I love her body.

"Um . . . it's just been a long time since I've been in a serious relationship, the kind that Kyle seems to be looking for. I'm not sure I can fully give him that. The last one I had, ended very badly."

"What happened?" Mom pushes and I'm at the edge of my seat, here.

"We should get these out to the guests; they're going to wonder where we are." CiCi rushes through her sentence and I can hear drag a serving dish along the counter until she probably lifts it.

"CiCi," Mom calls out.

"Yeah?"

"Kyle's a good guy."

"I know. Thing is . . . so was the guy that destroyed me," she admits, then I hear nothing but the door between the kitchen and living room swing open.

"You can come in now; she's gone." Mom says quietly.

See how I never got away with any shit, growing up?

I walk up the steps to the deck and head back into the kitchen. "There's just something about you, Winnie Cooper." I bring my mom in for a hug and kiss the top of her head.

"Hmm." She pats my back and I let go. "You all done with your temper tantrum now?" she asks just as she begins to stir the rue she's making.

"Yep, I think so." I sigh then look up as CiCi walks back in. "Hey." I offer her a warm smile.

"Hey, yourself." She places a tray down and grabs another one. "Everyone is asking for you, Winnie."

"I'm coming right now." She pours the rue over potatoes. Mmm . . . looks like something I will need to test taste. "Leave that alone, Kyle, it has to go in the oven." She slaps my hand like I was reaching for it or something.

"I was only gonna brush the crumbs off the counter."

You believe me, right?

"I call bullshit, son." She gives me that "knowing" eye of hers before leaving the kitchen.

"She's got your number, huh?" CiCi smiles over at me.

"She sure does." I move closer to her. "I overreacted before."

"Ya think?" She turns to me, leaning her hip against the island.

"Yes." I nod, a little embarrassed. "I'm sorry."

"It's not a big deal. I get it. Most people don't want to think about their parents and sex at the same time. It's ok." She shrugs.

"No, it isn't. You only did the very thing that I love about you. I don't want you to think I would ever try to get you to change." I graze her hand with mine then lace our fingers together.

"You love that about me?" she asks apprehensively.

"Yes." I move in closer until our faces are a mere inch apart.

"Why don't you help me with these trays?" She backs away.

"Yes, ma'am." I bring her hand up to my lips and kiss the back of it. After releasing her hand, CiCi grabs a serving dish and hands it to me.

"Mmm . . . Mom's crab cakes." I almost moan.

"Try not to eat them all before you make it out of the kitchen." She raises an eyebrow at me.

I shove one in my mouth and smile big.

"Hey, I'm not the one you will have to answer to." She shakes her head, grabs a tray, and goes through the door to where the party is. I follow her lead, after swallowing.

After a few minutes of traveling around the living room (possibly playing, "one for you, one for me"), I find CiCi with her back facing me, talking to Joan Livingston, our long-time neighbor.

"Have you known the Coopers long?"

"Just a few months."

"Oh? How did you meet them?"

"Lindsay volunteered at my grooming shop. She was so wonderful with the customers and the animals, that I asked her to work for me. We've become great friends since then."

"Joan!" I step into their bubble. "I see you've met my girlfriend, CiCi." I put my hand around the small of CiCi's back and squeeze her towards me a little. What? I couldn't help it.

Joan's face lights up. "Oh, well, she definitely didn't get that far in her revelations." she giggles.

I watch as CiCi gives a tight-lipped smile, her body tense. "I'm not surprised." I nod. "See, we're still in our trial period. We have about three more weeks before we can make the final decision to go through with it, right, Ceese?" I nudge her.

"Trial period? Go through with what?" Joan asks in obvious confusion.

I lean in towards her, "The wedding," I say in a hushed voice.

"She's one of those mail order brides."

"Are you from Russia, dear?" Joan inquires, the sound of scandal in her voice.

"No, no. I'm the new American version. We come as equals, having our own businesses and such. I'm just required to be submissive in the bedroom." CiCi plays along. "It's very upscale . . . so much that we get a trial period."

"I mean, what if she snores?" I pipe up.

"What if he can't keep it—" CiCi points her thumb up in the air.

"I've already discovered she farts in her sleep."

"I do?" she asks, sounding appalled.

"Yes, dear. It's quite offensive." I shake my head.

"Um . . . well, I wish you both the best in your endeavors. I see Gertie is here and I've been meaning to talk to her about something. Would you mind excusing me?" Joan seems very flustered.

"By all means." I smile, move out of her way, and usher my hand out for her to go. Joan leaves us to our own devices.

"Let me guess, nosy neighbor?" CiCi's lips finally break into a smile.

"I've always sworn she's a double agent," I say through my grin as I wave to Joan's husband, Walter, across the room. I bring my attention back to CiCi. "Have I told you how gorgeous you look in this dress?" I give her a once-over. "It matches your eyes almost to a 'T.'" I circle around her. I lean in near her ear, "I meant to thank you earlier for doing as you were told," I say quietly, tugging on the material at her hip.

Her breath catches. "I . . . I didn't wear this because you told me to wear a dress."

"No?" I straighten up and raise an eyebrow at her.

"No," she states stubbornly.

Just as I'm about to call her on her bluff, my mom calls out for everyone to gather in the living room. Lindsay, who is never patient when it comes to opening gifts, is ready to open them. I grab the tray from CiCi to put down, and then take her hand in mine. Lacing fingers with her, I guide her to the center of attention.

"Where's Mickey?" she asks quietly.

"In the shed, crated till . . . now, I guess."

"What?!" She yanks her hand out of mine. "How long has he

been out there for?"

Before I can even answer her, she's already making a beeline to the kitchen. "Where are you going?" I catch up with her and grab her arm to turn her to me.

"Is it dark in there?" she practically yells and twists her arm out of my grasp.

"No." I sigh and roll my eyes as she storms off again. Shaking my head, I follow her outside and stop. She's too busy cussing me out, under her breath, to listen to me. I'm just going to stand here and let her have this moment of wanting to put her foot in her mouth later. *Christ!*

You know what she's going to find when she opens that shed door? She's going to find Christopher, my little 2nd cousin, in there with Mickey, keeping him company. She's also going to find that the shed has electricity, allowing lights and music to keep Mickey calm.

I lean up against the railing on the deck, watching as she opens the shed door. She stands there for a moment, then turns around and heads back. I cross my arms across my chest, as well as my legs.

"Did you meet Christopher?" I ask as she heads up the few stairs to the massive deck.

"Yeah."

"Yeah? That's it, just yeah?" I grill her. Do I sound like I'm looking for a fight? Yeah, I am.

"What do you want me to say?" She crosses and rubs her arms up and down. Eye contact? No.

"How about, gee, Kyle, I'm sorry I jumped to conclusions and thought you were some kind of asshole who would lock a dog up in a dark shed without food or water, for hours? You got something like that for me, Ceese?" I bite.

"Don't chastise me." Her eyes shoot up to mine. "I made a mistake, I'm sorry. Get over it."

"I'm sorry, get over it? What the fuck kind of apology is that?"

Just then, the back door opens and my dad pokes his head out of it. "Lindsay's opening her gifts, guys, and she keeps asking for you. I think you two have had enough alone time. This is her day." Before we can even reply, he's back in and shuts the door.

"Shit, he's right." She brings her attention back to me. She steps into my personal space more and looks up at me. "Listen, I am sorry.

About the assumption and my shitty apology." She toes up and lays a soft kiss on my lips. "We need to get inside," she adds. I nod and take her hand to lead her in. "I told Christopher to bring Mickey in in a few minutes, is that ok?"

"Yes."

"Kyle?" She pulls on my hand.

"What?" I look over my shoulder at her.

"Are we ok?"

I give her a slight, indifferent shrug. I don't know how to answer that. I look forward and continue to guide us through the kitchen, swinging door, and into the living room.

"There you two are!" Lindsay beams. Damn, I do feel like a big jerk for spending the better half of this day indisposed.

"Sorry, Linz," I offer. CiCi squeezes my hand as Christopher walks through the front door, holding Mickey's crate with a cover over it. "I hope this makes up for my getting sidetracked."

"What is this?" she asks excitedly. God, I love that about my sister, the childlike excitement. It's so pure and infectious. I hate to admit this, but it makes me sad at the same time. I feel like I'm missing something that she has a huge hold on. I think most people are missing it, though. Everyone looks at her with pity, a lot of the time.

Fools—all of them.

"Are you ok?" CiCi leans up and whispers in my ear.

"Yeah," I sigh before letting go of her hand to put my arm around her shoulder. She smiles up at me.

"Ahhh!" Linz screams. "He's so cute! Is it a he?" she asks as she unlocks his crate and brings him out. I'm not going to lie, I'm a little nervous.

"I knew it!" CiCi says excitedly in a whisper. We both stand here, watching as Mickey kisses Linz like a sweet little pup. Not the terror I picked up several days ago. A wave of emotion comes over me and I can feel myself tear up. What? It's my sister, for Christ's sake . . . she gets to me. CiCi has her arm around my waist and she squeezes me to her. I glance down at her and she's beaming at me, same glossed over eyes as me. We both let out a giggle. Well, she giggled . . . I chuckled. Men don't giggle.

Fuck it. I giggle. I'll just own that shit flat out.

"Christ, I thought the Livingston's were never going to leave," Dad grumbles as he reaches to the middle of the table for the pork fried rice. The party's been over for an hour. I should say Joan and Walter left an hour ago. The party actually finished two hours ago. Mom and Dad both insisted that Ceese and I stay for dinner. Since Chinese was on the menu, there was no way I could refuse.

"What was this business about you two having an arranged marriage or something?" Mom waves her chopstick back and forth, pointing at me then CiCi. I bark out in laughter. I think CiCi was about to but she had food in her mouth and she is now coughing up a storm. My guess is it went down the wrong pipe.

"You ok, baby?" I pat her back.

"Don't," cough, "call . . . me . . . baby," she continues to cough out.

"You ok, beautiful?" I correct myself. She nods. Ok. It has nothing to do with *me* calling her baby—it's 'baby' in general. Hmm . . .

"That would be a product of CiCi and me, having a little fun with our dear, nosy neighbor." I turn my attention back to my mom. I then fill her in on what it is we said, exactly.

"You two are *so* bad!" Mom laughs. "However, you are no match for me!" She points her chopstick in the air like "checkmate."

"Ah, what did my dear, sweet, wouldn't harm a fly, mother do?"

"Well," she begins, "Joan was very interested in my apron. Yes, she said, 'Well, now, Winnie, that's a very interesting apron you have on,' trying not to state the obvious."

"Make me proud, Mama, what did you say?" CiCi is already laughing. I'm digesting the fact that she just referred to my mother as 'Mama.'

I fucking hate how much I love it.

Mom giggles (Dad doesn't . . . ahem). "I think I may have, CiCi." She waves her hand at her in the way that girls do, ya know, the 'just listen' wave. "I said to her, 'isn't it lovely? CiCi knows how much I love to cook chicken. Always trying a new recipe. She said, 'Well, are you sure that was her intention behind the apron, dear?' She was behaving so skeptically. I said, 'of course, Joan . . . wait for it . . ." she trails off in a laugh. Mom goes from laughing to practically crying. It takes her a good minute before she seems as if she can finish. "I said, 'of course, Joan . . . what else would I do with a cock, besides put it in my oven?'" We all burst into laughter. "CiCi, I kept a straight face, too!" Mom boasts at her accomplishment.

"I can't even begin to tell you how hard I love you right now." She gets up and heads over to my mom, still laughing, and gives her a hug.

I'm not going to lie . . .

Pitter pat. Pitter pat. Pitter pat.

"CiCi!" Linz almost screeches as CiCi sits back down.

"What?" she asks, seemingly alarmed.

"I just thought of something!" Linz giggles.

"What's that?" CiCi encourages her.

"If you marry my brother, we can call you CCC!"

CiCi looks a bit panicked, people.

"I got one better," I pipe up.

"What?" Everyone says in unison. Well, except for CiCi . . . she still has headlights on her.

"Whenever CiCi gets pissed off at me, after we're married, we can call her . . ." I trail off.

Wait for it . . .

Wait for it . . .

"C-3PO!" I bellow out. Everyone laughs. Everyone except "Bambi." Suddenly, a smile breaks through her lips.

"And I'll be able to cuss you out in over six million forms of communication," she sasses.

"You know how many forms of communication he can speak?" I ask in awe.

"Duh . . ." she trails off and rolls her eyes.

"You just shot up on the "Hot Meter" by about ten thousand points, just so you know." I bite on my lower lip and think about the form of communication that I'd like to have with her at this moment.

If my parents weren't here, she'd be spread out on this table like dessert.

"I may or may not have a gold bikini."

I'd like to take this moment and pray for my erection.

It. Hurts.

"Kyle! Son!" Dad bellows out, snapping me back from my thoughts.

"Huh?"

"Where the hell did you go in that mind of yours?"

"Tatooine." I shake it off. "Sorry." I offer. Dad chuckles at me. CiCi is doing the little giggle she does through her nose sometimes. I'm sitting here, slightly mortified.

"I asked when you were leaving for Spain." Dad questions before shoving another huge bite of food in.

"Wednesday," I answer and avoid CiCi's eyes that, I'm sure, are now on me.

"How long are you going to be gone for?" CiCi asks quietly. She sounds sort of vulnerable.

"I'm not sure." I glance her way. "I'm training two of the guys so they can learn the ins and outs of the negotiations that we do overseas."

She doesn't reply. As a matter of fact, everyone seems to get real quiet. I don't know what CiCi's thinking, but I'm pretty sure it's not good.

I grab her hand as we stroll down the walkway from my parents. We have just said our goodbyes to them and now I've got to figure out a way to convince her to stay with me the next few days.

"So, can I stay with you tonight? I'd like to hit that shit again." She sways my hand and gives me a crooked smile.

"Sure. But I should warn you, my finger may slip in and play with your ass again."

"Look, it's a lot of pressure, but, nobody wants to be a party of one. Your finger should bring a friend."

My cock just twitched.

"Are you sure? I mean, we don't want to crowd your tight space. It could feel like a rude intrusion."

"True, but I think it's time I loosen up—get ready for bigger things."

I think it's weeping.

"If that's the case, you should just stay with me so I can better help you prepare for that." I spin her around, once we approach her car, so that her back is up against the door.

"I think that's a fantastic idea." Her rapid breaths match mine.

"You do? You'll stay with me?" I jerk my head back.

"Yeah, is that ok?" She seems a little uncertain now.

"That. Is. More. Than. Ok." I kiss her between my words.

Wow, that was easy, huh?

"Alright, I guess I'll follow you, then?" she asks, pulling away from our kisses.

"No. Just grab your stuff. We'll take my car. Why the hell did you park so far away from our house, anyways?" I add the last bit in quick.

"I wasn't sure how many people were coming, or if there was going to be old people, so I parked farther away. I'm only a few houses down; it's not a big deal." She points out the obvious. Me? I'm staring at her in awe. See, here's something that I'm not sure CiCi realizes yet but every time she drops a brick from her wall, I not only take notice but I soak in that moment. Why? Because it's not just that she was thinking of the possibility of an elderly guest, it was because she told me she thought of them. Look, I know CiCi is a good person with a heart of gold. The thing is that CiCi doesn't really like people to know. Did she say this to me? No. Did she have to? No. But with that all said, when she shows me this side of her, without any hesitation, that, right there, is the winning ticket. I haven't mentioned it once to her when she's done it. I think that's the way to go, otherwise, she'd be sure to pull that ticket straight out of my hand in the future. So, instead, I take in the moment, secretly celebrating, knowing I'm that much closer to her heart.

"Did you hear anything I just said?" She toes up so she's eye to eye with me.

"Oh, I'm sorry. I got lost in my thoughts. What did you say?" I glide my hands on to her hips.

"I said I have to work in the morning. I'm going to need my car."

"I'll drive you to work." I grab her keys from her to unlock her door. "Excuse me." I grab the handle to her back door and wait for her to move out of the way.

"Don't you get up super early to get down to Boston? Where do you live, anyhow?" She tilts her head like she's pondering.

"Here, in Windham, a few blocks away." I stop myself from further explaining why I live in the same town as my parents. That's probably because CiCi just gave me a knowing smile.

She's the only one who's ever understood.

Pitter pat. Pitter pat. Pitter pat.

She moves out of the way, allowing me access into her car. I grab her stuff, shut the door, lock it, and reach for her hand to lead the way to my car.

"You're car still has that 'brand new' smell." She sucks in another whiff once we're settled in.

"That's because I'm never home to drive it," I admit, inwardly cringing at my inability to omit certain truths. I don't understand it; I can do it in the boardroom or in the middle of negotiations but I can never do it with family.

"Oh," she sighs.

"Ceese . . ." I glance over at her as we head down the street. "This upcoming trip is so that I can change all of that. Mitch and I made the decision that it was time to hand over the reins for most of the overseas trips. We're both ready to settle down and have a life." I try to explain.

"It's good to see you two taking the plunge; you're a cute couple."

"Haha, very funny," I retort. She snickers.

"You know . . . when . . ." she starts and stops, hesitating.

"What?" I try to push her along as I reach up and turn my defrost on. There's a chill in the air tonight, causing my windows to fog up. I notice CiCi fidgeting with her fingers. I gently grab her hand and lace fingers with her before pulling it up to my lips. I plant several light kisses on the back of her hand. "Go on," I encourage.

"When Mitch went away . . . in the beginning, he and Charley almost didn't survive it," she finally spits out.

"First, those were different circumstances. You know the demon Mitch was battling. Christ, Ceese, I worked ten years with the man and never knew that part of his past till Charley came along." I shake my head; I still find that unbelievable. "Second, that won't happen to us. Please don't try to burden us with other people's obstacles." I say sternly but with a softness in my voice, trying to avoid an argument.

"Well, what do you mean by that?"

"I mean, we are us. We are not Mitch and Charlotte. We do not have the same situations as they do; we're not coming into this relationship with their baggage. Don't make *us* about *them*."

"I'm not so sure there should be an 'us,'" she says cautiously. It seems to me that she's trying to get a few things off of her chest without leading into an argument, as well. Considering that possibility, I try to take in some calming breaths before I react.

"Why is that?"

Radio silence.

"I'm not him. Don't punish me for what he did to you," I say, remaining calm.

"It's just . . . I don't know if I'm ready for all of this. My life has my head spinning right now; I'm all over the place," she barrels out, noticeably avoiding the issue I brought up. I know that's our main issue. I also know that I can't force her to let me help her with it. It's something *she* needs to work through herself. All I can do is stand by her side, being supportive and patient, as much as she needs me to be.

"You're feeling things and it's scaring you, right?" Before I let her answer, "I'm going through the same thing, Ceese. It doesn't mean we have to rush in to putting a label on it. I think that's where so many people go wrong. Why can't we just explore these feelings and see where they lead us."

"You say that, and I could agree to it, but you were in there, just as bad as they were, talking about marriage and stuff," she huffs. I can't help but chuckle at her dramatics. "Why is that so funny?"

"You're funny." I glance over again and give her one of my famous smirks. She pulls her hand from me, crosses her arms over her chest, and looks out the window almost in defiance. "Look at this." I pull into my driveway and point to my house.

"It's nice." She shrugs.

"It is. You know what it isn't?"

"What?"

"Vegas." I quip. "There's no Elvis inside, trying to marry us off." I tease. "It was just talk. Just a funny little conversation built around a 'what if.' Nobody threw a ball and chain on your leg. Stop making a mountain out of a molehill."

"It's what they expect. They are expecting us to have that 'Happily Ever After' ending."

"Of course they do. I'm their son. They want me to be happy and when they see that I'm with somebody that makes me feel that way, they're going to push. But, let's not think this is all about me; they want grandkids and I'm the only one who's able to give them that."

"Kids?" She turns to me with that wide-eyed, panicked look she wore so nicely at the dinner table.

"Yeah, we should get inside and get started on that." I wink. She whacks my shoulder. "You are going to drive yourself—both of us, actually—crazy. Nobody's looking to slap labels on harder than you, and I think that's so you can stamp it simultaneously with: *Denied!*"

She scoffs.

I wait.

"Well, that's it, then. *We* shouldn't be an *us,*" she states as if the problem is solved.

"You know what? Here's what we're going to do." I start. I'm pretty much done with the patience thing at this point. "You are going to stay with me until I leave for Spain. We are going to act like a new couple, like we should, and not let this conversation hang over our head. When I go to Spain, for however long I will be there, you will take that time to decide if you want to be in this with me. When I come back, I expect your decision." I unbuckle. "The thing is this, CiCi, we have been playing cat and mouse for a few months now, and I'm pretty much done. You're either in this or you're not. As much as I want to be in a relationship with you, I need to think of protecting myself, too. There is an expiration date on how long you can string someone along and mine is just about met. What do you say?" I cut off the engine and turn to her.

"That all sounds very logical, Mr. Spock," she teases. "Although . . . I feel some sort of graph or pie chart presentation would've really nailed that speech home."

"I'm serious, Birkita."

"I know you are and you're also right," she admits.

"About what?" I ask as I pull my phone out and get into my calendar.

"Pretty much everything. What are you doing?" She leans over.

"Putting this into my calendar."

"Putting what in?"

“You said I was right; I feel that should be documented for future reference.”

“Good idea, dipshit. Now, why don’t you put that in, as well. We can count up, at the end of the month, how many times you manage to make me call you that.” She pats my leg and kisses my cheek before getting out of the car.

Chapter Fourteen

The Odd Couple . . .

CiCi

"Holy fuck . . ." I trail off. I can't help it. We've just walked into his house and I have a desire to get down to the floor and lick it, just to prove how fucking clean this place is. This isn't "good, he's not a slob" clean, it's "this asshole comes down here and scrubs shit with a toothbrush, at three in the morning, when he can't sleep" clean.

Lord, I won't last a day.

"What's the matter?" he asks, looking around frantically then back to me.

"Nothing. I just thought of a new reality show that's sort of the opposite idea of *Hoarding: Buried Alive!*"

"Yeah, I'm a little OCD," he runs his hand through his hair, looking around.

"Little is an understatement, but better than you being a slob, right?" I nudge into him.

"Right. So, do you want a tour first, or do you want to . . ."

I lean up and place a lingering kiss on his lips. "So, tell me," I start as I walk away and head towards his stairs, "Why such a big house?" I ask. It's your typical colonial, found in this area, but on a larger scale. Looking around at the build, I can already tell it's a design by a local builder named, Cooper (ironically). Why do I know this? My dad was one of the contracted electricians on many of their developments. I've also, always, been partial to them.

"I bought it, imagining a family eventually filling it," he states honestly. I stop dead in my tracks but then move on so he won't notice.

"What if your wife didn't like this big ole' house? That wasn't thought out very well."

"Well . . . do you like it, Ceese?" He sounds worried. I feel slightly queasy.

"It doesn't matter what I think, Kyle, I'm not your wife." I retort snidely.

I fucking love his house. It's what I've always wanted.

Damn it!

Shut-up . . . I know what you're thinking!

"From a woman's perspective, Ceese, do you like it?!" he raises his voice a bit.

"It's nice. I like it well enough." I look over my shoulder and offer him a reassuring smile. Well, I didn't lie. My conscience is clear.

"Go to the left and it's the door at the end of the hall," he instructs.

"Is the west wing forbidden?" I thumb over to the opposite side of the house as a joke.

"That's east," he says flatly.

"It was a joke. I was referencing Beauty and the . . . never mind," I stop myself.

"Oh. Oh, yeah. Right . . ." he trails off.

"What's the matter?" I turn to him just as I approach the door.

"Tired." He leans in near me but goes for the doorknob, turning it, and opening the door.

"You weren't five minutes ago, don't lie to me." I reach up and fiddle with the buttons on his shirt, walking backwards into the room.

"No, I wasn't." He nods in agreement. He flicks on the light and as much as this nosy bitch wants to look around, I can tell something's not right, so I keep my focus on him. "Why don't you head into the bathroom and get ready for bed while I start working on settling you in," he suggests and quickly pecks my cheek.

We all know the time span on my patience, right?

Lawd . . .

"What do you mean 'settle me in'?" I let my hands drop.

"Put your stuff away, Ceese, what else would I mean?" He shakes his head slightly, narrowing his eyes.

"I'll take care of my stuff." I ignore his very obvious irritation with me. Normally, I'd be all "Can you iron my shit, too?" but not tonight. That bag isn't just full of my clothes. It has all of my bills—past due bills—in there. I don't want him seeing that shit . . . it's embarrassing.

"It's not a big deal."

"Right, so leave it alone!" Oh dear, I think I went a little over the top on that response.

"What do you have in there?" He goes for my bag.

"Stop!" I reach ahead of him.

"What's in there—drugs?" he almost yells in an accusatory fashion.

Say what, now?

"I'm sorry; I didn't realize we were in the middle of an after school special." I look around the room as if a camera crew should be there. "I learned it from watching you, Kyle. I learned it from watching you!"

"That was a TV commercial." He shakes his head, smirking.

"Same thing." I shrug.

"No it's not." He jerks his head back.

"Were there actors?"

"Yes."

"Were they relaying a message?" I cross my arms.

"Yes, but—"

"—same thing!" I cut him off.

"Whatever." He rolls his eyes.

"That dad's porn-stache was creepy. He was creepy, like it should've been a "Daddy, don't touch me there" commercial."

“Well, with all the coke snortin’, it very well could’ve been,” Kyle says with great thought.

“Word.”

“People still say that?”

“What?” I lean down and grab my bag.

“Word.”

“It hasn’t been stricken from the dictionary.”

“You know what I mean.” His frustration comes to the surface, again.

“Do I?” I live for this shit, honestly, I do. I place my bag on his bed and rifle through it, trying to find something remotely sexy that he can take off of me in five seconds flat.

I have a long-sleeved thermal shirt and flannel PJ bottoms.

I am a sex Goddess!

“Kyle, can I borrow a t-shirt of yours?” I throw my previous selection of hotness back into my bag. Suddenly, Kyle’s hands slide onto my hips and my breath hitches. His breath hits my neck as he pulls me close. My inside flutters at his touch, his closeness. No one’s made me feel like this in a long time. I almost forgot what it felt like; the world stands still but for the loud sound of my heart, pounding in my ears. *Wow, that was all poetic and shit.*

“Ceese,” he hums against my neck. “You won’t need a t-shirt . . . or anything else for that matter.” He starts to slowly unzip my dress. A chill runs down my spine, so powerful—it travels back up and around my ears, lingering there . . . buzzing. His hands glide up my newly exposed skin, up to my shoulders to push the material forward and off of them. My dress drops. I close my eyes and lean my head back on his shoulder as his touch retraces its steps down my back, then, moving forward, over my ribs and up to my breast. He gently cups them, his thumbs circling my already hardened nipples. Mmm . . .

Tug, tug, rub, and roll . . .

Tug, tug, rub, and roll . . .

“Tug, tug, rub, and roll . . .” Kyle chants in my ear. Wait—what?! I jerk my head to look at him. “What’s the matter, I can’t chant with you?” He smirks. His fingers are, of course, still doing, what we’ll now refer to as “TTR and R.” It may be a little difficult for me to concentrate on the answer for that question. I decide to ignore his comment and get back to the task at hand here, minus my public chant.

"I want you to listen to me very carefully," he starts, "We're doing this *my* way tonight. Do you know what that means?" He bites at my earlobe, sucking it into his mouth. I try to stop my leg from shaking like I'm getting my belly scratched or something. Oh, don't worry . . . *something's definitely getting scratched tonight.* "Well, do you?" his tone a little more authoritative. Fuck, I whimpered.

"No," I finally answer him.

"It means," he turns me abruptly to face him, "slow." His lips are barely an inch away from mine. He licks them slowly. "Deep."

I think my water just broke.

"I'm going to take my time, enjoying every inch of you. You will not rush us. And, you will keep this beautiful . . ." he nips at my bottom lip before pulling it between his to give it a proper suck, "smart mouth, at bay." He nips again, this time grinding my lip lightly with his teeth. It's all I can do to keep *my whimpering* at bay—*fuck my smart mouth.* My legs feel like they are going to give out from underneath me. This could be due to the tsunami that is happening in my panties. *Pull it together, CiCi.* "I'm going to make love to you like I wanted to the other night," he pants. I guess he's feeling what I'm feeling, right now. Or something very similar.

"I don't make love, Kyle." It needed to be said. I'm sure it's not going to go over well, but I had to put it out there. I want to make love to him; I can't. There's only one man I've ever made love to and what was so beautiful, in the moment, quickly became shadowed by ugliness. Ugliness that, to this day, makes me unable to connect—on that level—with anyone.

"You will tonight. You will," he murmurs, his lips making a soft path of kisses down my neck.

"No." I try to push back from him. "You don't understand," I say quietly and look down.

He palms my face and brings my eyes back up to his. "I don't know what he did to you and I'm not going to push you to tell me." He eskimo kisses me.

Fuck, I love when he does that.

"When you're ready, I'll be here to listen—I promise. Until then, I'm not going to walk on eggshells. It's not always going to be your way, Ceese. We're in this together. I feel things for you that I don't recall *ever* feeling about anyone else. I know you're not comfortable enough for me to express how I feel too much out in public. But, in the bedroom, I'm not holding back." He shakes my head slightly as if to emphasize. "I want to make love." Kiss. "That's what we're going to do." Kiss . . . suck. Mmm. His hands slide down to my girls. My nipples harden again as his thumbs trace circles around them. He pinches them slowly, building up the pressing, causing me to moan. The pinch gets harder, tighter. The feeling is painfully erotic and I can't help but yelp into his mouth. Ok, it was more like a whimper, but holy fuck, Batman! "Ceese," he groans against my mouth, "I wanna taste that sweet pussy of yours." He guides me back and onto the bed, finally releasing my nipples from his finger's death grip.

"You may need a poncho for when you get down there . . . just sayin'," I pant, half serious as I climb back onto the bed.

Kyle smirks, as Kyle does in most situations.

However . . .

This smirk comes equipped with some lip biting action.

It makes me want to fuck his face . . . *hard.*

His hands slap down on my hips. He then, grasps the sides of my black panties and pulls them down and off. I'm almost a little embarrassed to have him see how wet I am for him. He may call in the Coast Guard. "Bring your knees up. No!" He stops me as I bring my legs up and reach to take my shoes off. "They stay on. Now, pull your knees up." My breathing is starting to get out of control. "Open them—wide." I do so. Kyle looks down. "*Fuck!*" he breathes like it's painful. He quickly unbuckles and whips his belt off. His pants, next. I look down the middle, between my legs, and see his hard, thick cock, pointing at me like I'm in big trouble. I think I might be.

"This," he flicks my piercing, "does things to me that make me feel crazy. You're so fucking hot, beautiful." He slaps the inside of my thighs with both hands; his thumbs strum up and down either side of my lady licorice. "So fucking wet for me . . . so needy." He licks his lips and applies pressure to my clit with his thumb. I rock against it. "Yeah, beautiful, that's it. Show me how badly you want me balls deep." He slaps the inside of my thighs again, his thumb reapplying pressure.

Slowly, he lies on his stomach, situating his head between my legs. "Hold your legs back tight. Eyes down here, Ceese. I want you to watch me clean up the mess I've made." He nips at my mound. I hold tightly under my knees, making sure that they are spread apart and out of the way. I watch. He lays two soft kisses up my center finishing up with a kiss and slight suck near my piercing. *Fuck, I love when he does that.* He keeps his eyes on me as he leans down again and with one long, slow sweep, he licks up my center. He groans. I watch his tongue poke out of his mouth and gently stroke my clit over and over again. His fingers slide down my center, circling my opening. He pulls my wetness. "Taste how badly you want me, Ceese." He lifts his fingers to my mouth. I let him slide them in. I suck my taste off, greedily. Not because I enjoy the taste. But because I enjoy watching him and how much this turns him on. "Mmm good, right?"

He pulls them and puts them back to work, not waiting for my answer. *Oh, shit!* Feeling the pressure I felt earlier, I lean up a little bit more, at the same time, pulling my legs in tighter. I watch as his tongue dips shallowly, teases me, and then, plunges deeply. I scream out. That's not the only thing he plunged in me. I rock (as best as I can) and I let out guttural groans. This only seems to fuel his fire. He plunges deeper; his finger brings a friend . . .

"Kyle!" I yell . . . well, gasp, really. I let go of my legs and bury my hands in my hair, pulling to relieve the tension in other places. Kyle's left forearm pushes my legs back to get me back at the angle I was at. The hair pulling is not working, so I let my hands fall to my girls. Say it with me.

Tug, tug, rub, and roll . . .

I lay here, rocking, feeling every sensation he and I are both putting me through and I let go. The tingling starts, causing me to clench my pussy around his tongue. It travels deep, getting stronger . . . stronger. *Oh, fuck. Holy shit.* He pulls my hood back and swipes my clit with his tongue. "Faaaaaaccccckkkkk!" I scream out.

You know when a fish is out of water and it spastically flops?

That would be me . . . right now.

Kyle climbs up my body, trailing kisses. He stops to give Birkita some love. "I love watching you," he confesses. "Do you have any idea how sexy you are?" he asks. I just keep my eyes closed, listening to his smooth voice, trying to steady my breath. "I bet you don't even realize that you are still touching and playing with your nipples, lazily. So sexy . . ." he trails off, moving my left hand and taking my nipple into his mouth. He's slow and methodical, making me needy again. Releasing it, he leans over the other one, nudging my hand away with his face. I thread my fingers through his hair, encouraging him. "Touch your pussy," he commands softly. I don't even think; I just do. I ride my hand, my fingers slipping through my center with ease . . .

"Kyle . . . gah." My hips jerk up over and over again, helping me to find my pleasure.

"That's it . . . that's my girl." He attacks my neck. "Is this what you do, when you're in bed at night, thinking about me? Do you touch yourself?"

"Please," I beg, wanting to feel him inside of me. As soon as I reach my climax, his mouth is on mine, our tongues aggressively petting each other.

He pulls back abruptly, getting on his knees. Oh, thank Christ! I watch him jerk his cock up and down. It looks painfully hard and I can't wait for it to slam inside of me. I widen my legs for him some more, and give my pussy another rub or two . . . a pep talk, if you will.

"I'm so ready for you, Kyle," I breathe. He gives me a little smirk.

"Patience, beautiful." He grabs my left leg and brings it up against his chest.

Patience? What?

Kyle slips my shoe off and starts to massage my foot slowly, deeply. Oh, you have *got* to be kidding me! See? I'm not cut out for this shit. I want to get right to—oh. He's nipping at my insole. He chuckles lightly at my reaction then, carries on, nipping at the skin up my leg. The only way I could describe the sensation that is happening to my entire body, is to say it feels like "pins and needles" but at the very beginning, when it feels sort of cool. I'm on sensory overload, the more he travels, the more my anticipation builds. Just when I can't take anymore, Kyle flips me on to my stomach. Yes, I yelped. I wasn't expecting him to go all ninja on my ass!

It won't be long now. You know how I can tell? Kyle's hands are beginning to massage me a little more aggressively. The pressure feels awesome. The sound of his rapid breaths—even better. Suddenly, his hands both slam on to my ass, squeezing my cheeks harshly. He pushes them up and I feel his tongue slide along underneath my right cheek before giving me a good bite, then . . . whack! "Ah, Kyle!" Holy fuck, that was hot.

Please do that again.
Please do that again.
Chant with me—it helps. (Shut-up . . . it does!)
Please do that again.

Squeeze. Lick. Bite. Smack. *Dear God, baby Jesus, and all them bastards, who hauled ass, through the desert—thank you.* "You have the most gorgeous back," he murmurs, dragging his lips up it.

"Kyle?" I ask, trying to keep my voice level.

"Yeah?" He makes his way up my neck.

"I'm going to get on my knees, so you can take me. If I don't feel your cock slipping inside of me in the next ten seconds, I'm going to push you off of me and grab Purp," I state as clearly and calmly as I can.

"Purp?"

"Yes. Purp—vibrator to the gods."

"You shouldn't have done that," he says in a tone that reminds me of being a kid and hearing "ooh, I'm telllling," remember that?

"What?" I snap lightly. I mean, honestly, I'm hanging by a thread here.

"You shouldn't have told me you have a vibrator with you. You are *definitely* not getting any rest tonight." He flips me back over again. Sure, I love being treated like a ragdoll. "Is it really called Purp or is that your name for it?" He smiles down at me as he settles himself between my legs.

"I named him," I reply quietly, honing in on his eyes and lips.

"Why Purp?" A flicker of amusement comes over his face.

"Because he's purple and . . . he does magical things." I bite my smile back.

"Magical things, huh?"

"Mmm hmm."

"What kind of things do I do to you, Ceese?" His previous amused look falls.

He waits.
I stare into his blue eyes.
The silence is so loud.

"You do things to me that take my breath away. Amazing things. Things that frighten me." I hit him full force with my honesty, no fucking around, no bullshit.

No wall.

"Frighten you, how?" His fingertips dance across my cheek like a feather and I find myself leaning into his touch. I close my eyes; relishing it. I don't know if I have the right words to answer his question. If I did have them, I'm not certain that I'd want to lay them out. I think that's what frightens me the most . . . not knowing which side of the fence is the better side—the right side. "You're not going to answer me?" he almost whispers.

"I don't know how." I let my eyelids flutter open.

"It's ok," he breathes before his lips caress mine. It's light and sweet at first, but quickly turns urgent. Our intent, coming back to focus. I feel him slide my right leg around his left hip as his tongue licks hard into my mouth, warranting a submissive groan from me.

"Please, Kyle," I beg again.

"You ready?" he baits me.

"Yes, please," I pant, secretly congratulating myself for keeping my smart mouth under wraps. *Am I ready? Wtf?*

My hips respond wildly to the sensation of him rubbing his cock up and down my center. He leans in towards my ear, "You're the first woman I've ever brought home, here, and made love to. I have every intention of making you the last."

I tried to respond, but my words got cock-blocked . . . ahem.

"*Fuck,* you're so tight," he grunts. I'd respond to that, as well, but my body is still arched and my mouth's open, in a silent scream, as I try to accommodate him.

Yes, Imma little concerned for my lady boom boom.

Just give me a minute . . . I'll be all right.

Lawd . . .

The tension in my back finally lets up and I ease myself down only to be greeted by his hungry lips. He reaches down and hikes my leg up higher on his hip as he pulls out and slowly begins to fill me again. Just as I'm almost full to the brim, he pulls back, taking with him the satisfaction of that final stretch. SLAM! *Oh fuck, oh fuck, oh fuck!* He pulls my hands off of him and whips them above my head. "Keep them there," he commands as he releases them and brings his hands to my hips. He pushes up on his knees slightly; lifting my hips with his movement, tilting them up for a better angle. Once he seems to have me the way he wants, he hovers over me again, pinning my arms down, conquering my mouth, and guiding his cock to hit my g-thang over and over again, merciless.

"Kyle," I break away, "please!" I feel as if I'm on the verge of tears. It's too slow, too full—too much. The intensity of the dragged out pace is more than I can bear.

"Shh . . . I'm almost there." He attacks my lips again. His breath becoming more labored, his hips, pumping into me at a quicker pace. I scream as he slams in to me. He holds it for a moment then thrusts little, yet deep, thrusts into me. It feels like he's pulsating deeply inside. I squeeze around him to stop it, but that only eggs him on more. He bites the ever-loving-fuck out of my lower lip as he releases my hands. Quickly, he reaches for my legs and whips them up and then down on either side of my head. "Relationships. Are. All. About. Compromise," he pants. Huh? He plants another kiss on my lips, and then he leans back on his heels, holding my legs back, and he lets me have it.

"Kyle! God, oh God—Kyle!" I'm a mess. I can't organize a single thought as he pounds so hard into me, his cock almost becoming my cervix's wombmate.

"Are you there, baby?" he grunts, barely letting up.

"Yes . . . Oh, God, yes!" I practically scream. "Don't call me baby." I add. Kyle just growls at my comment and may have found his second wind on the whole pounding thing. I grab at him, the sheets, my hair . . . anything and everything to help me. And then . . .

He lets out a barbaric groan.

My toes curl, painfully.

I look down and watch his cock slide in and out of me for the last few pumps. *You made it, boom boom, you made it.* My head collapses back onto my pillow. Kyle's head collapses onto his or, as others may call it, my boob. We're both gasping for air like the fat kid in gym class. What?!

"You frighten me, too," he suddenly says in a low, almost too quiet voice. I have nothing to say on this matter. What can I say? Instead, I let my fingernails trail up and down his back, comforting him without words. Soon enough, I hear the tempo of his breathing change. He's asleep. Before I join him in slumberland (Oh, and I will soon!), I put some serious thought into my feelings and actions.

Maybe I am ready for this. Maybe this is just what I need. It's been long enough; God, I'd love to just let go of the past. The thing is; I don't remember feeling *this* way with Drew. I remember being in love with him, but that was love in your early twenties. It's different when you're older, right? You've experienced the world a lot more. You know more of what you want and what you don't want for yourself. It's different. I feel different.

At the same time, I really haven't a clue as how to handle *this* in anyway. And I can't begin to tell you how angry that makes me. It's like, in every other aspect of my life, I'm thirty-four (almost five, but let's not really mention that. Also, my behavior, around the GEGs, does not count in this equation; we are a separate entity.), but with love, it's as if I'm stuck at twenty. I never let myself grow in that department. What Drew did to me really did ruin me in a way that makes me hate him even more, thinking about it. I think what makes me mad the most is that I feel somebody else would've moved on a long time ago. I hate that I'm not over it—that I have no peace with the past.

Here, I have this amazing, gorgeous, patient man in my arms and . . . I don't know what to do with him! I mean, I *know* what to do with him. It's the emotional part. I don't know how to *allow* myself to do that. I have to try, though. He's different. He feels right. For him, I will try.

"Go to sleep, Birkita," he mumbles.

"You're awake?"

"Mmm hmm." He squeezes me.

"I'm not surprised."

"No?"

"Nope. We've just had some nasty hot sex, I'm sure you want to get up and sanitize everything," I tease.

"Shut-up," he laughs lightly. I join in a little.

"So, is there something you feel you should tell me about?"

"What?" He lifts his head. "What do you mean?"

"You've left one shoe on me. My guess is that you have a secret fantasy about fucking a one-legged woman." I point out, though he's not bothering to look.

"You have a really warped brain, you know that, right?" He nudges my nose and gives me a quick kiss.

"Why, thank you," I smile. "It takes a lot of work to think up these strange thoughts and ideas."

"Hmm, c'mon, let's jump in the shower." He gives me another quick kiss, and then pulls out. I let out a disapproving sigh. It only takes a second to be reminded of something that shouldn't have happened. Kyle's baby batter trickles out of me. Yes, I could've said something, given him a reminder, but in all fairness, he wasn't rushing with urgency, and I was completely incapacitated what with all he was doing to me. I can't help but question whether he has a motive or not. However, we've had a busy day with up and downs, as it is. Also, I don't want to ruin our evening by arguing over something that can't be changed now. *Oh, but it will be,* in the future—I can guarantee that.

I take his hand, following his lead into the bathroom. One thing, of course, leads to another and Kyle is showing me his version of "leave-in conditioner"; know what I'm sayin'?

I try to move. Not only is my body arguing with me over this, but Kyle's body is preventing me, as well. I'm trapped. Very carefully, I slide Kyle's arm and leg off of me. It's no easy feat, I tell you. Slipping out of bed, I grab my yoga pants and t-shirt out of my bag, quickly dressing. I sneak out of the room as quietly as I can before running downstairs. I need to hurry and get back before he wakes up. Spotting Kyle's car keys on the little table by the door, I snatch them up and run out of the house. I climb into his Lexus—who gives a fuck model—SUV. It's goldish-tan, that's all I can tell ya! I start it up and back out, slowly. I hit the GPS and the motherfucker starts talking to me! I need one of these puppies. I tell it what it wants to know and, like magic, I arrive at the closest pharmacy. Within twenty minutes, I'm out and heading back to Kyle's house. As soon as I pull up into the driveway, a very fucking hot-as-hell Kyle darts out of his house, towards the driveway . . . in only pj bottoms. There's a sudden weather alert going on in my pants. They say, "It's going to be a *wet* one!" Yup . . . pretty much!

He whips the door open, anger all over that beautiful face of his. "What's the matter?" I ask innocently.

"What's the matter?" he seethes. "Oh, I don't know, Ceese. Could it be the fact that I've been dealing with fire and police up until five minutes before you came back home?"

"What are you talking about?"

"You left without the damn code to the alarm system."

"Oh, shit! I'm sorry. I didn't mean to do that."

"Where the fuck did you go? It's five in the damn morning, Ceese!" he whisper yells then slams the door after I get out. Kinda defeats the purpose behind the whisper yell, but I won't mention that to him.

"I needed to go to the store." I attempt to throw my small pharmacy bag into my purse.

"For what?" He grabs it from me as he opens the door to the house. I follow him in, not knowing how to prepare for any reaction from him. Kyle stops dead in his tracks. My heart races a million miles a minute. "Did you take this already?" he asks, not even looking back at me.

"Yes."

"Wow, ok," he sighs. Shaking his head, he tosses the bag onto the counter as we enter the kitchen. He turns around, leans up against the counter, and crosses his arms.

We stare.

Not eye fuck stare.

Just regular "Who's going to talk first" stare.

"I think it needs to be said that if I did, in fact, get you pregnant, it doesn't mean I would leave you," he pipes up first (there's a shocker!).

"Well, then, it should also be said that if you did, *in fact,* get me pregnant, it doesn't mean I would stay with you," I counter.

"Touché."

"Look, I don't want to argue about this. We are both at fault here. Let's just move on and make sure it doesn't happen again." I toss out a white flag before one is truly needed.

"Oh, I agree. But before we lay this to rest, I need to tell you how I feel about this." He stands up straight. "You just said we were both at fault, no?"

"Yes."

"Well then, don't you think we *both* should've been involved in your little decision here?" he asks and I notice a little tick-like action happening in his jawline. I may also be a little mesmerized by his slight flexing and releasing of his chest and arm muscles. It's like he's fighting back an eternal battle or something.

Flex.

Release.

Flex.

Release.

"CiCi!" he yells, bringing me back to focus.

"It's my body, Kyle. I'm the one who decides."

"It's *my* baby, too!"

"We don't know if I got pregnant, so just stop. You're taking this to a place it doesn't need to go." I try to calm him down.

"What you did is against *everything* I believe in, regardless as to whether or not a baby was created."

"Listen, if you're going to get all political on my ass, then I'm leaving. I don't have to listen to this bullshit." I head towards the stairs.

"It's not bullshit. It's a life and it shouldn't be canceled out because you don't feel like being responsible for it!" he seethes.

"Whoa! Back the fuck up, Jack! First of all, don't talk to me like that. Second of all, where do you get off judging anybody? You know, Kyle, I share those same views as you—to a point. But, there are *always* exceptions." Oh, fuck it to hell; my blood is boiling.

"Was my sister one of those exceptions, Ceese?" he asks in a condescending tone.

"Oh, don't you fucking dare! Don't you bring her into this conversation! This has nothing to do with her!" I stalk towards him. "You think I'd terminate a pregnancy over downs syndrome?! You *asshole!*" I poke at his chest.

"There are no exceptions. Even in the worse conditions, there's always adoption. So many couples who can't have kids are waiting. Look at Ava and Trent." He pushes into my finger.

"Don't *you* tell me about *my* friends!"

"Don't tell you. Don't . . . don't . . . don't! That's all you've got! What can I tell you about, Ceese? Can I tell you that being adopted is probably a hell of a lot better than being—oh, I don't know—*dead?*! How about the burden of the mom's decision, weighing heavier than the burden of raising that child?" he yells in my face.

"No, Kyle . . . you definitely don't need to tell me about that burden."

Fuck my chin and it's quivering.
Fuck my eyes and their inability to fight off my tears.
And fuck my heart that has been breaking for fifteen years.

Chapter Fifteen

Dancing around the white elephant in the room . . .

CiCi

I don't know how much time has passed. All I know, is I somehow ended up on the floor, in Kyle's arms, gasping through my horrific-sounding sobs. "Shh . . . shh," he whispers against my temple. "I'm so sorry . . . I'm sorry," he adds and kisses my hair. *Stop, CiCi, stop. Oh, God, he wasn't supposed to know—nobody was supposed to know! Think. Think. Think.*

I wipe my face and try to get out of his arms. "I need to go," I say casually as if I didn't just have a mental breakdown (or whatever that was).

"No!" He jerks his head and stands up with me. "You're not going. We're going to sit down and you are going to talk this out with me. You're not running away from us or your past anymore. You're done with it. It's time, Birkita. It's time to let it go." He guides me to the living room.

Anyone else singing, "Let it Go" from *Frozen,* in their heads now?

Jesus, that fucking song! Thanks, Brooklynn!

We sit on the sofa; his thumbs, caressing the backs of my hands that he has a strong grasp on. "What happened?" he encourages me to begin. I don't want to begin, though. I don't want to talk about this, at all. So I cried, who cares? It was a moment of weakness. I got it out, now I'll be fine for a while.

"It's Sunday, isn't it?" I try my hand at avoiding.

"Yes, it is."

"I was thinking today was Monday, last night when we were figuring out the cars."

"I wasn't really thinking about anything but being with you." He leans in and pecks my lips softly.

"Do you go to church on Sundays? I go to church. Sometimes I don't go with the family. I go by myself to St. Christopher's. It's an Episcopalian church. I like it there. It's very similar to my Catholic church but it has a cozier feel to it. My family and friends don't know I go there. Well, Maddie knows. She's the secret keeper in the GEGs. She's also our captain. She's great. I pretty much tell her everything. I think we all do. Do you have somebody like that?" I sit and wait for him to digest all of my ramblings, deeply hoping that it was enough to distract him from his previous agenda. He gives me the warmest, closed-lip smile I've ever had the pleasure of being on the receiving end of. And I remember . . .

He gets me . . .

"I don't go to church as often as I should, but I would love to come with you to St. Christopher's. It could be *our* secret. From the few times I've met Maddie, I'd say I agree with your assessment of her. Although, I'm not really sure at this point in your life what having her as your captain means but I'm sure, knowing you girls, I will probably be holding my gut, laughing, once I find out. The person I tell everything to is my mom. Mitch comes in at a close second, though. Did I answer all of the questions to your satisfaction?" He reaches up and pushes some of my hair behind my ear. I lean into his touch. It's becoming an annoying habit of mine. I hate being so needy. But then I feel the weight of his lips on mine, his tongue gliding across them, encouraging them to part. And suddenly, any thoughts of this new habit being annoying are erased. I open, allowing him to deepen the kiss and everything just feels right in the world. I'm not sure how to really explain it because a part of me wants to fight this so bad—these feelings. The rest of me wants to come home and Kyle feels like he's the key in helping me find the way there. Slowly, I lean back, pulling him with me. "Ceese," he murmurs against my lips, "we need to talk, beautiful."

"I need you." I lean up to taste his mouth again.

"Baby, I—"

"—Stop. I have asked you several times now, not to call me that." I place my hand on his chest to create some space between us.

"Is that what he called you?" He sits back up.

"Yes, he and every other damn guy on the planet. You're different, Kyle, in every way. Especially, the way I feel about you—it's different. It's special, don't make it ordinary." I do nothing to hide my irritation.

Kyle stares at me and it makes me feel even more awkward from having diarrhea of the mouth. "I just have to say this," he starts. I cringe. "Hearing the words that just came out of your mouth makes me want to take my inner vagina, throw it out there, and beg you to let me have your baby."

My eyes, I imagine, are bugged the fuck out.

I suck both of my lips in, attempting to not die from laughter.

Fuck it!

"Bwahahaha," shoots out of my mouth at full force. I can't even stop. I mean, who talks like this besides me? I find myself slowing down, wondering, did he ever talk like this before meeting me? If not, is this a good thing for him? Am I good for him?

"Whoa . . . what's going on in there? Why are you so serious all of the sudden?" He tilts his head as if to figure me out.

"I just love you—I mean, I love that you . . . uh . . . um, that you have no problem saying shit like this to me!" *What. In. The. Actual. Fuck?*

"Stop." He smirks.

"No, but I . . . I mean, we don't . . . we haven't . . . it's only been three months and only recently . . . look, I don't want you to get the wrong idea or lead you on." I finally blurt out.

"You don't want to lead me on?" He bites back his smile. Motherfucker is eating this shit up.

"No. I don't," I say in a voice full of defeat.

"Well, let's clarify things . . . make sure I'm fully aware of where you stand, so I don't feel lead on, okay?"

"Um, ok." I look at him, curious as to what he's up to.

He pushes back on the sofa and pats the seat cushion between his legs. "Come here," he invites me. I give him a meek smile and climb into the space between his legs, settling my back against his chest. *Mmm . . . perfect.* "See this, right here? I love this, Ceese; how perfect you fit in my arms. From the sound of your sigh, am I right to assume you love it, too?" his voice is so soothing next to my ear. I close my eyes, enjoying the extra squeeze he's giving me. "Well?"

"Yes, I love it."

"Do you love the way I kiss you?" He brings his fingers up to my chin, turning my face and tilting it up to his. Kyle's lips collect mine and it's like Heaven the way our tongues glide over each other.

"Yes," I breathe when he pulls away.

His hand slips down from my chin, my neck, the center of my chest, until he reaches the hem of my shirt. I'm not going to lie; my breathing may be a little labored at the moment. "Do you love how I caress your skin, beautiful?" His hands travel under my shirt, his fingers gliding across my stomach, nonchalantly.

"Kyle," I gasp lightly, my head rolling back onto his shoulder. My hands grasp at the material of his pj bottoms in anticipation of being driven out of my mind. *Fuck the way he affects me, damn it!*

"Do you? Do you love when I touch you?" His hands become less nonchalant.

"Yes . . . yes," I pant.

Kyle's breathing becomes labored, as well, the higher his hands travel. "Damn it," he seethes. I'm pretty sure his tone is not due to him being angry with me. He quickly brings his hands back out into the light of day. "What else do you love, CiCi—tell me," he demands, running his hands through his hair.

"Um . . . I—"

"Spit it out!"

"I thought you like it when I swallowed." I crook my neck and give him a coy smile.

"Oh, that goes under the category of 'love.' CiCi, I love every bit, every part of having sex with you. Let's avoid that aspect. I want to know what you love outside of the bedroom, okay?" He nips at my bottom lip.

"Okay." And suddenly, I, CiCi O'Brien, am feeling shy. Without a blink or slight change of shade in my cheeks, I could easily tell Kyle that I love watching his big, fat cock, pounding my pussy. Telling Kyle that I love his eskimo kisses has me on the verge of fucking hives. I don't know where to begin. There are so many things to choose from; I'm not sure if I should say the little things or the things that are *huge* to me. Funny thing is, it's the little things that are huge to me.

"Wow . . . you have to think this hard about it? You're kind of giving me a complex, here, Ceese." He picks at an imaginary piece of lint on his pants, and then rubs his palm against his knee.

"No! No, Kyle." I start to get up but only to turn around onto my knees to face him. "There's so many things that I love, I'm having a hard time organizing them in my head," I try to ease his insecurity. He slides his hands onto my hips and it's all I can do not to attack him. "I love that you find ways to touch me," I blurt out. He starts to open his mouth and I'm pretty sure it's to remind me that I'm not supposed to make this about sex. "Wait, I don't mean it in a sexual way. You always manage to grab my hand to hold, place a hand on my back . . . stuff like that. It makes me feel good. It doesn't sound like much but, if it was another guy, I really wouldn't give a shit." *Hi, CiCi, welcome back! Now stop being a pussy and tell him how you feel.* Encouraged by Kyle's boyish grin, I carry on. "I'm big on family; being an O'Brien, you really don't have a choice." I chuckle a little. "I love that you are, too. I especially love how close you are with your mom. I'm very close with mine too, so it's nice that I won't ever have arguments with you about that. I love that you're brave enough to say obnoxious things to me like I would say to you. I love it even more that you not only think to do that, but can pull it off, too. I love that you get me—not many people do." *Fuck the knot in my throat.* "I love that you don't give up on me. That you have a level of patience with me that should be scientifically researched."

"That may involve probing." He shakes his head, "I prefer to probe and not be probed."

"You give good probe, Kyle." I deadpan. He gives me that smirk where he bites his smile back at the same time. "I love when you do this smirk right here." I touch his mouth. "It makes me want to slap you in the face with my pussy."

"I can't think of anything better to be slapped in the face with," he chuckles. "Do you have anymore?" He shakes my hips, tightening his grip on them.

"A ton more, but . . . I don't want to reveal all of my cards at once. Besides, wouldn't it be nicer to hear over time instead of all at once?"

"Good." He leans up and hugs me to him.

"Good?" I jerk my head back, unsure of what he's referencing.

"Yes. Good. Over time means you've made your decision already." He smiles up at me.

"What are you talking about?"

"Our discussion, last night? About you, deciding what you want while I'm in Spain?"

"Oh," I sigh.

"Oh?" He pushes back on my hips. "What does that mean?"

"It means, oh. I wasn't sure what you were talking about, you reminded me. I said 'oh.' I believe that is a normal response." I answer. I'm sure he's not satisfied with this answer but, oh well. I don't want another argument with him.

"Well, just a reminder about that patience you think needs scientific study—it's running out." He lifts an eyebrow at me.

"C'mon, let's go back to bed and get a few more hours of sleep." I get up and wait for him to do the same, but he's not budging.

"No, Ceese. We came in here to talk about what happened. Sit back down." He grabs my hand and tugs.

"Yeah, I'll pass, but thanks, though." I try to pull my hand away.

"Why?"

"You're kidding, right?" I snap lightly.

"No. I'm not kidding."

"Kyle, I just revealed to you how you make me feel. That was very hard for me. Two seconds later, you make me regret saying anything at all. I would rather go upstairs with you and let you fuck me in the ass because that would be more comfortable than sharing something so personal and painful with you." I manage to finally free my hand from him and make my way to the stairs.

It's six in the morning. There's no one I would dare call at this time. I'm pretty much stuck here, as far as rides go. I can't even call anyone to vent. I grab my phone and check my timeline on Facebook—*somebody has to be having a shittier morning than me.* Oh shit! Julie's on.

Me: Hey, Asswhore! What are you doing up this early?

Julie: Trying to put an awesome fucking book down with no success!

Me: Ooh! Can I borrow it? I want to make sure I know all the tricks to awesome fucking!

Julie: It's all about the good steady pace and most importantly, a great climax.

Me: Is there a lot to swallow?

Julie: It's been described as "copious amounts." There's a lot for the heroine to take in.

Me: I know the feeling.

Julie: Kidding aside, I think you would like this book. It's called Whispers by Hailey Trent.

Julie: Wait—what?! Are you letting Kyle plunge into your secret abyss?!!!

Me: Is it really a secret?

Julie: Well, with the way you always walk around, scratching your balls . . .

Me: Those are lady balls and they need scratchin' too (they're bigger than mens').

Julie: Well????

Me: Yes. Kyle and I are together. I actually could use your ear. Later, though. Kyle just walked in. Ok. Love you, bye!

Julie: You know why I don't mind cliffhangers in books? Because having a best friend like you gives me plenty of practice at "getting over it." Bye! Love you, too! Full snatch report later, please!!

"Is this where I come to get anal?" Kyle quips.

"I wouldn't have pegged you to be that type of guy, Kyle—kinky bastard. Well," I pat the bed, "bend over here and I'll get the lube and my vibrator for you." I wink. He smirks then sits next to me and grabs my hand. Drawing little circles on the back, he opens his mouth several times as if in an attempt to speak, but closes it again.

We seem to be at an impasse here. It doesn't need to be this way. I don't *want* it to stay this way. I feel like I'm at one of those crucial moments in your life where you could easily make the wrong decision and spend the rest of your life wondering what would've happened if you could go just back and choose correctly. Here's the thing; the me from three months ago would've made the wrong choice, not giving a fuck because it scared her. The me, today, is still scared *as* shitless but I'm tired of it and I do give a fuck. Something has clearly changed in me. I'm not sure *exactly* when it happened. It may never have happened, had he not come along. But here it is and . . . here I go . . .

"When I was in college, I met and fell in love with Andrew Spofford. We were inseparable. He was *it* for me. We'd stay on the phone for hours, talking about our future: when we would marry, how many kids we'd have, where we'd live. I believed in him. I believed in us. I gave him all of me; not a second thought. As you can imagine, from our conversation earlier, I found myself pregnant." I turn my head, lifting my eyes to meet his. He gives me a nod of encouragement and squeezes my hand. I take in a deep breath.

"At first, I fucking freaked out like most girls do that end up in this predicament. But then, I thought about how much we had gone over our plans. Sure, it was a lot earlier than we had talked about, but we would manage. It was meant to be; otherwise it wouldn't have happened, right?" I widen my eyes for emphasis. Kyle gives me a curt smile. "So, instead of dread, I allowed myself to feel happy about the little monster growing in me. I mean monster is sweetest of ways. I imagined him being like cookie monster or something, with snacks all over his face." I chuckle a little but it doesn't help the knot that's forming again. "I fell in love, for the second time in my life. I couldn't wait to tell Drew, but I wanted to do it in person. He and I were so busy with exams and stuff, I just couldn't find the right time." I stop to take another deep breath. I'm actually surprised how easy this is flying out of my mouth. "Finally, I had decided to surprise him. It was a Thursday night. I had made plans with a few of my friends but decided to cancel, knowing that he was staying in. I thought it would be great to not only surprise him but tell him about the baby. Neither one of us had classes the next day that would force us to cut our talk short." I stop, fighting the bile that is making its way up from my stomach.

"He didn't want the baby?" Kyle speaks up.

"He never ended up knowing about the baby."

"What do you mean? Did something happen to him?" He starts rubbing my back. I know he's wracking his brain while trying to soothe me, but I can't even stop the sobs that have come so hard.

Finally, I pull it together to give him the answer. "No. Nothing happened to him. I never told him because I was too distracted by being mortified and having my heart broken all at once."

"You found him cheating on you?" he asks and I can hear the anger in his voice.

"No. He never cheated on me. I wish he had. God, I wish he had. What he did was far worse than anything."

"Did he rape you?"

"No."

"What the hell did he do, Ceese?!"

"Look, Kyle, I really can't. I'm not ready to discuss that part. Please. I just want to tell you about the baby." I turn to him, grabbing his hands—pleading.

"Ok, Ceese. I'm just trying to figure everything out. I want to help you try to find a way past all of this." He rests his forehead against mine.

"I know. I need you to be patient, though. You're the only person I've ever told this to. Nobody knows, Kyle. Do you understand how big this is for me? I'm not even a hundred percent sure that I'm doing the right thing, here."

"You are! I promise you are, Ceese." He grasps my hands in his palms and I bring my eyes up to his. "I will never do anything to make you regret telling me, I promise." He thumbs my tears away and lays several soft kisses on my lips. He pulls back, "Now, tell me, what happened?"

I reach over and grab tissues off the nightstand to blow my nose. I ball up the used tissues in my hands and mindlessly start playing with them. "Don't do that," he stops me, "It's unsanitary." He grabs them and throws them in the wastebasket.

Me? I can't help but laugh at him. "Honestly, Kyle, I don't think that was the most unsanitary thing I've done in the past twenty-four hours."

"That's different." He smiles then proceeds to squirt antibacterial shit in my hands.

"I'm sorry but you've lost your title as Mr. Spock. I am now calling you Monk."

"I don't even know what that means except it's probably another TV show. You need to do something better with your time, beautiful."

"Should I do *you,* instead?"

"You should—at all times! Now . . . you are slowly working yourself away from telling me what happened, don't think I haven't noticed." He darts an eyebrow up.

"Yeah," I sigh. "So, basically, what he did to me mortified me so bad, I felt destroyed. I could never face him again. I could never face anyone there. I left. I left him, school, my dreams—everything." I pull my hair tie out and shake my hair out with my hand: nervous energy.

"Then what?"

"I scheduled an appointment to terminate the pregnancy. I did that Friday morning. I didn't give myself much of a chance to think. All I knew was that I couldn't face him ever again. I know my parents would've helped me but I couldn't even face them at the time. I couldn't face my baby. I . . . I . . . never." I stop and try to collect myself. "I wanted no part of him. What I failed to see, at the time, was that I was giving up a part of me. I've had to live with that decision every day of my life since. Do you have any idea as to what kind of a personal hell that has been? Every time Charley had another baby, my other sisters, it was like a slap in the face. The worst, though . . ." I trail off, feeling my emotions hitting me full force again. "Watching my best friend, struggle to have a baby for *nine* years. Kyle, the guilt is unbearable. I can't even talk to her about it. I can't listen. I make a joke and look for a reason to get off the phone, or I try to change the subject in person." I lay my head into my hands and let myself cry.

"I bet she would understand if you tell her what happened. Ava seems like a wonderful person, I'm sure she wouldn't want you to feel this way one moment." He rubs my back again then suddenly stops. "I don't understand something, though."

"What?" I lift my head back up.

"This has haunted you all of these years? You feel as if you made a big mistake, right?"

"Yes. Kyle, you have to understand, I believe that women, given the right situation, should have the right to choose. But it's not something I could ever see myself doing. I wasn't thinking." I grab another tissue.

"Can I ask you why, then, you decided to take that pill this morning. If this has all been haunting you, if this is not you—why did you take it?" he raises his voice.

"I lied," I say quickly.

"What the fuck are you talking about?"

"Well, I didn't *lie,* I did take it. Then . . . I made myself throw it up. I thought I could do it. I couldn't. I'm in a different place in my life. I'm not as selfish as I let on. Kyle . . . say something, please." I reach up and touch his face. He pulls back.

Crack.

That was my heart.

"If you lied, why leave the box for me to find easily?" he asks apprehensively.

"If you recall correctly, you snatched it out of my hand." I shift so that I'm facing him better. "Also, I wasn't sure if you were being intentional in your actions. You know, you're joking about marriage, waving the reasons behind buying such a big house in my face, at the same time, asking me if I like the house that you bought for your future wife. How could I not think that you have an ulterior motive? So . . . me leaving that box in there was my way of saying I wasn't going to be trapped."

"Christ, Ceese! I wasn't trying to trap you!" He shoots off the bed and begins to pace. I lean back on my hands and watch him wear out the floor. He comes to a halt. "Ok. I can see how it definitely looked that way, but it's really not the case." He gets down on his knees in front of me and grasps my hips. I open my legs for him to come a little closer. "I don't have a real good excuse, only that when I'm with you, I'm not thinking straight. Normal things that would usually cross my mind—responsible things—just don't. I'm *always* careful. Maybe that's because I've *never* been with someone I've felt this way about. I don't know," he adds quickly. "I don't have the answer. It was irresponsible and I'm sorry."

"Hey, we're both at fault here." I put my arms around his neck. "I could've just as easily reminded you. Guess I was in the same fog as you." I smile.

"Ok. So from now, until you get on something, we will stop behaving like teenagers, deal?" He kisses my nose.

"Deal," I agree. "Are we good, Kyle?" I ask for merit.

"You know, I think we are. It's good that we talked about it right away, Ceese. Are you feeling ok, having discussed all of that?"

"I really am. Thank you." I kiss him. "I think maybe we should get some sleep now. I'm exhausted," I say looking over at the clock. It's going on seven in the morning.

"Sounds good. Get up so I can pull the covers back." He stands up and pulls me with him. I move out of the way and proceed to take my clothes off while he situates the bed. He turns around, holding his hand out to the bed for me. His jaw drops. "You know I'm going to fucking molest you now, right?" he asks as I climb in.

"I wouldn't expect anything less." I shoot him a playful wink. I watch as he strips down and climbs in, curling up behind me. His hands waste no time, having their way with me. Mmm . . .

Chapter Sixteen

A whole new world . . .

Kyle

Her hair fans over the pillows. Fast asleep, she's making cute little noises. I suspect it's from crying so much, she's still a little clogged up. I can't help the gleeful mood I'm in as I watch her—in my bed—while I iron her clothes. What? I can't just hang them up wrinkled! Don't laugh at me; I couldn't sleep. Also, her bag of clothes was bothering me. I just imagined them all wrinkled and shit.

I also found something else all wrinkled up that I wasn't expecting—past due bills. Not just past due, some were shut-off notices. It seems that if CiCi is embarrassed or uncomfortable about something, she lies her way through it. I don't like that. I actually have a *big* problem with that. But I'd be lying if I didn't say that I figured that out about her from the get go. I think what bothers me more is that she didn't come to me. Not for money, but to help her figure things out. Yes, I would've tried to *take care* of it for her; however, I would've also tried to help her figure her way out of this slump. I know she's struggling with the shop. She's taken away some of Lindsay's hours. Hours she has no right giving to my sister in the first place—she can't afford it. My sister, God love her, that kid has a heart of gold. She's been trying to help CiCi out in secret.

"What are you doing?" CiCi asks sounding half asleep. I look up from my ironing.

"Ironing."

"You like to iron?" She stretches. Mmm.

"It's relaxing."

"Well, don't be shy then, let me get you my clothes to do, too." She pulls the covers back.

Boobies.

Wow. I really just thought that word, didn't I? I swear to God, I was not like this before I met her. "I already have them." I hold her blouse up for her to see.

"You went through my damn bag, Kyle? After I asked you not to?" She darts out of bed.

"Yes. I did. I also saw the bills that you didn't want me to see." I put the hanger in and place it over the back of the chair, until I bring them all in to the closet.

"Don't bother hanging them up. Just put them right back in the bag." She goes for her bag but I grab it first.

"You're gonna run? Is that your answer for everything?" I ask. She gasps. I look up at her. Her eyes are wide and tearing up. *Shit!* "I mean with me, Ceese. I wasn't referring to the past. I wasn't even thinking about that, I swear." I reach for her. She visibly relaxes. "Look, it's not a big deal. You know that I know that you've been struggling. Did I know the extent? No. I do now. Let me help."

"No. It's not your problem. Don't ever go through my shit again, okay? I don't like it."

"Fair enough. I wasn't looking to find stuff, though. I just wanted to save your clothes from being terribly wrinkled." I admit. She chuckles at me and shakes her head. I turn the iron off. "Now, I need you to do me a favor." I put my hands back on hers.

"What's that?"

"I need you to get back on my bed so I can wake you properly like I had planned." I kiss her.

"Properly, huh? Why do I get the feeling that this is going to be something very improper?" She gives me a playful grin.

"It could be to others, but I think you'll rather enjoy this. So much so, that whenever you stay with me, we'll make this your alarm clock." I waggle my eyebrows as she crawls back on to the bed. "Now open those gorgeous legs for me," I order and settle myself onto my stomach as she does. My hands slide under her thighs and around to her hips. I grasp them and pull her forward, face planting myself into my favorite place. I look up at her under my eyelashes and watch her chest rise and fall quickly. I love watching her anticipate my moves. I love surprising her with moves she's not expecting. I lace her sweet, plump lips with soft kisses. She lifts her ass off the bed, encouraging me. Flattening my tongue against her center, I give her one slow lick up it. She whimpers and begs. I'm not going to lie; I'm about to do the same. If my dick gets any harder right now, it'll burn a hole into this bed. "Touch yourself, beautiful," I command as I slide my hands off of her hips down to her mound. My left hand pulls back on her hood and my tongue darts out to play with her ring. *Fuck, I love that little ring!*

"Kyle, please!" She writhes and grasps the sheets.

"Touch your tits, now, Ceese!" I demand in a harsher tone and watch as she complies.

Tug, tug, rub, and roll . . .

I know she's chanting that again—her lips are moving to it. I love all of her quirks, I really do. I move my eyes down to the task at hand . . . er, mouth. I lick up her folds and let my tongue softly play at her clit. CiCi slams her pussy into my face. I chuckle.

"What are you laughing about?" she asks, frustration lacing her tone.

"I believe I've just been pussy slapped." I look up at her and grin.

"Yeah, well, get back down there; I'm not done slapping you." She reaches forward and pushes my head down.

"So abusive . . ." I mutter teasingly. I go at her again but this time, I'm relentless: licking hard, biting, and blowing on her clit. "Fuck, you're always so wet for me, B." I plunge my tongue deep inside of her. She lets out a guttural groan that shoots right to my painfully, engorged dick. Christ, I'm not going to last much longer—I need to make her come! I pull my face back and slide two fingers inside of her. Her body arches to my intrusion. I climb up on my knees; fingers still in place and bring my left hand to lay on her mound. My thumb slides on to her clit and meticulously begins to rub it in circles. I reach inside of her, feeling for just the right spot. CiCi gasps and jerks and I know I've reached my destination. Slowly, I motion my fingers as if I'm saying "come here" with them. The irony is—I am, aren't I?

"Oh God, oh yes, Kyle . . . right there," she mewls. I swear to God, if you had asked me ten seconds ago if I thought CiCi could get any hotter, I would've said no. I would've also been wrong. She's just planted her hands and pushed her body up in the air to rock into my fingers. *Holy fuck,* she's gorgeous. I feel hypnotized, watching her. I snap out of it the moment her pussy clenches around my fingers. She throws her head back and gives into her orgasm with panting moans. It's taking everything in me not to come while watching her. Finally, her body begins a slow descent as she comes down from her climax. I let my fingers slide out and give her clef a sweet kiss.

"I'm going to need you to turn over, Ceese. This is going to be fast and hard." I warn. Poor baby looks spent as she complies. "All the way up and grab a hold of the headboard." I shuffle my finger towards it as I grab a condom out of my nightstand. Sliding my hand up and down my shaft, I rip the packet with my teeth and roll on the condom, pinching the tip of it. *Fuck, I'm so hard.* I move behind her. Oh man, she's perfect; spread so nicely for me, ass in the air, holding onto the bars. I run my fingers up her center, collecting some of her wetness and bringing it to her ass. "God, Ceese, I can't wait to fuck this tight, little, pretty ass of yours." I slip a finger in, then two. I watch as she welcomes my touch, leaning back into it. Hmmm . . . her whimpers drive me mad. Trying to control myself, I'm still slightly shocked that I can speak so candidly in bed with her. I would've never said that to another woman in a hundred years. But, CiCi isn't just any woman, is she? "You want it too, don't you?" I ask and bite my lip hard as I watch my fingers fuck her diligently. She moans lightly. Quickly, I pull them out and slap her ass. "Hold on, beautiful, this is going to be lightning speed." And with that, I grasp her ass cheeks, pushing them up high, allowing the maximum exposure, and slam into her pussy. She lets out a scream that unleashes the beast in me and I fuck her harder than I've ever fucked anyone. Closing my eyes, I'm fueled by the slapping sound of her taking it from me. My balls tighten, "Gah!" The surge travels up into my cock and before I know it, I'm gasping for air as I find my release. I hear her scream my name as I ram into her again and again. Her pussy milks me in a way that would have angels singing if they could feel it. One last thrust and I collapse on top of her. CiCi continues to rock a little. Mmm . . . she always wants one more. I slide my hand underneath both of us and reach down, finding her clit. Her hand joins mine and we rub another one out of her together.

You know that feeling you have when you're awake but your eyes aren't open yet and you can feel it? No. Not *that.* Although, that is raring to go. I mean, feel someone staring at you? I'm always amazed how quickly we can go from a sound sleep to complete awareness.

"I'd find your pussy breath offensive if it wasn't from my pussy being plastered all over your face," CiCi says lackadaisically.

"Mmm . . . you have a way with whispering sweet nothings." I smile; my eyes still closed.

"I do, don't I? Listen, I'm going to need you to drive me to my car soon." She brushes my hair off my forehead.

"Why?" My eyes pop open and I push myself up on my elbow.

"I have Sunday dinner at my parents in a few hours."

I stare at her blankly.

She must know why I'm staring.

Jesus Christ, do I have to spell it out for her?

Yup.

"What time do we have to be there?" I'm going to go this route and see what happens. She immediately gets that same look on her face that she had at my parents' house. "What time, Ceese?" I ignore it.

"I didn't ask them if you could come," she says quickly as if the thought just came to her.

"Well, here." I reach over to the floor and grab her purse. "Call them and ask."

"It's such short notice."

"Then cancel." I suggest, trying to keep my irritation at bay.

"I can't."

"Why?"

"It's rude."

"I think your parents are used to your behavior." I whip open her zipper.

"Do not go into my purse!" She snatches it from me.

"Sorry, I thought I'd help you find your big girl pants."

"I'm just not ready," she states quietly.

"You're thirty-four years old—get ready!" I snap.

"My age has nothing to do with this."

"Make a decision." I say through my teeth.

"You know, you're getting all bent out of shape and my hesitation has nothing to do with you or me, so stop being a fucking asshole about it." She yanks her phone out and tosses her bag on the floor. I slide around behind her as she makes her phone call, and plant soft kisses on her back. I love her back—it's fucking gorgeous. My hands travel around and up to her breast. I cup them before letting my thumbs roll over her nipples. "Stop," she whisper shouts and tries to push my hands away. "Mom—hi!" she says quickly into the phone, still smacking my hands away. I grasp at her more aggressively causing her to gasp and throw her head back on my shoulder. "Sorry, I dropped something. No . . . nothing new." She tries to sound unaffected.

I lean into her ear. "Moms know everything, right?" I whisper. "I wonder if she can hear it in your voice." I bite at her lobe. "I bet she can tell you've been fucked seven ways to Sunday."

CiCi jerks her face towards mine, eyes wide open. "Mom, is there enough room for one more tonight . . . I . . . uh, um . . . I'd like to bring Kyle," she finally spits out. "No, I'm fine. I'm just doing something," she says quickly.

"Yeah, you'll be doing my cock in a minute." I bite into her shoulder. She elbows me. I laugh. She joins. And . . . at this moment, I just fell a little harder. I hug her to me and hold her there for the rest of the conversation. The conversation that only ends because apparently, a dish towel went up in flames in my kitchen. "Shit, she's not going to call 911, now is she?" I ask, slightly panicked.

"No. She is the reason I was hesitant, though." She smiles back at me then, sighs.

"Why?"

"Because she will see us and run with it." She leans forward to get up. "C'mon, pussy breath, let's get cleaned up." She holds her hand out to me.

"Okay. I think it's time for you to get another dose of special mouthwash, yourself." I wink at her than slap her ass.

"It's good stuff; really whitens my teeth."

"Got a lot of protein in it, too."

"Wow, that is a plus!" she laughs and pulls me into the bathroom. I watch her ready the shower and I can't help but worry. For some reason, she's seen something in me that made her open up in ways that she hasn't opened up in years. While I'm happy about this and certainly honored, I can't help but worry that she won't always see me in this light. What if, one day, she wakes up and I'm not who she was hoping I would be. This relationship thing is pretty new to both of us (in a born again way). I don't have any baggage but I'm not sure if that's a good thing or a bad thing. Lastly, what if I'm just a phase for her? I've said it from the start; she could possibly destroy me.

"Kyle." CiCi turns to me. We've just pulled up to her parents' house and she's been a ball of nervous energy the whole trip here.

"Everything will be fine. I'm not such a bad guy. I don't think they will hate me or anything." I grab her hand and bring it up to my lips to plant several kisses.

"That's not it." She shakes her head.

"What is it, then?"

"My mom. Kyle, my mom has MS," she starts.

"I know, beautiful. Mitch told me a while back." I offer her an encouraging smile.

"Can you let me finish?" She smacks my leg. I nod. She takes in a breath and stares out at the house. "She's coming out of remission. Scratch that—she's out of remission. Right now, she's moved past denial and fast-forwarded right to doom and gloom. I'm not knocking anything she's going through; it fucking sucks. It's just . . . you're the first guy I've brought home since Drew. She was weepy just the other night, worried that I wouldn't find someone. When I told her I met you and that you were a good guy, she—"

"—you told her about me already?" I cut her off.

"Yes. Is that okay?" She furrows her brows.

"That's more that okay, that's amazingly fantastic!" I hug her to me.

"Ok . . . calm down, killer." She pats my back. I pull back a little and stare into her eyes.

Falling . . .

"Go on." I nudge her nose and peck her lips.

"She became extremely excited and relieved, all at once. So, I want to warn you that by the time we leave, she may have our first-born named." She smiles meekly.

Falling . . .

"I'm sure I'll put in a good fight if I hate the name. C'mon, now." I give her a chaste kiss and open my door. I jog around to her side of the car and help her out.

"Alright, skipper, take it down a notch; nobody's looking." She rolls her eyes at me.

"Actually, both of your parents are doing their darnedest to not be caught while they are—in fact—looking. However, I would do this anyhow. You know that." I pull her to me.

"They're watching?" she asks a bit panicked.

"Yes. Would now be a good time to shove my tongue down your throat . . . maybe grope you a bit?"

"Sure, but they may come out and instruct you on how to do it right." She winks and gives me a quick kiss before turning to head up to the door of the house.

Before we even finish climbing the steps, the door is thrown open. "Dolly!" An older gentleman calls out. My guess is it's the famous "Happy" Jack O'Brien.

"Hey, Dad." She kisses and hugs him. "What's with the overzealous welcome?"

"What? Can't a dad be happy to see his daughter?" He acts hurt.

"Hmm . . . you're not fooling anyone." She squints her eyes at him then slips by him into the house.

"Mr. O'Brien." I put my hand out for a shake.

"You fish, Kyle?" Is how he greets me while shaking my hand.

"Uh . . . I haven't in a while, but yes."

"Good. You can come with Mitch and me next Saturday." He pats my back and guides me in the house.

"I'm sorry, sir, but I'll be in Spain for work." Fuck if I'm not off to a bad start!

"Spain?" he asks, sounding surprised.

"Yeah, Daddy. He's going to train to be a conquistador—olé!" She does some weird funky move with a snap and pose to finish. I can't help but laugh at her carefree nature. I think that's what I love most about her.

"I'm actually taking our new team over to do *their* final training. Becoming a conquistador may not come off of my bucket list this time around." I rub my chest and shake my head, emphasizing the disappointment. I sigh.

"Mitch said you work with him. I think it's great that you boys are doing this. Let the younger kids get some of the action. There comes a time in a man's life where he needs to settle down in one place and get some roots in the ground." He eyes me the whole time he goes through his spiel.

"I couldn't agree more with you, sir." I nod and get a quick glance in of CiCi, who's being extremely productive shooting eye daggers at me. I'm guessing that's her mother standing next to her, productively shooting hearts out of her eyes at me. I wink at Ceese.

"Well, come on and make yourselves at home. Kyle, you can follow me into the kitchen so we can get better acquainted." She smiles and reaches out her hand to me.

"Sure, Mrs. O'Brien." I grab her hand and follow.

"Call me, Ma," she says, waving her other hand.

"Call her Shannon or Mrs. O'Brien!" CiCi calls after us.

"What are you making, Ma? It smells good in here." I ask real loud then turn back to Ceese and stick my tongue out at her. She flips me off.

Falling . . .

"I've made your favorite. Now, reach up into that cupboard and get me that colander." She points.

"How do you know what my favorite dish is?" Curiosity may

very well kill this cat.

"What's there to know?"

"Well, you've never met me before." I scratch the back of my neck as I try to figure her out.

"Colander." She whacks my stomach with the back of her hand. I turn to grab it. "I'm a good cook, Kyle. Everything I make will be your favorite."

"Word is bond, yo! My mom's cooking is the shiznits!" CiCi bellows out, walking into the kitchen.

"Have you started watching that MTV Raps show again, Carissa?" Her mom shakes her head at her.

"Yes I have, Mom. Now that my time machine is working again, I've been going back and making the 90s my bitch." She pops an appetizer in her mouth and laughs when her mom whips her with a dish towel.

"You getting a taste of Frick and Frack?" Happy says from behind me, making me jump. Sneaky bastard.

"Yeah. It's like they were separated at birth." I stare in awe.

"We were, dipshit. You see me walking around attached to a placenta?"

"Carissa Catherine!" her mom gasps. I know why her mom is panicking. Here I am, the first guy Ceese has brought home in over a decade and she speaks to me like *this?* A guy might be pissed. Not this guy, though. I fucking *love* that mouth of hers. It turns me on to no end. I decide to lash out at her in our own little coded way.

I eye fuck her.

Hard.

Throw a little lip biting and nose flaring in to show her I mean business and I can see the heat rise up into her cheeks. She reaches up to her necklace, playing with the cross, sliding it back and forth on the chain as if to comfort herself.

"Don't worry, Ma. CiCi's mouth doesn't offend me in the least. In fact, it's one of the things I love most about her," I add, throwing a smile her way before noticing CiCi's eyes growing big.

"Well, thank God for miracles!" Charlotte calls out as she and Mitch enter the kitchen, followed by her three kids. This is a pretty decent size kitchen, but it's completely crowded now.

"Kyle!" Mitch shakes my hand, slaps me on the back, and leans in. "How in the fuck did you two go from being done to having family dinner in a matter of days?" he inquires secretively.

"Let's just say, we've come to an understanding," I reply and pat his upper arm before he pulls away. Mitch's attention gets pulled by one of the kids. Shannon is clanking things. Charlotte is right next to her diving in to the finishing touches. Happy's gone off to answer the door. The buzz in this house is electrifying. But none of that noise catches my attention quite like the pair of green eyes I see, staring back at me from the other side of the room. I walk across, eliminating the distance between us. Her hands immediately lie on my chest and slide up and around my neck. I pull her to me, hugging her as tightly as I can.

"Sorry," she whispers into my neck.

"I have no idea what you're talking about." I chuck her chin and lay several kisses on her lips.

All of the noise stops.

CiCi and I look around.

"You all waiting for the money shot?" she asks. Dear God, she seriously just asked that question.

"I think it already happened in Kyle's pants," Mitch bellows out. I shoot him a look that hopefully tells him to fuck off. I don't even know this guy anymore! "Relax, Kyle." He slaps my back. "If you're going to be around this family, you may as well learn to loosen up. Anything goes in this house and it takes a lot to offend someone."

"Alright, everyone, get the hell out of my kitchen now, goddamn it. The girls will be here in a half an hour and I don't have a thing ready!" Shannon yells as she pulls two cooked meatloaves out of the oven.

"The girls?" CiCi panics.

"Yeah. It's that time of the month." Shannon shrugs.

"Jesus, I thought I was feeling cramps." CiCi shakes her head and sort of looks pissed off. "C'mon!" She grabs my hand, drags me out of the kitchen, past the living room into a smaller room, and closes the door. "I need to prepare you for this," she states urgently and begins to pace.

"For what? I've met all of your friends, beautiful. There's nothing for you to worry about." I grab her hands, removing them out of her hair. "Stop." Kiss. "Worrying." Kiss. "So much." A little tongue slippage.

"But, Kyle, they haven't been around you since we've . . . I mean . . . we're very new and they are going to be relentless." She pushes away.

I grasp her hips and close the gap between us. "I think I know a thing or two about being relentless." I murmur before attacking her lips.

"Why are you so relaxed and comfortable with all of this?" She shoves off from me again.

"Why are you not?" I counter.

"I'm not used to it. I just don't want them making a big deal out of it. We're fucking, so what?" She throws her hand out for emphasis.

We're fucking?

You caught that, too, huh?

"C'mon, let's get back out there." I open the door and wave her out. She lets out a frustrated groan and storms past me.

"What the hell is her problem?" Mitch asks after he watches her continue out of the living room.

"Do me a favor?" I direct my attention towards him.

"What's up?"

"Are you able to contact the rest of the GEGs?"

Mitch whips out his phone and starts laughing. "I feel like we should be whipping out a special phone when a line like that is dropped. Group text?" He looks up, still slightly chuckling.

"No shit, right?" I have to laugh. It's true and I can't help but imagine Mitch and me in black and white, in an office, smoking cigarettes, racing to call the GEGs on the big black office rotary phone.

"Dude, what do you need me to say?" Mitch waves the phone in my face.

"Just tell them the CiCi and I are together and to please not make a big deal out of it at dinner."

"I'm not telling them that. That's like ammunition, man! Besides, CiCi will be *pissed* if they don't make a big deal out of it." He puts his phone away. "Stop worrying so much."

"What's he worrying about?" Happy inquires as he walks in.

"The girls making a big deal out of him and CiCi being together," Mitch answers.

"Eh, those girls have been best friends forever. Their more like sisters, really. They make a big deal out of everything. Love those girls." He shakes his head, smiling. "It's like I have eight daughters instead of five. Speaking of," he looks around, "I'm glad I got you fellas alone. I want to give you some advice," he says with a secretive tone.

"What's that, Dad?" Mitch comes in a little closer and we almost look as if we're going into a huddle.

"Look, I don't know if you're aware of this or not, but I, myself, was in a very similar situation as you both. My brother-in-law, God rest his soul, was my best friend. He was married to Shannon's sister. I'm telling you two right *now,*" he points at the ground authoritatively with the most serious "life or death" face I've ever seen before. "Never *ever* assume anybody knows what *you* know!"

"Dad, what the hell are you talking about?" Mitch asks. I'm glad he did because I'm standing here just as fucking clueless.

"Don't assume because you tell each other stuff about the girls that the girls know anything you know," he repeats is a less confusing . . . no, wait . . . that's still confusing.

"Ah! I think I know what you're getting at, Dad!" Mitch waves a finger in the air.

"Good. You want to enlighten me?"

"It's like, what I told you about Charlotte. Nobody else knows, except for Ava. Shit! You didn't say anything to CiCi, did you?" Mitch grabs my shoulder and I can see the panic spreading like wildfire in his eyes.

"That—*right there*—is what I'm talking about." Happy pokes at my other shoulder.

"No. I didn't, but shit—Happy's right! I wouldn't have known not to!"

"See? Always and I mean, *always* talk to each other first and make sure you know who knows before you assume shit and everything goes to hell in a hand basket!" he reiterates. "Now, clearly, I have no idea as to what you are talking about but since three of my girls are involved, I want the goods."

"We're actually going to discuss this over dinner, Dad." Mitch shuffles his hand through his hair.

"That's fine, but you'll tell me now. I know I've been married to Shannon for almost forty years but that doesn't mean I don't need a heads up on how to deal with her reaction to stuff. You'll never have them fully figured out, fellas, but that's half the fun in being with them, isn't it?"

"Hey, Dad, how's Mom doing?" Mitch softens his voice.

Happy's face drops. "Not good, Mitch," his voice scratches. "You know me well enough, Mitch, to know I don't let much get to me. But I'd be lying right now if I told you I wasn't pissed off," he chokes. "That's my sweetheart in there . . . suffering . . . and there's not a *damn* thing I can do but sit by and watch. I just want to take it from her! She's a good woman; she doesn't deserve this." He rubs his face, catching a sob. "You know, Shannon . . . she's sayin' this is the end of the road, that she's got nothing left in her. It was bad the last time—really, really bad! I don't know if I could disagree with her if it gets like that again. So, not only am I worried about her getting that sick, but pulling back out of it. What if it gets her this time—*this lousy, fucking beast*—and I lose my Shannon all the while sitting next to her and watching it happen. You're supposed to protect the woman you love. I don't have a sword powerful enough . . . not even a white horse to sit upon to give her hope. I'll tell you right now, fellas, forty years is a long time but when it comes to losing the love of your life, it's no longer than a minute. You'd do anything for another forty." Happy is letting his emotions go and he is full on crying for his woman. We are, officially, in a group huddle, snot collectively dripping onto the floor from all of us.

Yes. I'm dying to wipe it up.

"Dad, it's going to be ok. You just have to stay strong for her. We will be there for both of you in any way we can." Mitch pats his back.

"Absolutely!" I add my word of wisdom.

"Ahh, you're a good boy, Mitchy." Happy lets go of us, grasps Mitch's face in his palms and pulls his face down to kiss Mitch's forehead (we both have a few inches on him). He then proceeds to wipe his nose on the back of his hand before reaching for me.

Dear God, no!

Happy's palms slap my face and pulls me down. I'd mention the suspicious moisture in those palms, but I'm desperately trying not to think about it. "Welcome to the family, Kyle. We're a crazy bunch but we love each other hard." And with that, he plants a kiss on my forehead. I'd like to say it was his seal of approval. He pulls his hands away and . . .

I feel it.

Slime, snot, booger juice, or the million other names for it.

It's right there; side of my left jaw.

Breathe.

"Is everything okay?" Charlotte asks as she walks in, looking at all of us with concern.

"What's the matter with you three?" Shannon pipes up, following Charlotte in. Then, CiCi and the kids.

"It's the Patriots," Mitch wipes his face, seemingly trying to pull himself together. "They just lost the game with three seconds on the clock."

"Are you boys for real?" Shannon shakes her head at us.

"It was a close game, Shannon! We've worked hard all season and now we can kiss the Super Bowl goodbye!" Happy defends us.

"Grandpa, they have another game next week, what are you talking about?" Brogan asks.

"Nah, Brogan." I shake my head. "It won't matter if they win that one. We've lost too many," I add and throw in another little grief-stricken sob as I grab my handkerchief out of my pack pocket to wipe my eyes, sliding it down to my jaw.

See what I did there?

Just then, we all hear a ruckus at the back door. "Shit . . ." CiCi trails off. I take this time to go searching for a bathroom.

Chapter Seventeen

The peanut gallery . . .

Kyle

Ever notice how loud the dinner table can be when no one is talking at it? Everything is louder: clanking of dishes, silver scraping the plates, the sound of drinking, moving bowls around, etcetera, etcetera. If you listen closely enough, you can hear the rhythm of it all. It's kind of cool. It's also the kind of thing you think about when you're sitting in the hot seat. I dare to glance around at everyone and try to contain my amusement as they all quickly avert their eyes.

I pick up my fork, clink my glass, and clear my throat. Everyone gives me their immediate attention. "CiCi and I took the company jet to Vegas last night, got married, and flew back. Mitch can you pass me the gravy bowl?" I ask as I grab another slab of meatloaf and wait to see how many more minutes this silence will last.

“I motherfucking knew it!” Julie is the first one to burst.

“Julie, you watch your goddamn mouth at my table!” Shannon yells at her. “You better be fucking kidding me, Kyle, goddamn it!” she directs her wrath towards me. I have no idea what anybody else is saying because they are all yelling over each other. Me?

I’m smirking.

I turn my neck to catch CiCi’s smile, except . . . well . . . she’s not smiling at all. She’s staring down at her plate, moving food around with her fork. “Hey.” I nudge her. She ignores me. Realizing this was a fun plan gone drastically wrong, I wave everyone down and finally put my fingers in my mouth and let out a whistle. Everyone collectively shuts up. “It was a joke.” I say as soon as I have their attention.

“No. Kyle.” She places her hand on my arm. “I should tell them. They need to know in case they are questioned.” She brings her attention back to everyone and lets out a long sigh. “They were going to deport me back to Ireland,” she says so straight-faced it actually scares me. How much wool has she been able to pull over my eyes?

“Carissa, you’ve never been to Ireland a day in your life—how could they deport you?” Shannon looks completely miffed with her eyebrows tightly knitted together.

“They’ve got me mixed up with somebody else, Ma.” CiCi shrugs. “I tried to explain it to them. They wouldn’t listen.”

“They *who?!*” all of the girls practically yell.

“The people in charge of deportation. They didn’t want to hear my song and dance. They said they were giving all single, full-blooded Irish people six months to give them a solid good reason not to deport us. They’re trying to make room in the country, they said. I didn’t check my mail. I thought it was junk, so I always threw it out. They came to the shop the other day and told me, in person, that I had one week to get my affairs in order and leave. Kyle was there and told them we were engaged. They wouldn’t give me an extension so we went to Vegas.” She grabs her drink and takes a sip.

“These past twenty-four hours have been the happiest of my life.” I smile over at her.

“What did ‘they’ look like?” Maddie chimes in after studying CiCi the entire time.

“They were in black suits. One was a tall black man, the other, an older white man.” She acts as if she’s really concentrating. “They wore dark sunglasses."

"Yeah. And there was strange theme music in the background every time they talked." I snap as if I thought of something extremely important. CiCi and I look at each other and start bobbing our heads to the beat. "Here come the men in black," we both sing.

"You two are fucking assholes!" Charlotte yells out in frustration and throws a roll at each of us. CiCi and I hold our stomachs, laughing. I mean, you should've seen how these guys were falling for it.

"So you two are not married and you're not being deported?" Shannon tries to clarify.

"No." I laugh.

"Oh, I'm going to deport her ass, all right!" Charlotte attacks her potatoes.

"She's just mad because she falls for this shit all of the time," Ceese informs me then lays the sweetest kiss on my lips—in front of *everyone.*

"Let me see some tongue action, Ceese!" Ava, who's been relatively quiet this entire time, finally adds to the mix here.

"Pipe down, Ava! And, CiCi, you keep that tongue of yours in *your* mouth!" Happy intercepts.

"Ok, everyone." Maddie waves her hands out above the food. "Let's go around the table. Who's starting this month?"

"Jesus Christ, Maddie, you always make it sound like we're at an AA meeting." CiCi complains then bursts out laughing.

"What?" I chuckle, watching her.

She wipes away her tears and tries to control herself. "The first time I met your sister, she asked me what that meant," she says then starts laughing again. All of the girls start laughing with her.

"What did you say?" I ask, but she can't stop laughing. "Do you girls know what she told her?"

"They don't know, man. One of them gets like this; they all get like this in anticipation." Mitch looks over at Charlotte and rolls his eyes.

"I said," she starts but another roll of laughter comes out of her. "Asswhores Anonymous!" She finally screams out. I believe that was the only way she was able to get it out. All five girls are wailing now. Mitch, Trent, and I all look at each other and laugh at our predicament.

"Well, one thing is for sure," Trent says over their laughing fit.

"It's nice to finally have company. For the past ten years, I've been the only man brave enough to stand in their shadow. Welcome to the club, gentlemen." He picks up his glass to salute us.

"Where did we go wrong, Shannon?" Happy looks around the table at all of the girls, who are finally calming down.

"Nowhere, sweetie. I wouldn't trade their laughter in for the world." She smiles. I sit here in awe. Honestly, you would think that Maddie, Julie, and Ava were their kids. There's something pretty damn terrific about that.

I can't help but think about how lucky I am to come from a great family that I can be comfortable around. Never mind find somebody whose family makes me feel the same way—that's gold.

Everyone finally settles down. "I'm going last," Charlotte waves.

"What are we doing?" I ask CiCi.

"Oh. This little dinner with all of the girls only happens once a month, so we go around the table talking about anything new in our lives or interesting stories for Mom and Dad to catch up. It's become tradition." She takes my napkin and wipes the corner of my mouth. "I'll go first," she calls out but keeps her attention on me. Everybody stays real quiet. "I fell in love this week." She turns back to everyone. My heart races a mile a minute. "New client. He's a scotty dog named, Sir, but I call him Sir-licks-a lot. He's so cute. That's all he does the entire time, give me kisses while I'm grooming him," she carries on. I look over at Mitch. He does a slight hand across the neck gesture, telling me to let it go. Of course, I'll let it go, I mean, we're only fucking, right? "Oh, and I started seeing this guy." She directs her thumb in my direction.

"We'll pray for you, Kyle." Julie laughs.

"Thanks. I appreciate it." I hold my glass up to her.

"Me next!" Maddie dances in her seat.

"He brought me coffee again!" Maddie actually sings and does the cabbage patch in her seat.

"Madelyn, is this the same guy who was bringing you coffee last month?" Shannon inquires.

"The Viking." She sighs as if in love. Hmm . . . funny concept, huh? "He's so handsome and smart. He's a giant."

"I love you, honey, but I don't want to hear about him until he's putting cream in more than your coffee." Shannon pats her hand.

"Mom!" Maddie screeches.

"I'm sorry, Maddie, but right now, coffee is as boring as shit! What else is going on?"

"I have a new type of client I've never had before," she leans in as if the HIPPA police will fly in here out of nowhere. "He has hippopotomonstrosesquipedaliophobia." She widens her eyes.

"I had that once," Julie quips, "one little blue pill and it was gone."

"Uhh . . . I believe that was something else, Julie," CiCi says.

"Maddie?" I grab her attention. This kind of stuff fascinates me. "Is that the fear of long words?"

"It is!" She waves her hand at me excitedly.

"For the love of God, please tell me you say that word to him every chance you can!" Ava laughs.

"Oh my God, I totally do. How can I not—I mean—come on!"

"How do you keep a straight face with these nut jobs?" CiCi asks.

"Don't say that. Having fears doesn't make you a nut job." Maddie shifts in her chair and pushes her hair behind her ear.

"I don't know, Maddie, CiCi has a lot of fears, most people tend to think she's nuts," I snort.

"True dat!" Four of the girls say. I look over at Ceese and she's biting the inside of her cheek.

"I'm next!" Julie drums the table. "I've decided not to model anymore. Also, since it seems that CiCi now has a solid man by her side, I've decided to become a lesbian and make Maddie my bitch with her being in the same situation as I."

"I've waited my whole life to be your bitch, Julie." Maddie bats her eyes at Julie.

"I know, short stack. It was just a matter of time. Hold my hand under the table, will ya? This can be our first date."

"Oh, you girls," Happy laughs.

"Are you two numb nuts done?" Charlotte asks then leans back and looks over at the kids' table.

"Hey, Miss Observant, your kids went into the living room to watch TV fifteen minutes ago." CiCi snaps in her face.

"Oh. Good," she states with the sound of relief. "I have some news to share with all of you. It's actually mine and Ava's to share."

"Charley's letting me borrow her vagina," Ava beats her to the punch.

"Why, Trent getting tired of yours?" CiCi quips.

"No, asshat. I've agreed to be Ava and Trent's surrogate mother. And . . ." she trails off.

"We're pregnant!" she and Ava scream.

"Shut the front fucking door!" Maddie yells. They all get up to hug Ava and Charlotte. Everyone except for CiCi.

"Hey." I lean over and nudge her. She looks at me, her eyes filled. Her nose flairs and the tears plummet down. I grab her hand. "Go congratulate her." I lean into her ear and whisper. She nods and gets up.

"I'm so happy for you, Ava," she says before hugging her.

"Are you? I have to say, Ceese, you don't look like you are." Ava cringes as she says it.

"No! I am, I promise. I'm just surprised. I think this is wonderful. You deserve it after trying for so long. I really am happy for you." She pulls her in for a huge hug and I watch as my girl cries. I'm sure Ava believes it's for her and so she's crying with her. I know it's that and so much more and my heart is just aching over her pain.

"C'mon, boys, let's clean up this mess while the girls talk." Happy stands up. "Charley, I'm so proud of you, honey. And, Ava, I'm so thrilled for you, sweetheart." Happy heads over to her and kisses the top of her head.

"Thanks, Dad." She smiles up at him.

"Thanks, Daddy." Charlotte grabs his hand.

CiCi makes her way back to me. "I want to go," she whispers in my ear.

"No."

"What?"

I lean into her ear. "I said no. You are not going to run because something is hard for you to face. That is *your* best friend over there and *your* sister. They both need *your* support. I understand that you are feeling some things right now and want to be left alone to feel them. I agree; you need that. But for right now, you need to push that aside and be here for them. You got me?" I grab her chin gently with my thumb and forefinger to bring her eyes to mine.

"Yes," she simply says then nods.

"Good girl." I kiss her lips.

"I'm going to have to fuck the shit out of you later to work through this, just so you know."

"Whatever it takes to help you cope, beautiful." I bite my smile back.

"Go ahead and clean-up with the guys. I know you got a hard on the moment Daddy mentioned cleaning," she teases me.

"I don't know how I'm going to walk, balancing this thing." I kiss her quickly before grabbing some plates. She heads back over to the girls but steals a glance at me. I give her a wink.

Mitch told me after dinner that once it was time to leave, the actual event of leaving wouldn't occur for another hour. I didn't understand what he was really talking about until everyone started to announce their departure and it indeed, did not occur for another hour. I don't even understand why everyone was standing around. They were just reiterating the plans for the next dinner over and over again. "They linger, it's like a disorder or something." Mitch leaned into my ear.

"This is fucking nuts, bro. I was ready to leave at eight." I looked at my watch again. Finally, I had taken charge by grabbing CiCi's hand and just yelling our goodbyes to them as we left.

Safe and sound now, in my car, I can't wait to get her home to help her fulfill her coping plan. But first, I have to nip something in the bud before it eats me alive. "What am I to you?" I glance over as I make a right turn off of her parent's street and onto the main road.

"Jesus Christ, Kyle. Don't fucking start." She sighs and looks out her window.

"Are you going to see other guys while I'm in Spain?" Just as I finish the question, we hit a downpour. I flick my windshield wipers on but it's no use. I pull over and put my hazards on.

"Are you going to see other women over there?" she asks quietly while looking down to her lap.

"What other women? You're the only one I've been able to *see* for months now. Nobody compares to you, Ceese.

"You were *seeing* giggles. What was up with her hair, too? I kept hearing the theme song to Buck Rogers." She laughs.

"The year was 1987 . . ." we both say in unison. *Holy shit.* I can't believe she knows the opening.

"I kept calling her Twiki." I laugh. "Anyways, she was nothing and you know that. I was trying to forget about you." I grab her hand.

"How'd that work out for you?"

"It didn't and I'm glad."

"Let's play fact or fiction." She taps my hand.

"Um . . . ok."

"I'll go first and you tell me if it's fact or fiction."

"Go ahead."

"I love the color purple."

"Fact."

"Yes. How did you know?" She smiles.

"You have it everywhere." I chuck her chin. "My turn?"

"Yes."

"I graduated college a year early."

"Fact!"

"Fiction. I could have but I added a ton of classes I didn't need for my degree."

"Why?"

"Because I wanted to learn about those subjects."

"Nerd," she teases. "I've never had sex in a car before."

"Fiction." I scoff.

"Fact." She pokes at my chest.

"Well, that's just un-American."

"Want to change that for me, Kyle?" She begins to unbutton the front of her dress. Slowly she reveals her breasts to me. I lean forward and cup her right one. "Well?"

I sweep her lips with mine. "The rain is letting up, beautiful. Let's just go home." I pull her dress back up.

"Seriously?" she asks in disbelief.

"Yes." I situate myself back in the driver side and signal to get back on the road. "Ceese . . ." I try to get her attention. She stays quiet. "When I start, I'm not gonna want to stop. That's why."

"Oh."

I reach my hand out for hers and feel her soft fingers lace with mine. "What were all of the girls handing you tonight?"

"What are you talking about?"

"I walked by the room you girls were in and I saw them all handing you a check. Why?"

She clears her throat. "That's none of your business."

"Can we just sit down and go over your stuff tonight?" This is so frustrating. I wish she would just let me help.

"I have it figured out, Kyle. You need to stop. Just slow the fuck down." She lets go of my hand and grabs her phone.

"What are you doing?"

"Checking my phone."

"I'm trying to talk to you and you're checking your phone? Why?"

"Kyle, what do you want?" She turns her whole body my way.

"Just you."

"Then stop. You're crowding me with your need to swoop in and fix everything. I can figure this out. I already have a plan. Can you just have a little confidence in me?" she pleads.

Damn. She's right.

"Sorry. When you are comfortable enough, will you at least share your ideas with me? I'd like to hear them." I turn the wipers off. My street doesn't even look like it got one drop.

"When I'm comfortable, Kyle, yes." She throws her phone back in her bag as I pull into my driveway.

"Can I just give you my final two cents on this?" I ask, turning the car off.

"What?"

"What if you do indeed have a fantastic idea but I have just the thing to tweak it to make it better? Or, what if I come up with an idea that you hadn't thought of? This is hard for me, Ceese. I'm a closer. That takes a good amount of research to do it well. I'm really good at research. I don't ever think I've missed an angle. You're looking at this as your boyfriend trying to come in and save the day. And, yes, that is partly true but you need to remember that I am a business man with my head in the game at all times. My company does so well because I help Mitch stay at least two steps ahead of the other guys. I just want you to stop and think about that, Ceese. This isn't just what it feels like; I actually know what the fuck I'm doing," I finish.

"That was more than two cents," she laughs. "Kyle, I will think about what you said. You do have a valid point but I like to figure shit out myself. If I can't figure it out, I will come to you, okay?" She lays the side of her head against the seat as she stares at me.

"Okay." I palm her cheek and plant several kisses on her lips. "Ready to go in?"

"Does Pinocchio have a wooden dick?"

I roll my eyes and let out a small laugh. "C'mon, sweet cheeks." I open my door.

"Ugh! Don't call me that," she complains as she climbs out of her side.

"No?" I chuckle.

"No." She looks over her shoulder at me as she walks up to the door.

"Alright. But you know, it would be nice to hear an endearment from you."

"What are you talking about? I have an endearment that I use for you all time."

"*Dipshit* really doesn't fall under that category." I reach past her and unlock the door.

"It does in my book. That name is reserved for the special people in my life." She walks in ahead of me.

Falling . . .

Chapter Eighteen

Playing house . . .

CiCi

I'm going to keep my cool.
I'm going to keep my cool.

I don't think I'm going to be able to keep my cool. I stare at the clock. I have a half an hour until she gets here. Since the day I met her, I have never once been angry with Lindsay. I'm fuming. Yet, I can't be or, at least, I can't project that rage at her. Kyle told me this morning what he discovered that she was doing. God, her intentions were so sweet but this is not how you do things. She invaded my privacy and she needs to understand that while her intentions were great, she really can't do stuff like this. The biggest problem? I am the one who has to correct her on this. Me!

Fuck my life.

What did she do? She took some of my bills and tried to make payments on them. Of course, I didn't notice because I have every bill five times. For some reason, these companies think by simply sending you another bill, stating the same exact thing, that you will magically be able to pull money out of your ass. I haven't shit green since I was a baby. Look, I get it—I really do. She's just trying to be a good friend and at the same time, she's making sure I don't let her go completely. But, man . . . going through my personal shit? That's not okay; it just isn't.

"Bark Avenue," I answer the phone. God only knows how long it was ringing.

"Hey, beautiful," Kyle's sexy voice greets me. I may be willing to admit that my anger and anxiety have just climbed down about ten notches.

"Hey, yourself," I sigh as I sit down and play mindlessly with the phone cord.

"Do you find Mondays a good day to be open for business?"

Is he fucking kidding me, right now?

"If a certain somebody doesn't cut out his shit, I'm going to be closed for business this Monday—know what I'm sayin'?"

"How are you doing?" Smart man, changing the subject like that.

"Freaking out." I tap my pencil continuously onto the appointment book.

"Just try to remain calm. Remember where it's coming from. Then . . ." his voice gets lower, "remember how you woke up on the right side of the bed this morning." I can hear his smile and mine easily matches it. Kyle introduced me to the alarm clock at his house this morning—his tongue. I woke up, coming all over his face; it was beautiful. Honestly, best fucking way to wake up—*ever!* Kyle told me to expect that wake-up call every morning with him. So, if you see me, on any random day, looking like I had my Wheaties, you'll know I spent the night with Kyle. Also, I think I may patent that idea.

Pussy-licking alarm clock.

Fucking gold, right?

"Oh, I remember," I say flirtatiously.

"Mmm," he moans and I get a flash flood warning in my panties. "Yeah, I'll be right there," he calls out to someone. "I've got a meeting I need to get to, sweetness," he says.

"You're just trying them all out there, aren't ya?" I laugh.

"Ugh! Can I call you after lunch?" he asks.

"Sure. Are you going straight to your meeting after hanging up?"

"Yes, why?"

"I just want to tell you something really quick."

"Go ahead."

"There's just one thing I want you to think about while you're in your meeting."

"What's that?"

"My pussy. You've made it so sore that every time I sit, I can feel you thrusting inside of me. I've been here ten minutes, Kyle. I've purposely sat twenty times. Have a good meeting, *babe.*" As I go to hang the phone up, I hear him say, "Jesus Christ, Ceese!" Ahh . . . that ought to make his meeting a little *harder* for him.

A moment later and my phone lights up with a text from him.

YOU ARE FUCKING EVIL!

♥

Just then, Linz walks through the door. As soon as she sees me, her face beams with the biggest smile I've ever seen in my life. *Damn it.* "Hi, Ceese!"

"Hey, Linz." I smile back. I just want to forget the whole thing. I can't though.

"Do we have a busy day today?" she asks as she heads into the back to put her coat and stuff away.

"We have a few on the schedule today," I answer then blow out a big puff of air that I let quiver my lips. Eww . . . what? You know what I mean, right? If not, too fucking bad. I don't have time to sit around here, drawing you diagrams and shit.

"Who's coming in today?" Linz brings my attention back to her.

"Uh . . . some newbies. Hey, listen. We need to talk."

"Oh no, you're not cutting more of my hours, are you?" she asks and seems to be on the verge of crying.

"No." I answer quickly. "However, I realize that your fear of that happening has inspired you to do something you really shouldn't have." I give her the "eye." Only . . . I'm not so sure she speaks "eye." It's really uncomfortable when you run into people who don't speak your language.

"What do you mean, CiCi?"

"Lindsay, I know that you took some of my bills to put money towards them," I say as calmly as possible. Her eyes immediately tear up.

"I just wanted to help. You're my best friend. I didn't want to lose you." She wipes at her tears.

I grab her arms lightly. "I want you to listen to me right now. You will *never* lose me. I really appreciate what you were trying to do, Linz, honestly I do. I need you to understand, though, that what you did, good deed aside, was wrong. You can't take someone else's bills without them knowing and pay them. You're violating that person's privacy. That's what you did to me. I understand why, but you need to understand that it wasn't right or your place to do so." Rant done.

"I'm sorry, CiCi." Her chin quivers. "Am I fired?"

"God, no! I just wanted you to understand why your decision to help me wasn't maybe the best way to go about things. Do you get it?" I sort of cringe. I'm not sure if what I'm saying is actually sinking in. I kind of take for granted that I treat Lindsay like a normal person every day. Sometimes I even forget that she has downs syndrome and I certainly don't know her capacity of understanding certain things.

"I do. I'm sorry if I upset you, Ceese." She hugs me.

"Alright, enough of this now, let's get ready for our clients." I push back a little, smiling at her.

"Okay, boss!" she says and I can tell all of her usual excitement has returned. I'm glad.

"Are you ready to get some real thrusting," Kyle bellows out as soon as he walks through the door. I can hear him as he goes through the house calling for me, and finally finds me sitting at the dining room table. "Ceese? What's wrong, sweetie?" He quickly kneels in front of me and wipes my tears away.

"Addie died today. Cancer. I didn't even know." I say, feeling like I'm in a trance.

"Oh God, sweetie, I'm so sorry. Was she a dog you groomed?"

"What?"

"Was she one of the dogs you groomed?"

"No. She was a friend. She ran the shelter. A family member called the shelter to let them know. The new girl, Megan, called me. She's the one I do the groom-a-thon for. Pearl is her dog. Oh, Pearl. What are they going to do with Pearl?" I start to sob.

"Give me numbers. I will get all the info you need." He pulls a pad out of his briefcase. I nod and give him the only number I have.

"Can we take Pearl if she doesn't have a home?" I ask. I'm not sure why I'm asking him but it just seems right.

"Absolutely. Anything you want, beautiful." He kisses me then grabs the pad and gets out his phone. And just like that—he's on it.

I love him.

Shut up . . . I'm distressed.

She looked tired. Why didn't she tell me? Did I hug her back the last time she hugged me? Did I? Why don't I want to hug people? Did I hug her? Oh God, I can't remember!

"Ceese, I got as much info as they have now. I did find out that you are mentioned in her will." He kneels in front of me.

"What?! Why?" This is too much.

"I don't know, Birkita. You need to be strong." He kisses me. "Pearl is with her family right now," he adds.

"Don't go to Spain," I say it before I even try to correct the thought.

"Oh, Ceese, honey, I have to." He rubs my arms up and down. *Honey?* That's a new one.

"I need you. Please don't go." I start to cry. The thought of him leaving, for God knows how long, is just too much for me right now.

"I have to go. Please understand that I *want* to stay here with you. I'm doing this so I don't have to leave you much in the future," he pleads.

"I. Need. You!" I say forcefully.

"I'll see if I can postpone, is that okay?"

I just nod my head and start crying again before I lay it down on his shoulder.

"First, let's get something to eat in you. Then, I'm going to draw you a nice, hot bath." He kisses my head.

"I tried to take something out to make for dinner but you have all kinds of codes on the packages in the freezer. I didn't understand them so I didn't take anything out."

"Codes?"

"Yes. You have codes written on the packages." I repeat. He starts laughing. "What?"

"Oh, beautiful, those aren't codes," he continues to laugh. "They're dates."

"No. They start out with zeros." I try to correct him.

"Yes, I put zeros in front of single numbers."

"So, pizza?" I ask. I don't understand the point of putting a zero first and I'm too wiped to inquire about it.

"That's fine." He smiles at me.

The doorbell rings.

"Damn, that was quick. I didn't even order yet!"

"Shit! That would be your nephews and niece." He rubs the back of his neck before heading to the door. "Charlotte has an appointment tonight. Mitch is going with her and your mom is too wiped out today. I told them we would watch the kids." He opens the front door.

"Aunt CiCi! I here!" Brooklynn comes barreling towards me. I scoop her up onto my lap.

"Uncle Kyle, do you have a play station?" Brogan asks as he takes his coat off.

Uncle—fucking—Kyle?

I hone in on Kyle's face—he's beaming. I'm trying really hard to breathe through this, right now. But I'm starting to get the cold sweats you get right before you get the shits. "Broge, why are you calling him that? He's not your uncle." I ask him casually (well, I try) as he walks into the dining room.

"He's Mitch's best friend so Mom said he's our uncle now." He shrugs. Shit. I didn't even think of that. In my family, we always respect close family friends with the title of aunt or uncle. I wish I had thought of that before I said anything. I caught Kyle's face as Brogan was answering me. Let's just say it was a mixture of disappointment and anger covered up by a whole big pile of "let's just act like that shit didn't bother me."

I bounce Brooklynn on my lap, making her laugh and direct my attention towards Bennett, who's just walked in. "Benny . . . what's the matter, bud?" I reach out my hand to him.

"I don't wanna eat here!" he cries as he comes in for a hug.

"Why?"

"Cuz' I don't like it here," he continues.

"Honey, you've never been here before." I try to soothe him. It's hard with Bennett. You never know how he's going to accept change. Sometimes we anticipate a big blowout and nothing happens and other times, we think it will be fine and we end up consoling him for hours. "You know what?"

"What?"

"Uncle Kyle and I were just getting ready to order pizza and we will get it from your favorite place, okay?" As I say it, I notice Kyle do a quick roll of his eyes.

"Where are your parents, bud?" he asks Broge.

"We're here, we're here! Sorry!" Charley rushes in. "Where's your bathroom, Kyle?" You can hear the urgency in her voice. I swear my sister has to pee ten times more than the normal amount a pregnant women needs to. She should just live in the bathroom when she's pregnant.

"Go down the hall here and it's the first one on your right." He points.

"Thanks!" She rushes past him.

"Don't dawdle!" Mitch yells after her as he steps into the house. "Sorry, man, I got a little tongue-tied." Mitch waggles his eyebrows at Kyle.

"Hey, kids, why don't you go into the media room and put on some TV. We'll be right in."

"A media room? Cool, where is it?"

"Go through the living room there and you'll see double doors. It's through there." Kyle gives him the info and I put Brooklynn down so she can run after the boys.

"Kyle, since Mitch is here, do you want to ask him about Spain?"

"What about Spain?" Mitch asks as he jerks his head around like he's looking for something.

"Nothing. What are you looking for?" Kyle jerks his head with him. I'd sit here and laugh at these two douchebags but I'm still trying to swallow that fact that Kyle said "nothing."

"I'm hungry, man. You have any snacks?"

"Yeah. Hold on." Kyle heads to the kitchen.

"What's the thing about Spain?"

"Can that meeting be postponed? My friend, Addie, died suddenly and I'm not sure when the funeral is but I'd really like to have Kyle here with me."

"Who died?" Charley asks as she walks back in.

"Addie." I can feel my eyes filling up again.

"What? How? When?" She pulls a seat up next to me.

"She had cancer. I didn't even know. She never told me." I start crying.

"Oh my God, Ceese, I'm so sorry." She hugs me.

"Here, dude." Kyle tosses a small package at Mitch.

"Goldfish, man, really?"

"I like them." He shrugs.

"In individual packets? What are you, five?"

"It's all about calorie control, man. Besides, they go well with Capri Suns." He smirks at him. I see Mitch quickly flick his hand by his throat like he's telling him to shut up. Oh yeah, I know what that's about and I can't help but laugh a little.

"So, Spain?" Mitch opens the package. "I'm going to need about four more of these." He pours it in his mouth.

"What about it? We're good to go," Kyle says. My head jerks back and I stare at him in disbelief.

"CiCi just told us about her friend and that she'd like you to be by her side. I can see what I can do," he offers.

"No." Kyle shakes his head. "That's not a good idea. We made a commitment and we should stick to it. If we start giving mixed messages as far as our commitment level, then companies will stop trusting us. No. I'm good for Spain on Wednesday."

Companies—my ass!

"You know what? He's right. You don't want them to think you can't back up the level of quality in the product you *put* out there. They'll stop believing you and soon enough, stop bothering with you completely." I stare straight at him. I bring my attention back to Charley. "Have a good appointment, sis. I'm gonna go in the other room and order the pizza." I give her a quick hug. I get up and head out.

On the way, I hear Mitch ask, "So, I'm postponing then?"

"Yes." Kyle simply states, although it did sound as if he said it through his teeth.

I order the food then head in by the kids. They, of course, are fighting over what show to watch.

After a few minutes go by, Kyle walks into the media room. He picks up the remote and lowers the volume. "Where did you order the pizza from?"

"Gio's in Hampstead."

"Jesus," he mutters under his breath. "I'll be back in about five hours," he says sarcastically and heads back out.

"Uncle Kyle, wait up!" Brogan chases after.

"Put your coat on!" I yell. "So, what do you guys want to watch?" I ask Bennett and Brooklynn after I hear the front door slam shut.

Slowly, I blink my eyes open. I jump up in a panic and glance around the room. The kids are gone. I get up and race to the door. *I can't believe I fell asleep!* Whipping it open, I hurry across the living room and stop dead in my tracks. Kyle and the kids are sitting at the dining room table, laughing and eating. "Again!" Brooklynn screeches.

"Ugh . . . Oooo kaaay," Kyle says and turns around. When he faces forward again he has two pizza crusts hanging from under his top lip like a walrus. "Do I have something on my teeth, Brooklynn?" he asks her. I wouldn't say the question came out very clear but I'm fluent in Dipshit. Just then, Kyle notices me and pulls the crust from his mouth. "Hi. Are you hungry?" He gives me a warm smile.

"Yeah." I return it.

"Come on over, I have your plate right here." He lifts it for confirmation. Nerd. "Isn't your aunt beautiful?" he asks them as I sit.

"Isn't your uncle a dipshit?" I match his poetic tone.

"Don't worry, Uncle Kyle, she calls everybody she loves a dipshit." Brogan says and I laugh. Charley would fucking kill me right now.

"Not everybody, Broge," Kyle disagrees.

"Yes." I say before I even think about it.

"Yes, what?" Kyle asks.

"Yes, everybody," I say quickly and shove my mouth with food. I can't even look at him right now.

Kyle clears his throat. "So, Mitch told me he's taking you boys to the Sox game this weekend, are you excited?"

"I can't wait!"

"Me too!" Bennett does a little dance in his seat.

"I go!" Brooklynn sings.

"No!" Both boys yell.

Headlights shine into the dining room windows. "Wow, they're back already?" And then we hear them, arguing up the path. "I don't care!" Charley yells as they walk in.

"Jesus, why are you guys arguing so much lately? This isn't like you." I say as soon as they get into the dining room.

"It's because of the white elephant," Charley snaps and grabs a slice of pizza angrily.

"Well, that's just racist."

"What?" she yells at me.

"Nothing." I shake my head. "Holy shit, Mitch, you've got a live one on your hands."

"Please don't stir the fucking pot, Ceese." He throws his hand up in the air.

"Mama sad." Brooky pouts.

"I'm not sad, Brooke." Charley says . . . sadly then starts to cry. "I'm sorry, Mitch." She sobs into his chest. "I'm so all over the place. Fucking hormones."

"Shh . . . shh, baby. I know it's the hormones. I'm not helping though, either." He consoles her. "Everybody finish up and we'll go get Mommy her favorite ice cream." He kisses her head. The kids all cheer. I'm a little jealous. *I want ice cream, goddamn it!*

"You sit and eat, beautiful; I'm going to start cleaning up." Kyle shoots me a wink before getting up to do so. I'd offer to help but I have an inner lazy bitch who holds me back something fierce.

I finish up and walk mi familia to the door. Charley and I watch as Mitch parades the kids down to the car and gets them in. "He's so good to me, Ceese. I wish I could stop snapping at him." Her chin quivers.

"Whoa! He's not always a Miss Suzy Sunshine." I defend her.

"Oh, don't I know it." She widens her eyes. "But with the exception of his foot-to-mouth disorder, he's a wonderful man. He's just not happy about me doing this. He's proud of me but he hates the idea that I am carrying someone else's baby."

"I think that's understandable." I shrug.

"It is. It just doesn't make things any easier. Alright, give me a hug." She puts her arms around me.

"You're lucky we're both tired and cranky tonight or I'd be chewing your ear off about doing all of this behind our backs."

"We wanted to make sure it stuck first. Ava's been through so much, she couldn't handle being asked constantly about this, too." She lets go of me.

"I get it, but still . . ." I trail off.

"I'll talk to you tomorrow. Go have some great make-up sex. That's what I'm going to do!" She clicks her tongue and winks before heading down to the car. I turn around and walk back into the house. I can hear dishes clanking in the kitchen but rather than go in there, I decided to venture back into the media room. There's a whole mess of reality TV I need to catch up on. I'm sure Mr. Belvedere won't mind.

After a while, I hear the water running in the bathroom upstairs. I guess he's decided to take a shower. I have to say, this back and forth with him is getting old already. We both do it and we both need to stop. Kyle's a very intense person. Part of that is definitely due to his OCD. I feel like I'm an item on his life list that he checked off and now we're supposed to automatically act as if we've been together forever. But, at the same time, I need to remember that we have played cat and mouse for several months, we're older, and I sort of love that about our relationship even though it scares me half the time. So maybe it is mostly me. I want this and I'm afraid of it. Poor guy is probably getting whiplash. I know I am.

"C'mon," he says softly, holding his hand out to me. *Jesus!* I didn't even realize he'd come in here. Fucking ninja! I grab his hand and stand up in front of him. Without saying another word, he turns and leads me out of the media room and up the stairs. The butterflies in my belly are going a little haywire and my pussy is tingling. He guides me into the bedroom, right to the master bath. The tub is filled (huge claw foot—it's gorgeous.) and has bubbles. There's candles lit everywhere. *I'm trying my hardest not to ask him why he has all of these candles. But only because they're mismatched in color and sizes.* There is soft music playing in the background. Kyle grabs the hem of my shirt and pulls it up and over my head. He tosses it in the hamper then circles around me. I can feel his hot breath hit my right shoulder before his lips do. My girls breathe a sigh of relief when the pressure of my bra is released. He guides my bra off of me. His hands reach around me and unsnap the button of my jeans. I lay my head back on his shoulder, listening to the sound of him unzipping them. I raise my head back up as he slowly glides them down over my hips. I step out of them as well as my panties.

"Jesus!" I yelp as he nips at my ass. I gasp as I feel his fingers slide between my folds. He groans. My guess—there's no drought.

"Step into the tub, beautiful," he says when he stands back up. I walk towards it and he holds my hand to help me in. "Get your hair wet so I can wash it for you," he says as he picks the remainder of my clothes off the floor and places them in the hamper. I lie back and get my hair completely soaked. I watch as he undresses. I bite the inside of my cheek when he completely unveils himself. His dick looks as solid as steal and I feel the ache in me grow. "Scoot forward so I can get in."

"Well, since you're pointing and all . . ." I slide up and he gets in.

"Now rest back against my chest," he commands gently. This obeying shit is becoming a real habit of mine. After several minutes of just laying here like this, in piping hot water that smells of coconut, I finally feel every nerve ending in my body relax. "Birkita . . . we have to stop behaving this way." His voice is just as soothing as his fingers, leisurely travelling up and down my arms.

"I know," I sigh.

"I get that you're scared. Having feelings for someone is very scary. I know because I feel the same way about you. Purposely hurting each other to protect ourselves is proving to not be a very good idea."

"I know."

"Ok. Well, if you know and I know, then it stops right now. Yes?"

"Yes." I turn my neck to give him a kiss. "Can I ask you a question, though, without you getting upset?"

"Of course, especially when you put it that way," he teases.

"Have you stopped and thought at all this weekend that maybe we're moving a little too fast?" I cringe.

"No. That's society telling you that." He sighs with frustration. "Look, I don't know who the hell came up with the rules as to when the appropriate time your heart should start feeling stuff—it's bullshit. You feel it when you feel it. Ceese, we're in our thirties. We're not some teenage couple having 'I love you more' battles after two days. We both have life experience under our belts—it's different. Besides, I've been chasing you for a few months now. It's not like you haven't gotten to know me at all yet. Is this one of the things that has been bothering you?" he asks as he brings all of my hair over to my left shoulder.

"Yes. It has weighed on my mind."

"Well, tell *it* to shut the hell up. Now, let's get a move on in here because I really want to fuck you." He nips my ear.

"I want to fuck you more." I play.

"No. I want to fuck you more." He chuckles.

Bottom line: we're both gonna be *fucked.*

Chapter Nineteen

Check please!

CiCi

I'm not going to lie. Watching him board that plane right now is just about destroying me. I begged him to stay but he had already put the trip off by almost a week. What a week it has been. Kyle and I, since our talk in the tub, have been solid. No, honestly. Something inside of me just clicked. I know it's only been a week since said clicking but I can't even begin to describe to you how freeing it is. To just say, "fuck it" and throw all of my trust into him . . . into us. Yesterday was the only day we really got into a scuffle—if you want to call it that. You see, by Wednesday night (which coincidentally was Addie's funeral) I was emotionally spent. Between Addie's death, trying to get my head in the game with work, and figuring out the shit with my house, I finally broke down and told him everything: the bills, what I was doing with my house, and my idea for the shop. Kyle was amazing about it all, he really was. He helped me organize everything and make lists. Then, he asked me to move in. Okay, he didn't *exactly* ask me—he told me. I didn't freak out (I *totally* freaked out, but I kept it to myself.). I simply told him that I would think about it. Thursday came and I had to leave work early to go to the reading of Addie's will. She left me Pearl and the shelter. She left the shelter all of her money. Needless to say, her family was pissed and thought I had brainwashed Addie. I don't give a flying fuck, though. They can all kiss my ass. I may have said that while I kissed my two birds off at them before storming out. Immediately following that . . .

I hyperventilated.

Let me tell you a little something I've learned about hyperventilation. When done long enough or quickly enough (not really sure of that equation because why the fuck would I be?) it causes your muscles to contract (picture how your toes curl during an orgasm.). This occurred just as I made it down to the lobby where Maddie and Julie were waiting for me. I didn't know what was happening. Jesus Christ, I thought I was having a stroke. "You're not having a stroke," Maddie said. "Just breathe."

"I. Am. Breathing. Bitch," I said in quick pants.

"No you're not."

"Is there a priest in the house?" Julie yelled; spinning around to look or to turn into Wonder Woman—either was a possibility. "My friend, here, needs an exorcism!" She then, opened her bottle of water and started to shake it so it would splash on me. "The power of Christ compels you! The power of Christ compels you!" she yelled. Now to get full appreciation of the scene displayed before strangers, you must understand what my hands looked like as I raised them at her, yelling. They were gnarled up as if I had been suffering from Rheumatoid Arthritis for twenty years without a single dose of treatment. I couldn't pick my nose if I wanted to! All I needed was a witch's cackle. Those bitches laughed their asses off in between telling me to breathe and taking pictures of me. *Fucking assholes!* In any case, yelling was the sure fire thing to get me breathing correctly and I was miraculously cured. I immediately posted one of the pics to my Facebook timeline. What? It was fucking funny—after the fact.

So, moving on here. Thursday night, Kyle came home and I unloaded everything on him. As if I wasn't stressed enough about my business, now I had to worry full-time about the shelter. Kyle didn't miss a beat; he comforted me right away and assured me that everything would be all right. He also took about two minutes flat to fall in love with Pearl. He even told her that he was going to be her daddy now. Don't worry, I told him never to say that to her again. In other news, Pearl, we've learned, is a visual fucker as well! How did we discover this? Ha! Kyle was balls deep, pounding me. It was so good. *Fuck me—it was sooo good!* He held my legs down on either side of my head like he always does when he fucks me this deep. And when this is happening, I grunt and groan with every thrust. Every time he would thrust in and I would grunt, she would yelp simultaneously with my grunt. Sometimes she would even yelp right before I did. And when I came hard and let out a prolonged cry of "ooooooh oooooh" like I was singing the chorus of a New Kids on The Block song, she howled with me.

Friday—Pearl got her own bedroom.

You know what else happened Friday? A guy in front of me switched to the other lane just as the light turned green. The douchebag that was in front of him, for some reason unbeknownst to everyone, had his car in reverse. He hit the accelerator and, having enough room and good pick up, slammed right into my car. When Hondas get hit in the front, the engine drops and the car is totaled. Silver lining? Kyle pampered the shit out of me and I get to use his car while he's gone.

Then Saturday came and our scuffle. We stopped by my house only to find a shitload of people coming in and out, placing things on a moving truck. I jumped out of his car and raced inside, cursing the whole way because I was sore from the accident. I started screaming obscenities at these people until Kyle grabbed me by the arm to get my attention. "Ceese, I paid for them to come here and pack up your house. I wanted you to have one less thing to worry about. They are moving this all to our house and they will unpack it for you there." He waited for my response. I was fuming. I told him I was going to think about moving in. I didn't say yes. This is how the rest of the argument went (all one-sided, mind you).

Me: "Dude!"

Him: Eye fuck.

Me: "I love your house," I conceded due to soakage of my panties from said eye fuck.

Him: Smirk.

Me: "I'm gonna go change my panties."

Kyle helped me usher myself into the bathroom. He also helped strip me of my panties and bend over my sink vanity so he could fuck me from behind.

Banner fucking week, huh?

Now today, I had to say goodbye and only God knows how long he'll be gone for.

Three weeks and counting . . .

Pulling clothes out of the dryer, I hear the chime for Skype ringing through my laptop in the bedroom. I hurry up and run to the bed, plopping on my stomach and hitting accept. Kyle flashes up on my screen. I may have sighed.

"Hey, beautiful." He smiles.

"Hey, yourself." I push the laptop back a little. And then . . .

We stare.

Lips (his) and inside of cheeks (mine) are bit.

Smirks are made.

"Shut-up!" I say. It's become a habit of mine to say this after we stare for a while.

"I can't help it, there's so much to say." His usual reply. Thing is, at night (my time), we have nothing left to say because we talk constantly throughout the day. So we just take this time to connect visually. Sometimes we have a continuation of the day's events that we'll share. But mostly, it's just us looking at each other and exchanging how badly we want to be together. The subject of video sex comes up—*all the time.* I won't do it. I have no problem with phone sex. I just can't do the video. He asks me why and I give him the same answer—personal choice. He's not happy with that answer but he sucks it up.

"So, I have some good news." He rubs his eyes.

"How do you already have any news when it's six in the morning there?"

"The meeting for today got cancelled."

"You're coming home!" I practically screech.

"Well, no, not exactly." He rubs the back of his neck. "There's an issue in Germany. I'm flying there today."

"Listen, you can't solve Germany's problems. Don't they have a president or something there?" I'm not going to lie—I'm pissed.

"Beautiful, are you talking about Germany as a whole or are you on the same page as me and know we're discussing our plant there?" I can see he's trying to fight a laugh; he's not doing a very good job.

"Of course I mean your plant, dipshit." I lie. "Don't you have a head asshole in charge over there?" I ask.

He eyes me suspiciously but I think he decides to let it go. "We do, but he's clearly not doing what he's supposed to be doing. I need to head over for damage control. I'm sorry, Ceese." his shoulders slump.

"How long?" I look away. I don't want him to see me tearing up. Not to sound like a selfish bitch here, but I've got a lot going on and am more than ready to throw in the towel and let him help me in a more hands on approach (both on and off the court—know what I'm sayin'?). Ok, fine, I'm being a selfish bitch. Whatever; I'll own that shit. I just want him home.

"I don't know. I will try to get home to you as soon as possible. Hey!" He sits up straight. "Come out here!"

"What? Kyle, I can't come out there!" He is out of his damn mind.

"Why? You're not that busy, close the shop for a few weeks."

"I have bills that need to get paid. I have a shelter I am now in charge of. Oh, and I'm trying to sell my house. Do you really think taking off to Germany so lady boom boom can get some action is really a good idea?"

"I think I just fell for you a little harder . . ." he trails off.

"Huh?"

"Lady boom boom." He bites back his smile.

"Stay focused, please," I plead. He sighs then does a little shiver. "Jesus Christ, are you breaking out the riverdance now?"

"What?" He laughs. I imitate him. He laughs harder. "I miss the hell out of you, Birkita," he says as he comes down from his laughing fit.

"I miss you, too." I frown.

"Then come."

"I'd love to come." I waggle my brows at him.

"Ugh!" he grunts. "C'mon, say you will."

"I don't have a passport." My hands fly out in emphasis.

"How is that even possible?"

"I stick to my turf." I shrug.

"Where's that—in the middle of *West Side Story?*"

"Haha, very funny, asshole."

"Get the notepad with all of your lists in it." He shuffles his finger at me. I roll my eyes, him and his fucking "lists." I get up on my knees then reach over to the nightstand drawer where my trusty notepad is. "Stretch a little more," he says softly. I jerk my head back to see him checking me out. So now I gotta get all dramatic and shit. I shift my knees so that he gets a full view of my ass. I will neither confirm nor deny that I may be moving in such a way that would be suggestive of getting it from behind. "Fuck and Jesus Christ," Kyle says under his breath. Oh, I should probably mention that I'm only in my lacy G-string. While we're on the subject—I hate these fuckers! I'm only wearing them because I ran out of my usual faves. Hence: laundry night. I don't feel sexy wearing them; I feel like I need to pick my wedgie—all day! Kyle, apparently, does not agree with me. I hear Kyle let out a low groan and I suddenly don't feel very good. I look over my shoulders and there he is . . . working things out on his end. I immediately turn to my laptop and shut it.

I sit in silence.

For about one minute till my phone sounds as if it will explode. It rings. It buzzes. It chimes. It sings. Wait for it . . . wait for it. It vibrates. I open my notepad to my list of things to do.

22. See a therapist.

The house phone starts. Not sure why he even has one since he's *never* home. I finally take it off the receiver. I know this seems like very odd behavior on my part but if you only knew . . .

Ten minutes goes by and my cell rings again. I glance at it and see that it's Charley.

"What the hell is going on?" she asks as soon as I answer.

"What do you mean?" Always play dumb first—just in case.

"Kyle is a mad man right now!" she yells in a whisper.

"Why?" Always get more info—just in case.

"Ceese, he thinks you have another guy there!" Urgent whisper.

"What?! No!" I sit up quickly. "Why the hell would he think that?"

"He said you abruptly ended your skype call with him and won't answer him on any outlet."

"So his first assumption is that I'm cheating on him?" My heart just dropped to the floor, people.

"No, but it's the one sticking out the most. Look, Mitch is on the phone with him now, trying to calm him down. What the hell happened?"

"Tell Mitch to tell him that I will talk to him tomorrow. Also, that I would appreciate it if he would just drop this. It was totally my fault and had nothing to do with him." I give her as much truth as I can.

"What does *this* have to do *with,* Ceese?" I can hear her frustration. I'm right there with her.

"Just tell him." I hang up. I immediately text Maddie.

I need to see you for an office visit tomorrow.

I can't hang out tomorrow.

No. I need a real office visit. I'm ready to talk.

I have 9am.

Ok.

I love you. It's going to be ok.

Ok.

Is it, though? Is it really going to be ok? I've let something like this affect me for fifteen years now. Am I really going to go into Maddie's office tomorrow, tell her everything, and magically—all will be well? My phone chimes to the beat of a text. I look. It's from Kyle.

I don't know what happened tonight. I'm sorry for my part, though, if I made you feel uncomfortable. It's just . . . I miss you so much. I miss touching you.

You are the only one I want.

I'm sorry I thought differently for a moment.

I'll fix this.

I wish I knew what you were REALLY talking about.

Goodnight.

Goodnight, beautiful.

And with that, I plug my phone into the charger, get dressed for bed, make sure the house is locked up and security system on. I climb into bed and pray that I will find sleep soon.

"I love you, baby," Drew murmurs against my neck.

"I love you, too."

"Are you sure you're ready for this?" He brings his head up to stare into my eyes.

"Yes. I am, Drew. I love you so much." I slide my hands up his arms and thread my fingers into his hair, pulling him to me for another kiss. He reaches down and finds the hem of my dress. He kneels in front of me on the bed, allowing me to sit up so he can pull my dress off.

"You're so beautiful, Ceese," he says breathlessly as he runs his hands up my legs. I unhook my bra and listen to him groan as I lie back down. His hands immediately cover my breasts and I arch my back to his touch. I feel them slide down to the waist of my panties. He tugs and I lift my ass off the bed. Drew wastes no time yanking his clothes off. Between playing football and working out, he's got a great build.

"Gah Drew!" I gasp when I feel his hot tongue licking up my center. Holy shit! Drew has fingered me before but he's never gone down on me. Umm . . . ok, I don't think Drew has ever gone down on anybody before because this feels a little uncoordinated and sloppy. I sort of want him to stop. "Drew, please." I beg. He stops slobbering on me and climbs his way up my body, stopping to suck at my nipples. Mmm . . . that's nice.

"Did that feel good, baby? Did you like it when I licked your pussy?" he asks before he kisses me.

"Mm hmm," I lie. But that's what you do when you're in love, right?

"Are you ready? This may hurt you a little." He rubs his dick up and down my lips and I feel a deep ache in me grow.

"Yes," I pant.

"I love you, baby. I love you so much. I can't wait to make you my wife." And with that, he plunges into me. I grab at the sheets as

my head arches back. My mouth is open but no sound is coming out. "God, baby, you're so tight," he groans near my ear. I'm never going to walk again after this. "Baby, I need to move." He starts to pull out and then plunges in again. I feel like I'm being torn in two. "Baby, you need to relax." He does it again.

"Wait. Wait. Oh God, please wait, Drew," I plead. He's not giving me enough time to acclimate.

"Are you ok, baby?"

"No. It hurts." I whimper.

"I know, baby. It will feel better in a minute, I promise." He kisses me. I open my mouth at the beckoning of his tongue. I moan slightly, enjoying the simplicity of this kiss. But then he pulls back and thrusts again. My yelp breaks our kiss. "Shh . . . shh," he soothes me and pumps a little quicker. I'm actually glad—I want this to be over with. Finally, after a few moments, I relax, realizing it's not so bad anymore. I'm also able to move my hips with his. "That's it, baby . . . that's it." He wraps my leg around his waist and I groan at the newer fullness. Before I know it . . .

"God, Ceese—yes!"

That's it? Wasn't I supposed to have a "come to Jesus" moment? No. This must be wrong. I've watched videos with Jay. I'm supposed to be making an "O" face right now. This is it?

"Oh, baby, God I'm so in love with you." He lifts his head off my chest. "Thank you." He smiles, kisses my nose, pulls out, and rolls onto his back.

"Drew, I think you punctured something," I say in a panic as I feel the blood pour out of me. Drew looks between my legs (God, how embarrassing.) and bites back his smile. His fingers start probing me. "What are you doing?"

"This is so fucking hot, baby."

"Me, bleeding to death is hot?" I practically yell.

"Baby, that's not your blood." He swirls it around then plunges his fingers in again. "That's my come, pouring out of you. It's fucking hot as hell."

"You came in me?" I feel the panic rise up in me.

"You're on the pill, baby. It'll be fine." He kisses me. "C'mon, we need to get dressed and head out before all the guys get home."

"Oh, ok." I sit up . . . ow. Within a few minutes we are dressed

and heading down the stairs.

As soon as we are outside of his Frat house, he stops me and pulls me into his arms. "Are you okay, Ceese?" He pulls back and there is concern painted all over his face. He seems more like him than he was twenty minutes ago.

"I'm ok." I offer him a meek smile.

"I love you so much. I never want to do anything to hurt you. You are the love of my life, baby." He palms my face and I can't help but feel concerned with the pained look in his eyes.

"Are you ok?" I grasp his wrists as he continues to hold my face.

"Yes. I'm sorry. I'm just stressed out with this whole Fraternity thing. I suddenly have the feeling that you were very right about me not bothering to join." He lays his forehead against mine.

"Don't worry, Drew, you'll get in!" I try to boost his confidence.

"Oh, I'm pretty sure I will—that's what I'm worried about." He gives me a quick kiss and then let's go of my face so we can continue to walk. I don't really understand where this is coming from. That's been his biggest focus for this year; to get into the same fraternity his dad was in. He didn't get in last year and it about destroyed him. Drew's top priority, in the year I've known him, has always been to make his dad proud. I will never understand this since his dad is such a fucking prick. I don't even think the man knows he has a son. I know Drew is going to be different with our kids. He talks about it all the time. Maddie says Drew's behavior is pretty typical for kids who have parents that are self-absorbed, never taking notice of anything unless it directly affects them.

Douchebags.

"May I take your order?" The guy behind the window at the ice cream shop asks. I look up and see Kyle with a Hitler mustache. What the fuck?

"She can't have any ice cream, Kyle, because she threw our baby away, didn't you, Ceese?" Drew says from beside me.

"What?"

"You threw our baby away!" he yells.

I sit up, screaming.

It was just a dream.

It was just a dream.

I look over at the clock and see that it's a little after seven in the morning. No time to sit here and cry. I need to get a shower and get ready to see Maddie. I'm so thankful I called her last night. I need to talk to her more now than ever.

Chapter Twenty

What is . . . I need to find this bastard?

Kyle

"Who is Constantine the Great?"

"What is the Scientific Method?"

"What is Meroitic?"

Little known fact about me: I win *Jeopardy!* every week. My parents tell me all the time that I should go on there. I'd probably choke up. Instead, I sit in hotel rooms, watching it on my laptop and yelling out the answers. It amazes me that I know the names of ten different extinct languages but I know not a damn thing about what my girlfriend is going through. I'm not sure I'll ever know . . . if I depend on her to tell me.

I take in a deep breath. "Fuck it." I'm going to do this. She doesn't need to know. I fire up the program to do a background check. That's just step one. I put in all the info I have on him, which is not much. I do know that they went to Tufts together and I know his name—that's a good start.

My phone starts to ring and the only reason I am prying myself away is because I'm hoping it's CiCi. Instead, it's my dad.

"Hey, Dad, what's going on?"

"Uh, Kyle?"

"Yeah, Dad?"

"Mom's in the hospital. She had a slight heart attack today." He sounds so somber.

"What?! Is she ok? What are they doing for her?" I jump up in a panic and start repacking the suitcase I've just unpacked.

"She's in surgery right now. They're putting a stent in the blocked artery," he says in his most calming tone. "I will call you as soon as she comes out."

"I'm going to get the jet ready and head home."

"Kyle, you can't do anything right now. You finish what you're supposed to be doing. I'll keep you posted." he reiterates.

"Like hell, Dad! I need to be by my mother's side—that's what I need to be doing!" I yell. I know I shouldn't yell. I'm just upset.

"Alright, son, whatever you think is best. I called CiCi and asked her to take Linz and Mickey for the night." He sighs. "I'm just so grateful that they were able to help her at the hospital. They've all been wonderful." He gets choked up.

"Was Linz there when this happened?"

"No. She was at the shelter, volunteering. She doesn't know."

"It's going to be fine, Dad. I'm going to call Mitch now."

"Okay, son. Talk soon. I'll leave a message if you're in the air."

"It should go through, Dad. Either way, I'll touch base with you soon." And with that, I hang up and dial Mitch.

"Hey, I was just going to call you," he answers.

"You already heard about my mother?" How the fuck does he know before me?

"No. What are you talking about?"

"My mother had a heart attack today. They're operating on her now. I need to bail, man. Can you fly out here and deal with this shit? I need to be with my mother." I pace back and forth, not that I think Mitch would say no to me.

"Well, that's already a done deal."

"Huh?"

"I was just going to call you and tell you that we're switching out duties. I'm flying there in the morning," he says quietly.

"Why? What's going on?"

"It's CiCi."

"What?! What's the matter with CiCi?!" I yell. This only makes my newly formed headache pulse harder.

"She's ok," he says hesitantly. "Look, man, she went in to talk to Maddie about some things. Maddie called Charlotte and asked her to see if I could get you home. She wouldn't tell her what they discussed but she really feels strongly that you need to be here while she's going through all of whatever the hell it is she's going through," he finishes.

"Okay."

"You all right?"

"I'm not sure but I'm going to call Erica now to get the jet ready. Not sure how feasible that will be since we only landed here this morning. If the pilot hasn't slept at all today, I may be stuck here till tomorrow morning." I throw my shoes into their bag a little more aggressively now that I've realized my possible predicament.

"Nah, man. You're all set. The jet's ready to go."

"Thank Christ," I sigh.

"Well, thank him later; you gotta get to the airport in an hour. I'll catch you on the other end! Fly safe!"

"Ok, Mitch. Later!" We hang up and I get the rest of myself packed. Erica, our assistant, texts me that my car will be downstairs, waiting. I grab my stuff and am out the door.

I tried to sleep on the plane, knowing the time difference would kill me, but I couldn't. Between worrying about my mother, whom thankfully made it through surgery ok, and wondering what the hell CiCi revealed to Maddie. Now in the car, I'm completely wiped out. I need to stop by the hospital first, just to see with my own two eyes that she's ok. Luckily, it's a short ride from the Manchester airport. The driver pulls up and drops me off in the front of Catholic Medical Center. I head up to ICU.

"Dad," I whisper and shake his shoulder. He jolts awake

"Hey, son." He stands up and hugs me.

"How is she?"

"Sleepy. She's been awake a few times but only for a few minutes. I thought you were going to head straight home."

"Nah, Dad. I needed to see her first." I shake my head and head over to my mother. She's sleeping soundly. I give her a kiss on her head. "I love you," I whisper. I feel my father's hand on my back. I turn to him. "Can they bring you in a cot or something?"

"I'm alright. You know me; I can sleep upside down if I wanted to." He chuckles a bit.

"I'll be back in the morning. What do you want me to tell Linz?"

"I'm not sure. Talk to CiCi and ask her what she thinks. I just couldn't deal with her knowing today. I know it was wrong of me but I was a little beside myself."

"Dad, I get it; you don't have to explain." I pull him in for a hug. "I'm just sorry I wasn't here to help you through all of this. This must have been terrifying for you."

"You're here now, Kyle, that's all that matters. Now, go home to your sweetie." He pats my upper arms.

"Ok. I'll see you tomorrow," I say then turn to my mother again. "I'll see you in the morning, Mom. Get better." I kiss her on the forehead and leave.

It's a nice, crisp fall evening. Thanksgiving is just a few weeks away and boy do I have a lot to be thankful for. My driver pulls up. I rush in and tell him to take me home.

The twenty-minute drive seems to take forever. I can't wait to touch her . . . smell her skin. If I close my eyes and concentrate hard enough, I can smell the scent of her lotion. Uh, finally! "Thanks, Teddy!" I pat his shoulder and get out of the car.

"Mr. Cooper, your luggage, sir!" he calls after me.

"Shit, sorry!" I smile and turn back to meet him at the trunk. He hands me my suitcases and says goodnight before I run off. I unlock the door and walk in, ready to punch the code for the alarm.

"Kyle?" CiCi stops short as soon as she sees me.

"Hey, beautiful." I smile, flipping the cover back up on the alarm pad.

She runs to me and I drop the rest of my bags before she jumps up on me, wrapping her legs around my waist. "I can't believe you're here!" She kisses me over and over. "I've missed you so much." Now my face. I'm not going to lie . . . I wasn't expecting *this* kind of reception but damn if it doesn't make my heart bounce all over the place.

"Hey . . . hey, why are you crying?" I finally take notice.

"I just really needed you today and well . . . here you are, like my knight in shining armor." Her chin quivers as she tries to calm down.

"Of course I'm here, and just so you know, I was coming home today anyway. I was switching with Mitch. Unfortunately, I ended up with two reasons to come home." I frown. She doesn't need to know that my coming home was Maddie's doing. All she needs to know is that when she *needs* me, I'll be there.

"Really?" She sniffs. "Oh, Kyle, I'm so sorry about your mom. I tried to see her today but I didn't have a good window; she was still in surgery. I haven't told Linz yet but I don't like keeping this from her. Why are you looking at me like that?" She finally shuts the hell up.

"Where's my sister?"

"In bed, sleeping."

"Are you sure?"

"Yes. I checked on her a half an hour ago," she says and I see her beautiful green eyes turn a shade darker.

Oh, we are so on the same page, right now.

My lips attack hers and we're like wildfire, spreading. She yanks at my jacket as I climb the stairs with her. I hold her with one arm, releasing the other so she can pull the sleeve off. I switch hands. Once my jacket is off, she tears at my shirt—buttons fly everywhere.

Yes, I want to stop and clean up the buttons.

I don't think that'll go over well, though.

I run a little faster up the stairs when she moans how badly she needs me. I don't know where the fuck this energy is coming from. Actually, I do . . . but if I explain it to you, it would bring the sexy meter down and we don't want that, do we? I bust through our bedroom door. Shit! I go back and close it nicely, locking it. Not an easy feat when the woman you love is sucking the ever-loving-crap out of your earlobe. I collapse onto the bed with her and immediately yank her pajama shirt off of her.

Boobies!

Shut up—it's been a while!

I attack them, simultaneously pulling at her bottoms. She pulls my undershirt off then goes right for my pants. "Please, I need you right away," she begs. Look, I'm ready to bust at the seams now; I'm more than ok with no foreplay. "Come in me; we're good to go," she adds.

Lord, it may happen before, if she doesn't *shut-up.*

I yank her bottoms off. I let out a ferocious groan. *Just fuck her, don't lick her. Just fuck her, don't lick her.*

Lick.

Lick. Suck. Lick.

Groan.

Lick. Kiss. Lick.

"Kyle!" she yells.

"Okay, okay!" I travel up her body—*licking*. Finally, my eyes meet hers and it just washes over me.

"Don't say it," she whispers looking straight back. How did she know? How did she know it was on the tip of my tongue? I close my eyes.

I love you.

"Okay." I say instead. I lean down and collect her lips. She brings her legs up higher, encircling my waist.

"Please," she begs against my lips. Just a little shift and I thrust into her. Her body arches like it always does. I take her slow and deep, showing her how much I love her instead of telling her. Every time she opens her mouth to oppose my pace, I shut it with mine. Finally . . . she gives in and regulates her hips to my pace.

After several minutes, CiCi starts clenching down on me. I groan in appreciation. "Oh God . . . Oh, Kyle!" she moans sinking her nails into my back. Her legs, shaking, around my waist. I let go, pounding into her harder—finding my release. I should mention that she was egging me on, telling me how good her pussy will feel, loaded with my come. I know, right? How could I hold it any longer? I collapse on her chest and we lay her like this for several minutes. It's soothing—listening to her breathe, feeling her in my arms—I'm in heaven.

I look up at her. She greets me with a warm smile. "I love you." There—I said it.

"I'm so in love with you," she admits with shaky breath. I reach up and palm her face before I caress her lips. Somehow, when I kiss her this time—so different. Good different. Forever different. I reach under and engulf her in my arms, nestling my head on her chest . . .

Mom's been in the hospital a few days now and they've finally moved her into a regular room. CiCi, Lindsay, and I are on our way up to visit her. "I hope her roommate isn't a douchebag," CiCi says.

"I'm sure you'll find reason to believe she is." I tease her. She laughs then elbows me. I have to say—I'm the happiest I can ever remember being. CiCi and I have been *amazing*. In and out of the bedroom, of course. "Best behavior, please," I beg as we enter the room.

"Yeah . . . sure." She laughs.

"Hey, Mom!" I greet her, overzealously paired with a huge grin as we walk in.

"Oh, Kyle, knock it off! I'm fine!" Her hands push away nonsense at us.

"How do you like your new room?" CiCi asks.

"Love it," Mom says cheerfully. She then mouths "Pain in the ass" and points to the person on the other side of the curtain. I'll tell you right now; this person must be bad if my mother is saying something like this. It's either that or surgery has changed her. In all fairness, we can hear her whimpering and complaining.

"What's going on over here?" CiCi walks over and asks.

"Ceese!" I say in a hushed whisper.

"I'm sorry, Miss, my mother is having a hard time adapting." The gentleman says.

"What's wrong, ma'am?"

"Ceese!" I try again. All she does is draw back the curtain.

"How can I live?" The woman cries.

"What happened?" CiCi inquires.

"They want me to be all sunshine and flowers when this is my life now!" The woman screams.

"What's up, buttercup?" CiCi continues. Christ, I wish she would just come back over here.

"Look at this!" she yells and pulls back her covers. I look because how the fuck can I not? And I see that she has had her foot amputated. "They want me to carry on like life is so wonderful! They are all avoiding what has happened to me, as if I'm supposed to forget! Look!" she yells. "What do you see, miss?" She points at her missing foot.

"It looks to me like you have one foot in the grave," CiCi says without any hesitation. I want to fucking die right now. I'm just not sure if it will be from embarrassment or laughter. The woman just stares at her for a while and then, she breaks out in such a hearty laugh it seems to scare her family. "You know, I know a great nail tech. I'm sure she will give you half off. I mean, you are giving her half the work, right?" CiCi offers. The woman is rolling.

"Thank you, miss." The woman is practically in tears—serious ones this time. "Thank you for stating the obvious. These bozos are acting as if nothing happened, like I would forget if they did so." She reaches to hug CiCi. I laugh to myself, knowing inner CiCi is cringing right now. But my girl does it; she goes in for the hug. I'm a proud man, right now.

She makes her way back over to us. "I love you," I say in awe. She blows me a kiss and gives me a wink.

"Backatcha, handsome!" I love how open she's been about her feelings. I'm just as scared, though.

"This makes my heart so happy; seeing you two." Mom smiles at both of us.

"I don't think you're alone there, Mom." I grab her hand and kiss the back of it.

"I knew from the moment I met you, CiCi." Mom reaches out her hand to her. CiCi gives her a shy smile and pushes her hair behind her ear. *There's something so sweet and innocent about her when she gets embarrassed like this.* "You're really made from special stuff."

"Thanks, I'll tell my dad you said so," she replies. *And . . . there it goes, as quickly as it came.* Mom smacks the back of her hand, teasingly. "So when are we busting you out of this joint?"

"Well, if I'm a good girl, they said maybe tomorrow."

"You better behave yourself then!"

Mom just lies there, staring at us. She grabs my hand with her free one and brings it together with Ceese's. We both sit on the bed, on either side of her, holding hands on her lap. "I can't tell you how heart happy I am, right now." She tears up.

"Oh no, we're not doing any tears, lady. We purposely came in at this hour because it's the no crying hour." CiCi shakes her head.

"I love you," Mom says through her free running tears, completely ignoring CiCi's comment.

"I love you, too, Winnie Cooper. I have a question, though."

"What's that, dear?"

"You say you love me but . . . what would you do if I sang out of tune?"

"I'd sing back up . . . just as badly." She laughs.

"I wish I met you last year."

"Why?" Mom laughs apprehensively. We've all gotten used to CiCi's quips. You never really know what is going to come out of her mouth.

"Because, I would've totally thrown you a twenty-fifth anniversary party! I mean twenty-five years of having a name that is the pun of many a cheesy joke—that's epic!" She whips her hand out to emphasize.

"Well, we'll do it for the thirtieth!" Mom suggests. CiCi gets quiet. I have a feeling I know why. Mom just implied that CiCi will still be here with me in four years, without question. I can't imagine anyone else in her shoes. The question is—does she? She fought her feelings for me for so long that it's hard for me to squash these insecurities that rise.

"You promise me that you will do everything in your power to make sure you're here for it and I promise you that people will talk about that party for *years.*" CiCi's voice shakes. My heart just did a flip in my chest. Her hesitation had nothing to do with her being unsure about us and everything to do with worry over my mother's health.

"No expense spared," I add before planting a kiss on Ceese's shoulder.

"Why is everybody crying?" Linz asks once she sees us.

"Where did you go?" I ask her as I wipe my unshed tears away.

"With Daddy to the gift shop. I bought Mickey this stuffed animal last time and he already tore it into shreds. He cried for it today but I had thrown it away." She waves the puppy at us. "Why are you all crying? Is everything ok, Mom?" She furrows her brow.

"Everything is fine, Linz," I answer for our mother. "We're all just really happy to be together and to be family." As I say this, I squeeze Ceese's hand so she knows I'm including her in on this statement. She squeezes back and kisses my cheek.

"Speaking of family, Kyle and I want to have everyone over for dinner when you're feeling better. I want you to meet my parents. You've already met my sister. Also, she'll be the one cooking—you two can bark recipes out at each other like it's a competition." She reaches for Mom's pillow. "Sit up," she commands. Mom sits up and CiCi fixes the sheet on it and flips it before returning it behind my mother. "There." She holds it until mom rests back.

"I'd love that! I've heard wonderful things about your parents." Mom beams.

"They are awesome. I'm really lucky. I can see you all hitting it off."

Just then, my phone rings. I look down and see that it's the P.I. in Washington; the one I hired to find Drew. My search results didn't get me much further than the state he was living in. Not sure why, I've never come across that problem before. Don't ask me what I plan on doing with all of this information because I really don't know. Whatever it is, it can't be something that will fuck up my relationship with her. I won't lose her over this piece of shit. Yes, I know I should wait for her to be ready to tell me what happened—I will. I just need to know where this son of a bitch is for when she does. "I gotta take this, beautiful." I give her a quick kiss before letting go of her hand and heading out of the room.

"Cooper," I state when I answer. No, I don't normally answer my phone like this; but being in P.I. mode, I feel it's fitting. Simmons begins to fill me in on his findings. I listen while quietly asking the nurse for a pen and paper. I see why it was hard to dig up much info on him; Simmons believes his job with military defense gave him top clearance. He's not even sure of his exact title. He was able to uncover that Drew is married with two daughters. The last piece of information he gives floors me. "Okay, thanks, Simmons, I'll send the rest of your payment now." And with that, I hang up.

"Hey, sweetie," CiCi calls out to me. *Sweetie?—that's nice.* "Your mom wants to take a nap, are you done with your call?" She walks over to me. "Hey, what's wrong? You don't have to fly somewhere, do you?" I can hear the panic in her voice at that possibility.

"No. Sorry. I just got news that I wasn't expecting on a lead. It's ok, though, nothing to worry about." I open my arms to her, wrapping them around once she walks into my space. I stand here and hold her for a few minutes. I always wanted to feel this way about someone, I just wasn't sure it was ever going to happen. It's amazing; the best feeling in the world.

"C'mon, let's say goodbye to your mom so she can get some sleep." She looks up at me.

"Sure thing." I kiss her.

Chapter Twenty-One

Family, friends, and holidays—oh my!

Kyle

I love mornings . . . you know why?

Lick.

Lick. Kiss. Lick.

Bite.

Groan and repeat.

"Jesus, Kyle—*Jesus!*" she screams out. Mmm . . . she's awake—it's on now! My arms slide underneath her thighs and wrap around. I pull back on her hood and have at her. And by that, I mean aggressive tongue fucking—just the way she likes it. I chuckle lightly as she goes all Linda Blair, thrashing on her end of things. And now . . . the back massage. Ahh . . . What's that, you ask? Mmm . . . CiCi always rests her feet on my back when I do this. And, for some reason, when she gets close, she starts rubbing them up and down my back like she's actually climbing a rope. It not only cues me that she's close, but it also gives me an awesome massage. Of course, she denies that she does this. I don't argue with her because I'm not really interested in her *not* doing it.

She whimpers.

You have no idea the power her whimpers hold over me. It takes everything in me not to come on the spot. This morning, I'm pulling out the big guns to prevent the inevitable—I picture the real life cat lady. You know the one I'm talking about; she had all of those surgeries to look like a cat. She creeps me out.

Whimper. Cry. Begging whimper.

I tear myself away from her and off the bed. I pace and take deep breaths with my hands on top of my head. I bring my attention back to her when I hear her moan. Her hand is in between her legs, rubbing ferociously as her pelvis rises like she's fucking the air. Good God, she's beautiful. I rush over to her and pull her hand away as soon as I climb on the bed, kneeling before her. I wrap her legs around my waist and slam into her. She gasps as if someone is cutting off her air supply. Like a fucking teenage boy, getting a piece of ass for the first time, I unload inside of her in the matter of a few fast pumps. It's all good, though; she was already there, and I just sealed the deal, hitting her in the right spot. I collapse on top of her. "What you fucking do to me, CiCi—what you fucking do," I pant.

"Do you know what you do?" She matches my rapid breathing. "You give good tongue fuck, Kyle—good tongue fuck."

I look up at her and bite back my smile. "I'm glad you're happy with my services, ma'am."

"Yes. You are the best alarm clock I've ever owned." She wipes my sweaty bangs off my forehead.

"Oh, you own me now?" I laugh lightly.

"I've got the receipt around here somewhere."

"You kept the receipt? Why, in case you want to return me?"

"Psh yeah! What if you break? Other than that, you're a tax write-off."

"First of all, if I break, it'll be your fault what with how hard you ride my cock sometimes. Second of all, how am I a tax write-off?" I play along. I love the shit that comes out of her mouth. She never has to stop and think; it just flies right out as if she's rehearsed it a million times.

"First of all, you're the best riding cock I've ever had." She winks. See how that shit just flies. Instead of riding crop—cock; amazing. "Second of all, you're a tax write-off because you are medicine to my soul—healing me. Everyday my heart gets stronger, more trusting—freer. I love you, Kyle. I love you more than I ever thought it was possible to love someone." She lightly plays with my hair, avoiding my eyes.

"Marry me." Holy fuck—I just said that out loud, didn't I? I am completely in awe at what she just said to me. I wasn't expecting that at all. I think it clouded my judgment. Oh, I definitely want her to be my wife—don't get me wrong. I'm just afraid that asking that simple, yet fully loaded, question may just be the thing that sets us back. The fact that I have all of this time to have these thoughts, because she's not saying anything, pretty much confirms my fear. "I'm sorry. I shouldn't have . . . let's just get up and take our shower. We have to get the turkeys in the oven. Everybody's going to be here in a few hours," I ramble on.

"Yes."

I take in a quick, shaky breath. "What?"

"Yes." She palms my face. "Yes. I would love nothing more than to be your wife." She leans in and kisses me. I pull back, feeling unsure of what just happened. That's that insecurity rising again. "Kyle, I mean it."

"I . . . um . . . holy shit, Ceese. Holy shit! You said yes!" I practically yell as I get up on my knees.

"I did," she laughs.

I jump out of bed and pace with what I'm sure is the biggest, goofiest grin I have ever made. "Holy shit. Shit! Shit! Shit! I can't believe it!! Wooo hooo!" I scream and do a double fist pump (get your mind out of the gutter!). CiCi lies back, watching me and laughing. "Who should we call? We should call our moms!" I rush to my phone.

"Wait—no!" She sits up quickly. "Hold on there, killer. Let's just . . . can we just keep this to ourselves right now, please?"

"Why?" Yeah . . . I just snapped at her. Can you blame me?

"I want it to just be our little secret for right now. I want to keep it to ourselves. Not long, though, I promise."

"No."

"No?" She moves her legs to the side of the bed.

"No," I confirm. "If we tell people, then it's real, and that's why you don't want to say anything."

"That's not fair, Kyle," she says with defeat in her voice.

"Given your history with me, I think it's very fair."

"So, basically, you trust in me—in *my* love *for* you—enough to ask me to marry you. But, you don't trust in me enough to know that I mean what I say?"

"This has nothing to do with trust issues," I retort.

"Uh, yeah . . . it actually does." She gets up, her face red with frustration (or it could still be residual from the orgasm, who knows?) as she storms by me and into the bathroom.

I think I have just been involved in the shortest engagement ever.

Go ahead and congratulate me—I'll wait.

"Ceese?" I call out as I follow her in. She's already under the shower. Damn if that's not the best silhouette I've ever seen. She ignores me. She might not have heard me under the showerhead but ignoring me seems more dramatically correct for this situation. *Okay, I really see why she calls me Mr. Spock now.*

I open the door to the shower and walk in behind her. My hands slide down her sides and rest on her hips. I lay my forehead down on the top of her head and let the water pour over me, forming awkward streams on my face.

I don't ever want to know what it feels like to lose her.

CiCi takes in a sharp, whimpering gasp before turning around and into my arms. We stand like this, holding each other, for several minutes—in silence. Sometimes the best thing to say is nothing at all. I think it's very clear how we feel. Words would've ruined our moment.

The idea for hosting Thanksgiving came to us in an inebriated state. Yes, it would be awesome to have twenty-one people and four dogs here all day! Don't you think so? We've been jokingly cringing over this but I know we're both happy to have our family around. CiCi is kind of down that her other sisters and families won't be able to make it. She's been talking about them a lot lately. The drift between the girls really bothers her.

The sisters that *are* coming, besides Charley, are the GEGs. Sometimes I'm really in awe at how these five women can still be so close after all these years, especially with the way they talk to each other. But, it's their own brand of crazy and it really wears well on them.

"It will be a miracle if today doesn't end up a hot mess," she says as she closes the oven and turns around, leaning up against it.

"I think it will be fine." I cross the room to her.

"I think it will be *mostly* fine, however, we have a few that we're not used to having around. Oh, and we have Julie's mom—that ought to be a blast." She rolls her eyes.

"Why do you say that?"

"If you looked up narcissism in the dictionary, you would find Cynthia's face. Everything gets rolled back to her. It's the biggest reason why she and Julie aren't that close." She takes in a deep breath. "Man, Kyle, we're both really lucky we have the parents we do."

"Oh, for sure!" I agree. "So what's the scoop with Maddie bringing the Viking?"

"And his kid—don't forget that! Not really sure. Hopefully, he meshes in well."

Just then, the doorbell rings. Knowing that Mitch was dropping Charley off early this morning, CiCi goes to let her in. I take off to the media room and enjoy the calm before the storm . . . or at least till Ceese starts yelling for her cleaning captain.

Chapter Twenty-Two

Turkey thyme and lots of whine

CiCi

It's noon and just about everybody's here. We're waiting on Maddie and the Viking to arrive. Shit—I've got to stop calling him that. Fuck it. He'll always be "The Viking." I just can't wait to see what this son of a bitch looks like!

"Oh. My. God! I'm going to choke her! Why do I subject myself to her?" Julie yells in a whisper, making sure her mother doesn't hear her.

"Look, there are a lot of people for her to spread her sunshine to, don't sweat it."

"Easy for you to say; she avoids you like the plague." She rolls her eyes and grabs a celery stick filled with cream cheese. "That's the beauty of being a 'bad influence' on me." She chomps into it.

"Yes, of course. Although, I think I've really let her down, I mean, why aren't you a crack-whore yet? You've been around me long enough." I open the oven to check on the turkey. Actually, I wanted to get hit with another strong blast of turkey smell.

"I know. You're such a disappointment. I mean, I'm not even a proper alcoholic. Hey, is that a new apron?" She touches my arm to turn me.

"Yeah. Kyle's mom gave it to me." I look down at it with her.

"Don't stop basting your turkey in my oven, 'til my buzzer goes off!" she reads aloud. "Kyle's mom gave you that?" She laughs. "Oh, Imma like her for sure!"

"Aww, she's great. I adore her." I beam.

"Whom do you adore?" Winnie asks after sneaking up from behind me, placing her hands on my upper arms.

"Oh, were your ears ringing?" I tap her hand gently.

"They must've been. What can I do to help?" She stretches her neck around to see what's what, I'm guessing.

"Nothing really. Shall we pass out your appetizers?"

"That may be a good idea; I think the natives are getting restless." She puts her hand up by her mouth, like it's a secret.

"What are you girls up to?" Mom asks as she heads in.

"We're just waiting for the rest of the women to pile in here so we can all hold hands in a circle and sing "Kumbaya" until something miraculously pops up that needs to be done before dinner is ready," Julie replies. She's my smartass understudy and sometimes . . . I'm hers.

"Oh, I know all of the words! I could lead you all in like I did for my college choir. I was the main soloist." Cynthia chimes from behind us. We all collectively roll our eyes before acknowledging her.

"It was a joke, Mom. We all want to help, but there's nothing to do right now." Julie rubs her temples. I feel for her. The problem is that Julie's mom has been self-absorbed for as long as Julie can remember, so even the tiniest thing her mom says sets her off.

"C'mon, Cynthia, let's go see if anyone's made any clutter for us to clean up yet." My mother puts her arm around her shoulder and guides her out. I don't know why, but my mom has always had extra patience for Cynthia even after knowing what Cynthia has said about me. I think it's my mother's own personal way of saying "fuck you" to her but she will neither confirm nor deny that if asked.

"I'm pretty sure Kyle has more than a handle on the clutter situation," Winnie says after my mom and Cynthia walk out.

"Yeah, what's up with that?" Julie grabs another celery stick.

"Ha! People think *I'm* bad!" Winnie laughs.

"Oh, leave Mr. Belvedere alone." I head over to the fridge. Do you know what excites me about this time of year besides the obvious? Egg nog. I fucking love me some egg nog! I will watch the amount of stuff I put in my mouth just so I can overindulge on this instead.

"Isn't that your second glass?" Julie grabs a glass out of the cabinet and places it next to mine.

"You know you wouldn't be getting any of my shit if it wasn't Thanksgiving." I grab her glass aggressively and pour her some.

"Yeah, yeah . . . shut your pie hole and fill 'er up!"

"You know, when she says that to me, it's got a completely different meaning." Blake pipes up from behind us.

"Jesus! What is it with everyone sneaking up on us this morning?" I turn around, almost dropping my glass.

"Sorry, love," he says before placing his hands on Julie's hips. He leans down and plants a few kisses on the back of her neck. Julie belches—loudly.

"You are one sexy bitch," I say in aww.

"Isn't she? I've come to believe that she does this kind of stuff to deter me, but in all honesty, nothing turns me on more than to know she's comfortable enough with me that she will belch like a trucker." He grinds into her a little just to show her how much, I'm assuming. I watch as Julie closes her eyes and bites her lip. I wish she would just give in already. Blake is a great guy.

"I bet you two have hot-ass-sex."

"I haven't had her in the ass yet, but as soon as I do, I'll let you know if it was hot." Blake smiles. Can you tell he's been around us for a while? Julie stomps on his foot. I'm sure that would have some oomph to it, but she's barefoot.

"You should be nicer to him, Julie; he's the only one that comes back for more." I nudge her with my elbow.

"Shut-up, Ceese," she says quickly and under her breath.

"What's this, now?" Blake asks, confusion all over his face. Just then, Cynthia walks in and huffs dramatically when she looks at Blake and Julie.

"What is your problem now?" Julie snaps at her.

"I just don't know what you are doing with your life." Cynthia sighs.

"What do you mean by that?!"

"You don't have a solid job and your boyfriend is going nowhere fast with you. He's just with you for your money, you have to know that." She pushes her hands out at nothing.

"Now you wait just a bloody second, you daft cow!" Blake yells.

Holy fuck.

"She has three solid jobs doing the things that she loves to do!" he continues.

"Oh, modeling? Please!" Cynthia laughs. "Do you think she will look like this for the rest of her life?" She waves her hand at her daughter.

"Not just the modeling. She spends her days promoting authors with her blog and tour services! She's got a knack for it and is very sought after!"

"Blog?" Me and the other girls ask as we are all now standing front and center to this shit show.

"I don't even know what that means." Cynthia rolls her eyes.

"No, you wouldn't, you know why?" he asks through his teeth. "Because that would require you to stop thinking about *you* for one moment of your life! As far as your comment about me, that just proves to everyone in here what a self-absorbed, ignorant lady you are. You should be ashamed of yourself, the way you walk around, judging people. Look in the bloody fucking mirror, Cynthia!" his voice crescendos before he slams his fist on the counter. I have *never* seen Blake like this.

"Ha! What do you know? Look at you, fighting so gallantly for her. Meanwhile, you're not the only egg in her basket . . . or her bed, buddy!" she laughs.

"Mom!" Julie yells.

Let's get something straight right now; Julie lies. She tells us all about these guys that she's sees—one night stands. It's bullshit. However, I'm the only one who really knows that. She's been a one-man woman ever since Blake came along. She won't even admit it to herself, though. So, as far as everybody else knows, she's been the same ole same ole.

"Alright, now, that's the second time I'm hearing some sort of comment like this. What is going on, Julie?" He grabs her arm and tries to turn her to face him but she doesn't budge.

"I was only kidding with my comment," I say quickly, trying to lessen the blow.

"Are you still seeing other guys?" I can almost hear the lump in his throat as he swallows.

Don't do it, Julie. Don't do it, Julie.

Julie takes in a deep breath. "Yes. I am," she states, still not looking him in the eye.

She never listens.

"Are you sleeping with them?" he asks in a much lower voice. I'm pretty sure I'm not the only one who heard him as most of us are all standing here . . . listening. Yes, we're all assholes but we just can't help it.

"Yes." Her eyes fill up.

He hesitates for a few moments. Opens his mouth and shuts it. It's almost painful to watch. I can see him fighting back the anguish he must be feeling. His nose flairs once again. "Right. I suppose that's my cue, then. You all have a lovely holiday. He nods towards all of us then heads out of the kitchen.

"What are you doing?" I grab her arm and pull her. "Why did you lie to him?"

"I'll tell you why she lied," Kyle interjects. "Because, just like you, she's afraid of how she feels for him. She's pushing him away on purpose. It's asinine! I don't know why you women pull this shit," he starts to raise his voice. "It's clear to me and everyone else here that you are not only destroying that man, who clearly cares about you, but you are destroying yourself! It's all over your face, Julie, don't even try to deny it."

"Kyle, this really isn't—"

"—any of my business?" He finishes my sentence. "No, it's not. But I know exactly what that guy is going through. You did the same damn thing to me and it killed me every time! And for what?!" Kyle yells at me.

"I'm so sorry I did that to you." I grasp his face in my palms. "I really am." I lean up and kiss him.

"What's going on here?" Maddie asks grabbing our attention.

"The Viking . . ." Yes, every woman in the room just said that in a collective sigh. Except for Cynthia, she doesn't know about him.

We hear the door slam and Julie lets out a small sob. I turn back to her. "Kyle's right, Julie. I did that to him and it was awful on both of us. I stopped doing it, gave into my feelings, and have never been so happy in my life." I plead with her. Kyle's hands slide around my waist and he hugs me to him. Julie looks at me apprehensively. "Do you care about him?" I ask. She nods frantically. "Go after him, then. Tell him the truth; otherwise you're going to lose him."

"Oh God, you're right." She gets a look of panic across her face. "Excuse me." She rushes by us and out of the kitchen. Slam goes the door again.

"Well, I don't know why she's bothering. He's not good enough for her anyway." Cynthia shakes her head.

"You wouldn't know what's good for your daughter if it slapped you in the fucking face!" I yell.

"Why you disrespectful piece of trash!"

I swear not a minute has flown by yet and Cynthia is screaming.

Ok . . . my mother may have thrown a pie in her face.

I look around to see where my mom is. Oh . . . it was not my mother who threw the pie. She's too busy climbing Daddy like he's the ropes on a wrestling ring and she's Jimmy "The Superfly" Snuka. Who the fuck threw the pie? I look around the room again and my eyes finally fix on a very pissed off Winnie Cooper who's heading towards Cynthia with a wet towel.

"You have some nerve, coming into my son's house and disrespecting his girlfriend like that. I don't know where you come from lady, but you have no class. CiCi is damn good friend to your daughter. She's a damn good friend to anyone who needs one. I've heard nothing but nasty things come from your mouth since you got here." She hands her the towel.

Cynthia takes it, wipes her face, and heads over to the sink. "I don't know what you're talking about," she says almost too quietly.

"Oh, you most certainly do. You just didn't know anyone heard you make those comments to Julie. Now, I can tolerate a lot of things—Lord knows I have—but I refuse to listen to such downright nastiness. Not one word from your mouth had an ounce of truth to it. I think it's high time, lady, that you stop and reevaluate your life. Try to take the time to figure out why people don't like you and, for the love of God—change it!" And with that, Winnie Cooper leaves the kitchen to collect herself, I'm sure. I'm also sure that someone needs to scoop Kyle's jaw, and mine, off the floor.

Now that it's quiet, we can hear the yelling that is going outside. So we do what anybody would do when they know two people are arguing right outside the house . . .

We all run to a vacant window.

I can't really make out what they are saying. I can tell that Julie is pleading with him and crying. He keeps trying to look away from her except for when he yells at her. Finally, I see her nodding repetitively, like she's agreeing to something. She starts crying again and lays her head against his chest. He looks up to the sky like he's asking for a little help from the big man upstairs. He then wraps his arms around her as he looks back down. He kisses the top of her head. She looks up at him and his hand threads into her hair before he brings her in for a kiss.

"That's so hot," I say under my breath.

"I can top that," Kyle says quietly in my ear.

"I bet you can." I smile up at him.

"Shit—they're coming!" Ava announces and we all find something random to do. Yeah, not suspicious looking at all, are we?

Cynthia heads to the door just as Julie and Blake walk in. "Mom? What the hell happened to you?" Julie's eyes are wide but there is humor dancing around in them. I know she is doing everything she can not to laugh at her mother. Her mother, who still has apple filling, flattening her hair. The pieces of pie crust add a nice texture, as well.

"It's been made very clear—as you can see—that I'm not welcome here."

"What did you do?"

"I didn't do anything but state my opinion."

"She called my daughter a piece of trash in her own home! She's lucky I didn't mop up that floor with her, goddamn it!" Mom raises a fist. One hundred percent Irish—that's all I'm sayin' 'bout that.

Julie gets out of the doorway and holds her arm out. "Goodbye, Mother."

"You're not coming with me?" Cynthia seems shocked.

"No. I'm spending Thanksgiving with my real family." She snuggles into the side of Blake's chest.

"I'm your family." Cynthia's eyes fill.

"Only on paper. I'm done with this. With your behavior. With always trying to have a relationship with you. You're miserable and the only thing that makes you happy is to put the people around you down. There's no reason for me to subject myself to this kind of abuse anymore. Please leave." Julie opens the door wider for her.

"Abuse?" Cynthia's voice cracks.

"Yes. That's exactly what it is . . . what you have been doing to Julie, Cynthia." Maddie speaks up.

With all of us standing and staring at her, I think Cynthia's light bulb finally comes on; she leaves. As soon as the door closes behind her, Blake wraps his arms around Julie as she sobs into his chest.

"Hey, Blake," Maddie places her hand on his forearm, "can you let us take over from here?"

"Absolutely." He nods and gives her another quick kiss before letting her go.

We immediately encircle her. "I just can't anymore. I've reached the end of my rope," she cries. "Now I feel guilty that she's going to be all alone."

"Are you kidding me? Now she can go have a pity party and invite anyone who will listen. She's probably as happy as a pig in shit right now." Charley scoffs.

"Hey, ladies, not to break up your super power Asswhore meeting, but I can't contain these kids any longer." Mitch interrupts us.

"I'm sorry; did somebody mislead you into believing we would give a shit?" I ask.

"Mitch, send them out to the kitchen to meet Hunter and help us set up their table. That will keep them busy for a few." Kyle waves Mitch in.

"Thanks, man," he says. "C'mon, kids!" he yells over his shoulder. They come parading out, past our huddle (unfazed, mind you), and out to the kitchen.

"Dipshit," I say under my breath at Mitch.

"Love you, too, Ceese," he calls out.

"C'mon, girls, let's get in there." Julie wipes her eyes. "Oh my

God—Maddie! I'm so sorry! What a first impression to make on the Viking!"

"Oh, fuck it! I warned him that you were all a bunch of crazy bitches. He knew not to be surprised by anything." She pats Julie's back and rubs it. "Let's go." She nods her head in the direction of the kitchen.

"He's Australian, right?" I ask as we walk.

"Yes."

"Well, see that? We've introduced him to a proper American Thanksgiving!" I say.

"For sure! What's Thanksgiving without yelling, crying, and laughing?" Ava asks. "Rock the fuck on with Kyle's mom, by the way!" she adds.

"I love that woman." I do. I really truly do.

"Here is your mission, if you choose to accept it," I start and give Kyle, Mitch, Trent, and Blake the "stare down."

"What if we don't choose?" Trent asks. He's been around us girls the longest; I don't even have to say what we're after.

"No puss 'n boots!" Charley, Ava, Julie, and I all say in unison.

"Is that a new one?" Blake laughs.

"No!" Kyle, Mitch, and Trent answer in unison.

"How do you know about puss 'n boots?" I ask Kyle, trying to recall if I've ever said that to him.

"Mitch told me," he replies quickly.

"Look!" Ava hands jerk out in front of her. "That is our best friend out there, and . . . our captain," she says the last part with a burst of giggle. The rest of us girls collaborate on the giggles. Ava finally gets herself under control. "We need to know that his intentions are good. No fucking around fellas! Remember, if we're stuck with a douche-bag—*so. Are. You!*"

"I think you ladies grilled him enough over dinner." Kyle grabs a paper towel and wipes up something off the floor.

"Do you think you would be here, Mr. Belvedere, if these guys didn't grill you first?" I eye him.

"First of all, yes, because this is my house. Second of all, I was never grilled." He looks at me as if I'm crazy. I don't need to say a word—the other three guys are looking at him like he's crazy.

"Look, you're all lucky," Trent starts, "I didn't have any of you! I got grilled by these crazy bitches." He holds his hand out at us. "They're just lucky I absolutely adore them."

"Good save, Trent—good save." Charley gives that statement the back-up support of a nod.

"Alright, you guys know what you need to do; let's get dessert out there." Julie finally adds to the conversation. *She was probably too busy thinking about sucking Blake's cock tonight to seal the deal on his forgiveness.* Yes. Yes, I think about my friends having sex with their significant others, don't you? Shut-up . . . you do, too! *Dipshit . . .*

"CiCi, stop daydreaming and grab the damn pie!" Ava barks at me.

"Dude, what's up with you being all bossy and shit today?" I can't help it; she's been a little off from the usual sweet and innocent Ava.

"I called your name like five times," she huffs.

"Get over it, there was some hot shit going on in my brain." I grab the pie from her. Kyle smirks at me. I'm not even going to explain to him that something hot had nothing to do with us.

We take the dessert out to the dining room. Winnie and Mom had already brought in the coffee and drinks for the kids. We all sit down. "Ding, ding, ding . . ." I make the sound of a bell for the second round. "Where's Brooklynn?" I ask, looking down the table.

"Napping," Charley says before shoving chocolate cream pie in her mouth.

"Trent and I are pregnant!" Ava squeals out of nowhere. Mitch drops his fork in such a dramatic force; I believe it will later be remembered as "The fork drop heard around the world." Charley squees with Ava. Kyle and I look each other. I'm pretty sure we're thinking the same thing. You see, Mitch was not really on board with Charley being Ava's surrogate. They had just started getting serious. I'm not sure how or why he finally agreed but I do know it wasn't without some massive arguing. The fact that Charley is now pregnant by surrogation (not a word? It is now, bitch.) when he didn't want her to be, only to have them turn around and finally get pregnant? Oh boy! I'm pretty sure Mitch is ready to bust at the seams and not in a good way.

I look over at him.

I think I see steam.

"So, now you guys are going to have two babies! How are you feeling about that—has it sunk in yet?" Maddie, God love her, can never stop asking people how they "feel about that." She never hangs up her therapist hat.

"Three! Three babies!" Trent says wide-eyed and looking paranoid like he might want to shoot himself instead of going through with this.

Mitch clears his throat. "You're having twins? How long have you known?" he asks, not even looking up from his plate. His ears are fire engine red.

"Oh, um . . . we found out about a week after Charley. We wanted to wait to tell everyone, though, given our history." I can hear the trepidation in Ava's voice.

"Well, that's just great—perfect. Congratulations." Mitch raises his coffee mug. I look at Charley and she's like a deer in headlights.

I take this as my cue to change the subject. Only, how the fuck do I change the subject? I would look like a total bitch if I was all . . . gee that's great . . . did you all see the Patriots game last Sunday? I look at Kyle and widen my eyes for him to do something.

"I bet Yoga will be wonderful for the babies. Speaking of that, I was just telling CiCi the other day that I'd like to come by your studio and take a class." Winnie saves the day.

"You should! It would be so good for you. I teach at night but I have a few girls that help out during the day," Ava carries on.

"I have the best future mother-in-law in the world," I whisper in Kyle's ear.

He gives me a shy smile. I furrow my brows at him. He leans into my ear. "I wasn't completely sure you still wanted to marry me," he whispers in my ear.

"Of course I do." I kiss him.

By the time dessert is over, things have simmered down quite a bit. The last of the dishes are being done and the girls are all getting ready to leave. I'll see them in the morning because we crazy bitches love us some Black Friday!

"So, have we scared you off, Declan?" Charley asks the Viking.

"Not at all. I have to say, though, there wasn't a single moment I was bored. I actually feel as if I should've paid admission." He leans down and gives her a kiss on the cheek.

"Why? Does Maddie usually charge you for *her* freak show?"

"CiCi! Shut up!" Maddie snaps.

"No. She pays me for mine, though." He winks at me. Maddie blushes and looks up at him with a big smile. The Viking has a least a foot on Maddie. I'm figuring that she gets a running start in when she wants to climb this mountain of a man. The more I look at them (and picture them having off the charts, amazing sex) the more I see how well they look together despite their height differences. I knew he had blond hair and blue eyes, but I didn't expect it to be down to his shoulders, have a little wave to it, and look fucking sexy as hell. I also didn't expect him to be a Cellist. He's a little on the shy side, but we'll whip him into shape in no time.

I look around at all ten of us. Everybody, for the first time in a long time, seems genuinely happy. I'm not gonna lie; I'm choking up a bit. Oh, fuck off—I'm not losing my edge! I love these bitches; they're my family. Of course, it pleases me to see them happy.

"Why are you giving everybody the stare down?" Julie asks.

"We're all fucking hot," I reply. "We could be the new version of 90210. We should have a reality show." You have no idea the emotions that are going through me from this brilliant idea taking over my brain.

"Ooh, what would you call it?" Lindsay pipes up from the back. She always thinks my ideas are brilliant, too. I think I love her a little more because of it.

"The GEGs of New Humpshire," I say with great thought.

"Humpshire?" Ava laughs.

"Yes!"

"Kyle, clearly, you're not giving it to her enough," Maddie pats his chest, giving him a disappointed look.

"I've given her all I've got, Captain!" He does the worst Scotty impression—ever!

"You should stick with Spock." I shake my head.

"We're going! See you all later!" Mitch randomly bursts out. "C'mon kids, say goodbye to everyone . . . again!" he calls out. Charley gives me a pleading look.

I grab her hand and walk her to the door. "Just do whatever he wants tonight. Even if you're tired, just give it up. He's *pissed;* it's all over his face. You need to try and simmer it down."

"That won't work." She bites her lip and knits her brows together. "Ceese, he hates not having control of things. It's a trigger for him. He's not going to touch me at all tonight," her voice trembles. "I'd rather him scream at me than not touch me." She wipes the tear away that manages to escape.

"Baby, what's wrong?" Mitch grabs our attention.

"Hormones." She smiles at him and waves it off.

"Well, go get your pretty, hormonal ass in the car. I'm sure you're wiped out." He chucks her chin before giving her a kiss. She sighs.

Dork.

I'm glad I'm not like that with Kyle.

Shut up—I am not!

Charley leads the kids out to the car but Mitch stays back. This may be due to the death grip I have on his arm. "Go ahead; lay it on me." He looks up at the ceiling. This is his "I'm going to keep my cool till I can't anymore" move.

"Don't take this out on her, Mitch. They've been trying for nine years. There's no way she could've known this was going to happen." I try to stay as diplomatic as I can.

"I know," he sighs and brings his gaze back to me. "I'm not going to deny that I'm pissed, but I'm not pissed off at her. I'm not even pissed off at Ava and Trent. I'm just pissed. But don't worry; I'll make sure she knows I'm not upset with her." He gives me a half smile and pulls me in for a hug.

"Alright, see you later, dipshit." I pat his back.

And so begins the filing out . . . finally! Kyle and I just stand here at the door like the receiving line at a wedding. A load of guilt washes over me when I realize that I was so busy getting wrapped up in helping get the food on the table and other people's drama that I really didn't spread my quality time out to everyone equally. Oh well, they'll get over it. It's not like they were racing to be up my ass.

"Goodnight!" we both yell before closing the door.

"Oh my God, do you hear that?" I lay my forehead onto the closed door enjoying the first moments of peace and quiet.

"Yes," he groans. "Do you hear this?" he asks and I hear him unzip his pants. "That's the sound of my dick finally gaining the freedom he's been fighting for all day." He breathes next to my ear. His hands hike my skirt up and grasp my ass. "What a little cock tease you are, Birkita, wearing this dress that only comes down mid-thigh. Let's not talk about these thigh-high suede boots and how fucking hot they look on you. That wasn't enough, though, right?" His right hand reaches around and dives inside of my panties. I let out a gaspy whimper and throw my head back onto his shoulder. The feeling of his fingers slide towards my backend and his cock slipping in over my panties the other way—Lord, hear my prayers. "You had to keep bending in front of me, didn't you? Do you know how hard it was to keep my hands off of you all day?" he asks, almost angrily, through his teeth. His left hand rips my panties away then travels up my back, unsnapping my bra. "Do you know how many times I've bent you over something and fucked the shit out of you today?" His hand slides around to my breast.

Tug, tug, rub, and roll.

Tug, tug, rub, and roll.

"The only problem is that it was all in my head. We're going to fix that right now, aren't we?" He bites at my earlobe.

"Yes," I pant. It's all I've got. I'm fighting off an orgasm right now.

"You know where I fucked you—each. And. Every. Time?" He nibbles at my neck.

Get me off this mountain; I'm climbing too fast!

"The table? Counter?"

"Yeah but . . ." He moves his hand from my clit and I want to scream for him to put it back. Suddenly, I feel his cock slide up to my "do not enter." His tip is so wet from me. "I fucked you here—so hard." He pushes against me and I feel myself stretch slightly for his tip.

Oh God . . .

He's going to make me earn my cape.

At the front fucking door, for Christ's sake?!

"Kyle, please," I beg. His fingers return to my clit then slide down further until they're fucking me slowly. He pushes a little further. I jump. "No!" I pull away and turn around. He seems a little shocked but it quickly turns into embarrassment as he tucks himself back in and looks everywhere instead of me for a moment. “Wait, wait! I want to.” I place my hands on his chest. “I just don’t want to have sex in an area of the house that would make it easy for people to see us. We can go upstairs . . . or the media room if you want different scenery. I just . . . I don’t want to do it where people can easily see into the windows.” I stare into his eyes, hoping that he’ll understand.

“Upstairs now, Ceese.” He jerks his head in that direction and keeps a stolid expression on his face. Jesus, he is so fucking hot when he gets like this. I don’t know why, but I become like putty in his hands every time. “Now!” He moves out of my way, grabs my arm, yanking me towards the stairs, and slaps my ass.

Ouch!

Also . . .

Mmm.

I charge up the stairs, looking over my shoulder. Kyle is walking up them in a slow, seductive prowl while unbuttoning his shirt and keeping his eyes glued on me. I half expect him to open his mouth and roar. I move even quicker, pulling my dress over my head and flinging my bra. That’ll bide me some time because you and I both know Mr. Belvedere will stop to pick that shit up. I head into our room and peel myself out of these boots. I don’t care if he has plans of me wearing them while he impales me; they need to come off. What is it with guys and fucking women with their shoes on, anyway? I don’t get it. I crawl onto the bed but I’m not exactly sure how I should pose myself. On my knees, ass up? On my back, legs spread? On my side? What?

“Ceese? Why are you circling around on the bed like Pearl does when she’s looking for a comfy spot?” He slightly chuckles. *Fucking prick.* I give up and just sit, legs dangling the side of the bed.

“You know, you have a rude habit of pointing at me,” I mention and eye his rock hard cock.

“Lie back; I want to make you come.”

“Well, you don’t have to tell me twice.” I smile playfully and lie back.

“After I make you come, I’m going to give you a choice of what’s going to happen next.” He stops talking and slowly traces my clef. I lick then bite my lip. “You either let me take your ass tonight or . . . I spank you for not letting me, and then I’ll take your pussy.” His fingers dive in, making my head jerk back.

I bring my head back up and study him. I almost can't read him. "Kyle, are you okay?"

"Yeah," he answers me quickly. "Why?"

"You're just very serious. I wanted to make sure."

"Ceese, my cock is about to explode . . . this is a very serious situation. Now tell me, how are you taking it from me tonight?" his voice takes on a more urgent tone.

"What do you want?"

"I want both."

"Ok."

"Open these beautiful legs." He kneels onto the bed. I open. "Fuck, you're dripping for me," he groans.

But I always am, aren't I?

Cue the curtains

I know . . . I'm such a bitch.

Kisses a bird off to you

Night, bitches!

Chapter Twenty-Three

The blackest of Black Fridays . . .

Kyle

One hour and forty-five minutes. That's how long I've been staring at this envelope. I've turned it. I've flipped it. I've considered steaming it open. I've stopped myself from going through with it. Finally . . . I call Maddie.

"Hey," she answers like she already knows who's calling her.

"Hey? Is this how you always answer your phone? Aren't you a professional?"

"Yes I am, but I'm studying a new profession as an asshole. How am I doing, master?" she quips.

"You have me programmed in?" I ignore her comment. You eventually learn to do this, being around these girls a lot.

"Of course I do," she says in a tone like I'm crazy for asking.

"Whatever, listen. Don't say anything."

"Why the fuck are you whispering?"

"I don't know." I say at regular volume. "Listen! A letter came in the mail today for CiCi." I wait.

"I know this is the age of technology but there's no need to panic when you receive mail the old-fashioned way."

"Knock it off, Maddie! It's from *him!*"

"What?" I can hear her stop in her tracks.

"What should I do?"

"Don't hide it from her, Kyle," she says secretively.

"Are you around her?"

"No."

"So, I should give it to her? I don't know, Maddie. She's been doing so well, like she's finally able to move on. Don't you think this will undo all of her hard work?" I run my free hand through my hair. I'm not going to lie; this all makes me very nervous.

"Yes. Please give it to her. Let me explain something to you." I hear her take in a deep breath. "CiCi has not come out and told me a thing about what happened fifteen years ago until you came along. Suddenly, she's allowing herself to recognize her behavior as sometimes being a direct result of what happened to her in the past. That's huge, Kyle. She's in a great place now, thanks to you. She's ready to face this. If you weren't in her life, if she hadn't made the recent progress she has made; my answer would be different. However, I recommend that you be right by her side when she reads it. Don't allow her to do it alone. I don't care if you stand on the opposite side of the room—she needs you, whether she wants to believe it or not. You have become her rock, Kyle. I don't know how you did it, dude, but kudos to you and we all love you for it. She's a great person; she deserves to be happy." I can hear her getting choked up. This right here is why I love these girls so much . . . what I respect about them—they truly love each other. It's an amazing thing to witness. Oh, they're all bat shit crazy, but that's part of their charm.

"I'm not her only rock, Maddie. You girls are the wind beneath her wings," I say with a smile. I'm mastering "GEG talk."

"You're a dork. Love you, too. Gotta go—incoming!" she says urgently. We say quick goodbyes and hang up.

It's a thick fucking letter. I fight off the last urge to open it for myself and place it on the counter. Man, I wish I knew how long it was going to sit there for. These girls have been shopping since three in the morning. It's now eleven. I mean—what is there left to buy at this point? I'm just glad I went back to sleep this morning. I wouldn't be able to take a nap once she's opened that letter. As a matter of fact, I should keep the letter from her until she has, at least, had a nap. I grab it and place it on top of the fridge. I head into the media room to watch *A Christmas Story*—classic.

Before I know it, my mind is wandering to last night. God, last night was *amazing*. I close my eyes to get the full visual. Ok, I got a little carried away with the spanking; her ass was pretty red. I couldn't help it. I was feeling a little insecure. Do you think I missed how she was staring at Maddie's boyfriend? No, I didn't and I can tell you right now, I wasn't and am still not happy about it. What the fuck was that about anyway? I don't like how she was looking at Blake, either. I don't like her looking at any other guy that's not me—not in that way. I kept it to myself, though, just in case I was overreacting. Besides, feeling insecure is one thing, acting out because of that insecurity is another. Anyways . . . there she was, on her knees, ass up. It was red and she was soaked. I swear to Christ she's going to turn me into a two-pump-chump. I can barely keep it together around her.

She was trembling.

I was nervous.

We were about to have a first—together.

Oh, you thought I've done that before? Nope. I've never even had the desire; truth be told. With CiCi . . . I desire everything. She was so wet. I made sure to pull most of it to lubricate her naturally. And then, I sunk into her, plunging several times to relax her and thoroughly coat myself. I pulled out and slowly slid my cock up to her other opening. We both panted in anticipation. I pushed against her opening. Her breaths became more rapid. "Take in a deep breath, Ceese then exhale and try to relax." I know; easier said than done. But she did as I said and as soon as she fully exhaled, I pushed all the way in—maybe a little too quickly. She gasped and whimpered. Oh fuck, how she whimpered. You know what her whimpering does to me. It took every ounce of my strength to contain myself. I focused on the newer sensation. How tight it felt. But mostly, it felt like taking a bite of forbidden fruit, and I can't even begin to tell you how much more erotic that thought made it feel. Every time I pulled back and dove in again, I felt myself getting harder from her response. I'm not even going to go there about the visual. I'm sad that Ceese couldn't see the way my cock slid in and out of her ass. She's a visual fucker like me and I love that about her; it's hot as hell. I made sure to describe it to her, though. Let's just say that not only did she acclimate herself quickly, but that dirty fucking mouth of hers was open for business. God, I love her! She had me shattered within minutes. I, of course, shattered her this morning with her favorite alarm clock.

"Wow, Rosie palm and her five sisters are really giving it to you good!" CiCi bellows out of nowhere!

"Shit!" I open my eyes, jumping at her voice. She's eyeing my crotch while biting back her smile. I pull my hand out of my pants. "I don't even know how it got in there." I try to act shocked.

"Funny how that shit happens, huh?" She giggles as she walks around from the back of the couch, pulling her scarf off.

"Is it snowing?"

"No. I have really bad dandruff." She rolls her eyes and shakes out her hair before pulling her coat off. She struggles with her boots but manages to pull them off. "Scooch, I'm freezing my ass off; I need a snuggle." She smacks my leg. I get on my side and push my back against the couch. She lies next to me. I pull the blanket over us and we spoon. Not even five minutes goes by and I can hear the tempo in her breathing change. *Poor baby.* I snuggle closer and breathe her hair in. This is the best place in the world.

"Kyle?"

"Yes?"

"Your dick is poking me," she says around a yawn.

"Poking you is his favorite thing to do."

"Tell him nobody's home."

"He can hear lady boom boom's faucet running. Drip. Drip. Drip." I whisper into her ear.

She laughs lightly, "Dipshit."

"C'mon, you've been sleeping for two hours anyway; you should be getting up now otherwise, you'll be awake all night." I pat her hip.

"I'm sure I could come up with a way to tire myself out." She grinds her bottom into me.

"I could help . . . I'm useful like that," I murmur between kisses to her neck.

"Ugh . . . you're right; let's get up." She stretches then sits up.

"I've been up for the past few hours and it's done nothing but cause me pain."

"Shut-up." She slaps my stomach.

"You're very aggressive this morning." I sit up, as well.

"Hmm. I'm hungry."

"Let's have some lunch and you can show me everything you bought." I stand up and reach my hand out to her. We walk out to the kitchen hand in hand without a care in the world. And then I remember. *Shit.* I'm going to let her eat first. Then, *I swear,* I'll give her the letter.

We quickly fix ourselves some Thanksgiving sandwiches—my favorite—and head back into the media room to see what Christmas movie we can find. I love that she loves Christmas. I'm the same way. My mom always played Christmas music while prepping for Thanksgiving, and for me, that was the start of the season. I guess things were the same way for Ceese in her family.

"Kyle, if you shake your leg one more time, I'm going to fucking break it," she snaps and slams her hand down on my leg. That makes it the third time she's yelled at me for that. We're on movie number two and my anxiety over this letter has been going through the roof.

"Sorry," I sigh and rub my face.

"What is the matter with you? You've had nothing but nervous energy the past two hours."

"Fuck it, I've procrastinated long enough." I get up. "Wait here, I'll be right back," I say before heading out to the kitchen. I grab the infamous letter and head back . . . slowly. "Ceese, this came for you today." I hold it out to her.

"Today? But it's a holiday." She furrows her brows.

"Only to the crazy people, who get up at two a.m. to stand in lines for the best deals."

"Really?"

"Yes. I know; it's hard to believe."

She grabs the letter from me, skimming it until she sees what I know she sees—the sender's information. She drops the letter and stands up; moving away from it like it's going to explode. "Why didn't you just throw that out? Why would you subject me to anything that bastard has to say?" she yells.

"I think you should read it. It might help you to have some closure on whatever he did." I lift the envelope and hold it out to her again.

"I don't want to read an apology from him. That won't bring me closure! Seeing him burn in hell will give me closure!"

"You just might be getting your wish, Ceese." I look down.

"What do you mean?" she asks. I ignore. "Kyle! *What do you mean?!*"

"Don't get mad," I start. Brilliant way to go about it, right? "I did a little digging on Drew."

"What? Why?!"

"I just needed to know where the son of bitch was, what he was up to, and if there was any criminal record on him. That's all—I wasn't going to do anything with it. Not at the moment, at least." I close the gap she caused between us. "I think you should read that letter. Look, I don't know what he did and I'm not going to force you to tell me. I don't want you to tell me until you are ready. However, this letter might have the answers to the questions you've been asking yourself for fifteen years. Don't wait another day, baby. It's time to heal fully from this—if you can."

"Why would you call me 'baby'? I've asked you time and time again *not* to call me that!" she screams, her eyes welling up.

"Ceese, it's time. Open the letter." I put it in her hands, ignoring her misplaced anger.

"I don't want to. There's nothing important enough in there for me to do this to myself. Is that what you want, Kyle? You want me to read this letter so I can freak out and start pushing you away again? Are you done with me—looking for a way out that won't make *you* look like the jerk?!" She pushes me.

"Stop it." Push. "Stop it, Ceese." Push. "Stop! It!" I yell in her face.

Slap.

I no sooner bounce back from that and she's pounding on my

chest with her fists. I grab her by the wrists. "Goddamn it, Ceese, *stop!*" I pin them behind her back. She hocks back. *Oh, hell no!* My left hand lets go of her wrist and I grab her face from underneath her chin. "Don't you fucking *dare* spit in my face! You can beat the shit out of me, but you *will not* spit in *my* face. We *will* be through. Do you understand me?!" I hate to admit this, but I have such a hold on her face that she couldn't spit at this moment if she wanted to. I'm not proud of this, you must know, but I will not tolerate being so disrespected. Slowly, the tension leaves her body and she starts crying. Her right hand comes up to my left arm and she grasps it gently; she pats it. "You good, now?" I ask. She nods and I let go of my hold. She falls forward, into my chest, and sobs her beautiful little heart out. All I can do is just stand here and hold her . . . be her rock.

I take in a deep breath. "He's dying, Ceese."

Her head jerks up, "What?" her voice cracks.

"He's dying. He has Hodgkin's Lymphoma. Treatment was unsuccessful for him."

"No, Kyle. How could you even get that information?" She shakes her head in what seems like disbelief.

"You hire people who know people, beautiful. It's not as difficult as they would like it to be." I push her tears away with my thumbs.

"I don't . . . I don't think I can do this." She takes in a shaky breath. "Can you read it to me?"

"If that's what you need, I have no problem doing that for you." I tilt my head, studying her to get the final ok. She nods slightly then points to the couch. We head over and sit. She takes in another deep breath.

I wait.

"Okay," she says after a few minutes have gone by.

"Okay." I copy her and open the letter. "Wow. He writes like a girl," I chuckle to ease the tension of this moment.

"I know. I used to tease him all the time." She laughs then, as if she remembers, her chin quivers. Christ, it's like everything that happened is still so fresh for her after all these years.

"Ready?

"Yes."

I look down.

Dear CiCi,

If you are reading this letter, it's safe to say that I am no longer in this world. My lawyer had explicit instructions not to mail this till after my passing.

"Wait—what?" CiCi cries.

"He's gone, Birkita." I repeat then watch as she falls apart, sobbing for someone that once held her heart in the palm of his hands. I'm a little shocked at her response and at the same time, not so much. CiCi loves fiercely and gathering from her response, she's the type who will always love you no matter what happens. I have mixed emotions, myself, about her response. She waves me on. I look back down.

I have played this conversation over and over again in my mind for the past fifteen years. And yet, I don't know where to begin. You were the love of my life and I destroyed everything we had become and everything we had planned to be because I needed to be accepted by that son of a bitch I call Father. I can't tell you how so very sorry I am for what happened.

One thing is for sure: you deserve answers. If this letter leaves you with nothing else, at least you will know why I did what I did. As you know, I was desperately trying to get accepted into Psi Gamma Alpha for the second year in a row. My father gave me hell for not making it the first time. He said I was an embarrassment. I was determined and it paid off. I made it to the secret challenge. It took them three weeks to get it from me. I kept postponing, saying I didn't have it yet. Then, with the deadline looming and another horrific argument with my father, I caved.

I told myself, "She'll hardly ever see these guys. Once we graduate, she'll never see any of them again." I wish I could go back and knock some sense into myself. I knew what they were doing was wrong. I knew I was wrong for not only allowing it but being a part of it, as well. What a fucking coward I was. And I thought I had the right to walk around calling myself a man. I wasn't a man; I was a very stupid, lost boy, trying desperately—at any cost—to have his father "find" him.

You never knew the rage that I felt at that moment, when I was allowing them to watch, my father to win. I had gotten up to turn it off and end my pledge. But then I saw you and the horrified look on your face.

"Ceese, I'm lost. What the fuck happened?" I stop reading and glance up at her. She is silently crying. I grab some tissues off the table and hand them to her.

She lays her head in her palms then runs them down, vigorously wiping her tears away and rubbing her face. She takes in a deep, shaky breath. "As you know, I went over to his frat house to tell him about the baby. It was a surprise visit. Well, no one was more surprised than I was. When I heard a bunch of the guys cheering and carrying on in their big living room where they watched movies and sports, I headed down the hall and into the room. At first, I was slightly chuckling at the way they were carrying on. That is until I looked to see what they were watching that was causing all the commotion." She tries to start the next sentence but she's hyperventilating a little bit.

"Shh . . . shh. Take your time." I go to hug her but she pushes away.

"I can't . . . I don't want to hug right now. I just need to get this out," her voice finally steadies again.

"Okay." I nod.

"When I looked at the screen, I realized it was me. Drew, unbeknownst to me, had videotaped the first time we made love; when he took my virginity."

"What?!"

"Yup. And there they were, all of those sick bastards, cheering Drew on, congratulating him on how fucking hot I was. Yelling out all kinds of personal questions: was I really tight, was I a squirter, did I let him fuck me in the ass. I was horrified. That night I lost my virginity was so beautiful to me and within moments, it became the ugliest night of my life. Drew's right. He did look as if he was about to turn it off, but then he saw me. The color drained from his face. I didn't care, though. I ran over to the TV and ripped out the video. I think they were all just in shock because no one tried to stop me. I ran. I ran so fast and hard, I fell . . . like one of those dumb bitches in a horror movie." She chuckles slightly at her last comment. That's CiCi for ya, always trying to find the funny in the worst kind of situations. And, damn it, if that isn't one of the reasons why I love her so much.

A lot of things are making sense to me now: no video sex, the alarm over somebody seeing us through our windows, and the infamous wall. I'm a little unsure about the whole visual fucker thing, but it does make sense when you think about it. It's her way of controlling who sees her pleasure. That's my take on it anyhow, but I'm no Maddie St. Claire.

"Sometimes I get so mad at myself for letting this one incident hold so much power over me for so many years, especially when you came along, Kyle. I should've gotten over it a while back."

"CiCi, are you fucking kidding me, right now? Get over it?" I look at her as if she has five heads.

"Well, it's not like I got raped." She looks down.

"What he did was a violation to you. First, he taped you without you knowing. Second, he showed it to others! Why would that be something you would *just get over?* You only consented to sex. You did not consent to the others. How could you not be traumatized by what he did? Don't ever under validate the magnitude of responsibility his actions have over the length of time you've grieved or the mistrust you've had in relationships since." I palm her face.

"You sound a little like Maddie." She gives me a weak smile.

"Good. Maddie's a smart chick."

"You're a smart chick, too." Her smile gets bigger. I groan with frustration and love before I plant a big kiss on her lips.

"Do you want me to continue with the letter?"

"Yes, please."

I pick it back up and scan over to find where I left off. Ah!

I was frozen. No. I was a coward. After a few minutes, I finally pulled myself together enough to run after you. I stopped the moment I got to your dorm. Your light was on and I could see you moving around, shifting stuff; and I knew. I knew that I had lost you. It didn't matter what brilliant line or two came out of my mouth; I had destroyed us.

I wasn't surprised the next day when several people told me you were dropping out. My guilt, though, went through the roof. I not only destroyed our future, I possibly was single-handedly destroying yours. I could only pray that you would transfer to another school for spring. I know that you never became a veterinarian like you had dreamed of. I am happy that you did at least become a groomer and opened your own business up. Yes, you can add creeper to the many names you have probably called me over the years. I couldn't help it. I never stopped loving you. Of course, I wanted to make sure *you were ok. But you weren't, were you?*

I know about the baby.

I stop and look up at her when she gasps. She has her mouth covered with her hand and she signals me with the other to keep reading.

One of our project buddies in the English class we took together came up to me, asking if you were okay. She said she saw you coming out of one of the parenting clinics in town, crying. I knew there would only be one reason for you to be there. I know you, Ceese. As much as you understand both sides of the argument over abortion, you always said you would never go through with something like that—it had to be a dire situation for you to do that. I did that. I put you in such a dark place, it made you do something you would've never done. I had realized at that moment—I succeeded. I was now just like my father. He too had put me in such a dark place, it made me do something I would've never done.

Before I continue, I need to tell you not only how deeply sorry I am (again), but that not a day goes by that I don't think about our baby. I wonder if he would've had your beautiful green eyes. I wonder a lot of things about him. I only hope God is gracious enough to have allowed me to be with him as you are reading this. I call him Henry. That's what we said we would name our first son, right?

It's important for me to tell you what happened after you left. I often wondered if you thought that I carried on with my life as if nothing had happened. No. Never. You were always in my heart and on my mind. Since the day I learned about the baby, I made a conscious decision to do right by you in any way that I could. Every day I tried to right my wrong, even if it was the smallest of gestures.

I accepted placement in the fraternity. Not for the initial reasons, for very new ones. I planned to make my way to the top and by the time I was a senior, I wanted to make the secret challenge obsolete. I succeeded. The secret challenge died once the seniors before me and my brothers left. Going through the files, we found that not only had they been doing this for the past forty years (one way or another) but they had a record of the brothers who did the secret challenge and who their virgin was. I saw my father's name on this list. His virgin was my mother. And that was the day he was dead to me. I no longer wanted to be his son and I definitely didn't want to follow in his footsteps. It was clear they only led down a path to hell.

I went into the military instead of business. I was going to make a career out of protecting people. I needed to do something for not being man enough to protect you. I became a Navy Seal. Hard to believe, right? I loved it. Mostly, I loved that I could distance myself from people . . . from ever falling in love again. When I was on leave, I'd visit friends, but mostly, I spent my time checking up on you. Haha . . . that just reminded me of Forrest Gump. Remember when we'd talk like him all day to each other? God, we were such dorks. I loved and miss that most about us. Sorry. Anyways . . . I always had mixed emotions when I would get information about you. Happy that you weren't married with five kids and sad about it all at the same time, guessing I was the cause. That breaks my heart, knowing that I hurt the one person I loved so much, like this. I never expected you to come back to me. My prayer for you has always been that you would find happiness. You deserve it, baby. You deserve a good man who will never hurt you like I did. You deserve a shitload of kids. God, you'd be an awesome mom. Ceese, there's a light in you that shines so brightly, people can't help but want to be in it, to feel it's warmth. When you walk away, even just out of a room—people notice because you take the warmth of that light with you. And it's something nobody could ever snuff out—it's that powerful. I know that I don't "know" you anymore but I'd bet everything I can in the world that that hasn't changed about you. How could it?

Moving on here. After several years of being a Seal, I was injured. Let's just say I was in traction and you would've laughed your ass off at me. That's when I met her. I didn't want to fall in love with someone else; Lord knows I didn't deserve that kind of happiness. Susan wouldn't let me have my pity party, though. A part of me thought that maybe I needed to move on for you to finally be able to move on. So, I let my guard down. I married Susan six years ago and she is one of the best people I know. We have two daughters. I'm glad we have daughters and not sons for two reasons. One, I had a shitty example of how a father should be with his son. Two, I have always felt in my heart of hearts, that our baby was a boy. I wanted him to have his own place in my heart. Does that make sense?

Everything in my life was going great. I wasn't able to go back as an active Seal but I was able to train future Seals. Susan and I have been extremely happy and our girls have been healthy. I stopped checking up on you. Six months ago, I found out that I have stage four Hodgkin's Lymphoma. Nothing has worked and I'm down to mere weeks with my family. Funny thing, Karma, huh? I must not have done enough right. That's how I feel many days. Most days, I feel blessed. I have had the honor of being loved and loving someone greatly, twice in my life. I have these two beautiful, intelligent girls who call me Dad and think I'm made from some kind of wonderful. That's the ONLY memory (emotionally) they will have of me, and I couldn't ask for them to have a better one.

I hope, for your sake, that you can find it in your heart to forgive me. It's not about me hoping to get to the big pearly gates. My fate is laid out no matter who comes up to bat for me. My hope is for you to find the happiness you so rightly deserve.

I'm sorry, CiCi. I'm sorry for everything and anything I took away from you that day. I'm sorry that I wasn't man enough to keep you protected. I'm sorry if my actions had a long-term negative affect on your life.

I love you. I always have and I always will. Despite my poor actions when I was with you, I am a better man today and you are the sole reason for it.

I've enclosed a few pictures of us. My lawyer will be shipping you the rest of our things that I've kept. Susan knows about you. However, she thinks you are dead. I let her believe that so that she would never have a problem with me keeping our stuff. I understand if you want nothing to do with any of these things. I just didn't want to take your option of deciding that away.

To this day, you are still the most amazing woman I've ever met in my life. I love you—always.

Love,
Drew

P.S. Whenever I hear "You Could Be Happy" by Snow Patrol, I think of you. I love you, Ceese.

I put the letter down and fix my eyes on CiCi. She has cried through the entire reading of this. "I call him Henry, too," she says then unleashes a wail I have never heard come out of anybody before, let alone CiCi. I can't help but let her grief wash over me as I listen to and watch her sob. I want to hold her but I'm not sure if that's what she needs right now. I reach for her. "I need a minute, please." She backs away, gets up, runs off.

I don't know what to do.

CiCi's been in bed for three hours now, not wanting to get out of it. I've had Maddie here to check on her but she won't really talk to her, either. All she will say is that she needs to be alone right now. All I can do is give her that space and try to find something to do besides stare at the clock.

I grab her folder marked "Plan B" in the office and flip it open on my desk. I'm so proud of her. She really listened to me and now has everything neatly organized. This reminds me, I need to call Roger on Monday to see how things are going with the sale of her house. It shouldn't take long at all. It's reasonably priced and we've just had everything fixed that needed to be fixed. That was a battle and a half. She gave me a hard time whenever I took the bill for something. I was getting annoyed by it and when the last contractor approached me with his bill, I shot her down with a panty-melting look. Well, that's what she called it. I was just trying to tell her to shut the fuck up without actually saying it. It worked to my benefit—twice.

Oh, what do we have here? I didn't know that she was already looking at models for her grooming van. I can't help but laugh. She has two sides: What CiCi wants and What CiCi can afford. The one she wants has all of the bells and whistles; it looks like a short bus (no pun intended). It's really nice but definitely out of her price range. According to her budget, she'll be paying this off for the next ten years. Not good. Then, there's the side she can afford. It's a beautiful, shiny red wagon with buckets next to it and some sponges. Her budget says, "Black Friday special—I can buy two=Rolling in it . . . literally."

Well, I think we can do better than a red wagon. I grab my phone and call the company. Yeah, I know, I'm gonna get a lot of shit for this. I'm slightly shocked that someone actually picks up the phone. Then again, it's Black Friday, who isn't buying mobile grooming vans today? I start going through the list of things she wants. "Colors? She didn't mention colors . . . uh . . ."

"Here, give me that," CiCi says softly from behind me and takes the phone out of my hands. She proceeds to talk to the woman on the phone, telling her everything she wants. I stare in awe at her, not only because she's not giving me a rash and a shit about ordering this thing, but she's walking around in only one of my t-shirts. She gives me a shy smile when she notices me staring then pads over to me. I lean back on the office chair for her to sit on my lap. She continues to go down the list with the lady while I rub her back. Finally, she finishes up the call. "We have to go down there tomorrow to sign all of the paperwork."

"Ok." I kiss her neck. "Thank you for letting me do this."

"It was either that or lugging all of my shit in a red wagon, going from door to door like some sort of moron." She shrugs.

"Why don't we get some soup into you?" I pat her knee.

"Ok." She stands up and I take her hand as we head out of the office.

"Can you put on pants?"

"I can. I think I learned to do it by the time I was three." She smiles back at me.

"Smartass." I tap her butt. "Please put on pants; I'm trying to control myself over here," I plead.

"Suck it up, buttercup." She opens the fridge. She bends over. I bite my fist. "What do you want to eat?"

"You seriously just asked me that question?"

"I want comfort food; let's order a pizza." She stands back up, closing the door.

"Do you want to talk about the letter and how you are feeling?" I turn her towards me gently.

"No. I can't right now."

"Okay. I have an idea." I place my hands on her hips and move her closer to me.

"Uh, oh." She laughs.

"Don't uh oh me." I sweep her lips. "Tonight, we will veg out in front of the TV like we had originally planned. We will not mention anything about the letter or what happened for the rest of the evening. Tomorrow—we will talk. Uh-uh, nope." I put my finger to her lips when she opens them as if to oppose. "You need to talk about this this, Ceese; you can't sweep it under the rug and act like you're alright just because you took a few hours to yourself. You've come so far. It would kill me to see you regress."

"I'm not done thinking about everything, Kyle. I'm not done working it out for myself. I need time to do that," her voice so vulnerable . . . so lost.

"It took you fifteen years, last time."

Fuck, I shouldn't have said that.

She averts her eyes and slightly sucks in her lips almost like she's fighting the urge to say something. Her head gives a little nod and she takes in a deep breath. "C'mon, let's order pizza and see what's on tonight." She pats my chest and frees herself from my grasp on her hips. As soon as she leaves the kitchen, I throw a couple of punches at an imaginary opponent then try to rip my hair out in frustration.

What?

It's a guy thing—fuck off!

Chapter Twenty-Four

Coming full circle . . .

CiCi

Lying on my side in bed, I stare at my engagement ring as Kyle plays with it. It's New Year's Day and I've had my Wheaties twice this morning already—know what I'm sayin'? Despite what happened over Thanksgiving, the last month has been wonderful. Kyle made things official before Christmas, surprising me with this gorgeous, platinum, split shank, double cushion halo engagement ring. He gave me a proper proposal but then asked me if he could do the one he was dying to do. Of course I agreed; the not knowing would've killed me. He then proceeded to ask me if I would allow him the honor of being my dipshit for the rest of our lives. How the fuck could I say no to *that?*! To say everyone was thrilled would be an understatement (The girls were especially gaga over the dipshit proposal). Next, my house sold! Booyah, motherfuckers—I made forty grand more than I was anticipating! Much to his dismay, I made Kyle take that money to go towards my new souped up groomin' machine. It wasn't easy; I had to grab him by the balls—again. In return, he did wicked things to me. I'd hardly call that punishment, though. This will be my first week soliciting customers. I've asked Winnie to come along and do the talking, so I actually get customers . . . a-hem.

"What are you thinking about?" He plants several kisses on my shoulder.

"Just how wonderful this last month has been." I snuggle closer into his chest.

"Mmm . . . it has been." He closes his eyes and a small, contented smile graces his face.

"Do you have a plant or something in Washington?" It's a random question but one I've been thinking about for a while.

"When do you want to go?" he asks as he opens one eye to look at me.

"As soon as possible. I need to meet her. I need to meet his family. I need closure, Kyle." I bite back my lip.

"Who will you tell her you are? Remember, he said she thinks you're dead."

"I know. I'm going to just say that I am a friend from College."

"She's seen pictures of you."

"Shit." *Fuck, I didn't think of that.*

"Tell her you're your sister, Caroline. That you are out on a business trip with your fiancé and you heard the news and wanted to pay your respects."

"It's a little scary how quickly you thought of that." I furrow my brows at him suspiciously.

"I'm a closer, Birkita. I get paid to think quickly on my feet." He kisses me and pushes my hair behind my left ear.

"And off of them." I wink at him. He whips me onto my back, proving my point. "This doesn't bother you; my wanting to do this?" I stare up into his eyes.

"No." His fingers play at my lips. "Not at all." He kisses me. "I'm relieved that you are taking any step, never mind this huge leap. It only reassures me more, beautiful."

"Reassures you?"

"That you really love me and that you're ready for our future. I'm not going to lie; a part of me still wakes up every morning, wondering if you will walk away from what we have. All that pushing me away in the beginning did a number on me," he says, his eyes focusing on his fingers playing at my jawline.

"C'mon, Kyle, I didn't push *that* hard."

"No. But if you were a politician, you'd have "flip flopper" stamped on your head in any opponents ads." He chuckles.

"You seriously just compared me to a politician?" I smack his ass. "Dork!"

"Mmm . . . again, mistress," he teases.

"Oh, shut-up!" I laugh. Bastard's always making fun of the books I read. You know what, though? I know he reads them when he gets a free moment because—*bam*—out of nowhere, he's doing some hot shit to me that I just fucking read about. You think I call him out on it, though? Hell no! I now fucking highlight the shit I want to try and make little notes in my reader. The other night, I crossed another thing off my bucket list for sex. Let's just say Purp and Kyle have become partners in crime, or . . . both lanes were open, know what I mean, jelly bean? Fuck, I think I'm still feeling the aftermath from that. "You remember what we did the other night?" I ask, my voice trembling a little.

"Jesus," he groans, closing his eyes.

"I think he might have been called upon that night, but I'm talking about the actual act." I giggle.

"Two lanes open?"

"Yes."

"You want to do that again . . . now?" His eyes instantly turn a darker shade of blue.

"Down, cowboy, down!" I tease. "No. I want to tape that the next time we do it."

"Are you sure? I don't know if I can handle watching it without exploding in my pants."

"Your honesty is so hot at times, Kyle." I roll my eyes.

"Well, it's true." He laughs. "But if that's what you want, and you feel this *is* helping you, then I'm on board. You know that I am. Anything you need, especially sexually, I'm there."

"That's good to know." I act indifferent.

"How about now? Do you need me now?" he asks quickly in a joking tone as he entices lady boom boom with his love muscle (haha . . . love muscle; I crack myself up).

"I always need you." I wrap my arms and legs around him.

"Do you think Maddie's idea of doing the sex tapes helps?" He suddenly gets a serious look on his face.

"Well, I thought it was a little crazy at first, but I have to admit, it does make me feel like I'm taking some control back. It gives power back to my consent. Funny how the mind works, huh?"

"I think it helps to know that they don't leave this house. You're the only one with the key to the box they're in so you know no one else will ever see them besides us. Not that I would do that anyway, but you know what I mean. Also, you can destroy them whenever you want."

"Oh, hell no! They are too fucking hot to destroy!" I widen my eyes.

"Thank Christ! It would be a fucking *crime* to burn those!" He laughs and I swear I hear a hint of relief in there.

"Back to the subject at hand, what are you gonna do about the leak down there?" I shift my hips so he can feel it.

"Well, ma'am, I'm gonna have to lay some pipe down," he plays.

"Are you sure you have the right pipe for the job?"

"It's a big pipe, ma'am, but you'll want that snug fit." He runs it up and down my center. "Does that feel like the right pipe for the job, Ceese?" he murmurs before taking my nipple into his mouth.

"The only pipe for the job, Kyle." I attack his lips. And with that . . .

He layeth the pipeth down.
And it is soooo good.

"Nervous?" He kisses the back of my hand as we begin our descent on the runway of SeaTac.

"Did Moby have a dick?"

Kyle laughs lightly. "Ceese, his name was Moby Dick."

"Same difference."

"Right, of course it is." He bites back his smile.

"Thank you." I squeeze his hand.

"For what?"

"For doing this. For being there for me even when I didn't want you to be. I really do appreciate it." I lean over and kiss him.

"I'd do anything for you, Birkita—I love you." He palms the left side of my face and I lean into his touch, relishing it.

Our moment breaks when the wheels hit the ground, making us bounce a little. Once we are taxied and cleared to get off, we head to the company car waiting for us. "Are we still going right there?" he asks.

"Yes. I think I only brought one set of balls with me and if I don't go now, I may lose them," I say as serious as a heart attack.

"I love your lady balls; let's not lose those." He smirks then leans forward to tell the driver where we are going. I sit back and close my eyes, talking myself out of changing my mind.

"Did you remember the gifts for the girls?" I open my eyes in a panic.

"Yes. They're in the trunk. How did you even know what they would want?"

"They were only married for six years so their girls have to be around five and younger. Girls that age mostly like the same shit."

"I wouldn't have known what to get."

"I'd entertain that comment with something smartasstastic but I'm too nervous at the moment."

"I'll be sure to say it again another time, when you're not. I wouldn't want you to fully miss that opportunity." He squeezes my thigh gently.

"Thanks. I appreciate it." I wink.

The thirty minutes to Bothell take forever and yet go by so quickly. I've never really understood what people mean when they say stupid shit like that, but today I do. We turn down their street and eventually come up to their house. The driver puts the car in park and gets out. He opens the door for us, then pops the trunk to hand me the girls' gifts. Kyle grabs my hand, gives me an encouraging smile, and we collectively take in a deep breath before heading up the driveway. Crossing over to the walkway, I look up quickly as I hear the door open.

She has dirty-blonde hair.

You know what's weird? I thought she would look like me. I don't know why; I just did. "Can I help you?" she asks as we approach her.

"Susan?" I ask meekly. I'm still unsure if this is, indeed, her.

"Yes. May I help you?" she repeats, and then glances over her shoulder.

"Hi. I'm Caroline O'Brien. I knew your husband." I am trying desperately to keep my voice from shaking.

She studies me for a moment and I can almost see a light bulb turn on. "Are you related to CiCi?"

"Yes. I'm her sister. This is my fiancé, Kyle." I quickly introduce them. I fucking hate lying.

"What brings you here?"

"I heard the news about Drew. Kyle and I are out here on business with his company and I thought I would stop by and pay my condolences."

My palms are sweating like a whore in church.

"That's so very kind of you. Please, come in." She smiles and leads us in. It's very spacious and open. There's a lot of blues, greens, and yellows. It's very calming. "I've just made a pot of coffee, would you like some?" She looks back at us.

"We'd love some," I reply.

"Please, have a seat." She waves to the table as we walk into the kitchen.

"Your home is beautiful," Kyle says quickly.

"Yes, I love this kitchen," I add. I look around and take in the white cabinetry, the black cabinet island giving a nice contrast.

"Oh, this was my baby out of all the projects we took on for the remodel, so thank you very much." She gives a quick look around as if to agree with herself before she pours the coffee.

"I've brought the girls some things. I took a gamble at their ages." I shake the bags a little before setting them on the table.

"Oh, they're four and two. That was very thoughtful of you. I'm sure they'll be thrilled."

"How are they doing?"

Fuck the lump in my throat.

"Oh, it's touch and go. It's still all so new. They keep asking me when Daddy's coming home. They think he's just visiting Heaven.

They don't really understand yet," her voice shakes and I can see the tears forming. "I just don't know how else to explain it to them." She wipes the tears away. I let mine pool. "They'll be getting up from their naps soon, so you'll get to meet them." She smiles and head over to us.

"I'd love that." I take my mug from her.

"I'm actually very surprised you are here. Drew told me a lot about CiCi. She was the reason why we struggled so much in the beginning." She sips her coffee after taking a seat.

"Yes, they had a falling out," I simply say.

"He would never tell me what happened; only that he made a very bad decision one day and it brought their relationship to an end." She places her mug down. Yeah, I know—she's fishing.

"I don't really know what happened, either. CiCi would never talk about it. She never spoke ill of him; she just wouldn't tell us what happened other than that they broke up.

"I'm sorry for your loss, as well," she says quickly.

"Thank you." I offer a meek smile. "I was surprised to find out that Drew ended up on the other side of the country."

"Yeah, well, being in the military, you end up *everywhere!*" she laughs. She then goes on to tell me about how he ended up out there. How they met and fell in love. Their life together. I can see why he fell in love with her. There's something about her; I don't know if it's her optimism or just the way you naturally feel comfortable around her, as if you've known her your entire life.

"What keeps me focused is knowing that it's all in the mix." She lifts her mug for another sip.

"In the mix?" I look at her quizzically.

"Life," she breathes. "Life is made up of all these events that happen. I think of them as ingredients. Everything we go through: joy, sadness, what have you; they're all ingredients. They get thrown in the mix. That batter, with all of those ingredients, makes up who we are and who we end up being. Sorry. I love to bake so I associate things with it," she chuckles.

"Susan, that analogy is perfect. I'd actually love to be here when you discuss losing your virginity with your daughters. I'm imagining a whole talk about cherry pie," I chuckle then glance at Kyle whose eyes are bugged the fuck out. *Shit!* I totally just said that to her, didn't

I? See! This is why I shouldn't talk to people.

"I'll be sure to, at least, record it for you!" She laughs. *Thank God.* Just then, we hear the girls call out. "Oh, that's my cue! I'll be right back." She pats my hand and heads up the stairs.

"How are you doing?" Kyle grabs my hand.

"Better than I expected to. Man, she's awesome, isn't she?" I ask in disbelief.

"Yes, she is."

"I'm glad we came. This was really good for me." I nod, agreeing with myself. We turn our attention to the sound of Susan and the girls coming in.

"They are very excited to meet you." Susan laughs as the girls come running in right to me screaming in a gleeful way that little girls do. They remind me of my niece, Brooklynn.

I gasp.

The oldest is a spitting image of Drew.

"It's like you're looking right at him, isn't it?" Susan asks.

"Wow." It's all I've got.

"You're pretty," the oldest says.

"That's nice, Carissa, but maybe you should start off with a hello first." Susan sits back in her seat and watches us.

"I'm sorry. What did you say her name is?" I'm fucking hearing things, I know it.

"Oh, where are my manners?" She grabs her coffee. "This is Carissa." She points to her oldest. "And this is Sophia."

"I love the name Carissa; it's unusual, what made you decide to go with it?" Kyle asks the question burning in my mind.

"That was Drew's doing. He begged me to let him name our first daughter Carissa Catherine. He wanted to name her after the girl he didn't protect when he should have. He wanted to be reminded of her everyday so that he would never forget to protect our Carissa. He didn't want to be *that* parent that didn't think stuff would happen to *his* kid. That was his way of keeping him straight on that. Between his reasoning, his passion, and the fact that I actually adore the name, I allowed it. I got to pick Sophia's." She smiles and runs her hand down Sophia's hair.

"Her name is beautiful, as well," my voice shakes. And no . . . I can't control these motherfucking tears.

Shit.

Shit.

Shit.

"Was CiCi short for Carissa Catherine?" she asks.

"Yes." Lord . . . please don't let the ugly cry come.

"I don't know what he did," she starts, her chin quivering, "but he was a good man. He never forgave himself for what he did but instead of wallowing in it, he gave us one hundred and fifty percent of himself."

"He was a good man. He just had a moment of stupidity." I cry with her. Kyle gets up quickly, grabbing the attention of the girls with their presents. He leads them into the family room adjacent to the kitchen.

"Good enough to forgive him, CiCi?" she asks. I stare at her. She gives me an encouraging nod.

She knows.

"How did you know it was me?" I barely get the question out.

"Instinct."

"But Drew told you I was dead."

"I didn't take it literally. Also, he didn't change that much, he was still a lousy liar." She laughs lightly. I join her.

"God, he was *awful* at it!" I wipe my eyes.

"Well?" She gets serious again.

"Susan, it's taken me fifteen years and the love of a wonderful man to say this; I forgive him. I never thought it would be possible, but I was wrong. It's freeing as fucking hell." Shit, it really is.

She takes in a big gaspy-like breath, "Oh, thank you. Thank you so much," she cries.

"Why are you thanking me?"

"His mistake was a huge burden on him that he took to the grave, and call me crazy, but, I feel like your forgiveness is the key to his soul really being able to soar away. Does that make any sense to you?" She tilts her head.

"Yeah. That makes a lot of sense to me." I nod and reach forward to hug her.

No lie . . .

We hug for a good fifteen minutes, crying.

I'm not even interested in letting go.

Free.

Epilogue

Two years later and counting . . .

CiCi

"Kyle! Jesus, Kyle! Shut-up! Oh God!" I scream. "Shut-up! You're gonna . . . oh my God . . . yes! Shhh!"

Two lanes.

Know what I'm saying?

Faaaaaaacccccckkkkkk!

Fucking bastard's behind me laughing and grunting simultaneously. I'm pretty sure it has something to do with the fact that I'm the one screaming out, yet, telling him to shut the fuck up. Whatever . . . he knows what I'm saying, that's all that matters.

Holy shit.

Brzzzjrrr.

"Jesus Christ, Ceese, Jesus Christ!" Kyle carries on.

Bbbbrrzzzzjerrrrzzz.

"Stop—don't stop, Kyle!" I've got my pussy bell ringing and my . . . my . . . Oh God.

Ding!

Cake's done!

I pull Purp out and fall forward, letting Kyle finish in the end (Haha . . . that's what I said.). Imma lay here like a hot mess. Kyle's mouth is running dirty a mile a minute and I love every fucking word coming out of it. I especially love the sound of his balls slapping against my pussy. Mmm . . .

God, I sound like a fucking whore.

Jealous?

I would be. This shit is hot!

Kyle lets out a final groan (like a wolf, howling at the moon . . . I'm that good, biatches!) then collapses on top of me. We lay here, trying to compose ourselves, like usual, for a few moments.

I look over at the monitor and see that Patrick is still sleeping soundly. Thank God. Oh, want to get a good laugh in? We named our son after our fathers, using their middle names. Our son's name is *Patrick Stewart* Cooper. Patrick Stewart played captain on *Star Trek: The Next Generation.* Guess when Kyle realized this and informed me. Five months after Patrick was born! What the fuck? Oh well, he and Winnie Cooper can hit some conventions together.

He almost didn't happen: Patrick. I had one of my moments again, after meeting Susan. Kyle and I were walking down a long block to get to our car after a retirement party for one of the guys at his company. We somehow got on the subject of kids and I freaked.

"Kyle, I don't think I want kids. I'm not really good with them."

"What are you talking about? You're awesome with Charlotte's kids."

"Now I am! Don't tell Charley but, I dropped them when they were babies."

"What? You dropped all three of them?"

"Well, it's not my fault! They're slippery little fuckers when they're first born!"

"Are you shittin' me?" he laughed.

"No! I'm terrible with them. Thankfully, the kids are relatively normal."

"I'll handle infancy, you can get the other ages." He pulled me to him. "Did you ever tell Charley?"

"Are you fucking kidding me? No!" I practically yelled.

"Well, I know she trusts you with their lives." He kissed me.

"If she knew, she wouldn't."

"Stop," he said then gave me that look. You know that look.

"I just want you to be happy and have everything you want. I'm not really sure that I'm what you need."

"You *are all that I need. I know that with every fiber of my being. Now, if you keep talking like this I'm going to have to take things away from you." He raised an eyebrow. I gave him a quizzical look. "No puss 'n boots."*

"Well, shit. I love me some puss 'n boots. I guess I'll shut-up, then." I slid my arms around his neck and pulled him down to me.

I never mentioned my insecurities again. I didn't have to. Kyle has made sure every day (especially since then) that I have no reason to feel insecure. I'm so glad. I can't imagine life without our son now. He's only a year old, but I swear he's brilliant.

We were going to wait until Charley and Mitch got married but what with everything that happened. Oh . . . that's right. Well, you're going to have to wait for Ava to tell you. I know . . . I'm such a bitch. Hold on while I shrug—get over it. Anywho . . . they told us to go ahead. We got married in my parent's back yard. It was a beautiful spring day—*best day of my life!*

I'm going to tell you all something right now. When love shows up at your front door without any warning, don't fucking run. Don't act like you haven't been waiting for that shit to come along. All you're doing is hurting that person and yourself. I've learned so much—grown so much—since Kyle walked into my life. I thank God every day for him and for the ability to open up my heart again. It wasn't easy. But anything worth the reward after the challenge shouldn't be.

Susan said something to me that has stuck like glue. All of these things in our life, whether big or small, really are the ingredients in the mix that is unique to us. Think about all of the people who have come in and out your life. Even if it was a brief stop, it's significant. Whether they teach you to trust or not to trust, they're teaching you something. It really does mold you. The key is to know the difference between the good stuff and the bad, how to balance it in *your* mix.

I didn't always balance it well, but I think I'm doing a pretty good job of it now. I'm happy and I'm really okay with that. That's huge. I'm still a smartass. That's . . . not a surprise. But, that's me. That's in my mix. Luckily, I have someone who loves *everything* that comes in my batter.

Eww . . . What?

Carry on . . . and for God's sake . . . laugh.

Life is funny, lemons and all—laugh at it.

Love,

CiCi

Acknowledgments

I am blessed beyond reason. My three kids see me at my laptop and get so frustrated that I'm not doing anything "cool" that they can participate in. It's even more frustrating when I'm on a deadline and shoo them out of the room, constantly. Grasping the concept that Mommy works from home, I'm sure, will not be happening anytime soon. Yet, they never stay frustrated, and somehow, still think that I hang the moon and the stars for them—thank God! They are and always will be my *greatest* accomplishment.

Next, I want to give a the hugest thanks to all of my readers whether you've been on this journey with me from book one or you just fell in love with my characters today. I'm now six books in and still completely blown away that there are people who not only love my books, but anticipate the release of the next one. It's the most amazing feeling to work so hard at a dream that you believed in and watch it become a reality. You guys rock!

Thank you to my family and friends for your continued support. A special thanks to my Aunt Madelyn for helping me keep my kids at bay while I write. Also, your sarcastic reply of "Does Pinocchio have a wooden dick?" anytime I ask you a question that has an obvious answer came in handy for CiCi. So, congratulations on being a smartass! I love you. Another special thanks to my Aunt Emma, who loved Under Contract so much, she tried to get the goods out of me for the rest of the books. I did not cave, people! Lol. I love you, Aunt Em, and it's pretty cool to see you so excited about my stories.

I can't thank my street team (The G-Team) enough. You girls pimp me relentlessly. It's awesome to see so many people believe in your work the way you girls do. You honestly keep me going. Deadline time is over and I'm so looking forward to hanging out with you girls in our room more . . . having completely inappropriate conversations! Lol.

CiCi had some fantastic beta readers!! A big round of applause to Nicola, Claire, Wendy S., Abby, Anna, and Wendy C. . You all did a fantastic job!

Thank you to Kari from Cover to Cover Design. You did a beautiful job on this cover!

Stacey Blake from Champagne Formats, I'm writing this before you even work your magic, but I know you are going to knock it out of the park!

A special thanks to Jess Huckins. She wasn't able to work with me on this one for edits but still helped me out where she could. You still rock! ☺

Rebecca Cartee, I can't thank you enough for taking me on as a last minute client! I'm so happy you fell in love with my characters! You did a fab job editing and it was really great to work with you on this book!

Drum roll please . . .

I have had the most unbelievable support system this past year. These ladies flew in with flowing pink capes and saved the day for my first release. Since then, they have become the dearest friends to me. Wendy Shatwell and Claire Allmendinger, what is there left to say? I'd be lost without you ladies! I can't wait to fly across the pond and give you the biggest (quite possibly the most awkward) hug I can give. I will then follow up with a crazy dance like The Carlton or something a little fancier that would require "jazz hands."

And finally, I want to thank the many bloggers who have shown me support by promoting me in anyway, especially with reviews and spotlights. I truly appreciate all the time you put into supporting authors, especially us Indie ones!

About the Author

I am a domestic engineer (born and raised in New Jersey) whose sole responsibility is guiding three young, impressionable kids into becoming phenomenal adults. This challenging yet rewarding work requires a lot of love (coffee), patience (wine), and determination (periodic exorcisms). I work all of this magic from the beautiful state of New Hampshire.

Before becoming a domestic goddess (not really), I spent over a decade working in the medical field, where I wore more hats than the queen.

I have loved the written word and the great escape it provides since I was a little girl. When I wasn't reading about people and the places they lived, I created my own characters and adventures. Finally, I started putting a pen to paper and allowing my characters to come to life. When I don't have a pen in hand, you can often find me laughing at the conversations my characters are having in my head.

Want to see what I'm up to? You can stalk me here at these spots!
Twitter: @JacquelynAyres
Facebook: https://www.facebook.com/JacquelynAyresAuthor
Pinterest: http://www.pinterest.com/jacquelynayres/

Coming Soon!
Crossing the Line (#3 GEG Series)
This is subject to change as far as order in the series
~UNEDITED~

Chapter One

Phobias.

We all have them. However, most of us don't walk that fine line between fear and just plain crazy.

I do.

Do you?

~~Fear has existed as long as man has~~

"No shit, assmunch!" I say almost under my breath, crossing out that last statement. Ugh! Why did I agree to write this article?!

"I'm sorry, were you talking to me?"

I look up quickly. *Shit—it's Wednesday!* It's "Viking Day." Did they have Vikings in Australia? If not then I think there's been a mix up; his family must've immigrated there.

His name is Declan Pierce. And it was only an hour ago that he was piercing the ever-loving-hell out of my love tunnel with his giant Viking cock. One look and I swore he wasn't going to fit, but he yanked my skirt up and pushed me down on my desk. His hand possessively, yet gently, grasped my neck. His fingers splaying the length of my jaw, holding me in place. He shushed me as his free hand found its way between my legs. I whimpered; I was so fucking wet for him and it put a cocky ass smile on his face. "It will fit. Let me show you how good it will fit, love," he said while stretching my entrance with his thick, Viking-man fingers. Because I'm one who likes to see proof—I submitted. Ever get fucked so hard and good, you can't keep your mouth from gaping open, or enable your throat to produce some sort of sound? That's how he fucked me. Gaping-mouth fuck. And I *loved* it.

He commanded me to come—I came.

He released my neck and pulled out with a thunderous groan. *"On your knees, Ms. St. Claire!"* I obeyed and was rewarded with his throbbing, swollen cock, filling my mouth until it exploded, releasing another wondrous, epic groan from him. Afterwards, he sat in the plush chair, most of my clients seem to prefer, and helped me up onto his lap where he cradled me. His large hands caressed my body in nonchalant manner. It didn't matter what kind of manner it was, he was touching me and that's all I needed. Then, he started talking lowly in my ear, saying deliciously naughty things about my pussy. The first thing he said is a must. And I'm sure you will agree with me.

"Mmm . . . any idea how amazing it was to feel your tight, little pussy, pulsating around my cock?"

See that right there? That's psyche 101 when it comes to sex talk. Men always want to hear about how big you think there cock is (in a positive light, of course). Well, women are no different! I don't care if her vag lips are flapping in the wind and you can stick your hand up in there to give a "thumbs up" to your cock while you're fucking her; tell her her pussy is tight! She'll love you and your "big" cock a little more! ;)

"Ms. St. Claire? Ms. St. Claire?! Are you alright?"

"Huh?" I snap back.

"Are you ok?" He places the back of his hand to my forehead.

"Yes, why?" I ask nervously because *he's touching me!*

"One minute I'm asking if you were talking to me, the next, your eyes glossed over, your face turned bright red, and you were breathing rapidly. Is everything ok?" He crouches down to me.

"Um . . . oh. Sorry." I shake my head. "I was lost in my thoughts . . . sorry." I say again.

"What on Earth were you thinking about?" He chuckles lightly. "I thought I was going to have to call a medic!"

I could easily tell him that I was lost in the thought of our impromptu "session" earlier but he probably won't remember it to reminisce along with me. That's because he wasn't really here. He was only fucking me in my mind. He fucks me there every day, at some point. Always on my desk. My own little—made for my mind—porno: THINK OF SOMETHING HERE!!!

"I don't even know," I say and give him, what I think is, my most perplexed look.

"Are you diabetic?"

"No. Don't be silly. I'm fine." I wave his idea off.

"Have you eaten?"

"No," I answer and feel my palms start to sweat. I'm just realizing how close his face is to mine.

"That's it then!" He slaps his knee. "Here, I've brought you a coffee." Taking it out of the drink tray, he places it on my desk near me. "Please, eat my muffin."

I'd like for him to eat my *muffin!*

"Thanks, but you don't have to do that." I smile, eyeing it. "Maybe just half." I give in before he puts in a fight. What? It's the—limited time only—banana muffin from Dunkin's. I'm not passing up on that shit! He nods, smiling as he pulls the plush chair (the one he was just cradling me on, telling me how tight I was . . . ahem) closer to my desk and takes his coffee out of the drink tray, as well. "You don't have to bring me coffee every week."

"Oh, I'm sorry. Did you want something else?" Declan reaches for my cup.

"No!" I smack his hand away and rescue my coffee.

"A little passionate about your coffee, aye?" His smile hits his eyes.

"Just a bit," I agree and take a sip. "I meant that you don't have to do this in general."

"I rather enjoy Wednesdays now, if I'm to be honest." He shifts in his seat. "This one hour of the week seems to be the only hour I get that has any normalcy to it."

"Why do you say that?" I cross my legs, letting my right one hang over the left and it bops . . . bops . . . bops.

"I have to tell you, that's terribly annoying." His hand puts pressure on my leg to make me stop. I stare at his hand, secretly wishing it to travel to my lady business. *Ugh! What is wrong with me?!*

"Sorry," I almost whisper. "So, tell me why you feel that way," I continue.

"I want to hear about your week. Tell me what's new with your friends?" He taps my knee then pulls his hand away.

"Declan—"

"—Dec"

"Dec, this is the third week you've popped in on me with coffee.

All we've done is talk about me. I'd like to hear some dialogue from you." I'm calm but assertive, I think.

"No." He shakes his head. "I'm not here for a therapy session. I'm here to talk to a very witty, charming, and beautiful woman. If I talk about me, you will turn this into a session and I will refrain from coming back."

"Um . . . thank you for the compliment. No thank you to the judgment."

"I'm not judging you. I just want to have coffee with you and pleasant conversation. I don't want to come in here and unload my bag."

I would so love for him to unload his bag!

Pull it together, Maddie! "Well, that's not fair."

"You listen to people all day, every day. Don't you want to take a break and be the one to talk for once?"

"I don't just listen. I coach. I talk it out with them. Don't slap a label on me." I may have come off a little pissed with that last comment.

"I didn't mean to state how you do your job. I just meant that I like to listen to you and . . . I don't know. I should just go. I'm sorry for offending you." He stands up.

I stand up with him. "Do you talk to anybody? Especially about your son?" I ask quickly.

"Have a nice night," he says quietly before heading out of my room.

"Declan! Dec!" I call after and follow him down the hall. "Stop!" I grab his arm.

He knocks on the door to Ted's office, ignoring my pull. "I'm sorry, we have to leave early today—something's come up." Dec says once he opens the door.

"Dec . . . wait." I try to get him to turn but he is of Viking quality and I'm just, as Pa Ingalls would say, a half-pint. Finally, I give up. He and his son head down the hall.

Good job, Captain Asswhore!

Sneak Peek

Rescue Breathing

The Breathe Series—Book One

Written by Zoe Norman

Rescue breathing, *also known as "the kiss of life," is a rescue technique where one person provides air for someone who has stopped breathing.*

- Excerpt from www.ask.com/health&fitness

CHAPTER ONE

Olivia

"There is a time in every woman's life when she needs to just walk away. This, Olivia, is that time."

That lovely quote comes directly from the mouth of my best friend, Charley, over the phone and across the country. She is giving me her version of a pep talk, which I am grateful is not currently including a stream of expletives directed at my ex, Jay.

About nine months ago, I found out he was not just cheating. Nope, that would have been too easy. In fact, at this point in my life, I would pay someone to turn the hands of time back and make it that easy. No, Jay provided me with a much more interesting betrayal. Wait for it. He was married. With kids. The whole time we were dating. All three years of it.

It's okay. Take a moment to absorb that. It's taken me nine months to just scratch the surface of taking that in. I am now at that special place where I'm just angry. Angry and decidedly spending the majority of my time fantasizing about different ways to remove Jay's testicles in a painful manner. Charley is all too willing to assist with this part of the grieving process, even from the polar opposite side of the United States, since dealing with sobbing, falling-apart Olivia is too much for her to bear.

"Liv, are you listening? This is your opportunity to have some fun. Get the hell out of the city and breathe a little. You need some space from all this. Even if you don't see him anymore, you need to get out of town. Come to this conference. I'll show you around Seattle. We'll go out with my girls here. It will be so much fun. Maybe you'll even get laid!"

The conference she is referring to is an American Psychological Association conference where I'm supposed to present my most recent research to be published about trauma and servicemen. I've spent the last nine months of my grief process interviewing nearly every fireman, policeman, and paramedic in the city of New York. It's amazing how productive hating someone else and being devastatingly broken can make you.

"Charley, I'm not looking to get laid. My God, that's the last thing on my mind!"

This is a lie. A big, fat, stupid lie. I think about sex every time I go to bed. Not with my ex—that sex wasn't even that good. No, I think about the kind of sex I've always wanted, with a man who makes me feel amazing and cherished and isn't afraid of a little fun. So basically I think about my dream-man sex on the body of a celebrity. Whatever. It works.

"Charley, if I come out there, you know I have to actually work. It's a conference. I'd be presenting at three different lectures."

I hear her sigh over the phone. "I know exactly what you're saying and I know you have to work. But you also have to have some fun, Liv. Hey, is that guy Rob going to be there? The guy you hooked up with at your last conference?"

I groan. Rob is a psychologist who presented at conference I attended in Chicago, several months after I found out about Jay. In a fit of sadness—and a tremendous amount of alcohol—I had sex with Rob in a stairwell of the hotel in which we were staying. Suffice it to say, it took me another two weeks to get him to stop calling me. The last thing I need right now is to run into him again.

"Absolutely not, Charlotte. That guy was like a leech. I have no interest in rehashing that disaster again."

I hear her giggle on the other end. "Liv, please. I haven't seen you in ages. I miss you. Just come out to Seattle. If there is a happy side effect, it's that you get out of New York, and if you're able to put some of the Jay stuff to bed, all the better, but at least we can visit, okay?"

I sigh. "Okay, okay, okay. I'll come out. I'll send you the itinerary when I get it. I do know I'll be at the Fairmont Olympic, but I could probably use a ride when I get there if you don't mind. Maybe we can have dinner the first night?"

"Yay! That's the spirit, girl. Oh my God, I can't wait to see you! Liv, you won't regret this. I promise you, I'm going to make it all better. I love you, Livvie girl."

I laugh as my heart clenches. Charley has been my best friend since we were in school together at Columbia. She moved to Seattle a few years ago for work and I miss her terribly. Not having her here during all this has been terribly difficult for me.

"I love you too, Charley. I can't wait to see you."

We hang up our call and I collapse into my couch. The conference is next week. I have a lot of work to do before I leave, not the least of which is call our travel coordinator at NYU and get my flight plan together. I pick up the phone and dial away.

***

My flight out to Seattle is tomorrow night and I'm still packing. I decided to take the last flight out in the hopes of getting a little sleep before my plane lands. It will mean arriving very late at night, but that will allow me a full night's sleep before the start of the conference.

I have all my clothes laid out in front of me. I have all the usual work stuff—skirt suits, pant suits, sensible shoes. But knowing that Charley wants to go out, I decide I should also pack some cute stuff too, so I've included some short black skirts that are fun, a couple of sexy tops, and some real fuck-me stilettos. I don't know who I think is going to fuck me in these shoes, but it's worth a shot, right?

Just thinking about having sex with someone else, despite all my late-night fantasies, makes my stomach roil. I wish my heart didn't hurt so much still. I'm lucky I never run into Jay at all. My guess is that he's—smartly—avoiding the places I might be likely to see him.

My discovery of his infidelity (it's easier to just call it that at this point) came on the heels of another revelation that I thought would be the best part of my life. I found out I was pregnant. Jay and I had always been careful, but fate has its way of intervening. And intervene it did. I had never thought anything about the fact that he'd never had me over to his place. Or that there were weekends he didn't contact me at all despite having had plans. Or that there were times of the year he was flat-out nervous. When you're desperate to be loved by someone, someone you are sure is your soul mate, you gloss over these items for which the rest of the female world scream, "There Is A Fucking Problem Here!"

So when I told him I was pregnant and he freaked out, I was stunned into silence. I mean, I wasn't exactly prepared for it, nor had

I been expecting it, but I certainly wasn't shrieking, "Fuck!" at the top of my lungs or "How the fuck did you let this happen?" From there, it was all downhill.

During his tirade, he said, "I don't want any more kids." And there it was. What other kids? What did he mean? And then, as if it were the most natural thing in the world, he told me that he was married, had two kids, and lived in a brownstone on the Upper East Side. And in that one quick moment, my entire life fell apart and his went back to normal.

Jay and I had been seeing each other for three years, since grad school. He was bright, handsome, and slated to be a very successful psychiatrist. He also seemed to be increasingly unavailable. Scheduled visits, phone calls where he was whispering. I talked at length with Charley about this. She told me that I was being paranoid, that it was in my head, but I knew it wasn't. And then, the "incident." Two weeks late on my period, vomiting in the morning, hypersensitivity to smells, and fifteen positive at-home pregnancy tests revealed what was now obvious—I was pregnant.

When I finally allowed Charley to convince me to go to the doctor to run a test and that too was positive, I decided that it was time to tell Jay. I called him and asked him to come over for dinner. He hemmed and hawed, complaining about some work commitment, but in the end, he agreed to come for dessert later in the evening. I was nervous, although I didn't know why. When I told him about the pregnancy, he blanched visibly and fell back into the couch. Not the response I'd been hoping for.

He wanted to know how this could have happened, where had I gone wrong with my birth control. I watched him, frozen, as he spewed accusation after accusation until finally he spit out, "I don't want any more fucking children, Olivia!"

Huh? More children? When had he gotten the first set? He turned and stormed out of my apartment and, eventually, my life. I had never been more broken in my life. I spent two weeks in a full-on fugue that then morphed into rage. Every day a little more bitter, a little more angry. By the end of the second week, I somehow found strength. Strength born by anger to be sure, but strength nonetheless.

After a doctor's visit where we discussed my no-longer-existing relationship and what was left of my options, my doctor started in on the "termination of pregnancy" talk. I listened to her speak, my mind reeling, my heart splintering. We talked about how abortions happened, what I could expect, did I have a friend who could take me? In that moment, I suddenly realized that I wanted to try and do this. This baby didn't deserve to not have a chance just because its father was a piece of shit. This baby was still part of me too.

I smiled the whole walk back to my apartment, eager to tell Charley I actually was as strong as she said I was. I was keeping this baby, damn it. So help me God, I was going to be such an amazing mother that I was going to blow all other mothers out of the water. We were going to do this together.

Two days later, I miscarried. I had barely gotten home from the hospital confirming the loss of my baby when I texted Jay.

No more worries. I lost the baby.

Have a great rest of your life.

There was no helping or consoling me. I would vacillate between deep, debilitating depression and almost manic work hours when I was trying to forget. My parents were devastated, my friends were full of sorrow and my heart was pulverized. From that point on, I had no interest in anything related to the opposite sex. Not dating, not sex, not marriage. Oh, in my heart, those were still things I wanted, but I mourned the loss of that dream lifestyle I thought I would have with Jay every day. It was safer to just close off.

The following months were a blur. It was as if someone had uncapped his bottle of lies and it came spilling out all over me. It turned out, people we had been friends with had all known. Every little thing I'd thought was real fell apart under his betrayal. I locked myself in my apartment for a week straight, crying and sitting in the fetal position on my couch. I didn't shower. I didn't eat. I didn't talk to anyone until my brother, Simon, and his fiancée, Reese, showed up one day and threw me in the shower, force-fed me some soup, and then let me sob in his lap.

For some reason, that pulled me out of my funk, and I returned to work. I threw myself into my research, everyone around me walking on eggshells and avoiding the topic of Jay. To this day, his name is not uttered by anyone I know, friend or colleague, with the exception of Charley and Simon. And good riddance for that.

***

I haul my bag out of the trunk of the cab in front of my gate at LaGuardia. The taxi driver doesn't consider helping me out of the cab. T*hanks, asshole. There goes your tip*. I'm early, but being that it was an evening flight, I didn't want to get stuck feeling rushed. I always carry on my bags. It's so much easier than having to wait for the carousel in an airport you've never been to before. I pop up the handle to my rolling suitcase and walk toward a bar I can see in the terminal. Charley suggested I get a drink since I hate flying—especially across the country. I decide that it isn't such a bad idea.

Other books by Zoe Norman:

Rescue Breathing (The Breathe Series—Book One)

Life Support (The Breathe Series—Book Two)

Where to find Zoe Norman:

Webpage: http://authorzoenorman.wix.com/zoenorman
Amazon Author Page: http://amazon.com/author/zoenorman
Facebook: https://www.facebook.com/AuthorZoeNorman
Twitter: @AuthorZoeNorman
Instagram: AuthorZoeNorman

Ransom by Faith S Lynn

Present Time

Sage

"Amanda, where are you going?" I ask as I try to keep up with her long strides. It's really hard considering I am wearing four inch heels while trying to navigate these damned cobblestone roads here in Savannah. It's still fairly early for all the partiers out, and River Street is crawling with them. She doesn't bother answering me, just keeps moving through the crowd until she turns down an alley. She stops at the bottom of a brick staircase that climbs the side of one of the buildings. The iron railing on the side is twisted, and doesn't look like it would be much help if you started falling.

"Now do you want to tell me what you are doing?" I ask, again.

I watch as her lips thin into a smile that screams wicked thoughts. I look to the top of the stairs and the red door that needs a new paint job, when the sign above the door catches my eye.

Roth * Psychic Reader
Palm - Spirit - Tarot

"No, you have got to be kidding me. There is no way in hell I am going in there." A chill runs down my spine just thinking about it.

Somewhere down the alley, I hear a cat hiss. Fuck this shit. I turn to take a step back down the stairs to leave when Amanda stops me.

You know, for someone who doesn't believe in this stuff, you sure are acting a lot like a pussy over it," she sneers. Ugh, she royally pisses me off sometimes. Still, she has been my best friend for ten years, and is the only other person in the world that it doesn't annoy me to be around for more than a few hours.

"I don't believe in it, but that doesn't mean I want to chance taking some freaky ass ghost or something home to haunt me forever. Nope," I say shaking my head dramatically.

She pokes one of her neon pink nails at my face and says, "Look here, Sage. You owe me one. I went with you on that stupid double date so you could make your shithead fiancé happy. I had to put up with that guy's incessant babbling about how he was God's gift to women, when really, he was just disgusting. That goodnight kiss he laid on me was enough for you to owe me forever!" She finally draws in a breath.

"Ugh. Fine! I swear to God, Manda, if I end up cursed or something, I will beat the shit out of you." She laughs in response as I storm past her and push through the door. A bell above the door sounds off with a sinister ding, and a chill runs down my spine.

It's dark except for the illumination of a few candles around the room. The shelf beside me is lined with old jars and leather bound books that look as though, if you were to touch them, they would turn to dust. Manda walks up beside me examining some of the items. One of her hands rises to skim over a tiny jewel, and I smack it down before she can.

"What the hell?" she asks.

"Are you completely insane? That crap could be hexed or whatever!" I say.

We both jump when a cackle like laugh comes from behind us. With Amanda's hand in mine, we turn to see a tiny old lady sitting in a chair in the middle of the room. I'm pretty sure she wasn't there when we walked in.

"Those are just some trinkets I keep around. I am no fool, the items that hold a hex are kept in the back," she assures us. Her voice is scratchy as if she has smoked one too many cigarettes in her lifetime. Her silver hair is so long that the ends are touching her hands folded on her lap.

"Come and sit." She extends her hand and points a finger to a small wicker couch across from her. A small table sits between it and her. Amanda tugs on my hand signaling that she intends to go through with this. We take a seat and I find my gaze going back to the old lady, whom I can only guess to be Roth, the name that was on the sign. She is so small. I bet she barely reaches five feet tall.

"What would you like to know, young lady?" she questions towards Amanda.

"I want to know how my life turns out. You know, the basics," Amanda explains to her.

The old woman scoots all the way to the front of her chair and puts both of her hands upright on the table. "Give me your palm, Amanda."

Amanda's and my heads jerk towards one another. She looks just as shocked as I do. I lean in and whisper, "She had to have heard me say it on the way in." My eyes shift to the old woman to see her thin lips turn up on the sides. Again, a shiver races through my body. I have always heard two superstitions for cold chills. We take our superstitions very seriously here in the south, which is not comforting considering that I am sitting in a witch's parlor.

Slowly, Amanda takes her hands and puts them on the table. Roth reaches over, pulls them closer to her and leans over them. Her thumbs move over Manda's palms, stretching and poking. She raises her head with an arched brow.

"My dear, your life is perfectly boring, to be honest. It turns out the exact way you want it. The man you are seeing now you will one day marry, and he will give you two beautiful children. The game that you two are playing now will come back tenfold in your futures. He will be miserable and cheat, because a zebra never changes its stripes, and you will be miserable but will stay with him for the status and money. The end." Roth doesn't even bat an eye as she tells Amanda of her supposed future.

"That's a bit harsh. Don't you think?" Amanda asks. Her face registers shock, but at the same time there is a sadness there, too.

"I am simply telling you what you already know to be true." Roth pats Amanda's hands before she turns to me. "Now what about you . . . Sage?"

Crap. Did she hear Amanda say my name, too? "I . . . uh . . . I came for moral support. I don't want to know anything. Thank you, though." I stand and grab at my still frozen friend. "Come on, Amanda. You got what you wanted, let's go!"

"Oh but Sage, I really think you should hear how your life is about to completely change," Roth says.

"No. No, I don't," I reply.

"Ok, then, but know this: Keep an open mind over the next few months of your life. Remember that you have had a very good life, but what you think makes you happy, the things you think you can't live without, are not what you really need." She takes a breath and continues, "He will open your eyes."

"Sure," I tell her, but it comes out shaky. Amanda stands and places a 100 dollar bill on the table and we walk out. We don't say a word to each other until we are back on River Street.

"I'm just going to head on home. I'll see you Sunday at the fundraiser. 'Kay?" Amanda says with a sniffle.

"Yeah, I'll see you then." I tell her before we turn and walk in separate directions. I take an alley head back up to Bay Street. I have lived here my entire life, but will never get over Savannah's beauty. Tonight I can't seem to enjoy it, though. Roth's words keep popping into my head. They don't make any sense. My life has always been the same. My father is a partner in the biggest hospitality business in the Deep South and my mother is always high on pills because, well, she can be. My only real friend is Amanda, and that "shithead" fiancé she hates, is Richard.

We have been with each other since my sophomore and his senior year of high school. He is really handsome, in that whole prep school kind of way. Smooth features, dusty blonde hair and green eyes. He is really fit too, because he was a swimmer in high school and college. The most confusing thing that Roth said to me was the part about how *he* would open my eyes. She didn't say a name. Could she have been talking about Richard?

A drunken woman stumbles from around the corner ahead and walks in my direction. She tries to smooth her kinky hair down with her filthy hands but only succeeds in making it look worse. Her clothes make her appear to be straight from some trailer park. Her top is a floral t-shirt with the sleeves cut off, leaving a gaping hole under her arms that shows off her leopard print bra, and her shorts could very well be men's. As she walks past me, she loses footing and rams into my side, sending me fumbling with her a few steps before I catch my balance.

"Why don't you watch where the hell you're going?" I shout at her as I shove her off of me to the ground.

She struggles to get back to her feet and when she finally does, she runs the back of her hands across her eyes and keeps her head tucked down. "I'm s . . . sorry."

"You're apology is worthless. What would be useful is for you to go back to the hole you crawled from," I bite out. She shrinks into herself more before she bolts down the street. Some people should really learn where they do and do not belong.

I am about four blocks from my house when I get the feeling of being watched. My mom has always told me that because Savannah is so old, there are all kinds of things lurking in the night. I stop walking and look around at the dark street. What light the street lamps put off isn't much but I use it to my advantage. There is a couple across the road leaned on a car making out and a man further up the sidewalk walking his dog in the other direction. I take a calming breath and tell myself it's just my imagination running wild from the night's events.

I continue walking when I am yanked backwards. I scream as I fall for what feels like forever. Pain shoots across the side of my head and down my neck. I blink a few times, but everything is a blur. A tall figure walks into my line of vision and bends down. I try to push him away, try to kick at him. It doesn't work. My limbs are like limp noodles.

Darkness is taking over. I do my best to stay conscious, but lose the battle. The last thing I remember is strong arms picking me up, and the scent of whiskey and honey.

Jag by Stevie J. Cole

Chapter 1

My mouth was dry, like someone had shoved a fistful of cheap off-brand cotton balls in it. I ran my tongue over my teeth in an effort to wipe the film of bourbon off of them. Yawning, I rolled onto my back and stretched out in the king-sized bed before lifting the sheets back over my body. The smell of the detergent floated up to my nose, and my lips curled up. No matter how nice the suite was, the sheets always smelled like that damn hotel laundry detergent. I couldn't *stand* that smell.

I heard someone next to me pull in a deep breath, and then the covers shifted off my body. Seconds later, I felt warm skin against mine, and then a hand wrapped around my stiff-ass dick. Fingers skimmed along its length, stopping to play with the metal bar lodged through the head.

Slowly, I opened my eyes. The sun was beaming in through one of the windows, and all I could see out of it was an overly crowded skyline. The sun glinted from the windows of the grey concrete skyscrapers competing for space; only a few slivers of blue sky managed to peep between them. I'd almost forgotten that I was in New York City. I couldn't really recall how she'd ended up with me, and I certainly had no idea what her fucking name was. To the best of my knowledge, I guessed she'd been at the club the night before. It wasn't out of the usual at all for me to wake up with an unknown woman beside me; it was habitual. One day, I'd probably luck out and bring back a psycho that'd try to off me, but I'd worry about that when it happened. *Most* of the time the sex was worth that small risk—at least it usually was when I could remember it.

Do I want to look over and see what she looks like, or not? That's one of the pluses about not letting them stay with you; you don't have to look poor judgment in the face.

Her grip tightened, and she gently stroked me in her hand. “Good morning,” she whispered.

I grunted and closed my eyes again. I hated when they ended up staying the night. That was never the plan because it was so fucking awkward the next morning when I was sober and trying to piece together what all we’d done. I hated having to talk to them; having to listen to them go on and on about what a big fan they are, how this is the most amazing thing that’s ever happened to them; and, worst of all, having them ask me if they can post the pictures from last night on Facebook, Twitter, and Instagram. Fangirls, they’re just dying to brag about having been bent over backwards and rammed by me, and rightfully so. It was quite the achievement.

Peeping through one halfway-opened eye, I saw a woman. *Okay. Well, at least I got that right despite being completely wasted.* She looked to be about twenty-four. *And thank God. She’s legal.* Her platinum blonde hair stuck up in all directions, and black rings of mascara were smudged underneath her eyes. This girl was an absolute mess. It was *obvious* I’d been there *and* had a good time marking my territory.

She wasn’t bad looking, but she was absolutely no different than the rest of the other privileged rich girls whose daddies bought their horny daughters’ way into the VIP areas. When she smiled, nothing on her face moved. When she abruptly sat up and slid her way down to my dick, her unnaturally round tits didn’t budge either. It was evident she’d already started with the plastic surgery addiction. This was the kind of girl I was used to: fake, horny, and willing to do anything for a brush with fame.

A slight giggle bounced from her lips as she tugged the covers off my naked body, and then her warm, slimy tongue, coated with morning breath germs, traced up my shaft. The sensation sent a small tingle shooting up from my groin. I looked down to find her staring up at me, her eyes locked intimately on mine as she sucked half of me back into her throat.

Letting out a short sigh, I leaned back and shut my eyes, no hint of a smile on my face. The way she was wrapping her tongue around me felt damn good, and even though I really had no interest in her being there, I wasn’t going to deprive her of the joy she’d get from watching me get off *one* more time. I tried not to be selfish with that privilege.

After just a few minutes of her head bobbing up and down, her hand twisting at just the right moments, and her choking on my length a few times, I felt my body relax. My legs stiffened up, and then my entire body heated from the overwhelming rush of endorphins coursing through me. It's amazing how quickly orgasms come when you're not strung out on coke, or a bottle of oxycodone, or speed. Quicker, but weak compared to the euphoria that drugs granted me.

When that initial warm and fuzzy feeling wore off, I was ready to get her the hell out of my hotel room. Sitting up, I said, "Thanks for the great blow job. Pretty sure the door's still unlocked," and I flung my naked ass back down across the bed.

I watched her blink a couple of times, shocked at how rude I was being. I mean, she *had* just given me the gift of oral pleasure, and who knows what I told her the night before. I may have promised her she could go on tour with us. She narrowed her eyes. *Here comes the 'OMG, I can't believe what a bastard he is' huff that chicks are so good at in 3, 2, 1 . . .*

A loud breath escaped her, and the springs of the mattress bounced as she hopped up. She mumbled to herself while gathering her things. I just laid there, staring up at the ceiling.

I tapped my finger in beat with her heels as they clicked across the tiled floors, and then they stopped.

Raising my head from the pillow, I glanced up at her, arching one brow in disinterest. The girl, whose name I'd never bothered to ask for, glared at me for a minute before a smile inched across her face.

"I can't believe this!" She fell silent and shook her head, then covered her mouth with her hand. "I'm," she paused. "Getting kicked out of *Jag Steele's* hotel room. OMG! This. Is. *Amazing!"* she squealed, and pulled her phone to her face, her fingers typing furiously and the grin growing wider by the second. I guess she had to check in on Foursquare and let everyone know she'd just become the one-thousand, five hundred and sixty-seventh woman to have her tonsils rammed by me—or some number close to that, because I sure as hell didn't try to keep count anymore.

Her eyes darted up at me, and I could tell she was considering something. I caught her pointer finger creeping down the side of her phone, and I cleared my throat. "If you take a photo of me like this and post it, my lawyers will be in touch with you." I shot the biggest, most asshole smile I could shape over at her. "Got that, princess?"

Her excited expression relaxed and her jaw dangled open. She managed to huff out a dejected, "Uh, yeah," as she lowered her phone and dropped it in her purse. And there she stood, frozen, by the door.

Still nude, I rose and brushed past her, opening the door and circling my finger in the air before pointing directly out into the hallway. "Enjoy the rest of your day," I said.

Ms. No-Name skirted through, taking one last glance at me over her shoulder before I shut the door.

Rubbing my hands over my face, I made my way to the bathroom. I flipped the light switch and gave my eyes a minute to adjust to the artificial light. Sometimes I felt guilty after I kicked a girl out like that. I didn't used to be such a jackass. And during my fleeting *moments* of sobriety, I could recall that I used to actually be really nice, sometimes even shy. Funny how well-rehearsed you can become at being who everyone *thinks* you should be. There was no doubt that I was a different guy.

At this point, life just annoyed the shit out of me.

A few hours later I was leaning against a doorway, watching the interns scamper around with lattes and double shot espressos. My eyes traced over the black cords running from the cameras, and then up at the canned lights hanging from the ceiling. The bustling New York City crowd was visible through the large window at the far end of the room, constant movement of people going through their mundane daily routines. Every so often someone would stop, cup their hands around their face, and peer into the studio.

Two more hours until I had to be in front of those cameras, and my nerves were already tightly bundled up, my stomach uneasy; all I could think about was running to the bathroom and snorting a few lines real quick. The only problem with that was I didn't have any coke—oh, and I was supposed to be clean.

I hated being interviewed, especially when it would require me to rehash all the ridiculous shit that had happened over the past few years. Really, the biggest problem I had at that moment was my sobriety. I'd never done an interview sober, and I doubted that I could make it through this one.

"Excuse me, Jag." One of the hipster interns attempted to get my attention.

Turning, and not saying a word, I faced him.

The intern didn't glance up from his pad as he continued. "They need you to come back to the dressing room, do some makeup before they start."

I pushed myself off of the door frame, then followed him down the slender white hallway.

He glanced back at me, a slight grin shaping his lips. "Man. I know I'm supposed to act all chill and stuff, but I can't help it. Pandemic Sorrow is my favorite band. You're a legend."

Shoving my shades up through my hair, I forced my lips to curve up. I'd been told in rehab that I needed to act more appreciative, but when you're as numb and arrogant as I am, sometimes it's hard to act thankful about anything.

I forced out what I'd been told was an appropriate response. "Thanks, man. Really appreciate that."

The guy stopped, dropping his clipboard down by his side and staring at me through his thick, black-rimmed Buddy Holly glasses. He shook his head and looked me dead in the eyes. "You guys aren't really done, are you? Those are just rumors?"

"Nah. We can't go nowhere. Music's all we know."

Pleased with that response, he turned and continued to the dressing room.

About seven months ago I'd almost made my heart explode, or almost overdosed, if you want to get technical with it, but I think the exploding heart thing sounds much better, less accusing. I had been *forced* into rehab, kicking and screaming, because I didn't have a fucking problem. I just got a little too excited, a little too carried away, and snorted one too many lines. That's not a problem, that's an accident. Right after I finished my treatment and was told I was "cured" from my "habit," I threatened and swore that I was going to leave Hollywood behind in an effort to stay clean. Of course, when that happened, people thought the band was done for. I hadn't threatened that because I wanted to stay clean—honestly, it all just sounded like a hassle—but more so that I wanted to get the fuck away and have some privacy. At times, the idea of fading into the background, of having a life where each damn breath I drew wouldn't be scrutinized and slapped across the front page of every tabloid in existence—well, sometimes that just seemed abso-fucking-lutely amazing.

We stopped outside the dressing room, and I grabbed the intern's shoulder before he walked away. "What's your name?" I asked.

"Jay."

One side of my mouth flipped up in a halfhearted grin, and I said, "Why do you work here, Jay?"

A ridge formed on his brow as he stared at me, not exactly sure why the hell I was asking him that question.

"What do you want to get from this place? From working at MTV? Fame? Is that what you're running after?" I pointed back to the studio. "You want to eventually end up in front of that camera?"

Nodding, he said, "Well, yeah. I mean, who doesn't want to be famous?"

I shook my head in disgust and turned to enter the dressing room as I mumbled, "Yeah. Well, some people that are famous just wish they weren't."

Jag is available at eBook retailers.

Follow Stevie J. Cole to keep up to date with release information:

Facebook: https://www.facebook.com/authorsteviejcole

Twitter: @steviejcole

Goodreads: https://www.goodreads.com/author/show/7736491.Stevie_J_Cole

www.ingramcontent.com/pod-product-compliance
Lightning Source LLC
Chambersburg PA
CBHW021458240626
47154CB00002B/420

* 9 7 8 0 9 8 6 3 0 6 9 1 4 *